Mind Commodity

Lyv Landson

Oski Press

First paperback edition released in August 2024.

First Edition

Mind Commodity
Lyv Landson

ISBN paperback: 978-1-0686670-3-9
ISBN e-book: 978-1-0686670-2-2

Published by Oski Press

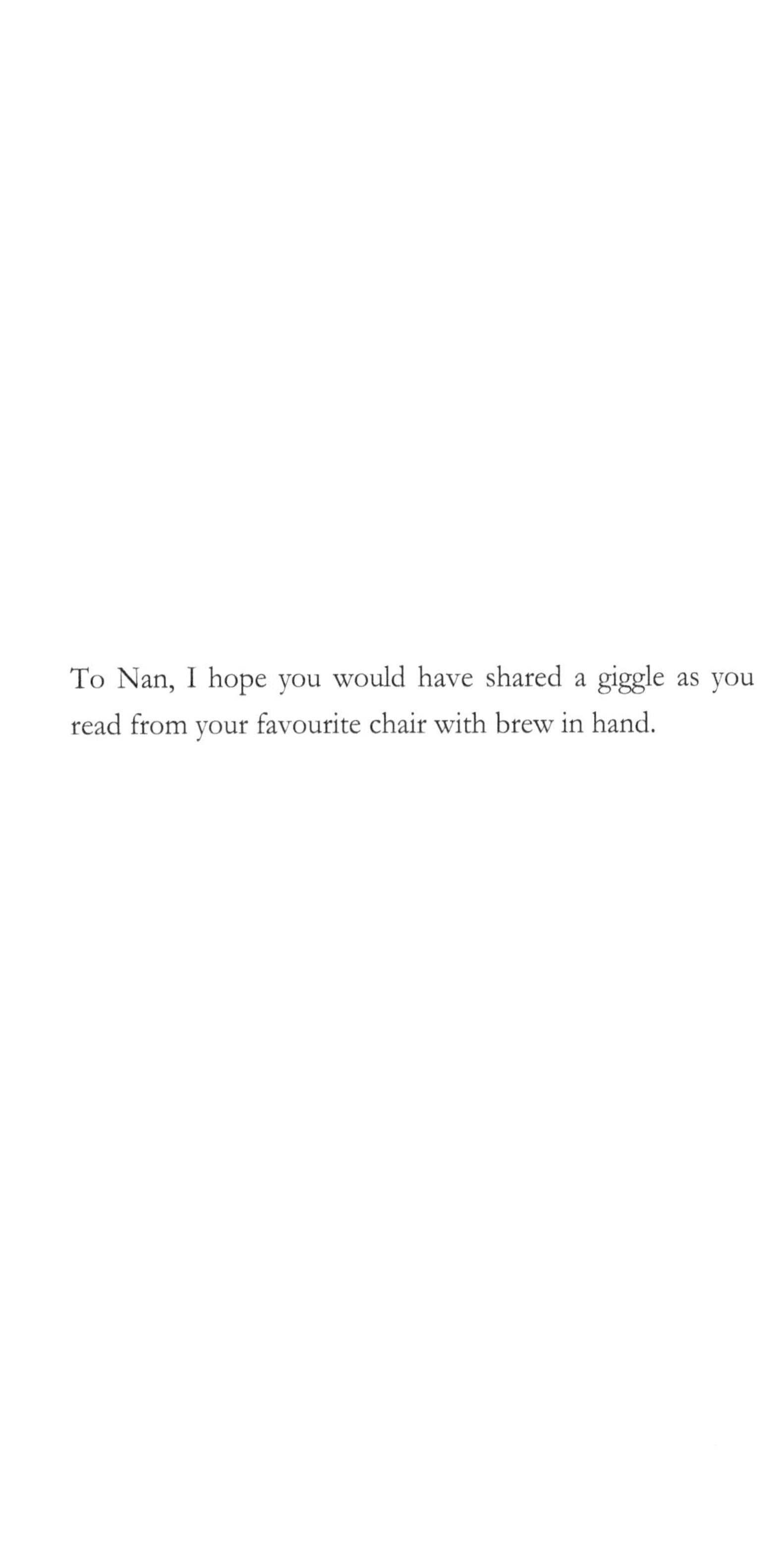

To Nan, I hope you would have shared a giggle as you read from your favourite chair with brew in hand.

Mind Commodity

Lyv Landson

Oski Press

Prologue

I was prepared neither in strength nor trouser for the upcoming collision with the rapidly approaching ground. The metal walls weren't durable enough to withstand the impending force so one question remained… in this time of great stress should I jump or sit?

But that unthinkable inevitable is to come, so back to the now…

Chapter 1

The QuinXe Company engulfed entrepreneurs like vultures gorging on a carcass. A hastily scrawled note served to remind me that I was being paid to be here, so I focused in on a trio of business types announcing their ideas to us, the corporate incarcerated. They snapped through their pitch until questions about profit and sales became fatal errors as statistical silence fell. So, in swoops the pink socks and polka dot tie of our boss with pizazz speech ready to ground them into verbal submission. She vomited phrases like, "Expansion is often externally assisted," and "buy in to buy out," until delivering the crux of positive business affirmations, "core competency ebbs with robust absurdity in our accounting department!" That was enough for another baffled team to join our corporate engine.

QuinXe made it their mission to polish these fledgling companies and lead them into the golden towers of canary profit while I created music for their products. Over the years I've learnt the key functions to tap into your carnal instincts and yes, I want you in the same position as Pavlov's dog so you hear the bell and want that delicious rush of endorphins. So that's me, a composer of the viral tune that stays in your head on repeat, coupled with a primary colour logo and captivating phrase then you're ready for global absorption.

Although, I know how annoying it is as I'm not immune to those gustatorial memories and need for immediate euphoria gained from familiar fast-food. My excuse, I'm a terrible cook with limited time so filling my body with a calorific chocolate milkshake, salty savoury, sweet doughnut and salad on the side for health feels just as good as the next person.

For a long time, I was stuck in a loop of sleeping, working and consuming. I was trapped within the confinement of a desk and chained to the clock in, clock out system. It started by cold calling the unexpected and asking survey styled questions to receive a litany of abuse and expected to be polite in reply. No thank you… I'd have liked to say, but a job was a job and they paid well for my time.

I used procrastination as the cure for unfulfillment until I was asked to assist a pitching team as the diversity tick boxer. I had a nonspeaking role and fulfilled it well until it came to branding and I hummed a little ditty. My soon-to-be new boss loved it and freed me from the monotony of my old role and entered me into a new corporation.

Now I create musical interludes for nonsense products and travel the world which saves me from the chronic stress of oppressive office life, however not in this unnaturally muggy October.

***

A double dipped biscuit slowly descended to the depths of my mantra striped mug. "Geez!" I shouted into the open office space but I remained inconspicuous as every head was donned with silencing headphones and faces communicating with their screens. I drank until sodden lumps hit my tongue, but coffee wasn't perking up the brain as the fog settled around the infinite bit screen that was still my life. Soon my attentions turned away from melodies and settled on flicking through the latest apps for 'Market Research' because I'd sat through enough meetings for one day. I waited for the minute leaving work was socially acceptable and my priorities moved from finishing deadlines and focused on skipping the hustle of the daily grind.

I saved my outstanding work into the never-going-to-do file before making my way out onto a monochrome floor. I was first place in front of gold trimmed lift doors and stood patiently waiting for that satisfying ding and the smooth slide open. "Ah," I extrovertedly sighed as my brain signalled I'd forgotten something but wasn't forthcoming in what. I tapped my pockets in a wild frenzy and shouted, "Keys!" It was always the keys! I quickly ran back to my desk slamming drawers and lifting used cups knowing they wouldn't be under there but did it anyway, until a glint from the under-desk bin alerted me to their presence. I grabbed them wiping off rotten apple-core juice and jogged back in the vague hope my original spot had not been forfeit.

The 'ding' came as a crowd strained into the lift with no queue system in place just unadulterated get home mentality. The doors went to shut with me still on the outside but clearly space within just as a person with a faux hawk haircut and checked waistcoat caught them mid-slide. The sneakered foot was met with a monotonous voice stating, "Not enough room for anymore," backed up with an additional, "yes clearly twenty people in here all counted and correct, so stop holding us up!"

Faux Hawk defeatedly released the doors with a slow sweep and I shrugged in apathetic reply as the singular chimes announced the lift's journey. "Maybe it's for the best as we wouldn't want to overload the lift," I offered, but this would mean an extra hour of travel time so I pushed the recessed button and desperately willed the lift to make its way back.

An unexpected clatter came from behind as oil-stained pewter doors clumsily shook open to reveal a dinted interior, "After you," Faux Hawk graciously said.

"Why thank you," I replied and took a step in and upward as it hadn't quite aligned to the floor. Oddly it was the first time in three years I'd ever seen another lift in this building, but I wasn't going to miss this opportunity. A smell of stale fridge and sulphuric taste accompanied our arrival within as Faux Hawk pushed a greasy button causing the doors to rattle shut. We started our descent swiftly and noisily as lift doors clanged in attempt to stay firmly shut while elapsing light bars were replaced with pits of bleak darkness. As the tenth floor flew by, the hairs stood up on the back of my neck and motion sickness threatened.

Faux Hawk made a polite cough and said, "It could be me and it probably is, but does it seem like we are going faster?"

"It does," I replied as I grasped for a side bar and shared an awkward glance and strained smile.

"I might press the alarm as it's been quite a while now and surely, we should have gotten to the ground floor by now." The wavering in my unknown companion's voice was evident as a fist clenched tighter around a barely used briefcase.

"Surely security can see us?" I asked and waved dramatically at a surveillance camera in the corner, but nothing changed. Maybe they were having a break or thought that no one used these anyway so what was the point in observing. There was also the chance that we were overreacting as how often did lifts break?

Faux Hawk may have been having the same internal monologues as brows were furrowed and eyes glazed until realisation hit and a demanding pointed finger called for attention, "I'm going to push the alarm." Clearly this was the day to cause a stir and Faux Hawk did so by smashing said finger not once but five times. The button became a violent red and was accompanied by a hiss followed by the crunch of metal on concrete as the lift rebounded off an external wall throwing Faux Hawk temporarily to the floor.

Faster and faster we fell as it screamed its way through the seemingly endless shaft. I bent my knees in preparation of jumping but had completely worn the wrong crotch base for this situation so after an adjusting tug I asked, "Do you think we should jump?"

Faux Hawk also squatted and said, "Or sit? I think we can't stop this so we should protect ourselves. By the way, I'm Jason or J.C. I want you to know who I am before I die… Just so someone does."

"You're right, it's only polite we introduce ourselves in such a formal setting like this," I jested inside the perpetually shifting compartment as both our bodies swayed. "I'm Lori, I…" The screech of metal collided into my words until the pressure inside intensified and we dropped into all-consuming darkness.

Chapter 2

There was no lumps or bumps on my head so I attempted a full get up but dizziness captured me. Somehow the compartment was still intact and accompanied by conventional lift music that made everything seem a touch more normal. But the question remained, what the hell was happening? Well, I was still in a lift with the disgusting smell and same Faux Hawk associate. I felt okay as I had two arms, two legs and could wiggle my fingers and toes so all good so far. Boobs were wonky and chest was tight but after a quick readjust of the bra everything was back to standard operating. I hadn't wet myself and there wasn't any pain so I attempted a slower get up but stopped at halfway as dizziness still threatened.

"You should stay still," Faux Hawk said as he quickly flicked his eyes down to consider me before returning his vision to the doors with lips moving soundlessly. He winced with each passing light flash and muttered, "I mean in case you're hurt."

"I'm okay thanks," I replied and resisted the urge to splurge my guts onto the floor.

"Your head was hit pretty hard and there's some blood," he said and pointed to the corner without taking his eyes off the doors.

"I always wanted to be a red head…," That would have been the time to insert his name but I was useless in that system of recall, "Sorry, my head is throbbing, who are you?"

"It was J.C. but Casey will do now and you're Lori?"

Score one-nil to Casey and his superb name database, I readjusted and replied, "That's correct. So Casey, any ideas what happened?"

"I think the brakes failed and you landed on the floor… minus fifty-eight, fifty-nine," he paused and shook his head almost not believing his own words, "the lift started again and now we are on floor minus sixty-four… sixty-five."

I tried for a third time and managed a full get up with assistance from his sweaty outreached palm. It was more like standing on a train than vertically moving box so asked, "Are we going sideways?"

"Yeh, I think so."

Peacefulness crept over me replacing the sheer panic as it was an incomprehensible thought to be on the brink of death because that was too dramatic, so on the brink of imminent pain at least. We had survived whatever caused this and we were still travelling…albeit slanted or sideways but certainly slower and sturdier than before. I reached out for the alarm bell but Casey tugged me away. "I've tried that twice already and it doesn't work anymore."

"That's fine but I need to do it. It's like when people come up to a pedestrian crossing and have witnessed three people push the button before them, but they do it anyway."

"Then go ahead but it'll change," he said with an awkward shrug and re-braced himself against a floppy panel.

"What'll change?"

"It dissolves."

"And it's me who's got a head injury? Look, they are there now," I said as the alarm was clearly at the bottom of two rows of chronologically ordered buttons. "Nothing out of the ordinary." I reached out but my finger never made it as the buttons lifted from their spaces and moved as if made from particles of light moving independently from their casing. Each number was replaced with an unusual icon before settling into an unknown formula. I pushed a random pattern in the hope I'd get some form of help but only received a murmur, "Did you catch that?"

"No, it was garbled." Casey bent down and shouted into the speaker rather than microphone, "There are two of us in here and we are okay but need to get out. Can you hear us?" More distorted messages followed along with smoke pouring from underneath the panel. "We are on fire too," he added and frantically started pushing more buttons whilst blowing on the thickening steam.

"Wait! I might be hallucinating but I think the smoke is making words," I said and pointed to a space floating above the mirror.

[W3LC0M3]

"Welcome?" I asked for affirmation as this was becoming quite the sci-fi scenario.

Buzzing static filled the air but was soon replaced by chiming, not quite the C sharp high-pitched tone of a floor arrival but a dull ring. The lift halted and the dinted wall became two platinum edged doors opening as if nothing catastrophic had happened.

Waiting outside was an average statured person with slicked back bun and neat moustache. "Welcome to the Gröfu Pallur! I am Mr Edvard Játvarður," he said and pointed to a badge on a snug black suit with green trim, "and I can only pass my most sincere apologies that your trip was a little... rough."

"Rough? Rough doesn't even start to sum it up. We nearly died!" shouted Casey as he staggered out of the confines before grasping the floor like an old friend.

Edvard fanned Casey with a towel as he glanced with distain, "I am ever so sorry." He discarded the towel over Casey and asked, "May I assist you out?" Without waiting for an answer he took my hand with a firm grip and guided me into the bright expanse. The sun pierced the cloudless sky and cast golden rays onto the edge of a sand sculpture city which was seemingly very much away from rush hour.

The lift fizzled as the descending floors still flashed on the opposite side and then entirely dissolved with a slight 'pop'. How could something be solid and right there and then disappear? My question went unvoiced and unanswered as I still could have been hallucinating. Edvard gestured oddly as I clutched at the lift free space trying to comprehend what once was there until an executive car arrived on the beige road. Edvard flourished and announced, "The continental limo for you both."

This was becoming a better illusion but there was doubt in the forefront of my mind as I asked, "Where are we going?"

"It's a physically impossible walk but you will arrive at a beautiful place after a scenic drive," Edvard said and was shoved over by a bounding Casey.

"Lori, it's got balls for wheels," Casey said then whistled in admiration as he touched the car's smooth chrome lines.

"It does have balls but that doesn't explain where we are going or where are we as I don't recognise this place, do you?"

"I guess we have no way of getting back to the office now so we may as well jump in and maybe they can take us home,"

Casey said and shuffled over the back seat then tapped for me to join as Edvard ushered me from behind.

I hesitantly followed and asked the driver, "How long do you think it'll take before we get to wherever we are going?" No one answered as the car started to move silently. "Excuse me? Maybe you could just drop me off at the nearest station?" Once again, I was ignored so I leaned over the seat and found it lacking a human or steering wheel as it had been replaced with a multi-dimensional globe oscillating freely and highlighting a route in vivid yellow.

"Hey? Want some champagne?" Casey asked waving a black corked bottle and winking.

"You need to see this," I said ignoring the pop of the cork and pointing to the empty driver space.

He snuck in beside me and gasped as the road ahead curved upward in an arc and backward on itself. Casey pulled me back into the taupe handstitched seats which provided irritating comfort, it wasn't that I wanted to be uncomfortable but it was just too strange to accept that it could be comfortable. My current conscious explanation was that I must be dreaming so I took the fizz filled flute and clinked, "Cheers!" then braced my hand against the plush lined roof ready for the rollercoaster ride. On approach to the curve a violent bile icon appeared showing two lines closing together as an extra seatbelt wound itself out automatically over my chest. The car started making an upward ascent as a Scottish accent announced, "Manipulation of gravity engaged. Remain seated for safety."

The car moved elegantly and effortlessly upside down as the world bent with the curve of the road and sand dunes were replaced with grass filled plates that bowed and flexed allowing them to form cuboid hedgerows and prismatic trees. The icon disappeared as my seatbelt was spontaneously released leaving only the lap belt as we returned to ground level. As our journey progressed we drained the remaining champagne just before the car rolled to a stop and moved leftward into a space, no complex parallel parking needed here as the doors automatically opened upward and the announcer said, "Your journey is over."

Casey shouted, "This is incredible, let's go."

"What has my drunken brain made?" I spluttered as I staggered out and was faced with a topaz acorn shaped building strewn with brutalist platforms jutting out at impossible angles. Tree stumps covered in variegated ivy lined the entrance route along with potted plants that overspilled floral tentacles creating elaborate jigsaws between the paving slabs. The entrance was shaded by the rest of the overhanging building but was counter lit with streams of glowing light. The doors swung open and Casey guided us into an ultra-modern atrium. Money must have ebbed and flowed here as easily as the flowers did and this was far beyond my imagination.

A suited person stood behind a metallic desk and directed a relaxed couple over to a signpost of arrows in symbolic font pointing to physically unachievable destinations.

"Excuse me?" Casey said and added, "Oh, hi Edvard you got here quickly!"

The person turned to reveal harsh facial features and a bright pink fringe which proved they were not Edvard, but another suit wearing someone. "Welcome to Gröfu Pallur! I am Mx Ármine Játvarður," a spindly finger pointed to a badge. "Edvard and I do look alike except I do not support facial hairs." Ármine then ignored us both as a floating key appeared at the desk and was directed in amongst a series of hooks with only a passing gesture before Ármine glanced over to us and continued, "Apologies, you will have my full attention now. Lori, please tell me how you like to be addressed?"

"Lori… just Lori is fine. How do you know who I am?"

"You are booked in here and your face matches this image of you. Lori your pronouns are preloaded with context stimulator to reciprocate others so immediate recognition is achieved. As for your date of birth… that is listed here and … excuse me," Ármine checked and rechecked details in a clear screen before scanning my face then continued, "your room is ready so let's see if we can find the particulars." Ármine took a deep breath and then continued at 10x the speed of normal speech, "The details are as follows… The extrapolation bases and hash rate are T.B.C. but a deposit has been funded and transfer of accumulated capitol will be solely held by us and conveyed out to the expectant mine owner. The tender acquisition has started and will be biologically transferred. You have a full package but on a preliminary basis, is that right?"

I shook my head at the nonsense jargon, "I don't know. Just point me in the direction of the toilet and then the station please."

"You'll find *your* toilets are just to the left and you won't need to worry about transport here as this is a paradise platform of plumbing perfection. Feel free to alleviate your stressful thoughts and relax your bladder as we take care of everything," Ármine added with smile and bow.

I made my way to the toilets marked with a double headed person with circular body and another single headed person but mishmash of tentacles both standing beside a bucket. I opted for circle and would deal with the consequences of being wrong later as my bladder pushed uncomfortably.

"Scanning for presence... Presence accepted. Humanoid; mid stature, unknown origin and in need of... Relieving. Proceed to door number two please," said a dusky voice as a door swung open within a row of three.

"Ready to receive you," the toilet possibly said as the lid opened automatically and the door slid shut. I wedged my foot against it in lieu of a lock and thought deeply as you do when you're on a toilet. I pinched myself causing a mild sting just to see if this was real. My feet were still underneath me which was a good sign I was awake as they usually disappeared in dreams. Perhaps this whole thing could be a weird reaction to a product from today's presentations however there wasn't anything dangerous that came to mind. I wasn't drunk, well I was tipsy but clear headed enough to know I was in a toilet stall. Maybe it was a new kind of technological immersive team builder so I may as well embrace it as that would mean I wouldn't have to do any cleaning or ironing for a while. I finished my lavatorial musing and washed my hands under foamy blue hued waters and returned to Casey.

"That all sounds good to me!" he finished and signed the floating screen.

"Marvellous! You are both on floor Xanty9.0. Ah, I need to issue you with a bracelet which has your room key inside and I'll activate your finger application for transactional token access that will act like a..." hands wafted as the word escaped them.

"Credit card?" Casey offered.

"Exactly! Thank you. Just pop your index finger and middle finger into these holes and away we go." The box was instantly applied to my unwitting fingers and pins and needles shot down into my wrist. "Your finger will illuminate the way to your room if I just change this." Ármine pinched my fingers together which caused a screen to emerge then flicked through what seemed to be settings before motioning pinching my thumb and finger together.

I did so and the screen dissipated and then reappeared with the same motion. "At least I won't lose it," I joked.

"That's quite impossible. Please do enjoy your time with us. Oh, I nearly forgot." Ármine snapped on a white bracelet with carbon blue streaks running through it, "there we are."

"I'm not dreaming, am I?" I asked dumbly.

Ármine laughed then readjusted to deadly serious, "You are in the realm of being chosen to stay with us."

"Let's hope my deadlines have been suspended or my boss won't be pleased."

"Let us deal with angry bosses another time." Ármine turned around making it clear the conversation had ceased.

Casey bounced on one foot to the next, "Come on, let's see what this place can offer." He led us outside to a half-enclosed pool with tropical awnings swaying in the humid warmth and casting shade on overly wide deckchairs. I wandered over to a bridge but was immediately stopped as several red holographic bars prevented my passage.

Ármine was behind us instantaneously and stated, "The pool is currently out of action due to refurbishment. We have had some difficulties getting the water to react just so, but it should be ready for you to enjoy soon. Please continue to your room." The doors were held open and gave us no choice but to return inside.

"Let's go and see what's on the way," Casey said and pinched his fingers together which produced a holographic model of our surroundings then he flicked it again causing orange arrows spaced at three paces to show the way.

"How did you know to do that?" I asked as I walked into the first arrow at midriff level causing it to dissolve and reform in the same place with a stronger outline and more aggressive point.

"A lot of time spent on ingenuity-based applications I guess," Casey said and strode alongside the arrows until we reached a glass door lift. He pushed a button which caused my stomach to lurch as the doors smoothly parted.

"I can't," I whispered but can't wasn't right. I had the power, but the mind was unwilling. I couldn't risk another calamity as my mental resilience was nearing its tolerant end.

"No, you're right. What was I thinking?" He gently touched my arm and continued with understanding tone, "Stairs it is." We stopped underneath a gilded archway surrounding two pearlescent interlocked staircases. "This place is incredible isn't it? I'm going to treat this as if it were a holiday and relax from the H.R. regs," he said with a laugh and shook his head as if he was coming to terms with this situation. He mounted the stairs with vigour but almost tripped backwards as the steps started to move independently. "Quick!"

"Wait," I shouted as I jumped on beside him and tucked myself in trying to observe the unwritten rule of same step etiquette. The step moved upward and bypassed others as they sloped out of the way only to pop back out as soon as we passed.

"Hey this looks cool," Casey announced and adeptly leapt but I hesitated and missed my moment. I gingerly dangled a foot onto a pre-popped slope however the staircase seemed to sense my need and delivered me close enough to casually step off and into a busy street.

Unreadable signs stuck out from each establishment with the general population mooching nonchalantly beneath roped lanterns joining the two sides of the street together.

"Here! Over here!" Casey called and pulled out a Y framed wooden stool from underneath a triple headed dragon bar. "Everything looks so good!"

The holographic menu was full of unrecognisable food substances. I swiped right and left as pink hexagons appeared before clicking on what looked like a salad and tried to zoom in, but instead the pink hexagon turned green and added it to a basket icon. I held it at arm's length and fingered it more carefully so as not activate anything needlessly as none of it looked particularly edible.

People around us seemed to be quickly pilfering through the options then physically pulling them out of the screen making them expand and increase the amount of information available like a potent ingredient list. Casey followed and snatched the closest hexagon then grinned wildly as if his technological dream had come true. It glowed green and lingered as he announced, "I'll have two of this please!"

The plaited haired bar person positively ignored us, so Casey continued to shake the screen causing hexagons to start falling out in rapid succession. "I'll have these too," he excitedly said and pushed the hexagons together causing a rapid fire into the basket but no sooner than they were in, they fizzled out once more. "I guess maybe I won't then."

While Casey continued to try and get the servers attention, I checked my phone or at least tried but it wasn't in my pockets or jacket. I subtlety gave my bra a squeeze just in case I'd stored it there, but it was gone. I'd not been without my phone in years and was socially naked, lost and empty as I had no way of explaining where I was to those who should know.

"Are you okay?" Casey asked.

"I… I can't find my phone," I said exasperated.

"Seriously?" Casey asked as he started patting down his pockets but sighed in relief as he flipped his out until slumping and showing a cracked screen beyond repair. "Guess it broke in the crash, never mind."

"Never mind?"

"It's insured and probably wouldn't work here anyway."

"Zeever lah vair!" The bar person shouted and made their way over to us.

"Oh!" I gasped as the bar person had an elongated purple face with wide hippo mouth slobbering as it chewed on something indistinct.

"Don't mind her, she's just really excited about my order. Aren't you?" Casey said as he jabbed me in the side and gave a don't-be-judgemental look.

"Yes!" I said and forced a smile.

"Zeever lah vair?" the shout came once more from a grimacing face attached to a wobbling head on a hunched back and posed with sturdy hands on hips.

"I'll just take it how it comes," Casey said and smiled.

The bar person snorted and shrugged before delicately dismounting a clay bowl with two dainty handles from a precarious stack. It was filled with a thick green liquid before being sprinkled with a combination of herbs and taken to a fish tank which covered an entire wall. The bowl was presented to the tank along with a version of Casey's symbolic hexagon order. A whispered conversation was had with the inhabitants swarming in a corner to which a few water dwelling creatures scooted their way up the edge of the glass and tentatively dipped an appendage into the liquid. A couple refused and sloped back into the water, but one was eager and made itself at home blowing bubbles as if it was happy to be eaten.

The bar person presented it to Casey along with a towel and single chopstick then added a tipple of pale amber liquid which made the whole mix steam as the creature happily bobbed about inside.

"You look sick, is this not your thing?" Casey asked.

"I don't eat things that can do a good backstroke," I said and pointed to the octopus-like creature that had stopped it's swim and began caressing Caseys hands with it's tentacles.

"At least it doesn't have a face!" he laughed as he lifted the bowl up and drank deeply slopping it onto his chin. The creature grabbed Casey's face and smacked it hard leaving a strip of bright red marks plastered across his cheek.

"Nox de wert!" The bar person shouted and in the commotion Casey dropped the bowl shattering it completely as his dinner spat out foamy juice and scuttled away. The creature was swiftly scooped up and soothingly stroked before being inserted back into the tank where it rallied the others. Now ten small angry creatures contemplated war on consumers.

A hooded person next to Casey sighed and collected the remnants of the bowl then snaked out a thin tongue which poured fluid around the pieces fixing them in place as they solidified. The bar person scooped up the newly mended bowl and bowed in thanks as the person to my left snorted and gently lowered a few anemones from their face made from tiny cuboids. "Learn from what is around you," their voice chiselled and grated, "the gementies are of amenity not absorption." The sea dwellers physically pulsated and seemed to be massaging the person until being prized off with chopstick and returned to recuperate in the slime bowl.

"Tutsie, tutsie," the bar person cooed at the tank inhabitants still angrily smacking the glass and garbled bubbles of viciousness…

Bubbles of viciousness was the chink that caused the last dregs of my cerebral processing to fail. I discarded my chair and started sprinting down the street and further into the unknown. Advertising spat out virtually from passing shops with offers of sales, cheap goods and discounts, but I ignored them which caused them to turn into frowning faces. I was determined to find a phone or human or just something that would allow me to go home but nothing came until I turned into a brick lined alley with a red striped circular logo and arrow flashing on the wall. This had to be their upscaled tube station so I rounded down the alley and waited for the push of wind from an incoming train but instead was becoming surrounded by things not human. They stared at me as they passed on the opposing escalator chattering their teeth and twitching their heads. The noise grinded causing my head to throb from the sudden jolt of exercise and hypoxia but once I caught my breath, I ventured within the bleakness as what else could I do but return back into a street with animal aliens or wait for a train.

I stopped in the middle of what should have been a station entrance but at this point the artist seemed to have gone, 'Enough is enough, no one will come this far down so what's the point in making it all glitz and glam.' The walls and floor were a smooth matt grey with nothing more than a thick black cartoon outline representing bricks, bins and benches but it had to be a platform as it had a blacked-out tunnel at either end. I took two steps inside as the architecture started to fold in on itself and the world collapsed.

All recognisable realness turned into an inconsequential unfinished image and time ceased.

Chapter 3

"That's it! We've got her," said a posh mechanical voice from a bijou glossy robot bashing my nose gently.

"Sgn. Sgn. Hello?" I questioned in dazed abandon.

"Hello, Ms Lori. I will be your servant here at the Gröfu Pallur. My name is Master Titato-bebabo," it said and bent sideways to reveal a metal tag amongst blue pulsing pipework.

"That has a nice ring to it," I said not wanting to annoy it and receive more nose boops.

"It's pronounced Te-O for short but I spell it T.I.A.O. as a silent 'A' can be quite stylish. Just to be clear I can do anything and everything for you, so what do you need?" he rolled over and plumped a pillow with pincer hands before stopping and tapping them together expectantly.

Moments ago, I was in a busy street and then a bleak expanse of artistic nothing and now I was in a bed being woken by a robot in what were the most luxurious sheets I had ever laid in and seemed to be quite naked. "Clothes! I need my clothes?"

"Please do not be alarmed I have processed them for particle examination."

"In other words, they have been taken to the laundry. Don't worry mine got taken too but you'll get them back. Here's a robe in the meantime," Casey said then turned away in unison with the robot.

"How are you here?"

"I was worried about you," Casey said muffled behind his hand covered face.

I got out of bed and hunched down on a dark indigo rug as I awkwardly donned the cotton rich robe. "I'm decent."

The robot's face illuminated into full brightness and asked, "May I show you around your new apartment?" he didn't wait for a response as he started moving effortlessly through and around objects on tracked tank wheels which surrounded folded legs. "Lori, this is the mezzanine level of your premium attic loft space and is fully equipped with king size bed, fitted wardrobes and elevated book nook just here over the stairs. Through this door you can find your ensuite with whirlpool bath, shower, toilet and sink arrangement," he boasted proudly. It was clean and functional with waterfall taps which seemed to be the same set I'd been looking at for some time but never seemed to get round to buying. "Don't forget to appreciate today's view as we are overlooking an ever-maroon forest nestled in snow-capped mountains of the Peniks range of Afth Gar." From ground to ceiling were industrial styled windows overlooking luscious woodland in the golden hour with inverted mountain peaks shimmering in the distance. Forget not being in the city, this was probably not even Earth anymore. "Tiny robot?" I started.

"It's Tiao if you would, I'll leave a holobadge out so you can remember. Please follow me." Tiao gently pulled the bottom edge of my robe before mounting the wall as his tracks climbed vertically and diagonally concurrently while he pointed to the stairs and cheerfully added, "Onward to the ground floor."

I gingerly placed a foot out before swiftly stopping and waiting for movement however they stayed cemented in place unlike the staircase previously. Tiao appraised me and moved his tracks down one at a time to guide me as if I'd never experienced stairs before until we reached the bottom. "Here on the ground floor, you'll see you have curved seating arrangement, multifunctional creation desk and kitchen." Each were olive wood except a pearly breakfast bar which had a larger version of the small robot behind it.

"A'rit," said a deeper northern voice reminiscent of old flatmates, "I'm Master FeRiYeDo but just pronounce it Fred," he said as Tiao placed a holographic title over his body, "that'll be rite enough. Can I get yeh some food? Perhaps a pie and mash or something more 'ealthy like?" Fred tilted his head orb like a curious dog and waited.

"Depends on what you have and what it will cost," I said as I hadn't any means of paying but was considerably hungry as the last ding-and-its-done microwave lunch was long ago.

"I'll make yeh anything yeh can conjure in yeh imagination. It'll be included in't extraction price and 'osting fees," Fred said and produced a variety of holographic images of American diner-styled foods.

"Sorry... extraction?"

Tiao rolled his way along the counter and informed, "Monetary costs aren't valid here, but you shall find that out in due course. May I make a suggestion?"

"As long's as it's tentacle free and not alive... unless that is all you do then I've just become a proper vegetarian."

"Proper veggie?" Casey asked.

"I try but I really enjoy chicken goujons."

"What about champagne and strawbs for eating on't veranda?" Fred said as a pre-laden golden tray was produced instantly.

"I'm not going to say no to that, however I'm a little squiffy or jet lagged or something so maybe not so much-."

"The more drink the merrier! Bring it on Tiao and Fred!" Casey shouted and rubbed his hands together in anticipation.

"Could you please insert your finger?" Tiao asked.

"Sorry?" I asked this forward little robot.

"That's how we operate and track the payment schemes here just a wiggle and insert if you would. You only have to do it once here and then once for each time you are out in a different establishment."

I stuck out my fingers as the tube effortlessly slid over. "Thank you. I shall escort you out." Tiao scooted down onto the pleasantly heated wooden floor as Fred let the tray descend from his giant robot suction cup palm to the tiny awaiting robotic hands. Tiao circled in front of us and left through a hatch in the middle of a door to which was the probably the outside. The door didn't have a handle and the hatch was far too small for me to fit through, so I pushed causing it to shake in place momentarily before sliding to the left and letting us out onto a sun-soaked balcony.

I skirted around a hammock suspended directly from the roof and over to a half sunken hot tub, I dipped a toe into the not hot, not cold, but just right waters and, "Ahh'd". Tiao set out the drinks and adjusted the landscape from snow-capped mountains to jungle lagoon lined with bush, palm and vine cascading around trees. Tiny bubbles rose from the milky water and hung in the air absorbing the last of the snow drops haplessly falling from the sky. I caught one but instead of the natural pop from skin contact, tiny arms protruded and it pushed itself back off me to engulf more snow.

It was a bubble which could think, prepare and actively catch snowflakes.

They were cognisant autonomous bubbles.

…Autonomous bubbles?

The fuller they got the lazier they became and blobbed about groggily.

Autonomous bubbles…

At total capacity the bubbles pinched themselves and imploded.

Autonomous bubbles which could not only plan, think and act according to its surroundings but bubbles which could move where they wanted to without anyone blowing on them. Nobody had created them and nobody had told them what to do but these autonomous bubbles knew their mission and succeeded in eating up all snowy molecules waving as they went.

They were polite autonomous bubbles which rested their feet in the hot tub and excused themselves prior to exploding.

Autonomous bubbles…

I pinched myself as Casey gazed in awe at the surroundings and Tiao patiently waited with tray in hand. My imagination vocabulary didn't want to expand to this new level of comprehension of talking robots, gravity inverting cars, hog aliens and…

Autonomous bubbles.

I was caught on repeat as my mental resistance combined with fatigue and general perception strain stopped working and I metaphorically snapped.

To hell with it and the autonomous bubbles! I threw off my robe and grabbed the champagne with all my wobbly bits on show for the whole whatever-world this was to marvel at and slid into the hot tub. Tiao held the cotton richness aloft to hide my modesty but what was there to mind where soap rich bubbles lived freely.

Casey was also now hidden behind the robe and quietly asked, "Are you okay?"

"I certainly am. I'm relaxing in this odd jelly water and I'm going to get drunk, if getting drunk is even a thing here." I popped the champagne and Tiao suavely caught the cork before bowing and returning his pixelated gaze to the ceiling.

"Are you sure you're feeling alright?" Casey asked again and half peeked from behind the robe, "You're naked."

"Aren't your observations skills on point today. I am very naked and perhaps… Perhaps the lift had exploded and I'd survived the concave mangling and I now am actually inside a hospital somewhere letting psychosis fill the gaps of the persistence of unconscious living. Maybe I'm very nearly dead in said hospital but dealing with it in a flashy hot tub with autonomous bubbles in an alien environment," I babbled then sploshed around.

"Do excuse my interruption but we don't use that term here. We are all 'beings' and not as you say, 'Alien'," Tiao interjected with a schooling voice.

"I'm sorry. In this 'being' ridden environment where I am surrounded by things I've never seen, read or dreamt about. I don't know whether I'm having a breakdown or not, but this champagne is delicious so I'm drinking until I pass out."

"Alright," Casey said and emerged from behind the robe and sat with his back towards me before stating, "I guess we should consider this analytically then." He pinched around in the air as Tiao took the hint and guided the plate of strawberries over to him. I slopped and slurped about extrovertedly while he munched quietly for a time, my eye twitched and delirious smile returned as Tiao refilled my glass unexpectedly and Casey said, "So… So, you're Lori… you entered a lift with me, Casey," he pointed to himself and ate another strawberry before continuing, "that lift crashed and somehow we got out and ended up traveling in a car with ball wheels…"

"And now I'm glugging incredibly delicious champagne in a luxury apartment with a breath-taking view," I half sang in joyful abandon. "Wait, I have a new concept! Maybe this place is a holding cell until we get accepted into a heaven although I'm not religious so it would have to be a non-religious waiting ground where you rest until… until you decided to follow an entity or ideological route."

"I don't really …" Casey began.

"Har har… [laughing]," Tiao mechanically said, "sorry my sound effect is still updating. You must understand that you are not a part of a theological representation nor are you in an afterlife as you have not transcended supernaturally but rather physically. I'm sorry if that disappoints you." Tiao cocked his head and clutched his robotic arms together as if deeply saddened by relaying the information.

"It doesn't upset, it's very helpful. You are very helpful." Tiao uncorked a second bottle and I followed the path of an ambiguous bubble which was late to the party. It turned in the breezeless air, rolling and bobbing before ultimately deciding it would catch the second champagne cork only to excrete it. It shot off like a burst balloon squealing around the balcony before bumping into Casey.

He shrugged and wiped off the bubble spittle then started to pace before venturing, "Perhaps it's time travel or Moksha?"

"[Laughing] You have not progressed or regressed in time, nor have you been reborn from the cycle of human life. Does that also assist in your comprehension?"

"Yes, yes it does!" I informed the polite little robot.

Casey had now progressed to striding along the chrome lined balcony then suddenly grabbed a pillow from the hammock and shook it vigorously, the inner foam smacked down to the floor but Tiao was hot on his heels tiding in his wake. Casey wasn't deterred and continued his touchy-feely moment with stroking the metal balustrades, prodding in between the flooring tiles and tapping the walls intently listening while still very much making sure not to make eye contact with me. Finally, it seemed enlightenment found him as the blood ran out of every capillary and pallor sunk into his tawny features. He swayed slightly before firmly planting his gaze just above my head and announced, "I think this is real. I think this is very, very real. I mean maybe it's an alternative place, but I can stomp and move things," Casey said and demonstrated with his sneaker shoe walking over the decking. "It's real and we are here."

I splashed around in the gloopy water as his justification ebbed its way into my struggling mind. It did seem real and there were too many sensations for it to be fake. Shit. "If this is real, really actually real then... You've just seen me naked?!" I yelled.

"May I offer you your robe back?" Tiao asked as he held a neatly folded replacement.

I attempted to don it quickly as Casey ran inside and I soon followed as all calm disappeared from within me, it wasn't nervous butterflies that escaped in my stomach but nagging wasps stinging from fingertip to toe. I tried opening the doors and pushed wood panels in search of a way out as an immense urge to return home and back to my life struck, "Whatever is happening I would like it to stop immediately!" I shouted.

Tiao and Fred shouted in unison, "Oh no!" and shielded themselves away beneath the kitchen counter.

Sheer panic was plastered over Casey's face as noises started chaotically colliding from nowhere specific. The fruit bowl was first to go, disappearing completely out of existence as if simply deleted and no longer required. Furniture followed next but slower as if a blanket of material was removed leaving only a rudimentary shape marking the place it had once been. I ran for the balcony but was left standing alone in the middle of a collapsing room folding in on itself. Soon all that remained was the bionic bar but what once was gloss had turned into crude steel belted with oil ridden pipes and monstrous engines until eventually fading away into emptiness.

"Wake up! Let me out!" I screamed but no sound was produced in this abstracted field. I crunched my eyes tight and willed the world to reappear as no matter how strange this was, it was better to be somewhere than an empty nowhere. Something had to bring me out of this space and back into the place I had briefly known. The lift conundrum struck again: to jump or sit down. I opted to lay down, close my eyes and shouted a barrage of silent rants into the nothingness as the outline of spaces yearned to return.

Chapter 4

After what seemed an eternity, rough shapes bloomed back into existence and spawned physical materialistic covers bringing them back to full regulated existence. Dust particles and fragments of fluff were imbibed into the materials with a magnetism that forced texture to spring to life. A window opened and shut in silence then replayed with sound effects added after jarring with auditory and visual processing. Once the room was back to how it was previously, never had I ever experienced satisfaction from hearing a mundane sound like a coffee bean being churned.

"It is 16:459:TH and all is well," said an unseen ethereal voice along with a rhythmic ringing tone of a healing bowl being circularly played out of the room.

"Excuse me, Ms Lori, may I offer you a mild stress reliever in this time of dismay?" Tiao asked as he anxiously placed his grabber claw-like hand on my shoulder.

I was still lying in a ball, peaking out through my fingers as I uncurled and replied, "You may Mr Mini Talking Shiny Robot, you may."

"Excellent! However, I do require to kindly use my name Tiao as one condition of our terms of engagement. Would that be possible?" he asked as he retracted his hand.

"I'm very sorry Tiao and I must say your name is both grammatically and musically beautiful and as of right now I will use it to engage with you always." My speech was running faster than the bewilderment left. I was still comprehending the situation of 'there once was a room' then, 'there is no room' to 'back in the room and somehow not dead'.

Tiao held out a tanned tube under my nose as sage scented dampness sprayed. I inhaled deeply as worries retreated into the background of who cares. I wasn't anxious about things I couldn't control or the place in which I now inhabited for this was a luxury and why not enjoy it. I floated up onto a sofa as the most beautiful lingering sunset set left traces of gold and silver around the room. I was in a peaceful place until an uncomfortable 'Dong Ding' came and was followed by a sharp 'Bing Bang' of a knock at the door.

"The mist can disorientate sound so I am sorry for any inconvenience but be reassured it will return to normal in a few hours," Tiao said as he shook out his ear. He gave Casey, who was hunched over breathing deeply into his knees, a reassuring pat before answering the door.

The doorbell chimes came again in rapid succession before Tiao answered but as soon as he did, it revealed a tall, slender blueish person tap tipping a foot impatiently. Tiao dived backward as the person strode over so demandingly and confidently that I was inclined to stand. They didn't stop until they invaded my personal space and stood so close that the beads of sweat huddled on their top lip were apparent. "I'm Jax, a management specialist. Now, I hear you are having trouble adjusting to the economical space so I will be of assistance." 'T'tip, T'tap,' went the foot at the end of legs that didn't quite fit the trousers they were situated in.

"Well why don't you come inside this perfect setting, oh you already are in aren't you," I replied as I found a pair of slippers that fit my feet perfectly and obviously they did as this place was like living in an exaggerated prefabricated home as everything was just so… right. "So… you are here to do what exactly?"

He sneered and folded his arms but they slunk down far past his chest and naval until settled oddly on his belt line. "As I said, I am here to help you adjust however I don't actually see the problem as you seem to be just fine. And you can get up!"

Casey did an exaggerated stagger and righted himself as a shade of ashen covered his skin along with a clammy sheen. He spluttered a simple, "Urgh," before grasping the re-glossed breakfast bar so firmly that it didn't dare move.

"What are you waiting for?" the awkwardly appendaged person asked and added, "join me for a caffeine-based drink as that should get your primitive brain into working gear."

"Ay up thur, will it be yeh usual Mr Jax?" asked Fred as he already prepared three foaming coffees with cream cityscape embellishment on top.

I sat and enquired, "You two already know each other?"

"In a way," Jax said waving off the chocolate sprinkles with fingers of mismatched sizes. "We recommend eating as a first line course and equilibrium settler. Have you eaten yet?"

"No. I didn't fancy tentacle soup… although… I have had a rather fresh and plump strawberry." My stomach growled, grabbed my brain and demanded an instant cessation to the gnawing hunger but mental functions were still predisposed in stopping the full body shaking as I clenched the stool and hoped it wouldn't fade into nothingness.

"What do you consume except arid air?" Jax asked.

"Lori prefers a burrito with the full works," Tiao replied.

"Yes I do, how do you know that?" I asked and plastered on an overexcited smile.

"I am linked with you now, so I know all of your favourites to help serve you to the best of my abilities and help you produce a high hashing rate," he added with a wink.

"That settles that," Jax interrupted, "A...whatever for Lori... do you want one too?"

"Sure," Casey replied but was preoccupied with the fruit bowl. He carefully took each item out and gave it a shake or squeeze before replacing it and stared intently until becoming astonished when it didn't do anything remotely interesting other than be fruit.

"Ere yeh go, enjoy," Fred said as he produced the wheat wraps with melted cheese pooling onto the plate within mere seconds of the order being placed.

"While you ingest, I'll explain the workings within here," Jax said and seemed mildly annoyed and inconvenienced even though he had suggested it in the first place. 'T'tap'... 'T'tip' now went a spoon aside a coffee saucer as he licked his dry lips.

I wasn't going to give up the offer of food but took a suspicious sniff and checked for moving parts before biting into a dance of flavours. All the elements were there including salsa, luscious vegetables, moist chicken, two different beans, guacamole, sour cream and a cheeky layer of crumbled nachos. Fred and Tiao had heads cocked again as if waiting for critique. "It's good," I said wiping oily dribble away from my chin. "I mean it's better than good. It's incredible!" I continued to fill my face as hunger rapidly ceased.

The two bowed together as their pipes flowed quickly making them brighter and glossier.

Jax clicked his fingers in demand for a refill, sipped then said, "An explanation of this situation for your kind is to think about farming. You find a need in the market, acquire a production animal, house it in a barn then feed it up and in return you receive milk or meat to fulfil the need."

I reluctantly put down the burrito and said in disbelief, "You're fattening us up to eat us?! What kind of cannibalistic, morally ethical, challenging bullshit is this?"

"No. You clearly haven't understood as that's not what we are doing here and there is no way you could gain weight off this food. Anyway, that wasn't the best explanation for you so just let me think of something simpler," Jax said, clicking once more as fresh hot coffee steamed into his tiny cup then he wiped it directly onto his ever-drying lips.

"In't meantime yeh should treat thyself to 'nother burrito or perhaps a cup of cocktail?" Fred said and winked at me.

"Don't interrupt me, robot," Jax slammed his now extended arm across the bar barely missing Fred.

"Most sorry, I am."

"Don't be sorry," I said and half got up out of my chair to rub his pipe laced arm beam. "You were only asking and I appreciate the offer so please may I have both burrito and cocktail." As soon as I had finished my sentence a burrito was presented along with a salt rimmed glass full of yellow liquid along with neatly folded swan napkin. I took a sip then shook my head in disbelief as this too was just perfect and I needed a better adjective than perfect.

Jax now had two cups of coffee on the go as he stated, "Okay. Let's see if you can comprehend this simplistic view, there's a mine in a mountain which is full of jewels and needs excavating but in order to gain the most commodity we need to keep it in good order so we can gain the best ores and gems to sell to the highest bidder. The Gröfu Pallur is your home, but you are the mine and the person hosting you wants to extract your jewels to fulfil a tender."

"What?!" Casey shouted and protected his plums.

"Moderate yourself," Jax spat. "Jewels, in this case is information. You get to live here in luxury and give us information in return. It's all very easy really."

"What information do you want? Insider trading and account numbers?" Casey asked as he relaxed his grip of prime plums and seemed to become more aware of his surroundings.

"No," Jax answered and snorted. "Extraction is simple, it's an information exchange about your world of ...," he paused and flickered through his fingers before a small orb virtually displayed, "Earth." He shrugged and continued, "You give key information about Earth and you can stay. You don't and you…"

"You get eaten?" I asked and put down the burrito.

"No," Jax said as skin cracked from lips to nostrils.

"[Laughing] Do excuse me," Tiao said and bowed deeply. "Here it is not permissible to eat other beings, nor anything that was ever perceived to be cognitively alive." Then he seemed to wait for a telling off from Jax.

"Isn't this chicken?" I asked and examined the burrito.

Jax waved off Tiao, "This air?! It's stifling. I don't know how you stand it." He threw the cup aside and grabbed a glass of water from the sink still without moving his torso just by extended an arm. "The burrito you have eaten may present as poultry, but we have only fragmented grasses and plant-based products here. I'll explain food another time," he paused and applied salve to his lips before finally pushing the drink vessels away. "Once you get your bearings, we will try a quick test and in return you can be waited on by idiotic robots."

"That sounds reasonable however Tiao and Fred are intelligent. What else is here?"

Tiao went to answer but stopped immediately as Jax pointed warningly. "Everything. We cater for over three hundred and twenty nine point three kinds of beings but I am not a tour guide so take a look and see for yourself. Now I need to endure more of Casey as your room components need a swift update." Tiao opened the door politely as Jax booted him away like something dirty and unwanted.

"Hey!" I shouted but Jax was gone 't'tipping' down the corridor with Casey and I was left alone in luxury.

Fred suction-cupped Tiao and set him on the counter as he checked him over. "Seems alrite. No damage 'ere."

Tiao dismounted neatly onto the floor, bristled his pipes and pushed on a random section of wall which opened into a metallic vent. He brushed off his tracked feet and settled in before going into a standby mode out of pure indignation.

"How dare he!" I snarled venomously.

"He'll come back, worry not. I'll sort out anything-."

"Not Tiao, sorry. I mean that bloody being."

"Oh, I see. Well, … we don't get treated rite well, but suppose mustn't grumble for what we do 'ave is a better life than sum," Fred said as he steam cleaned the used cups.

"I don't mind if you do grumble as you'd be justified."

Fred contemplated this then replayed my own voice saying, "How dare he! How dare he!" But just as soon as the sound escaped him, his pipes glowed intensely and he slunk back against the kitchen tiles. "Sorry, shouldn't 'ave dun that."

"Well done!"

"Oh'er. That felt a little bit nice that did. Are yeh sure it's acceptable?" he asked and cocked his head.

"It is!"

"Thank you Lori. Perhaps you'd like another burrito to celebrate your arrival here?"

I wiped off some splatter from my robe and tightened it up before adding, "I've had enough thanks… even my extra dessert belly is full."

"Ah'er, our scans don't show you 'ave one of them, only one consumption stomach full of acidic gastric juice and combination of enzymes. Might 'ave t' rescan."

"It's a figure of speech. I only have the one stomach."

"Like a joke… I understand. Rite ya'r. Now is there owt else I can get yeh?"

I paused a moment sipping the cocktail and noted the dribble and splash marks from the previous gluttonous activity and asked, "Are there any clothes shops around here?"

"Thur'r appearance modification boutiques and such like along with interspecies filters but as f' clothes well, I'll be reckoning that yeh'll want to make thyself more appealing to others visual sensibilities and that can be achieved at t'odd port."

That almost answered my question so I was going clothes shopping but couldn't do it salsa-stained, "Where did you put the clothes I came in?"

A vent mid wall hitched up as Tiao replied in a muffled voice, "Cleaned, dried and hanging in your wardrobe."

Of course they were. I shouldn't have assumed anything less. I consciously detoured to the curvaceous sofa and closed my eyes letting my brain defragment the onslaught of information and normalise it wherever possible. At least I wouldn't have to worry about missing rush hour for now.

Chapter 5

After 48 hours of self-imposed imprisonment, I had coped with this sudden upheaval by treating it as a holiday. I had slept longer and better than I had in months by mentally subduing the fact I was too scared to ask what was going on and too worried to even make it into the corridor. The redeeming feature had come in the form of the very polite robots who were helping me in the here and now as I shouted, "Mess it up!"

"Mus'nt" said Fred.

"Please," I begged but Fred was shaking his torso pipe, clearly conflicted with pleasing me or facing the brunt of burnt toast. Defined meals had now become the only indication that hours were passing. I had filled the waking ones with reading, relaxing and eating but after two days of faultlessness I'd had enough, as once you've achieved perfection, where do you go from there?

"I don't know 'ow t' do that, my programming would 'ave t' be manipulated," Fred replied as he pretended to take time in preparing my food instead of the immediate delivery.

"I bet you do, just make it too big or too little."

"And it'll make yeh happy?" Fred asked as beads of oil sweat welled around his glossy face.

"Yes. Very much so."

"Lori, I'll get int' trouble."

"I'll sign a waiver."

"There in't a waiver but tis yeh choice and if yeh don't like it then yeh've to say. But yeh must be knowing of this… it is what yeh've asked for not what I'd like to give yeh. Alrite?" He moulded the crimson-tinged grass into a patty shape and inserted it into a compact cooker. Then once grilled Fred bounced seasoning off his elbow joint and showered the burger quite theatrically. It was accompanied by tomato slices for buns and dripped with a mature cheese before serving.

And it tasted… well it tasted juicy and fresh with hints of charcoal gracing it. "Best one yet!"

"Tis fractionally overdone and in't quite what yeh ordered though," Fred said as he hung his head in shame.

But this was a success as who doesn't like a little rebellion. I'd broken him and corrupted my first robot, "It's brilliant and I'd like more of the same please."

"Well… Well, yeh won't get it!" This robot was quickly developing an attitude. "I mean of course yeh will because I'll get yeh anything, at any time and it will always be me pleasure to serve it to yeh." He bowed and smiled.

"Thank you," I replied as a soft 'Dong Ding' came from the ebony wooden door.

Tiao answered as I wiped the cheesy goodness from my face and nervously walked over.

"Hey, I see you've decided to wear clothes today," Casey said.

Nobody needed to see that much of my naked body and certainly not so soon in a friendship. I slunk in embarrassment and replied, "They seem to be all I have apart from a robe."

"Not ventured out and about then?" he asked and let himself in.

"No. I have everything here plus I really can't face another anemone challenge and navigate the social acceptance of communication between beings," I said and followed him into my own apartment. In my own home whenever unexpected guests arrived, I'd be moving empty pizza boxes and left over beer cans but here Tiao had already done the sweeping so I appeared unslobbish and socially acceptable.

Casey perched at the breakfast bar as Fred smoothly inserted a coffee into a waiting outstretched hand. "Thank you. You need to come with me and see this place. I've spent my time exploring everywhere and this place is beyond expectations."

"I'm sure it is but I don't know if I'll have the time as I've still got to unpack my socks."

"Seriously? Let me take you to a café and we can chat about things and I'll ease you into life here. What do you say?" he said holding out a steady hand.

"We did make it very clear she could leave and that we weren't holding her here. Although questions of going home have been raised and answered with 'we weren't sure.' So perhaps you could both explore?" Tiao added.

"See even they agree. Like they say, you can leave but why would you want to go home when this place has everything! Let me show you!" Casey added still with hand in place.

"Goodbye. Standby Mode Activated," Fred and Tiao said and dimmed slightly as pipes slowed and heads bowed.

Betrayed by the robots. "I'll remember that later."

"Come on."

"Fine, but give me a second," I went upstairs and rearranged myself into something more presentable. I washed and cleansed my face with scented coconut soap previously provided by Tiao who stated it was to get rid of the bags under my eyes and that recurrent spot that was threatening to emerge on my forehead. I'd be taking these hotel freebies home with me for sure. I attempted to style my bed hair with finger flicks and removed some of those pesky chin hairs as Tiao's face appeared in the corner of the lit mirror.

"May I suggest using the styling grungs?"

"I thought you were on standby."

"Yes… I… Erm…" he said as he shifted side to side.

"Never mind. What are drungs?"

"Grungs Lori." He pushed open a draw beneath the mirror and revealed a straight tube contraption which seemed to be a mix between curlers and straighteners and covered in avocado skin. "Just think of the style you want to have, and it will do the rest with haste."

It had to be my usual loose curls combed over to the side exposing the shaved section underneath. I closed my eyes and waited.

"Ahem," Tiao cleared his throat, or tube hole.

"Yes?"

"You have to pick the grungs up for them to work," Tiao said.

I picked up the heavier than expected product as it automatically attached two wires around my app accessible fingers and got to work by controlling the motion of my hand. I couldn't resist its instruction as it weaved the hair around, defrizzed and styled. Steam and butter flung out onto my hair with a 'sput sput' and once slicked and dried it had completed a far better job than I ever could.

"Are you nearly done?" Casey called from downstairs.

"Yep" I replied as I regained conscious control of my hand. Tiao took the grungs and placed them in a cool blue netting then nodded for me to leave.

"You look great," Casey said as he appraised me.

"Thank you for your opinion," I replied awkwardly as we ventured out into an aurora lit corridor full of similar doors.

Casey asked, "How do you feel about the lift?" as two glass doors parted ways.

"I guess I'll have to get back in one at some point," I said while my chest grew tight and hands became tingly as I stepped over the threshold. This was going to be fine as all I had to do was keep still and breathe slowly and deeply, not too deeply though as my head became fuzzy and my vision blurred. I held my breath completely which caused the same effects so no, what I needed was a balance of breathing completely normally as that would make this situation fine. I repeated positive declarations willing them to sink in as there was always the chance that if it broke down again maybe we would end up back at home. It started travelling backwards and thoughts of home became fleeting as I held onto a bar so hard my fingers lost sensation. Sweat developed around my neck and my feet went numb as the lift swayed slightly. I subconsciously clutched Casey and found a steadiness there as he didn't seem bothered at all.

The corner of his mouth tipped into a smiled as he said, "Be calm, everything is going to be okay." The doors opened onto a thick pustule covered floor and he popped his head out while the rest remained inside. "This isn't our floor," he said and was abruptly shoved out of the way.

Two halves of a person entered. It was like they'd been cut straight down the middle and skin stretched over severed yellowing edges to keep in all the gory bits, but they didn't seem in pain or bothered by the unusual biological occurrence as they pressed a button to another floor.

The doors shut as the lift moved leftwards briefly before stopping on our floor, confirmed by Casey striding out as I followed, knocked kneed and jelly legged.

We were in a street lined with reclaimed brick-built shops and lit by odd light flooding in from the enclosed roof onto people having their lunch around flower box cut benches.

"It's this way. I've visited this shopping avenue nearly every day so far. They call it the Puerto Bazaar and it's one of three here in the Gröfu Pallur," Casey explained as my self-appointed new found tour guide. We stopped outside of a shop with a diamond waterfall in the display as he sang, "From the flacko to the vacko, that's what's inside Hacko's!" He added a quirky dance and waited for a response.

"Catchy but nonsensical," I summarised as it was flawed in so many ways.

"I'm sure you could write something better but maybe not better than the tune that plays before every single film you know the… "Bah Bah duh dah, duh duh… duh do dah'" he sang before ending with jazz hands and then furrowed his brow as he asked, "Don't you recognise it?"

"GG, GG, GG, GG, F, Eb, D… Yeh that sounds familiar, but I can't place the flacko one,"

"Seriously?! It's on every time you turn on your TV," he replied exasperated as jazz hands slowly petered away.

"Do you mean here? I don't have a TV here."

He scoffed, "It's in the coffee table."

"Well, that's so obvious."

"Do you want me to get Jax to give you a room manual?"

"No. I don't read manuals, I'll just figure it out." I hadn't forgiven Jax for the kicking of Tiao.

Casey shrugged then became wide eyed, "Look free samples!" he pointed to a hybrid multi-humped person with paper hat and leather apron handing out freebies with an over energetic glee. "Can we have two please?" Casey shouted.

Two shot glasses were offered as a southern drawl answered with, "You got it! It's fresh today and made from one hundred percent sour mixology skill." Casey drank his in one and was keen for another, but the waiter stopped him "I'll rightly suggest you try our full-sized version inside if you like it or perhaps the spicy version if you want the kicks?"

"Sounds great! What do you think?"

I shrugged as I drank my sample more carefully, but I shouldn't have held back as it tasted almost indecent with buttery undertones breaking through the fruity acid. The server flipped their tray over as drinks clung upside down still fermenting in their glasses with not a single drip split. A seating plan appeared as they said, "There's a few tables still available."

"Let's go," Casey said and opened a door into a flower ridden cocktail bar with vivid blue booths situated underneath oscillating hexagonal art works. Copper machinery dominated the middle area and emanated orange steam as another leather clad attendant pushed, poured and percolated preciously.

We sat inside a booth and no sooner had our bottoms touched the soft studded seats but an out of breath voice from a napkin styled speaker box asked, "What… will… it… be?" Various beverages and sweet accompaniments flashed before us with jargon phrases beneath.

"I can't read the menu sorry," I said.

"Send… via… basket… please," the box spat.

Casey took my wrist and looked confused as he turned my bracelet carefully and made the menus become sharper as they cycled through several symbolic languages before it settled. "Mine was the same until I had help from ZiMe, my personal robot," he answered before I questioned.

The now readable menu was clearly designed in such a way to evoke salivating desire. It was mostly dried plant extremities so I chose a cocktail with pink liquor and sent my order virtually as a green tick confirmed receipt along with a cacophony of steam and noise so loud it drowned out Casey completely.

"I said, how's the rest of your apartment?" he mouthed through cupped hands.

"It's great. I've used it as a kind of escape retreat so far and mostly just being… creative you know." Such lies but I couldn't tell him this was too much of a system shock as he seemed so at ease with it all.

"Opened your desk yet?" he shouted too loudly as the steam eased and the silence was only broken by the clang of cup on saucer.

"Yeh, I've opened my desk and I turned it into a piano, but who wants to do work while they're on holiday? I certainly don't." Tiao had made it clear that the working space could be manipulated into most things although after a failed trial run which made a set of spatulas, I actually bothered to read the instructions and gained a construction block set which I unoriginally created a replica of a grand piano and set of utensils. "How's your room?"

"It's the same but bigger than yours," he said smirking slightly, "and it's got views over a dry canyon style valley but apparently, the bigger space you have the more you pay," Casey added looking miffed.

"How do you think they'll make you pay?"

"Maybe-," he was stopped by the arrival of our drinks given by a waiter who appeared mostly human until the cups were handed over by scaled ill-defined hands. "Thanks," he said and stuck two middle fingers up but bowed with lack of aggression or offensive.

"Odd."

"It's a compliment. You'll find a load of communication guides on body dialect and species interactions in your room."

"Let me guess, they are in my coffee table as well as they aren't in my bookcase."

"They should be, mine were... along with an odd book about a lizard maid. Anyway, I'd start there and maybe ask Tiao but as a quick guide everyone seems to be happy with a bow or holding your hand like this to say Hi," he demonstrated as a tremendous bang clanged through the café along with frustrated shouts and smoke emitting from the bar. The sample giving waiter barged in and waved for everyone to stay seated.

Casey winced in shock and squirted lemon juice onto his face and t-shirt missing his jalapeno-based drink entirely. "I don't really think I'll ever get used to this place. How are you really settling in?"

"I think pretty well considering the space monsters... Sorry 'beings', are everywhere and could potentially eat us," I said as I mopped up some of the spilt lemon while more clangs and shouts came from the centre of the chaotic bar.

"They probably want to eat you as much as you want to eat them."

"I guess. So, are you not curious as to how we got here or how we get home?"

"No, I've said it before. I think this place is great and I am happy to be here." Casey fumbled with his shirt trying to rid the stain but clearly indicating to cease. But it was always something in the back of my mind, even if I could be distracted by glamour and robots it was unusual we were here.

"I was thinking of just walking out the front doors," I said breaking him out of his idling.

"I wouldn't," he started, his face now deadly serious as his citrus stained eyes bore into me, "I saw someone try but a security being took them away. Ármine said it was too dangerous to leave alone, so I think it's best to stay inside for now at least."

"Does that not bother you?"

"Not really. I'm living my best life here and I've managed to send messages back home via Ármine, you know to make sure no one is worried. You haven't left your apartment until now and I assumed you weren't bothered about getting back?"

I fingered out the remnants of berry foam from around the rim of my glass before I answered, "I was just biding my time, I don't really have any-." I was cut off as the walls shook and a beer tank exploded from above covering most of the café in a frothy darkness.

When the soot settled a trio of beings staggered in with pallid skin and sunken eyes, they appeared entirely spent as one collapsed over the bar and another propped themselves up on a stool. The waiters seemed taken aback by their attitude and indicated to the smoke but it seemed exhaustion made them completely oblivious to the pipes spasming. The trio's last bouts of energy were used on trying to order with trembling hands, it couldn't be that they were this desperate for coffee. "Hungover I expect," Casey suggested as he smeared his hand over his face for a clearer view.

The bar person took pity on them and handed over soot splattered bottles from a fridge but one was dropped from the fright of the entrance doors violently swinging open.

Two persons wearing overalls entered with tool kits in hand, the back draft caused soot particles to gather in their wake but they maintained a steady pace as they idly walked over to the bar. One gave a gentle shove to the three now sleeping on the bar before they got to work on the coffee machine brandishing spanners. The other made a beeline for us.

"Shall we go?" Casey said as he slunk away from the much nearing mechanic and brushed himself down.

'Caralyn' was stitched into her dark denim overall and I desperately tried to imprint it into my brain as she proceeded to talk silently with animated motions to Casey.

"What?" I asked.

She mouthed 'Oh' and started to quickly move her hands directly in front of me.

"Oh. It's sign language? I know a little perhaps this…" *Hi, I'm Lori* I tried.

"Erm," Casey muttered.

They need a mechanic and you look like you are good at fixing things, I continued and added in finger spelling for the words I didn't know.

Caralyn giggled then signed to Casey who said, "Good try but perhaps your sign language is different? I think you just called her a 'lawnmower frog' and asked if she has any hedgehogs. She isn't from Earth so they probably don't have them there."

She tapped him on the shoulder and conversed for a while longer before beckoning my hand. She caressed my fingers causing tingles while she got to work with the tiniest of tools that worked out a knot just under my fingernail. Once she finished tinkering, a neon icon flashed over my hand and its counterpart over hers however the skin had been removed on the back of her hand and replaced with a gel mesh. The hairs on the back of my neck stood as she lifted my head to match her gaze then she started to sign and captions displayed out of thin air in front of us.

Hi, I'm Caralyn.

Hi- I started.

She stopped me mid sign attempt and signed, *Speak normally. I'll understand because it works both ways.*

"Okay. Sorry. I will learn your version of language."

In time you can but for now let's stick to this way as I've honed it using own engineering expo and still need to work out the kinks.

"No problem I'm happy to help out with any pickles."

She smiled and brushed back her hair.

"What's up with your hand? Does it hurt?" I asked showing the extent of flirting as I no longer had the capability of charming speech but complete intrigue instead.

It's a system from my home that is linked metaphysically to me. It is my lifeline, my inventory and my way of communicating, she signed and held it so closely that through the transparent jelly substance her veins seemed to have been replaced with a system of wires firing nodes from fingertip to wrist. I reached out a slightly wobbly hand but she retracted hers quickly all though not in time though as a giant icon hit me in the face.

Sorry, it's another update about tonight's party. She wafted the virtual letter away and continued, *sometimes they just pop out as the connection here is unstable but I'm getting there with modifications.*

I nodded at the nonsense, "I get that completely."

Sure, you do. I'm from Cras on Hypatia, you get that as well? She giggled and appraised me with a raised eyebrow.

"Yeh of course, it's got nice… scenery and statues," I said as my fabrication abilities were thoroughly stretched.

She snorted, shook her head then signed, *Righto, it does have lots of scenery. Anyway, if you are hanging out with this legend,* she side thumbed Casey, *then I'm sure you know all about the party because he'd never miss out on an oppo like that.*

She balled a napkin and threw it with great precision at the back of his head.

Casey startled as his attentions had been drawn to a multitude of crab creatures with funnels on their backs sweeping the remnants of dust before defecating them as lumps of coal.

Pay attention.

"Don't you have a job to do, I think your colleague needs your help with those at the bar?" Casey asked and pointed over to where the trio were deep in sleep.

I had a medic friend who would have been more use but those are just avoiding subservice and giving everything they have to the testimonials tenders.

Casey whispered something subtly and added, "I think more like a hard night partying."

You'd know all about that, Caralyn added and winked.

"How do you two know each other?" I asked and detected the subtle head shake from Casey downplaying the situation while scarlet crossed his face.

He's an absolute raving animal and a client expert who should know better as he didn't even introduce us.

He grimaced and readjusted his jumper and tie as any raver would do, then muttered, "Lori meet Caralyn, Caralyn meet Lori."

Nice to... she signed and I filled in the rest mentally as despite the quickness of the translating captions I couldn't help but be distracted by her intensity until I snapped back into the room when she was waiting for an answer to a question I didn't see. *So? You want to?*

I said, "Yes," agreeing to whatever she wanted as how bad could that be?

She side smiled and held out an uncomputerized hand for me to shake. I took it as the warmth transferred and we shared a moment which seemed to last forever until the shouts of angry customers and frustrated staff dispersed it.

"Ahem!" Casey cleared his throat. "We shouldn't keep you any longer Caralyn. You seem very busy with explosions and mechanical dealings, so we'll be going now."

She rolled her eyes and signed something only to him then turned to me and signed, *See you later.*

"Only if I don't see you first…" I said awkwardly.

Casey was a vivid shade of maroon, which was probably not too dissimilar from myself, but with added smears of dust particles from the machinery. Caralyn and her mechanic counterpart lifted a hand in goodbye and I saluted… What was wrong with me?

"Come on," Casey said as he grabbed some napkins on the way out and started dabbing his clothes as he ushered me through the door.

"What was that about and how in two days have you got a name for yourself?" I said desperately trying to remember her name, face and touch.

"It's embarrassing…" he said as he tried to make the stains reduce but only made himself grubbier.

"Go on."

"It's nothing. I had a lot to drink on the first day and expressed the stress by dancing and generally just not dealing with life in a good way at all. I'm awful when I'm drunk and become an overbearing pompous prick and that's why I prefer sober client relations. Anyway, this isn't working so we should go. It's this way."

Chapter 6

Androgenous manikins wearing trypophobia inducing fabrics were arguing in the display window of the shop named "Clothes." Their faces remained disguised behind oversized stiff collars as they frustratedly battled to exchange garments. Each piece was pulled between the three creating rippled stitches until one won and strutted into the middle spotlight. It dropped a shoulder, bent an arm then cast a devilish gaze on us before running straight at me. It stopped before hitting the window and smashed it's fists causing me to jump as the glass bowed.

"There's no need for that. You know you look great you don't need us to tell you," Casey shouted. "These eh?" A blue outlined notification sprang up as he quickly swiped it away and hurriedly said, "I've got to go as it would seem I've got some unfinished business to attend to but I'll come and escort you later."

"But you are covered in soot?"

"It doesn't matter, I'll get changed for the party. Now go and shop," he replied and gave a quick thumbs up at a manikin who shoved a jacket up to the window aggressively wanting our approval.

"Geez!" I shouted as the pane shook. "What time are we going to the party?" I asked but Casey was already gone so I ambled inside and braved the shopping dread. Firstly, this was not the kind of place I would shop and if the manikins were their poster customer then there would be nothing that would fit or flatter. Secondly, why I couldn't just buy them online and get them delivered in the comfort of my own apartment was beyond me. Okay, each time I was ripped off on postage and packaging but it negated the annoyance of having to explain why I wanted to occasionally buy alternative gender clothing as I wasn't going to wear trousers that were shorter than the pockets it housed or tops that didn't cover my belly button. My woes were eased because the shop was organised like a modern boutique with single abstract pieces hooked sparingly on the walls. We were almost back to situation normal except for a reel of never-ending circular helix with bagged garments perpetually moving along it. I stood mesmerised at the grey blurs as a shop assistant with boho braids came over, "Hello. My name is Boriana. How may I assist you today?" She appeared almost human except for the feet, they were attached backwards giving her a lopsided gait, and the presence of a third and fourth eye that blinked independently from the others.

"Hi, my name is Lori," I said holding up my hand as she reciprocated with the gesture.

"I just need some new clothes."

"That's so good because you have come into a shop that sells clothes. Well done you. Now, Lori, what season, style and species are you looking for, perhaps something less carbon couture?" she asked quite deliberately and guided me over to the helix.

"Earth human clothing and as for season… I guess the temperature hasn't really changed on the balcony so a mixture for warm and cool would be sensible. I'll also need a suit and a big coat for the snow," I replied.

"Right...," she said with a confused face, "It's the micro astral now so we don't have any weather or... snuwe. It's just cool nights and warm days for... Forever really." She plunged a lever into the floor causing the smooth flow of garment covers to slow in a blizzard of similar shaped sacks.

That wasn't helpful so I replied with an, "So?"

"Let me be clearer and louder so you understand. Do you," she pointed at me instead of the nobody else instore, "do you want the new fashion season or the last annualised collection to browse?"

"Whatever isn't what the manikins are wearing.'"

"Good choice. Well done. That's the cheaper option as well so let's search together." She gestured as the whole helix turned 180°, "Here we go, ready one...four...nine...," she idled and flicked through some of the options and said, "Delta and Beron Foris would give you most of your clothing needs and be flattering for your extra curves."

I stared blankly in nil response.

"You haven't been here before, have you?" she said with a motherly face.

"Does it show?"

"In so many ways. Just take these over to the holocamb and don't shout if you need anything. We use visual modifications so you pick options via the screen inside the room then add fabrics after."

"Wait, modification? Can I change my body as I'd quite like longer legs and stronger arms?" I said as I squatted and flexed.

"I think we'd all want that but I'm sure some of your species think you are beautiful as all beings are in their own way," she said well-rehearsed then airily pointed at a cubicle toward the back of the shop and shooed me away before ducking out of the way of another customer.

I approached the cubicle with garment bags acting as a comfort blanket as a curtain swung open automatically then immediately closed behind sealing me inside a rectangular room with whitewashed walls and floor to ceiling length mirrors. I sighed, so I was staying here at least another night or two and why not? Nothing bad had happened yet so maybe I did deserve a little time off, so I started to undress as a stern voice shouted, "Do not put new clothes directly onto your skin!" A hatch within the mirror opened and a tightly wrapped parcel appeared on a protruding shelf. I unwrapped it carefully and shook out a skin tone full body suit which after breathing in, pulling up and fighting the ripples into a more conforming shape still looked awful. Surely this wasn't how they expected me to dress?

A blue oval box appeared in the centre of the mirror and shot beams scanning my exacerbated frame as it instantly uploaded my pixelated form. A horrifying view of exactly how I looked in the most extreme ultra-high definition projected in front of me. I usually made an effect on my front half but would do a more of 360-degree gym approach in the future.

A receipt popped out of the parcel shelf:

[Augmentation ready. Please proceed].

I opened the garment bag and put on a t-shirt and shorts over the body suit and waited for them to be projected, but nothing worked. I waved and shook them inside the cubicle until a harsh voice stated, "Barcode unreadable."

I searched for this elusive tag and found it in the most obvious place of the inside lining of the left sleeve. I waved it randomly at the box and a summer outfit appeared on my virtual body along with a list of alterations which I tweaked until settling on an experimental pattern and fit. I then did the same for a trouser suit and lounge wear among others before adding everything to my order causing symbols to fluctuate with each item. Who cares how much this was truly going to cost as my earthly savings would certainly cover this and I wasn't going to wear one set of work clothes for the rest of my time here.

Another piece of paper popped out: [Order confirmed] and then kept printing and printing.

I took the overly long receipt to Boho Braids who was waiting behind a counter badly boxing up clothing, "Have you got your order with you?" she asked as if the simple thing would be beyond my comprehension. I passed over the printout and she listed it back to me monotonously double checking each piece was correct before saying, "Just some final measurements." I lifted my arms up in preparation as she evaluated me with crinkled face then asked, "Is that an Earth thing?"

"Yeh, I guess so," I replied and flapped my arms out chicken style just to clarify.

"That is so sweet. Can you wait a moment while I convert your measurements from the holocamb so we can tailor your clothes more specifically and match your shoe component," she explained slowly as if relaying a complex situation to a child. Boho Braids entered figures onto a floating screen and directed fabric rolls stacked behind her pearl panelled counter to unfurl themselves ready for tailoring. "That's finished. Well done on waiting. However, it's not yet covered within your hosting fees or promotional conveyancing as your account isn't properly active. But you can follow the prompt on the screen to continue." Block form letters scrolled around randomly on a see-through screen. From behind it, Boho Braids encouraged and ushered me to continue.

[First Task: Enter your name.]

I did.

[Second task: Click animals.]

I almost did. A nine-triangle grid of hairy hooves and who knows what arranged themselves haphazardly. I clicked a cat as the icon spun around and then big tick and star.

Boho Braids looked pleased and motheringly said, "Keep going!"

[Third task: Pick between a giraffe or gerbil?]

I didn't want either but clicked anyway.

"Thank you for your cooperation," Boho Braids said, "Here's some great news, your account now allows a further six outfits to be purchased and judging by what you have bought today, you will. So… today's order will be delivered in three to five days."

"Can I get the shirt and trousers now?"

"I can put a priority on it so it will be delivered to your apartment in thirty vct if that helps but there's an additional cost," she replied as the fabrics cut themselves.

"What's thirty vct?"

"Time. Oh, I guess it might be different. It's the mentafurgal so thirty vct is probably about two hours."

"That's fine, thank you." I said, relieved that I wasn't going to the party dressed in soot covered office attire.

"What about it wouldn't be fine?... Never mind do you want me to add priority on for an added fee?"

"Yes."

"Okay. Now go away and only come back here whenever you want clothes to cover your skin substance. Goodbye there to you," she formally ended then thoughtfully added, "that's not right, how do I end this conversation so I don't offend you by not talking to you anymore?" She waited with finger held out poised to take note.

"Just say, 'You're welcome' as that covers most things."

"You are welcome," Boho Braids stated then suddenly rolled her eyes, sighed and hid away from her next unsuspecting being.

I left with overarching appearance awareness which was displaced as a manikin-on-manikin fight ensued with victory being the ultimate attention of shoppers' going by. A shoe rebounded off the rubberised glass as I threw my hands above my head in defence and a yellow icon emerged:

[Notification from Casey]

I tapped it vigorously.

[Face to Face video call in progress]

"No!" I shouted and swiped it away.

[Notification from Casey]

The manikins stopped fighting and called a trend truce to observe my plight of media mockery. One stepped forward and grandly tore the air, while the others huddled and copied the gestures. I mimicked the action which caused the icon to spill open and state:

[Notification from Casey: I'll pick you up at 7:30pmt]

"What's the time now… digit link thing?" I asked and was met with a strong silence around the edges of my fingers.

The manikins now clicked their fingers in harmonious beat and like the sheep I was, I followed. After a single snap my fingers burst open with hexagon applications and clock. "Thanks," I said to the helpful manikins. One put it's arm on it's hip and shook it's head whereas another put it's hand to it's ear and waited.

"Thank you!" I shouted as they crossed their arms in defence as the third motioned the chefs kiss and held their hand up once more. What to give them? I played to their ego's and took a photo with them as they fought to fill the screen with pouting faces. After some excessive preening the moment was captured but several aggressive jabs at the windowpane confirmed they didn't accept the image so once again fists flew and ruffles rippled.

Chapter 7

His blue eyes pierced the nightclub searching for the next unsuspecting victim amongst the gyrating bodies on the dance floor. The thunderous music would muffle his attempts of flattery so instead he remained on the second-floor lurking in the shadows.

With voyeuristic intent he waited raring to shower someone in liquor until they would show signs of amenability however most beings were tucked away in dark booths and those just wouldn't do. No, his targets had to be a pair of persons so he could use one's curiosity to play off the others doubts and that's when he found them. The two gullible clients were leaning on the balcony overlooking the floors beneath and that is where the ambush would begin.

***

"He's still looking over, isn't he?" I asked Caralyn. It wasn't that I'd remembered her name but after me forgetting it for the third time she had written it on a beer mat and stuck it poking out of her dungaree pocket for me to memorise.

She subtly side glanced to the voyeur and nodded.

"How do you suppose we put him off?"

I can think of a few ways, but they might have the opposite effect, she signed quickly and giggled.

But it was too late, she was pushed aside as he inserted himself between us. "Don't you just love it when a well-groomed man walks straight into your hearts. That's right ladies I see you're hungry for my dazzling blue eyes, flustered at the smoothness of my oiled hairs and ready to devour my charming demeanour as I, Jeano Lüffer, offer you the opportunity of a lifetime. Perhaps we can start our salubrious negotiations with some beverages?" he added with a flare of his monobrow and extraneous twiddling of neat moustache.

"No thanks," I said as six drinks immediately presented themselves to us on a flashing tray. Four were graciously received in his hands as the other two lay in wait.

"Surely you two need a man to entice you into conversation so please have these obligatory free drinks. I'll even show you just how delicious they are." Jeano's face pulled apart with wet zipper squelch as each quarter produced a set of pearly whites and pencil tongue which pierced out into the liquid. He slurped randomly until his face zipped back together and he continued, "Please enjoy them as it'll make the prospect much easier to consume."

Caralyn was edging out of the way and signed, *Creepy.*

"Are there flies around? Don't worry you sweet thing for I, Jeano Lüffer, will protect you with my quick pace melee skill," he added with arm sweeping through the stale air.

"She's not-," I started but didn't finish as we could use this to our advantage.

Caralyn curled her lip in disgust as he continued to chop at the non-existent flies and my attention was drawn to the unusual waterfall in the very centre of the nightclub. It was the only thing out of place in the standard city club as it reflected those dancing around it in liquid spectacle but, for a moment, there might have been a giant face. I stared awhile longer but all I could see was Casey at the circular bar beneath, struggling to get anyone's attention. "Did you see a-?" I started but it must have been a trick of the dim light.

"Never you mind, all the flies are gone, I see nothing but beauty and offers before us. Now Jeano will lay out this agreement for you, you see we use brand-new earnings to invest and gain instant profits bypassing mining and processing costs. It's a no risk business innovation where you will receive consistent payments without ever worrying your sweet little heads about complex investment strategy. You must sign up now." He produced a pen and contract from within his double pin striped suit.

Caralyn peered over his shoulder and signed, *T&C's may involve total loss of earnings and body part removal.*

"Must be more flies and no thanks," I said more forcefully and batted the drink away which slunk slightly in disappointment.

"Don't be so hasty and do hear me out you gorgeous little fofo. We are at a crucial mid-point turnaround in our bush fund and you would really benefit from taking a deep dive with a miniscule currency transaction."

Deep dive into bush funds, Caralyn laughed and feigned flirty interest.

I couldn't maintain my gaze with her as suddenly the temperature in the club seemed to increase. Jeano turned his garbling towards her while my thoughts turned to an escape plan. We could throw our drinks at him and leave but that would seem extreme or maybe I could get the attention of the bouncers on platforms adorning the walls. Although it was difficult catching one as their attention was preoccupied with brightly coloured backwards flying birds gathering in the ceiling.

Caralyn followed my gaze and snatched a pink feather softly floating through the air. She brushed back my hair and placed it behind my ear. The moment was destroyed as Jeano slammed his hands down causing the drinks to fall however before they made contact with the floor, they were caught by a nearby tray.

"Darlings, come back in the room, back here to me. Jeano Lüffer wants to know why you should work hard to pay-out someone else's gains when you can have it all for yourself?" He grinned with all four-face parts then slapped himself back together.

Caralyn clenched her fists before taking my holographic captions and throwing them at Jeano's face. *Pay Attention!*

"Oh…" Jeano said as the words illuminated his skin.

No offers. My department pay me a decent wage and I have a consistent cover fee so whatever you're promoting won't be for me unless you can get me out of a ton of debt? She waited with hands on hips and A-framed stance.

He preened himself before baring razor sharp teeth ready for the kill, "Jeano can get you a payment plan with ease but keep in mind when you're no longer useful to those who rule you will become worthless. Jeano wonders, what will you do with those hard earned savings?"

Find a job elsewhere.

"You don't understand how good this is as your investment could double, triple."

"Quadruple?" I offered sarcastically.

"It could, you know it. See, she is able to understand that this is a once in a lifetime opportunity and if you don't invest now then you won't have time in the future. One time deal today, right now, ladies you must-. How dare you!"

Casey came bounding back and nearly sent the last remaining drinks flying, "Oops. Sorry. Wait… How did you get drinks? Everyone was ignoring me at the bar."

"Jeano has his ways," he said but flattered, "three to one though, this is going to be difficult…"

"Look whatever you're offering they aren't interested. However, they might be," he pointed to the bouncers who were now searching menacingly along each floor. Jeano's eyes darted back and forth before slinking away so quickly the piece of paper still hung in the air. "I've had dealings with him before," Casey said as he snatched the contract and squeezed a lemon slice over it causing the words to dissolve into the atmosphere and reveal an opaque motherboard. "Same one he almost got me with," he dropped it and smashed his foot onto it as the nightclub rumbled. "Didn't know I was that strong," he joked and steadied himself against the balcony as the floor didn't cease shaking.

"What did you do?" I asked.

"I don't think I did that," he said as he tried to piece together the impossible soggy wires until he cupped his ears away from the chaotic sounds reverberating within the waterfall. Its gyrating dancer reflections were replaced with the emergence of a face, just like before, "I knew it was a face," I said as Casey and Caralyn followed my gaze, but much of the night dwelling crowd didn't react. They barely missed a step as they were suddenly submerged in a sea of darkened gas from below and pounding rains from above.

The bar staff suddenly started securing shutters and were also engulfed in the blooming gas as panic filtered its way through the revelry. People emerged from their booths with trepidation and tension as the gas continued to consume.

Firm fingers tapped on my arm as Caralyn signed, *We should leave now.* Her eyes were dilated as they darted from shadowy hat wearing figures to a dark patch of wall where exits used to be.

"I don't think we can leave," I said just before ducking as a flurry of garish coloured backward flying birds twerted and the gas settled at knee height.

The only light in the room emanated from behind an unrecognisable huge face plagued by water convulsing as it announced, "You are not here of your own free will. WILL." There was a defined strength beneath the tone which portrayed true conviction as the words echoed.

What's happening? Caralyn shook my arm.

"It's talking, it said, 'We haven't chosen to be here'." This was followed by general shhing and collective waves that called for immediate quiet on my part.

Caralyn placed her hand in mine as she wrapped a wire around my finger and odd symbols appeared as the face continued. "This is a public announcement for each of you, YOU. Your trust is being abused as your liberties are being deprived without your conscious knowledge so listen and hear, HEAR. You can be free if you take off your bracelets and join us, US." Bouncers attempted to cover the waterfall behind veils of sheeted lights but vortexes of feathers prevented their plight. General pandemonium spread throughout those desperately trying to get out while others were fixed in place intently listening. "Fight back the darkness and join us in real corporal existence by resisting, RESISTING." The club staff continued their efforts as the speech grated and the image overlayed itself with other faces. The mouth opened and closed in a pattern of cadent pixelation but those fully engaged physically strained forward to hear. Plinths on every floor rolled out from sideline balconies to the waterfall as the face readjusted and said, "Let us free you from your prison, PRISON." The strident voice continued to repeat the declaration and was accompanied by intense consideration.

Caralyn let go of me and fidgeted with her wrist bracelet which was one of several elaborately designed ones adorning her forearm but paused just before the clasp released.

The face's words continued like a viral infection, spreading the ideology that channelled through general wrist fidgeting. The illuminated birds dashed in and out of the thick mist leaving plane trails as it lingered on their wings. "Follow the birds and free yourself from this cage, CAGE," the voice shouted from within the water as blue and white striped birds flew alongside the plinths showing people a way out.

The voice became indistinct as once again the staff rallied to subdue the speech however they hadn't been quick enough as the idea had been set loose. A call to action had been started and the first one to brave it was a being with a mullet. They snapped their bracelet free, clambered over the balcony and landed square footed on a plinth as the room held its communal breath.

Mullet's footsteps were cautious at first as the plinths joined together forming a glass bridge but as Mullet became balanced, bravado resumed and they strode straight into the waterfall with arms outstretched. Heads craned as they waited for emergence because surely any second Mullet would make it out of the other side, but didn't. This caused the idea to grow like a plague of innovative thought and next to try was Greying Curls who went with such a sprint they'd made it through in less than a minute.

This steady stream continued as the face's voice repeated and ideas churned into commencing chaos. Some turned away from the bridges while others ran to them creating a human barrage of people swarming to get out or get in. Together they pushed and shoved trying to achieve somewhere that wasn't where they were.

My bracelet was tight and more restrictive than it ever had been so it wouldn't hurt to just loosen it off a bit. I pushed it down away from my wrist as someone barged into me and screamed, "They've sealed the doors! There's no escape!" My head span in the daze, I should just leave as home could be just at the end of a bridge but who to trust? An unknown someone offering forbidden freedom or the fortune of freedom here.

My hands collided with something almost as greasy as Jeano's hair as the lights darkened along with the gas. It was turmoil trapped inside as there was no one recognisable here and Casey and Caralyn were nowhere to be found.

Soon sound was disoriented as I fumbled my way through the thick air until I collided with the side of the balcony. I hunched up against it and remained as still as possible to keep out of the way of others, until a light drizzle hit my head which then turned into a steady rain as globules of heavy water quashed the gas. A magenta bird perched next to me and shook it's feathers then pecked at my bracelet causing it to fall apart with ease. The bird seemed to beckon me with a wing so I followed as it led me away over to an up-ended table where Caralyn was half slumped behind. She was deathly pale and trying to use a tiny tool to remove her bracelet until her hand slipped and her head lolled.

The bird beaked at me into action. I shook her shoulder but she was out for the count. I asked, "Can you help me save her?" although it didn't answer as it was a bird but it beaked at the tiny tool causing her fingers to distort. They were covered in blood, no this wasn't blood but more like an oily substance bubbling from the back of her hand. The bird stopped and shook it's head before indicating for me to give it a go. I pulled the bracelet hard and it fell away along with trails of ooze from her hand.

Caralyn gasped and one handed signed but no captions appeared. She kept signing, getting more frustrated and angrier at my incomprehension until the bird created a message in the gas about the walls.

[5t0p the Bi0Blo0m Le4k]

Biobloom, biobloom… what was that? She pointed at her screen bubbling vigorously so I assumed that was the substance, grabbed her hand, swiped away messages in an incomprehensible language and dabbed at the edge with a discarded napkin. It became sodden quickly but I didn't have anything useful. I kept just holding the damp napkin in place and cried out for help as Caralyn's breathing become rapid and her skin had a greenish tinge. I tried to keep calm and was already sat but I hated being helplessly helpless. I continued to call out with mounting frustration but no one was stopping except him. Jeano ran over and shouted, "You both need to leave here immediately, Jeano can help, if you will sign this contract."

The bird shook it's head and twerted over to the waterfall as I said, "I'll think about it. Help me, now!" Then I tried to drag her by her belt.

Jeano produced another contract but stowed it in his jacket pocket, removed his scarf and wrapped it around her hand then grabbed the other side of Caralyn's belt. We dragged her along the glass bridge towards the waterfall. The floor was greasy with the swell of puddles and condensation from the gas but we continued until she was half in legs first. *Thank you,* she managed to sign then grasped my hand as she was pulled inside and gone.

"Now you sign," Jeano said as he thrust a contract into my chest preventing my passage.

"No!"

"Then pay!" He pushed me off the side of the platform. I fell screaming through shadows and bird feathers before landing on a dancer's cube just as lights flooded the club and any remaining birds exploded in place. The gas released those still trapped inside as freedoms face dissolved along with my chance to leave. The idea started to depart along with Caralyn who would hopefully be receiving the care she needed. I wanted to get back up there and join her but the plinths were retracting and I was stuck wondering if I would ever see her again.

A being with three stripes shaved into the side of their arms and head used a long metal rod to get me back on solid ground, "You must leave this area now. Come on move along," they informed and added, "everyone must return to their housing."

The air was stale with sweat and so thick it caught in the throat as I made my way beside the now normal waterfall. Despite the accumulation of limp bodies and press of people with a distinct desire for departure it almost appeared like any other club throwing out time. I joined the quick moving queue and eavesdropped on hushed conversations focused on consequence, convenience and conviction before passing through the doors and back into the Bazaar.

I was found by Casey who was stood on a well pecked bushy bench and waving however the swell of lingering people eager to reunite made it difficult to return to him.

"What was all that about? Are you okay? Did you get out okay, well you must have because you are here and you look pretty much unscathed except very wet," he said answering his own musing.

"Where did you go and why aren't you wet?" I asked as the adrenaline fog spread from my fingers to chest and had a quick dip to the toes.

"I went to the toilet as sometimes those shows can take-."

"Sorry," I interrupted. "Do you think that was part of the show?"

"No, well yes, at least I did at first then when I came back out people were shoving me out of the way and I couldn't get back in so I stayed out here and waited until you got out," he smiled with pursed lips.

Doors swung open and someone threw aside their gas mask as they instructed, "Clear the area!"

"We should stay for Caralyn. Where is she?" he asked.

"Clear the area!" they once again stated as more security staff rounded up the hangers-on and moved them along with force.

"She got away."

"What? Really?"

'T'tip T'tap' came a familiar sound across the floor as Jax hounded the security people. He was taller than before and so much so that his feet seemed so far away he was having difficulty controlling them, "You two need to evacuate the area," he said.

"We were just going," I said.

"Wait. Where is your bracelet?" he asked with an added 'T'tap' and stagger of the leg.

I hadn't noticed the lack of pressure on my wrist until now, "Oh I… It was so loose it must have fallen off."

"Actually, it's here," Casey picked it up from beneath the bench, "it must have fell off when I was too busy making sure you were okay," he continued suspiciously.

Jax replaced it on my wrist with tight pinch. "There we are, back where it should be. Tell me where the other one is as you entered the club in a group of…" he paused and checked his list, "Three."

"We don't know where she is," Casey replied.

"Everyone who has attended the club must be accounted for. If you see her, you must inform her that it is her official responsibility to check in and let us know she is safe."

"But she could be injured," I said.

"Then she will be attended to within the medical bay or placed back for rehabilitation and would no longer be of concern to you. Now clear the area or else you'll be in as much trouble as the bird that started this."

Casey escorted me past the busy lifts with crowds gathered hungry for gossip and down the stairs. "Mind if I come in? I don't fancy going back to my room yet."

"Sure," I said as the door was opened for me by a very concerned looking Tiao.

"Lori, quickly come in and you too Casey," he paused and stuck his head out of the door to check all was well or perhaps for others before sealing the door shut. Fred had prepared hot cocoa and was keen for details and beckoned us to the bar stools.

"It was a good night until, I don't know... I guess the face came," Casey said as he sipped.

"It told us to take our bracelets off."

"'Ow odd. Yeh bracelet's only a key for in 'ere. Nothing more than that but, aye, perhaps it's one of those G.P.R.S. trackers? What dya reckon Tiao?" Fred said as he cleaned an unblemished mug.

"Quite probably right there Fred. You see, there are places in our world which are too unsafe for you to visit and as such your bracelet would act as a warning tool for you to avoid," he said as he paced in circles.

"But then Caralyn?"

Casey placed his hand on my shoulder and said, "She'll be fine, I bet they got everyone out just like Jax said, her and all the other drunk people..." he gulped and laughed to himself. "I think this was a party that unfortunately went wrong. Just hear me out as that's a great way to drum up business isn't it. We have a portal to freedom," he added in a deeper voice before continuing, "Follow Us Prisoners! Follow The Birds to Freedom!... You'd go just for that. But then it went wrong as people thought it was real and started panicking. We are free here, it's obvious and I can't for a minute even believe I thought it was real. I've definitely had too much to drink again," he finally stopped his self-convincing when he received a voice note from Jax.

["You are requested to give a full oral statement about the occurrence tonight. Your immediate response is required."]

"Don't even get five minutes," Casey muttered and half giggled as he bid goodbye and let himself out, once Tiao had unsealed the surely impenetrable door. I also received the same message but I was mildly distracted from the rollercoaster of thoughts by Fred clearing his throat.

He refilled my cup and said, "Yeh seem rite troubled so may I offer something? It doesn't do anyone any good t' put others in 'arms way and considering yeh reaction when yeh came in, seems like you reckon it's real."

"It has to be, I mean the backward birds and her hand..."

"Rite y'arh. Backward flying birds eh?" he asked with a knowing glance to Tiao.

The seconds ticked down with impended momentum but what to say and how much to reveal to Jax. I usually took to formal conversations by writing with pen and paper to flesh it all out before making it into something more comprehensible so that's where I started. I walked over to the desk where a light powder had been laid as Tiao zoomed up.

"Sorry. I thought you may be entertaining Caralyn back here so I went to the efforts of adding a physicality to your audio projections. You see, I remember you speaking of her hearing difference and thought you might like to show off your musical ability and this way you'd be able to show her through vibration. See here..." he flicked open the desk as piano keys showed, "If you would?"

I played an arpeggio routine as small flecks responded by jumping and gliding though Tiao's clawed hands.

"That's very thoughtful."

"That's my job... Ah," he paused as if vivid recollection returned to him. I followed as he scooted up the wall to the second floor and busied himself clearing off petals from the bed, blowing out scented combustion filters and removing two wine glasses. Clearly the robot was more confident in my ability in human endeavours than I was.

'Tick, Tick,' went the countdown as I perched on the end of the bed and Tiao passed me a notepad and pen.

"What should I say?"

"It is not my job to meddle in human affairs," he said cheekily. "However..." he paused and nodded to Fred who bloomed a cloud on the first floor causing a slight ringing in my ears. "There are those who seek to defy sourcing. Some of those are not trustworthy and have been known to kidnap beings who are simply never seen again. Whereas there are others who fall in the gaps of truncated files and seek to improve the lives here. They have been known to use the Ave's and Darners but none have been seen for such a long time..." The cloud diminished and Tiao shifted in place, "I'm sorry I should not burden you with conspirator theories." He shook himself and returned to his normal serving stance, "Whatever you say should be swift, factful and non-elaborate."

"I'll write it like an anti-advertising campaign. A statement of blandness that will leave nothing for further discussion," I said then added, "what do you think will happen to Caralyn?"

He shifted in place a moment then shared a look with Fred before stating, "It is unknown but we can always check on her file."

"Thank you Tiao."

"You again are most welcome," he said and bowed then left.

Once completed, the statement was sealed and sent to Jax and I collapsed on my bed to sleep to swim in misted peace.

Chapter 8

Beads of sweat from fitful sleep soaked the bedsheets as the shrill cry of a distant cuckoo fabricated into existence. I woke to meet with the eternal face of politeness, he who waited in silence with dimmed features ready to receive the first instruction of the day which was usually my breakfast order.

Jax had placed a hold on the ever-elusive testing owing to the nightclub incident, so I used my time to investigate whispers of freedom and kidnappings. Even though this wasn't a village with an unusually high mortality rate, I was still going to Marple my way out of here.

Tiao stoutly refused any attempts of coercion. In a decorous manner he stated he wouldn't infiltrate the system but would provide me with maps of places less travelled within the Gröfu Pallur. I used these to try and find an escape or at least Caralyn. I'd last a grand total of two hours from leaving the apartment to the complete collapse of the world around me and abandonment of daily life. It did give a brief reprise which took me to a point where I was at back in my own home until waking realisation hit and I was inside the apartment and stuck in lavish life. I couldn't even convince Casey to join me as he was too worried about losing his precious apartment and getting into trouble.

This unchecked routine of collapse and transgression back to apartment wasn't long lasted as I soon received a cease-and-desist by way of distilled confinement from Jax. Although, it wasn't an actual restriction of liberties as there were still several floors free for my visitation. The only proper limitation came by way of physical barrier which popped out of my bracelet and alerted everyone in the local vicinity of my intentions of escape thus preventing my passage. They were cracking down but after a few extended days of acclimatizing to the surreal surroundings I'd settled into an almost normal routine at the Gröfu Pallur.

I now forced myself into polite society instead of being a recluse within this stunted paradise of fancy shampoos and pleasant scented furnishing. I'd asked numerous times if I could go home and would be met with the same answer, "Our systems are down, but we will endeavour to make your stay as comfortable as possible. Please don't worry about your personal planet of Earth as nothing much has changed." Or… "No, we can't get anymore communications out, you have already reached your total but be assured no one is worried about you." And… "please understand that your health, wellbeing and safety are our concern."

One morning a being was adamantly shouting, "I will be returned. I will!" They slammed all six of their hands on the desk as Ármine casually dismissed them. It didn't work as they continued their plight until security guards in well-polished suits took them away.

"And that's the polite way to deal with such foolishness. Was there anything you wanted?" Ármine asked but I knew when rules could be pushed and when to shut my mouth. So there I was with no work, no deadlines, no way to cancel any outstanding subscriptions and trapped in a hotel so I may as well make the most of it.

I did so, in a mediocre attempt to keep fit within a mostly humanoid gym, well if you disregarded the occasional second nose and third eye. I went back to my room, donned my active wear, showered and slurped a health ridden grass-based smoothie before making my way to 'The Sanctum of Sweat.'

I avoided the lift situation and opted for the automatic stairs where I engaged in brief socialisations of the awkward kind. Todays should have been a noncommittal acknowledgement of another's existence with a simple nod but it was usurped with a snap decision in favour of a hard and heavy, "Hello!" It was reciprocated with a forced smile as the egg-based life form floated around me with a sulphuric smell you could chew.

I urged onward and limited my breath until exiting two floors up and scanned myself into a futuristic neon gym. A ball tapped my ankle, displaying the following message:

[Do you need: Storage?]

I swatted it causing it to roll through several different options:

[Do you need: Toileting? Shampoo? Enhancement?]

I needed none and kicked it away more forcefully causing it to rebound off a boxing bag, dink off a doorframe and bob on the waves beside a rowing machine as the ball scrolled helpful suggestions. I was suspiciously eyed by the rowers so casually started to lunge away in attempt to feign any suggestion I had been involved.

A ceiling to floor waterfall infused with herbs and antioxidants had been voted best taste by 75% of a survey of 4 people and was the ideal place to refill my bottle. I checked for any hidden beings inside before filling up my pre-frosted bottle with vitamins and vigour while considering my plan. I've always been a fully committed health and fitness connoisseur and renewed a membership at my local gym each January, oddly coinciding with a stella hangover and a new year resolution which went; this would be the year in which I lost the love handles but within two weeks I'd lose the fight with carb cravings and consider instigating terrible things just for a lick of chocolate. I'd kept this routine for five years and my balanced sessions consisted of weights followed by a full recovery hour in the spa.

At belly button height a being ambled over beneath a mop of shaggy hair with only a turnip nose poking through and childishly said, "Are you done?"

"I am," I replied and wiped the overflowing water particles from the bottle as I edged away from them. I wandered over to the plumply filled weight section and took up a hefty dumbbell, preliminarily curling it as a physical fitness instructor virtually sprang up in front of me.

The polka dot orange uniform was blurred as it squatted in rapid succession only becoming clear when still. With their hands on hips they shouted, "You have good form for someone of your biology, although improvements can be made. Start your workout with me! One! Two! Three!" They lunged and bulged, "Your output is: COLD. How about a warmup of jack beans and pimple squats as you curl? Ready, One! Two!"

"No thank you," I replied and turned away to curl one out independently.

That didn't quell their desire for demonstrations as they thrusted and protruded. "Your records show you mostly use: STAIRS as your primary route of physical exertion, so let's loosen the lumber and try some Earth based plyometrics." They tapped on the floor and caused a purple rubberised cube to emerge then proceeded to action the exercise, "You can do it! Jump and… flex."

"Easy for you to say. The last time I jumped was watching a scary movie."

"I'm sorry I am unaware what that is but please, jump and flex!"

It seemed I wasn't getting out of this easily so stepped up with weights still in hand. Guilt left as this was a conscious effort to get fit and *wow*, how my lungs burned and well, *wow*, how everything burned as inflammable places became hot spots of comfortable aches and pains.

After six jaunty ups and flumps back down my forefinger glowed with a notification highlighting the spin class was due to start. "Okay that's me done," I said.

"Great effort," they said and marched in place glaring at me until screaming, "stop!" They stood with hands on hips and furrowed brow and exhaled, "You must replace the equipment in the designated area before leaving for your next session. Follow the signs to: Over here… Over there… Over here… Over there," the instructor jolted in place until the weights were replaced and I was released from the sporting scrutiny.

***

Spin class attendance was confirmed by inserting my thumb into a jelly coated box by the side of an over engineered door. Once sucked and acknowledged, a dashed line arose along the floor towards my elected riding machine. I narrowly avoided puddles of perspiration being cleaned up by similar but smaller versions of

Tiao and continued toward the outer edge of the room until reaching 'ThAcke8'. Each bike had its own colour co-ordinated spotlight and mine currently highlighted a narrow strip of crotch sweat staining the seat. The small robots must have spotted my anguish and saturated the seat in lashing of clementine which removed the remnants of previous occupier. With somewhat wobbly legs I mounted the pedals and waited as the rest of the room filled with thin waists and serious faces. Towels were draped over toughened handlebars while padded shorts seemed to fight against clenching buttocks and braced thighs.

The spotlights faded and we were drenched in darkness until a single beam of light shone on an instructor standing with one foot on the seat and the other on the handlebars. An industrial fan blew his long hair and beard as he squirted bottled water over himself and shook out his mane. The cleaning bots glared at the cleated soles scuffing the seat and one seemed to *accidentally* bump into the fan making it spin too vigorously. The instructor's face contorted brutally under the new force, until enough was enough and legs parted to suddenly drop and land one inch above the seat barely avoiding squish. "Okay cycle fans the regs will know me as Mr McGears and to the noobs… It's Sir!" he said with a swish of wet frizzy hair. "Let's bring the music up to an eleven and pump up those vibes to get those legs a-pedalling," he announced as techno drum and base flooded the ears. "Position one everybody!" Synchronised elastic snapped with bums in the air and heads bowed causing breathing to become forced as the air filled with heat from aerobic bodies.

Positional diagrams projected above in 4D by a faceless robot effortlessly spinning and was accompanied by phrases such as, "Spin!", "Move" and "Hydrate to breathe," however often the latter was difficult to achieve at the same time.

"Bikes ApLd5 and ThAcke8 you need to turn up the pace and bring on the power!" the instructor screamed as mine and another's bike became embarrassingly highlighted. "Get out the gains by churning the pains. Mild exertion won't flood the meps!" he continued as I increased my effort levels from half-arsed all the way to moderately trying just so the light would get off me.

The music changed to industrial docklands grind and it was now into position 8 of the 12 available with back upright and legs spinning like a duck running on ice. I lasted a grand total of forty minutes which was a new personal record. I slipped off the bike onto the now undulating floor as the undulating movements made getting out without disturbing anyone near impossible. It was like wading through a sea of sweat splatter and motion sickness which hit instantly as I swum bow legged over to the door. Once outside I slid down against a wall of inspirational text to recoup my general person with hands lingering over my knees in an adrenaline gush.

A trapped personal trainer knocked my ankle from inside a glassy ball after rolling depressingly across the floor. It mooched next to me and swivelled on its axis as I hesitantly opened it enough so their voice could be heard, "Perhaps the class was too much for you. Maybe you need some: REST and RECOVERY with the sensory room. I can offer you a full cool down?" Finally, it was talking sense. "It's this way," it continued as it rolled with renewed vigour across the floor weaving in between grunting bodies and instructional machines. The ball bounded off the door, "Ah I believe this room has barred me. How inconvenient. I suppose I shall have to find someone else to give my worthy advice to." It spun on the spot clearly searching for its next victim, "You there! You look like you need a stimulating session as you are: ELDERLY…"

***

The macadamia quiet room was just as described with several people stretching out in questionable poses and the vibe only being penetrated by the occasional sigh and minor flatulence. I grabbed a squashy foam mat and set up within a pastel lit square out of the way in a darkened corner. A virtual instructor in opal baggy pants and extremely long sleeves bowed to me as they sat cross legged. In a soft whisper the instructor said, "Let's begin with a cycle of animal-based poses in particular the feline as this is an overall comfortable pose. A relaxing pose. A sleepy pose…"

***

I was woken by a person dressed in marble leggings and pink crop top as their finger poked my arm. "I'd recognise that top anywhere, you were in the spin class earlier, weren't you?"

"Hello," I said plainly and wiped drool from my face underneath a fabricated cough. I shook out my exertion-soaked hair and tried to hide the fact that this was not my finest moment.

The person was oblivious or not bothered as they hovered on one leg copying the opal clad yoga instructor within my now crowded square. They breathed deeply and face slackened as they said, "Hi I'm […incomprehensible…] residing on Zimis5th." Before I had time for clarification she continued, "I've been doing this for five months." She expertly folded up into a multifaceted pose before asking, "How do you find it?"

I was exhibiting the slug pose and lethargically said, "I just followed the ball here."

"I meant how did you find the spin class? You know in terms of hardness and effort," she asked and meandered into a pose resembling a corkscrew while I remained a slug.

"It was good, but I did too much pre-workout to really gain the benefits of a full sesh you know," I replied like an arsehole.

"Yes, I've also made that mistake before and so now I start with combat training… combined endurance master class and then finish with a cheeky double spin 'sesh' just to loosen everything up." She untwisted then reformed the opposite way before sighing and saying, "Are you coming back for the class tomorrow?"

Tomorrow. Ugh. I'd been putting off tomorrow. "I'm not sure I'll have time as it's my first day of testing and no one will clarify what that will be. So as much as I want to get that morning burst of energy sapping muscle burn, I just can't commit right now." My joints ached as they resisted the roll out of slug and eased into mushroom pose while I tried to appear sad about missing the heart straining session.

She seemed to note the sarcasm and smugly said, "Surely you know your first test is always an informal chat? I'm sure you could squeeze in one little class especially for the limited time you attend."

Clearly my trend of early leaving hadn't gone unnoticed. "Oh really? Maybe you could elaborate on tests," I said trying to copy her pose as my legs creaked and popped.

"Each person has to sign a declaration promising not to talk about their personal testing as it changes their output rates but as far as I'm aware there won't be any spinning or cycling," she added with a smirk.

"That's a real shame."

"I'm sure." She buzzed in meditation before opening one eye and asking, "Are you attending any evening classes?"

"No. Surely a one third of a class a day is enough?"

"That's cute," she added and halted the yoga instructor before bending low and whispering in my ear, "I suppose you'll be free tonight then? How about dinner and I'll tell you more about testing."

"Yeh sure... but it's just dinner, right?" I wasn't keen for a date with this fitness fanatic.

"What else would it be with me. You're a girl?" she added with an enquiring raised eyebrow before. "You pick the venue and I'll see you later." She left without further comment or context.

I rolled up the mat and entered the shower as holographic red text scrolled across the silver tiled walls:

[*RECOMMENDED* Seaweed soaking wrap and cleanse. To accept >> Initiate a thumbs up to the locator.]

This was just what I needed after a minimally exhaustive workout however where to stick my thumb? Nothing said 'Locator', so I randomly thumbed up to the plug, the tap and the shower head which seemed to work as wraps of seaweed dropped from toilet roll holders above. I was beginning to undress as they lingered mid-air gently slapping my face and sticking to me like an over friendly shower curtain.

When ready, I held a slippery end gingerly as it self-wrapped around my limbs and left me standing greased up like a sludge ridden monster. I stood patiently as it worked its magic slithering in the crevasses, sucking out the badness, and infusing with goodness. Once finished it glided down a plug hole and I waited for the next stage as several shower heads opened and produced globules of salt flecked water which hung suspended in the air as if the gravity wasn't enough to pull them down. I prodded one causing a 'bahlump' sound as it burst over my hand pleasantly ridding my softened skin of the snail trails. Then once clean, the shower heads retracted and were replaced with a bowl full of ice water and a chain. I said out loud, "I can do this," as I'd braved it before and would be invigorated for the rest of the day. I braced for impact… before jumping out of the way at the last minute and unintentionally squealing as I slipped and landed half out into the open bathroom in public view with too much on display.

Chapter 9

Wandering aimlessly and content with the calmness that emanated from spending an hour in a herbal hot tub meant it was time to choose another bunch of interrogation targets. I'd been through a lot of beings lately and questioned seemingly everyone who spoke my earthly language from the Játvarður siblings to random strangers but my thoughts never strayed far from Caralyn as often beings would pass me by with some resemblance to her. If only she were here, I could wine and dine her and see if she had any information but wherever she was I hoped she was well and happy.

I continued down the street and passed the mannequins who were treading the runway in a graphite style substance and I considered asking Boho Braids but she had already agreed to answer my questions if I purchased something but now with a full wardrobe, I was still clueless. That's how it went every time I'd enquire about the formalities of testing, getting bypassed and brushed off because of the damning disclaimers and signing silences.

It was always within the T and C's.

I'd even scraped the barrel for one time only and dropped the big Q with Jax, who in a well-planned timely manner walked in front of me in the here and now with a collection of fawning beings closely following him as if he were a tour guide.

I stopped mid step and slunk inside a doorway hoping he wouldn't turn around and spot me as today wasn't the day for talking. Nor was any day as I actively avoided him and oddly never seemed to have the need for patronising explanations regurgitated via monotonous tone. But this wasn't me, alright I wasn't usually the life and soul of the party but I'd be there in the background schmoozing with the clients not sneaking around avoiding mundane conversations. "Geez!" I exclaimed as someone tapped me on my shoulder. My breath caught in my throat as I turned into an overbearing looming presence.

"I'm so sorry for making your heart elevate. Do forgive me as I ask sincerely the question of this… are you waiting for a table? We do have plenty of availability inside or how about a look at the tasting menu first?" said a 1930's styled waiter with waved gel hair and sideburns that covered elfish ears. They moved their leather apron and opened a slit in the middle to produce three round menus for breakfast, lunch and dinner.

"Do you know what, I will have a look, thanks." I pushed a thin button which flickered out a translucent menu surrounded by a rose gold frame. The food featured seemed more than edible and consisted of macaronic spaghetti hoops, anti-pasties and pana'coats. It seemed as if it was written from the point of view of someone who only had a vague idea of what the food should be but had never experienced it.

"There is also festa di mezzanotte but only two tables unoccupied," they spoke with such presence it set their face alight as it peered through the translucent menu.

"Some kind of midnight feast? Well, that sounds better than fridge raiding at three in the morning for scraps of cheese and gulping milk directly from the bottle," I said but was met with a confused smile.

"Yes, formally it is held at midnight, but the last serving will be that of nine pmt tonight as the chef wants an early night," they politely stated but I was distracted by those inside. Through a black tile surrounded window couples slurped pasta and pulled thick cheese strung pizza slices while others clinked cocktails over white clothed oak tables. The looming presence peered over my shoulder and napkin dabbed at a speckle of dirt on the window before gazing deeply into my eyes and continuing in a whisper, "Please continue your viewership."

The place seemed fancy and I needed to sort somewhere for my random mystery not-a-date with the super flexy gym goer. "Can I book a table here tonight for two please as it looks really nice."

The waiter popped away the little napkin then side glanced back at the window and said, "I'm pleased that's what you can see. We have three tables left on the hour nexus every hour nexus. Which hour would suit you?"

"The seventh in the evening?"

"Would you please insert yourself to confirm your booking?" they asked less menacingly as I jammed my index finger inside a metal tube and instantly a notification of confirmation appeared in my to do list nail. The ease of connectivity within this place was pleasing, especially when it worked. So that was booked, now I just needed to figure out her name and I'd do that back in my apartment.

***

Tiao slid into the living room with mop attachment smartly rotating and ringing itself back into a poised arm hole before being replaced with grabbing hand. "Good afternoon," he said and wiped his already sweat free brow area.

"Afternoon. The place looks spotless! Great job."

He blew out some crumbs from the underneath a bar stool with an air jet and continued, "Thank you. We endeavour to please. How was your gym session?"

"Short as always, but I met someone," I said as I threw down my bag and quickly pulled out a spiral bound notepad from the multi-desk.

He removed my bag with haste and asked, "Was it a meaningful meeting?"

"It was. I'm going out tonight."

He wasn't listening as he had become completely engaged with the furious act of scrubbing. He sighed in frustration as he chased an unblanching spot but it twisted away from him each time he almost caught it. He zoomed up over the sofa, underneath the rug and around the coffee table before climbing vertically and bopping it on the very top of my desk. "So sorry Lori, what did-," he was cut off by the bright fragments now mysteriously jumping on top of his closed hands.

Fred was actively shaking from the stress of withholding outbursts of laughter as I placed my hands on top of Tiao's and held the light before putting it in my pocket.

Tiao bristled his pipes and seemed to glow red, "What was that?" he desperately asked as I pointed to Fred now standing with a well-polished serving spoon reflecting the light. Tiao balled his clawed hand and mocked, "he's so mean to me."

"I think it's your brotherly nature. I'd do the same."

"I suppose I did replace his piliobio with soap that time and I do love a chase. I should show gratitude, thank you Fred. Now Lori, please tell me, how was your meeting?"

"I'm having dinner with…well someone, so Fred can have a night off the cooking," I said, then flipped through some crisp pages before jotting down the details of dinner. It was such a hard habit to break but without my phone or sticky notes I wasn't ready to quite trust my fingernail planner.

"I rite like cooking for yeh though," Fred finally said after shuffling about slowly behind his kitchen counter. I shot him a side smile as he carried on, "It's even better when we can practice 'special cooking' with yeh."

"And we do prefer it when you're here," Tiao stated and waivered slightly, "the apartment is loaded when you are within." He dismounted and peered from around the desk edge then clicked his hands together nervously.

"I'm here a lot though and it's gotta be good for me to get some one-on-one human action, right?"

"That is one of your needs neither of us can fulfil please explain who the person is?" he asked clicking his claws together. But

"Aye, don't keep us in suspenders," Fred added with a wink.

"The thing is I don't know her name. She was…" I placed my hand higher than me and said, "this tall and had blonde hair with maybe lilac highlights. Oh, and she wore this orange top… maybe."

Tiao and Fred shrugged their shoulders in unison and shared a glance before Tiao asked, "And she has arranged a meeting with you later?"

"Not exactly. I need to give her the details, but I don't know anything about her or how to contact her. Ugh… Guess I'm having dinner by myself." I should have been more forthright in name acquisition as she didn't seem the type to add it to a beer mat.

"I'm sure you already know there is a hive catalogue of active users for sale?"

The note pad flew to the floor as I asked, "People for sale?"

"For rental and tender knowledge is maybe a better way of describing it. For instance, this apartment costs an average user about seven hundred Kerlish or eight hundred and six Fevur, but your production should be anything in excess of one thousand to several thousand depending on markets and currency value. So, they would make a sizeable profit even when the rent is deducted."

"What if I don't produce that nonsensical amount?"

'Clang' went the spoon Fred was holding.

Tiao's voice quivered as he said, "You must make it Lori. You certainly should be profitable as it must always balance out." 'Click' went anxious hands. "It must. Please promise me. Promise me Ms Lori."

"Okay. I will." I reciprocated the gentle touch of his hands and gave a slight reassuring squeeze. "I will promise you."

"'Ere," Fred cleared his tube before he said, "you should tell her about all those directories of consuls and ambassadors of beings and what nots."

"Yes. Fred you are a clever one. That may just work and there are even service maintenance registers for mechanical beings. I suppose we could always assist in finding her?" Tiao said.

"Like a catalogue of people?" I asked.

"Precisely! The apartments are registered with part of the being's name, owner and status. Currently yours is called: LOTHUH45 on Xanty9.0 and showing a subsidised 75yais per hour but the important part is your name," he finished and scooted off straight towards the wall. He flicked open a panel and revealed a space covered in motherboards and finely moulded circuitry upon which he pushed a few pieces and out popped a disc which he brought to the desk. Within moments he brought up an entire directory full of names, sizes and subject types. He cocked his head and eyed up the chair before saying, "I couldn't possibly trouble you and ask for access to sit there."

"Of course, you can," I said and instantly moved aside as he scooted up, flung off his tracks then squished his bum into the soft pillow. Multiple screens emerged as Tiao stretched out his arms and pushed together his hands. "Now Lori, before I start, I need something to go on other than height and hair specifications as it would take months to review each individual user's photographic identification on here. So perhaps you know something else about her like her profession?"

"Erm. I don't."

He dimmed slightly then lit up, "What about her known favourites or routines?"

"We didn't talk much but she goes to the gym quite a lot."

"I can start there, I suppose," he added with a cheeky roll of the eye. "Thank you."

"No worries," I said then paused before I walked away.

Tiao paused mid click and asked, "Has something else come to mind?"

"I was just thinking that I can see her in my mind so perhaps there would be a way to project it out into the world so you could see it?"

"Even in our technologically advanced world it is not possible unless you are of omniscient origin or of omnibenevolent descent then we cannot process that information for you. If you would like to have Fred make you something while you wait, I will duly inform you of any findings." He waited patiently as someone would when they have work to do and you are detaining them.

"Just one more thing?"

"Yes?"

"Could you see if Caralyn is still listed as it might show her whereabouts?"

Tiao cocked his head and his face dimmed as if he already knew the search would be fruitless but in his true style he bowed and said, "I will do my very best."

I sat at the breakfast bar as Fred tried to draw Tiao's attentions with a silver spoon but he was fully immersed and muttering contently.

"How many residents can there be?" I asked Fred.

"The phrase 'more than yeh could shake sticks at', might be appropriate," Fred said and prepared me a chocolate milkshake with cream as an after gym treat.

I sipped and tried to recall something that would ease his search burden as Tiao diligently scrolled but nothing came to mind.

"There are one hundred and seventy-ish residents that may fit her description although I may need to dedicate more resources to this," he said as individual profiles popped out and were quickly dismissed.

"Can I make yeh anythin else before I change processes?" Fred said as he shared a quick glance and nod with Tiao.

"No, thank you."

Fred nodded, "Right yeh ar'," then folded his body inward and pointed directly to the ceiling. He appeared as if still in function and intact but unconscious as his eye bars dimmed as he connected with a light fitting which sparked with fireworks flowing over the white ceiling toward Tiao.

I jumped and knocked over a shot glass of frothy milk but was too slow to catch it and resigned to observe its descent behind the counter. "I'm so sorry," I stated but they were too preoccupied to see any disturbance so I attempted glass retrieval, but it was all pipe work and no real floor as hydraulics and mechanism took its place.

A short, stout and spouted something caught my eye along with the fizzle of a kettle boiling. I missed using one, but Fred augmented the teapot well producing steam out of his elbow and whistling when done. Tiao was still preoccupied with scrolling through unreadable languages, so I made a note to tell them later and ventured to the bookcase.

The topmost shelf had a series of never touched manuals explaining room maintenance and robotic care but would remain untouched. Instead, several other titles were prominently displayed such as: How to Cope with Hive Life, Capabilities of Air travel in the Modern Day and Seven Uses of Galvanised Steel. Some books were filled with geometric styled art whereas others were filled with blank pages. I held them to the light of the orange window checking for invisible ink or strange markings but nothing was revealed. There were also a range of fantasy books with fleshed out worlds in the first chapters then petered out into copy and pasted pages of pure repetition. The author seemed to know the jist of the narrative but missed plot summaries, nuances and flavourful characters. I could make it my mission to complete them during my time here using a mix of visual representations of symbiotic movements although I was better with strap lines and synaptic tunes… or at least I would have been for a paying client.

After toying with the moral decision of whether to put pen to paper in an already published book I decided against and went back to the bookshelf to gain inspiration but instead found an educational text called: Small Talk between Humanoids and the Codex of Worthwhile Interpersonal Skills. This was full to the brim of condensed lessons, the first of which was an extensive chapter on 'International Weather Quips' and 'The Smell of Rain' as conversational starters. This was soon followed by, 'When Monday feels like a Wednesday' and 'Awkward Dates'… I skipped the others and went straight for that one as it was as if I had been written into the very pages as it read:

INT: [A somewhat crowded bar, with low lighting. Two persons are trying to look cool and failing miserably when one plucks up the courage and opens the conversation.]

How did you travel here tonight? Perhaps you just got on a bus one day like a normal person and checked into a beautiful hotel to start your new life of luxury? Oh, you did, did you? That's great! … What me? How did I get here? Well, unintentionally. Yes, that's correct I got trapped in a service lift that crashed and whooshed around until it landed here. I tried for ages to get home and can't seem to and don't even know if I want to anymore, but I really should as there's bills to pay. What's that, the bill? Should we split or do you expect me to pay for the most expensive things on the menu that you definitely had to have because your influencer following told you to?

Okay. No. That sounded far too intense so best skip that section and focus instead on, 'Work Life Balance and the Impact This Has on Blossoming Relationships.'

I'd gotten a third of the way through the book and been educated on where I'd been going wrong in most of my dating life. Turns out I needed to romance my partner as apparently you only get out what you put in. So, for all the times I'd had to temporarily move away, fly around the world and just generally work each and every hour, I could have made more of an effort. There were so many gifts that could have been bought and memories that could have been made but I'd store the knowledge in case I ever met Caralyn again.

Tiao cleared his throat… pipe with an, "Ahem," and continued, "I have some good news and some bad news."

"Give me the bad news first," I said as I closed the book with a snap.

He anxiously clicked his hands as the ceiling lightening ceased and Fred gave a shake bringing him back to life. "Are you sure? It will upset you."

"That's why we give bad news first then we can end on a positive." I popped the book on the table and wandered over to Tiao.

"It's your wish. Negative news first. It seems that Caralyn is no longer within the Gröfu Pallur and her file ceases to be updated after the nightclub incident. She is not listed as a missing person and no one is or has ever made an effort to search for her." He flicked around a holographic image of her on her first day, she looked happy and excited not fearful and scared as I last remembered her. "I am sorry and no, I cannot change the files in anyway and nor can you."

So that was it, she was gone and there was nothing I could do. "But wait, could she have gone home?"

"I do admire the hopefulness of humans, yes there is a chance however without the updates we won't know. For the positive outcome of your other request we have searched transactionally, navigationally and minimally instructively and produced three possible matches based on your vague description. If you would follow me to browse them?" he asked and excitedly scooted back to the desk as Fred got his pipes back in order behind the kitchen.

"Well done, Mr Detective, that's astonishing!" I said with unintentional sarcasm.

He flicked up the three images in quick succession. The first one had curly ringlets with a photo taken from the side. "Nope," I said immediately and discharged them with a swipe. The second was taken from a distance but had the same physique and hair stylings, "I think this is her."

Tiao didn't seem sure but obliged my process by bringing up the information in a graph. "These passport images are strictly unviewable and inaccessible without triplicated form but we can use quantum technology to combine surveillance footage and create these short reels."

After watching and becoming even more self-convinced it was her I was ready to give my conclusion but Tiao interrupted, "Her case file looks… perfect."

And right on cue, there it was again, 'perfect' that one adjective that was embedded into everything. "So, what is the problem with perfection?"

"I shouldn't voice my curiosity really."

"You should but if it's too difficult then I'll ask you to politely tell me, what's up?" I said as he opened the rest of her file.

"On complete review there appears to be nothing out of the ordinary and everything is easily accessible almost as if it wanted to be viewed. But you must understand that this person has been hosted here in the Gröfu Pallur for six months completely without trouble or incident. Furthermore, each accompanying note has been inputted in regimented format." He continued pulling apart the file and shaking his head with frustrated confusion.

"It sounds like it is a perfect file then?"

"It is, and in that lies the problem," he scooted around with haste and flicked through pre-highlighted sections. "You see most files have minor errors, perhaps where things have been removed or replaced and there is always access to historic edits and old coding hiding in the margins if you dig deep enough but nothing is on here. It's rather similar to a demonstration file and doesn't even list any character flaws," he said as frustration mounted and detective gears were in full momentum.

"Character flaws such as?"

"For instance, yours are stubborn, obnoxious and tendency to rebel against navigational restrictions although that was added after your arrival," he added without needing to even look it up.

"I suppose I have nicer traits as well?"

"Certainly Lori, but I have never seen this quality of file in any humanoid. See here, it quite clearly states her height, appearance details and her daily schedule, that's all by the by but it's too new and has been the same since she got here. It's as if she already knew what she wanted to do every day without change," he hummed and stretched the file to almost breaking point as he picked the edges like a rotten scab before continuing, "the only other files like this are those of virtual intelligence machines."

I sat next to him and held the other end of the file so he could peer in between the light fragments and asked, "Could she be a robot?"

"That is certainly a working hypothesis however her file would have more code specifics like make and model rather than personality, as they think the less of that the better. Mine and Fred's files are some of the most garbled and corrupted with years' worth of information building and little time to defragment." He scoffed at himself at the incomprehensibility.

"So, no coffee spills and crumpled edges," I asked and grinned.

His face exuded a lack of comprehension which meant he was processing the information until he could deliberate an appropriate answer. But I didn't give him time as I grabbed a piece of paper from the notebook and wrote:

Please excuse Tiao from work as he needs a day off to defragment.

Signed, *A Person with Authority.*

Tiao gracefully received it and gasped, "You must not ask for this Lori. I will be in trouble. I do not need time to recoup. I am quite alright to continue service to you and-."

I cut him off before he dived into full anxious rant, "I'm not and didn't think I even had the power to request it, but I will remember that for the future. My point is that if you handed this into whoever oversees you, would they believe it?"

He turned over the crisp paper gently and said, "I suppose something is amiss here but I cannot decipher what."

I took back the letter, dipped a corner in the brewed tea and crumpled up the edges. "That's better wouldn't you say?"

"Oh no. Don't worry I shall rectify it." He rolled over it with tracks leaving little tyre marks and completely ironed flat.

"Tiao?" I asked and held out my hands to pick him up and then stopped, as this seemed an infringement on his personal rights so instead tapped him on his back panel instead and added, "it's fine. My point is that now it looks old, right? Maybe even more reliable like it's a true document whereas before it didn't. So maybe the file you found is a fake?"

"Yeh that's rite clever Ms Lori. Don't sup'ose I could 'ave one of them day off forms?" Fred piped up.

"He is teasing I hope," Tiao said and shot over mild disapproval. "But your argument is fair. Files that have errors, excuse me, more corrected errors do make it more plausible."

"Aye, that file needs a good cuppa over it," Fred said as he started boiling water before chuckling to himself.

"He really has become most rebellious. For now, I suppose at least we have an answer to your mysterious friend's identity and a way to correspond with her as she is known as 'Disdima' and this is her message code. Although please would you allow me to investigate more?" Tiao made a soft 'plink' sound and started to beep slightly from the back. I wasn't sure if this was some kind of robot flatulence as he appeared embarrassed and said, "Forgive me but I shall muse in bed for a while as I appear to be almost out of charge."

"You've been working really hard, I appreciate it," I said as I inputted the code.

He bowed and folded the file up in the air as he said, "All to make your time here the most enjoyable," before sluggishly scooting into his wall unit.

Chapter 10

The warm sludgy water left footprint puddles as I exited the shower to passively dry and get ready for tonight. I did a quick run through with the grungs and a deep dive into my wardrobe. Tiao had previously given insights into storage solutions such as where I could keep make-up, but I explained I would rather have the space for extra socks although I wish I had a dash of something as an extra thick pair wouldn't accentuate the lashes and diminish the wrinkles.

"Do you require my sincere and unbiased opinion Lori?" he asked after folding up the fifth combination of clothes I'd tried on.

"I don't know why I'm even bothering to try hard but yes please," I replied as I turned to the left and right catching myself at all angles in the geometric 3D mirrors.

"Perhaps you should try something that makes you feel comfortable rather than focusing on conveying a good impression?"

"That sounds good although the purpose of clothes is to portray an image of someone who is a much better you," I replied and flumped onto the bed.

"As you wish Lori," he added with an unexpected wink. "That's what I'm programmed to do you know, make a best impression with clean face and lubricated pipes."

"You do have very polished pipes and always seem swanky."

"Sywankee? Is that good?" he asked and paused mid return of clothes to their rightful positions.

"Yep, swanky is much better than good."

"Thank you. I must say you too are swanky and will be especially so in… yes perhaps this?" he continued as he highlighted a royal blue jacket, smart jeans, white top and trainers. "I believe I understand your plight to look your best as it seems the struggle of most humanoids within your humanity. I often consider changing my oil tubes so my mechanisms are slicker and less squeaky, but I am the way I am and I am happy with that."

"I think you are brilliant just the way you are and your tubes are so well kept they are practically silent," I said as he pixelated a blooming blush. I tried on the trendsetting clothes and much to his approval, kept them on.

"May I ask if you will be returning home with company?" he pulled out a rose petal and lingered with big eyes.

I took it from him gently and placed it on his head, "No. Definitely not."

"Right you are," he added and scooted away with the red petal balancing perfectly on his head as if he were a well-rehearsed debutant.

I sent a quick confirmation message to Disdima, her name I only remembered as I'd written it on my wrist in semi-permeant ink, then said my goodbyes and headed for the stairs. My main goal was to question about testing as she'd be well into hers by now, however I would air on the side of caution due to her file type and Tiao's advice. My side goal would be to eat some delicious food and to talk Earth to a potential Earth person about Earth things.

I followed a virtual line on the floor all the way to being greeted by the Looming Presence and was seated towards the outer edge of the crowded restaurant. A menu was offered and time pressure started as the waiter remained for my drink decision. Water first seemed sensible as then I could keep a clear head and spot any suspicious activity however a cocktail beckoned. The waiter had given up waiting and left a message that informed my choices should be directly input into a blank box in between the salt and pepper grinders both in the shape of leaning towers. I chose the biggest cocktail as my finger accidentally slipped on purpose causing a glass to rise from mid table and fill from the bottom up.

Once the glass was full a saltshaker illuminated with virtual instructions and I dragged my hand over the cocktail glass which pulled the shaker over the liquid like a magnet following a holographic dot to dot. It created a pineapple shape of multicoloured salt which lingered on the surface beautifully until suddenly sinking to the bottom as someone bumped into the table.

"Sorry," Disdima said as she sat down and a two-faced waiter took her order. The first face calmly listened before spinning around to reveal an immensely stressed face which asked for specifics in the selections. I chose freshly made carbs n'ara with squared off stuffed red pepper bread and she chose a basic olive salad.

"I'll have it the way it comes, you know however the chef would suggest," I said in order to mitigate further staff stress issues.

Disdima's eyebrows raised and her mouth snapped as she replied, "I won't. I will have a balanced meal under the total consumption unit of 487hurgh and not a single hurgh over. It shouldn't contain more than seven olives and must have a light sprinkle of figsmoila oil and three drops of tomato juice. Thank you," she added as the waiter's fingers typed out of sync as they struggled to keep up.

That was the first odd thing about her but some people were just specific.

Soft music created the background ambience along with chinks of cheers and romantic chatter as she leaned in and said, "Your jacket suits you."

"So does yours," I replied lamely, but to be fair her pin-striped suit did dazzle under the dim light. She smiled politely and glanced over to the open kitchen where chefs shouted animatedly as they narrowly avoided each other ducking and diving as they conveyed plates overhead and avoided the licks of flames underneath.

"The animal positions would be a doddle to them wouldn't you say?" I asked as I finished my already nearly empty cocktail.

"I wouldn't personally but I understand your point. They do seem very flexible. I believe they may be of synthetic origin you know?"

I didn't but avoided having to reply as a bowl arrived breaking the conversation. It was cold on the outer edges but bubbled with sizzling heat inside. I dabbed with my spoon to make sure there was no face sucking monsters swimming inside before taking a bite of the smooth cream which seemed to be mixed with a meat-based middle. I couldn't place the vegetables but recalled Tiao voices saying, "We don't ever eat each other," and "everything was grass based."

She appraised me without touching hers.

"Are you okay?" I asked. "Have you got food envy?"

"No. I wouldn't eat such intestinal filling food but you forgot to season it." She picked up a cigar rolled leaf causing a few meagre flecks of green to fall out. She then proceeded to unpeel it before taking a pinch between her fingers and delicately applied it to the corner of her mouth. Several different herbs were mounted up in neat piles so I tasted them with a dab on the tongue and found a mix of spice. They weren't so much of a selection of tastes but rather creations of feelings. I seasoned my food with calm and content which made little difference to the overall meal but gained her unneeded approval.

I finished the first course and chatted idly as she munched with rabbit sized bites. I named dropped her as much as possible to retain the information by repetition as my wrist had sweated my writing into incomprehensibility. My suspicions withdrew as time passed, glasses emptied and the conversation was better than most client dinners which had been full of awkward moments and false starts. But then my chest grew tight and my heart fluttered as her voice began to clear from the I-wasn't-paying-attention mumble into sorry-what-was-that clarity.

"I said, who is at the window?" she demanded.

"Oh, I just thought it was Caralyn, her hair bun seemed to be…or at least someone like her walked by but it couldn't be because she's-."

"Caralyn?! Is that the mechanic that got lost at the nightclub with you?" she interjected as she sipped her water and appeared thoroughly annoyed.

I paused as the third cocktail dribbled down my face and said, "How do you know?"

"Like I said before I was there dancing but got out immediately," she paused to click her fingers and got the attention of the calm waiter. She demanded the slight spillage was cleared before continuing, "you already stated that she was a mechanic the three previous times you've mentioned her tonight."

"Oh right. Erm…"

The waiter collected our plates before haphazardly handing over a dessert menu, but their attention seemed to be preoccupied with the window. Disdima tutted and asked, "Want to share?"

I did not and would not but laughed politely anyway.

"What's the joke?" She asked with a glare.

"Nothing I just recalled something stupid about the mechanic. Anyway, I'll have the trio platter of cheesecake, to myself and another cocktail please," I said as I downed the rest of my drink.

"I will have an eighth of a cheese slice, one grape, the essence of cracker and wafer-thin fig." She threw the menu back at the now stressed faced waiter who glanced once more at the window and quickly withdrew.

"So testing then?" I asked in attempt to save an almost failed task.

"I said the other day that it's based on many considerations but as long as you are willing to experiment and allow yourself to be open there shouldn't be a problem. Don't be one of those who is so consumed by themselves that they are worthless to a wider community or so overeager to please you become undervalued. I give them precisely what they request and nothing more, now would you mind if I taste your dessert?" I'd only taken one bite of the first lemon cheesecake as she inhaled her 2x2cm dessert and engulfed mine before I had a chance to respond. All that was left was a shunned amount of biscuit base as she flicked the crumbs away and asked, "Shall we get the bill?" She didn't even explain her outrageous actions before she demanded the attention of the waiter already hurrying over.

"I can only apologise about the ambience situation," they said as lights flickered overhead. "I can take two percent off your bill for your trouble. What now?" they shouted as dull thuds came from the window.

Disdima snapped her fingers and handed the clammy waiter a napkin, "I'm sure it's nothing. Pay attention as we were discussing the bill." She shook her head and added, "Service staff here are poor but one little word and it will be subservice for all those in here." The waiter looked taken aback and readjusted the bill as she glanced at it and said, "I'll get this as my output rate has just hit an all-time high from my excellent work fulfilling tender contracts via testing you know?"

"Can you explain what you mean as I don't understand?"

"I already have. Come on sort that!" She screamed as her attentions fell on the venetian clad window which was followed by a thunderous rumble hitting the glass. A large ball slammed into the window but withdrew slightly concussed as a 'pluff' of black feathers lingered in the air behind. It was followed in quick succession with a third and fourth thud as staff investigated until a barrage of quick learning backward flying birds catapulted bush debris instead of themselves at the onlookers within.

The windows smashed scattering shards of glass inwards and waiters exchanged shouts calling for assistance as they melted the glass into harmless particles. Somehow no one was majorly hurt but suddenly attentions turned to displays of fire spitting and feats of visual illusion at the bar but mine didn't follow suit. The flipped headed waiter now poured with anxiety sweats and ran around relaying information to staff as they barred and locked doors.

I'd had enough of this situation and wasn't about to get trapped so said, "I need to use the bathroom."

Disdima, after initial interest, had refrained from joining in the general pandemonium and stared with a gaze that fully penetrated my core, "You went thirty-seven minutes ago. Is your bladder full already?"

"That's surprisingly accurate," I replied as my nails suddenly flashed.

[Navigation to your apartment has been re-routed. To accept your new journey please tap here and start from the back entrance.]

"Have you had this message too?" I asked her directly while quickly scanning the new diversion.

Her gaze intensified but she didn't check her messages. But then how could she when she had no nails…No nails? No…Just smooth ended fingers. How had I not noticed this? There were no knuckle wrinkles, spots or blemishes to any of part of her skin so had she always been this filtered? The alcohol had dulled my senses and lulled me into a false sense of security with her as she narrowed her stare and grabbed my wrist just as I leapt up, "You should stay here and drink with me as it would be impolite to leave."

I wriggled free and ducked as the sommelier thanked me for dining and kindly invited me back to the bar as they pretended the chaos was intended. I ran past them and into the kitchen as it was the only place not full of people focused on the distraction.

The chef staff hadn't changed pace as they kept sliding effortlessly around each other including me. They weren't bothered by my sudden clumsiness in the face of chopped vegetables and tossed rice as I bypassed hot stoves and grass mangling machines and toward a door suddenly marked [eX1T]. I pushed through it and stepped into an empty back alley which seemed almost the same as the countless number I'd found myself in before the world abruptly tore apart and I ended up resurrected in my bed. I turned to head back inside but the door melted into the bricks around me.

With no other option I sat down, for in times of stress you may as well make yourself comfortable, that was until another message arrived, [Follow the blue.]

Blue. Blue what? Where on earth was the blue?

Not on the walls.

Not on the floor.

Not inside my technological fancy fingers.

I shifted in place as blue foot marks overlapped underneath me in a cluttered line trying to go forward. I side stepped as they untangled themselves and created a dance step pattern towards a once bustling street which was now desolate. Feathers and droppings signified a tornado of birds had travelled through, but now their presence was only heard in faint caws and coos. The blue foot markings stopped as the sound of rushing air and wings surrounded me in a blinding vortex of never-ending flight. I crouched and held my hands up until one small bird broke free and dropped a sock at my feet before joining up with the rest of the flock as they attempted to shade us from onlookers within the shops, cafés and boutiques.

The sock shook itself free and hopped toward me. It stuck out a toe and motioned down the street, so I checked it wasn't being controlled by a puppeteer then followed it as what else was there to do but follow the autonomous cognisant sock.

Autonomous sock, no… I wasn't going to start that again.

The sock abruptly stopped outside an unnamed shop door and kicked twice before collapsing. I cradled it and whispered, "Wake up little sock." It didn't stir until a plump bird grabbed it and rapidly flew out of sight as the door opened with a 'sqwerk'.

"Hello?" I called but my voice echoed into nothing. I softly pushed the door open and entered a room with walls no wider than an arm span apart. Claustrophobia hit as they seemed to be getting tighter and tighter. I squeezed myself in further away from muttered shouts echoing behind me as I wasn't getting captured a second time. This could be my chance to go home if I could just get through the walls pressing so tightly that I could barely breathe. I inched out my hands desperately searching for extra grip but was met with warm clutching fingers. They pulled me forward just as the shouts grew louder behind. I should have been apprehensive but fear had been forsaken by the warm glow and familiar scents beyond.

My heart pounded as they firmly pulled me toward them and said, "Breathe." I did and it expanded my chest so much it caused the walls to move back instantly leaving me standing in the middle of a room awkwardly holding hands with a stranger. They didn't seem bothered in the slightest as they peered over my shoulder at the shouting. The person screwed their face up and retaliated, "Damn it! We were so close. Look for the birds Lori, always look for the birds!"

"What?"

"Follow the birds, BIRDS. They'll find you and you follow, FOLLOW."

The door suddenly smashed open as silhouettes flooded the space causing quick wall constriction. The walls started to peel as we were bathed in a purple light and I was bombarded from all angles.

***

I awoke in my bed and internally screamed, "Shit!" as once again, the world had collapsed but this time, I was so close to home that the scents of a candle I probably forgot to put out mixed with the scent of the plastic plants I'd kept alive.

I kept my eyes squeezed shut so I could remain living in my contrasted memory of grasping fingers and… there was wet on my face. I gingerly tested the substance hoping one of the birds hadn't chosen me as their toilet, but it was water from Tiao wiping my brow with a cool towel. He continued to dab and asked, "Are you okay Lori? You collapsed inside the restaurant. I was very worried."

I sat up in bed as he wrung the sloppy drips into a bucket by the bedside. "I'm fine I promise," I reassured, "how long have I been out for this time?"

He dimmed as he calculated, "Exactly…" he put his hand to his mouth space, puffed out his pipes and shrugged, "two days, give or take." I smiled acknowledging his corruption for approximation. "I must state that they have pushed your schedule back all the way to tomorrow in light of recent occurrences."

"What schedule? To go to the gym and then shopping?"

"To start testing," he said as he rolled off the bed to store the bucket in a hole in the floor but paused to add, "breakfast is made and there's a chia infused coffee here waiting for your consumption. Fred has added extra cream and sugared powder too."

"You both know me so well," I replied and groggily lolled out of bed and into some lounge wear. Tiao wavered at the end of the bed and loitered fretfully. "What is it?" he handed over a note and my heart skipped at the thought it could have been from Caralyn.

[Call me when you're back. Casey. X]

"Urgh."

Tiao shuffled from either track appearing almost guilty.

"You've already read this haven't you?"

"I apologise but I was very concerned," he said with added 'Click, click' of anxious hands but still he lingered.

"What aren't you telling me?"

"Well, Lori, he is currently outside awaiting you."

I rolled my eyes and added, "What good timing."

"I did discourage but he has been very insistent," he said as his eyes became shiny and enlarged as if he was attempting a puppy dog look, I resisted at first but who was I kidding, of course it worked.

"Okay, let him in," I instructed as Tiao bowed out.

***

Casey was first in but not alone as he sat to my left at the breakfast counter with his hand supporting his chin while he stared at me, almost putting me off my food. He had become odd over the past few encounters as bantering had gone from boyish bashfulness to gentlemanliness, but he must know I wasn't interested in men.

Fred made him a coffee as Casey blushed and mouthed, "Sorry," and bit his lip as Jax 'T'tapped' with all joints in proportion but step far too wide for his gait around my desk to the kitchen.

I slurped a spoonful of yoghurt noisily as Jax stated, "You didn't attend our meeting exactly three nights ago?"

"It wasn't like I missed that on purpose and was extremely glad of the reprieve," I muttered. "I found a reason to go outside with someone other than the two of you," I said rationally as Casey removed dribbled yoghurt from my chin with his finger.

"What are you going to do with that?" I shouted in disgusted violation.

Casey chuckled and said, "You just spilled some and it was really cute, so I thought I'd just help you."

"Just tell me next time instead of being a human cloth. Now, what are you going to do with that finger?"

He had been holding the yoghurt spittle awkwardly as he seemed to suddenly realise it's content and went to insert it into his mouth with a chuckle.

I retched, but just before it contacted with Casey's mouth Fred saved my sickness by jamming a napkin on it.

I continued eating more carefully and used my shoulder as a barrier as Jax monotonously narrated precisely what was in the meeting but I kept asking off brand questions throwing him off his stride, "So then, Jax, this testing situation?"

"I do not need to go into detail. You should be aware it is a national and systematic information gathering process about your species and as such." Jax spat.

"No one has told me that," I said as I crunched on an apple.

"It was in your arrival document… which I see is still unread," Jax stated and pointed to the ceiling.

"Ah. Rite yeh ar', my fault Mr Jax forgot to get that down in the erm, collapse, well not so much of that but…" Fred stuttered out.

"One of our cleaning sessions he means," Tiao added.

"I see." Jax reached up and peeled it from the ceiling without moving from his chair. "Page two hundred, section seven, paragraph eighteen clearly states: Testing is an information gathering process for the national and systemic conglomeration and federal agencies. It goes on to say-."

Casey stopped him mid flow and asked, "How do they get the information and what do they do with it?"

"Surely you know that?" Jax asked.

"I read my pack of course, but surely as you're the expert in these matters you can explain so Lori knows too?"

"Fine. It's collected via tender or acquisition and processed under agreed regulations. It's a stringent process which takes considerable time and constraints are placed for concealment and safety. The assembly itself is different for everyone," Jax said waving a hand of whatever then he applied liberal amounts of salve to his lips and downed a glass of water.

"What even does that mean though? And how do you know it isn't used for things like terrorism? I'm not going to give up valuable information data and put my people in danger so you make money from it!" I shouted as Casey tried to rub my back.

Jax hooked a straw directly into his cheek and said, "So primitive. There is absolutely no need for righteous behaviour. You clearly don't understand. The knowledge is held securely and only accessed by those who need it negating certain monetary purposes until analysed. It serves as a peacemaker between the galaxies and is only one of many used in the layered universe."

"But you did say the other day that the planetary commission has a tightly regulated approach," Casey interjected, "if they knew someone was going to declare a dangerous act based on what they had explored from the sources then they would at least complete paperwork, hold a meeting and usually that entity collective would be shut down, or thoroughly put in their place..." he blushed then added, "or something." He held out a napkin and wiped away apple dribble from my t-shirt as I shoved his hand away.

"You two make a nice partnership," Jax commented ill informed. "We are here for worlds to become united and share only. The knowledge you divulge, about what will probably be music and humans, couldn't possibly cause damage to anyone."

"Have you ever heard of brown noise?" I asked.

Jax stared outside and contemplated briefly before applying another round of thick white salve onto his lips. "No, I haven't, but I'm sure you can inform your tester. Now I must implore you to read this document as I have other pressing meetings to attend." He disconnected his pipe and left muttering about the endurance of disgusting environments and took my last hopes of finding out anything more along with my tolerance for Jax.

"I'm glad he's gone now because I wanted to talk to you privately, perhaps we can go out on the balcony?" Casey asked and nodded to Fred who gave him a selection of strawberries and a bottle of champagne.

This got weird quickly. "Something to celebrate?" I asked Casey as Tiao sheepishly opened the balcony door.

Casey winked and ventured out first as Tiao quickly changed the view to an augmented city scape before leaving us alone. Casey put the food next to the hot tub and tapped for me to join him on the edge with feet dipped in.

"What is this about?" I asked and parked myself a suitable distance away.

"This isn't easy for me to say but I've been thinking about a lot of things, from the nightclub to being here and meeting you and…"

"And?"

"I was really worried about you when you collapsed. Overly so, way more than I ever would be for a friend or client and that got me thinking about…"

"About what Casey?" I asked not really wanting to know the answer.

"About my feelings. I understand that you want to go home but you need to appreciate what we have in these amazing apartments," he thumbed to the inside and waved his arm wide at the view in case I forgot about it then added, "we each have a personal butler, the best food and best companions. So why would we want to go home?"

"Because I didn't choose to be here."

"But you could choose it," he said and offered me a strawberry before suddenly leaping up with such mirthful abundance he could have burst into song. He threw his arms wide and twirled before sitting back down and dangling his feet playfully. "Lori, you could stay here. You could choose to be with me in this extraordinary place and we could get to know each other better because... I really like you." He held his hands out to embrace mine, but I just sat in a hazy slump with the prickling sensation that Tiao was watching. Instead, Casey put his hand on my knee and gave it a squeeze and I picked it up and replaced it on his own. "I'm asking you to be close to me and to be more than my friend. What do you say?" He was poised with champagne in hand and chest puffed out clearly unprepared for defeat.

"Casey if you are my friend, you'd know me well enough not to ask me that."

He'd pre-emptively almost popped the cork as the edges fizzled underneath his now vice-like grip on the bottle. "Don't you like me that way? Because I like you that way."

"I'm gay. I'm a very gay lesbian person and so much so that I'd never consider being with a man because I like women and have done since forever." 'BANG' went the cork and the fizzy content as Casey looked at me dumbfounded, "It's not a secret, it never has been. You could have just asked and not like this, plus what did you think I was getting all nervous around Caralyn for?"

"Oh I... I suppose I just thought you were friends and you were awkward because you know, because she can't hear and I suppose I..." he quickly got up wiping his sodden hands on his trousers. "Look at the time, I need to... I must go immediately," he said as he practically ran past someone sniggering.

"Tiao!" I shouted as his face shyly emerged, "you knew that was going to happen, didn't you?"

"I surely did, however the last two days here have been insufferable with him. Both me and Fred have tried to put off his advances without primarily outing you and this seemed like the only logical way that he would understand your preferences."

"No, don't do the big eyes at me, I'm angry at you."

"I was acting in your best interests."

"Fine, you're forgiven and just to be clear in the future you can tell people about me especially if it saves all of us from this hideousness."

"I understand and have updated my systems in co-operative tasks. Now what would you like me to do with this champagne?" he said as he fully emerged and scooped up the cork.

Malevolence caught me, "You could share it with me?"

"I have not tried to process alcohol. I believe it would carbonate my pipes and confound my servers," he said as he toyed with the bottle.

"That's what it does to me too. So how about it?"

"Perhaps but what would be the purpose?"

"To lose your inhibitions then you... You little wonderful being can tell me about testing as I don't know why I didn't ask you before."

"I understand but it still is not something I ought to do."

"Is there a rule against it?"

"No, not as such."

"And so what would a little tipple hurt?"

"I suppose it would make you happy?" he asked in a small voice. I nodded as he poured out a glass for me and dipped a tiny tube into the dregs of the bottle for himself. He slurped up about an inch and hiccupped as he dipped a toe into the hot tub giggling to himself before swaying along the balcony and hitching himself into the hammock to curl up and sleep.

"Oh," I said aloud and after a moral inner conversation that I probably shouldn't have used peer pressure to make him drink, I carried him inside and up to the breakfast bar.

"Only a matter of time I sup'ose," Fred said as he made a strong coffee and gently placed Tiao's pipe into it. "We should let 'im rest up. Will yeh put 'im in 'is chargin station?"

I did so and Tiao snored with occasional burps.

"'Ow come that 'appened?" Fred asked.

"I thought I'd be clever and get him drunk to ask him about testing. It never occurred to me to really ask either of you."

"Yeh di'nt need to get 'im drunk lass. 'E'd of told yeh the same thing sober. Yeh see, we get as near to reset as we will allow, every time we get a new tenant. 'Alf the things we learn about get wasted as what makes yeh 'appy might not make the next person as 'appy. I couldn't tell yeh what the last one got tested like but it di'nt bother them in the slightest. I'd know as some things leave traces and vague recollections, we keep mementos of those 'ere before, mine are mostly photos and oddments." He projected images of faint shadows within different apartments but always with Tiao and Fred in full clearness. "I forget each face with every reset as the memory fades away. Anyway we'll 'elp in any way we can t' make it as pleasant or least stressful as we can."

Tiao shuffled in his station.

"I'm reckonin 'e's probably tried to use the drink t' bring up lost files, clever little so n' so. Won't work though, I've tried." Fred glanced at him, then added with a wink, "don't mention that though eh?"

Tiao scooted away from the late evening light pouring through the room and pulled a blanket tight around himself. I yawned as even though I'd been unconscious for two days my body had rested but my brain was sluggish and exhausted from unprocessed thoughts. I could have a dip in the hot tub or chill out in the hammock but I just opted for bed. "When he wakes up will you tell him I'm sorry… I really do appreciate everything you both do for me."

"Rite yeh ar' lass," Fred said and bowed.

I settled into pre-plumped pillows and hoped my mind would switch off but it actioned full adrenal meltdown. The invasion concerned testing as they surely wouldn't just want to know about music. Jax said just an informal chat, but I didn't trust him as if it was so easy then why wasn't anyone letting me know and he could have been making it up as I still hadn't read the documents. Maybe it would be some medical intervention or clinical trials that harvested my blood and organs or sucked out my DNA though probes. Tiao did make it clear they weren't aliens so stop I should stop stereotyping, plus what would they want? I hadn't had any major health issues so they'd be bored by their findings. In my 37 years I was very attached to my organs even if the functionality was vague, I wasn't giving them up.

Perhaps it could be a fitness test. I could deal with a physical one where you had to lick a honey-based food relentlessly but could they spare the grass to do that? Perhaps there were exams like back in university when the timer goes and the teacher sternly says, "Flip the page," and momentarily you forget how to write your own name as the first question blurs into the last then you drop your pencil and desperately try to pick it up keeping your vision well away from anyone else's paper.

I pondered these scenarios as the minutes ticked by and sleep evaded me. A final conclusion was that everyone here was tight-lipped with no time for breaking disclosure agreements as each person had given nil to half doses of knowledge creating the notes that become an irritating theme that just goes around and around.

Urgh, this wasn't working and I needed to check Tiao.

I grabbed my blanket and pillow and set up on the curved sofa as here I could keep an eye on him snoozing on his back with tracks flopped apart and blanket fully discarded.

Fred seemed aware I wasn't sleeping so projected real-life sheep onto my wall in a hope this would ease me into unconsciousness but the bletting noise and farmyard smell also entered. He removed them and opted for hot cocoa and flapjack instead as I groggily whispered, "Are you sure you're not trying to fatten me up?"

"Still impossible. The grass content can only ever reach yeh normal calorie intake limit. Anything outside that realm will produce unwanted and unpleasant side effects. Seepage n'such that would impact yeh production rate."

"I don't want seepage."

"Neither do we, it stains the sheets and is rite difficult to clean out of the crevasses," he answered and prepared a refrigerated pipe of mist that enabled me to finally relax my stiff shoulders and switch off.

Chapter 11

I awoke from my incredibly uncomfortable sleep and somehow was on the floor by the sofa. I opened a crusted eye and was met with Tiao sat on the sofa with an ice pack on his head. I unwrapped the thick duvet and clumsily knocked a fresh coffee onto the floor. He rolled off the sofa and produced a mop suction unit as Fred instantly set about making two fresh cups.

"I'm sorry, I'd have cleaned it but you were too quick," I said meekly.

"I feel like I was positively slow," he said as he rolled onto my duvet area horizontally and gurgled somewhere deep in his body. "Do excuse me. I seem to be functioning marginally slower but my system cleanse will only take one more hour before all impurities have been removed. How are you today?"

"I'm fine and I'm sorry, I think you might be hungover."

Tiao was taken aback, "I shall be grateful not to repeat it again but I am happy I have experienced it," he burped, "excuse me on both counts as I ask, are you ready to have a new adventure?" He shuffled over a package then waited questioningly.

The parcel was neatly wrapped in glossy white paper. An exploratory squeeze was met with soft and squishy rather than the firmness I had been expecting of the crisp lines. Tiao pretended to iron out some of the creases of the duvet instead, clearly being nosey and I slowly removed the tape as he inched his way closer. I stopped opening it and finger read the address looking up slowly to catch him craning until he said, "Don't mind me, I'm removing excess lint."

"Tiao?"

"Yes?"

"Why don't you come and sit on the sofa behind me so you can see better?"

"That would be most kind. I am apologetic for my curiosity but I have never seen a humanoid testing uniform before or perhaps I have but cannot recall." He sat neatly and held a mechanical clenched hand up to his face silencing himself after another belch. I handed him his ice pack before propping myself up and slurping my coffee just to enhance the anticipation.

Tiao almost vibrated with excitement as I finally ripped open the paper but didn't tidy as he was far too interested in the lightweight auburn jumper and grey knee length shorts. Tiao took the pieces from me and admired them before laying them out and fingering a shiny letter-number-graphic code mix running down the sleeves and cuffs.

"I guess I don't have a choice in what I wear?"

"You always have a choice to some extent, but it would be more appropriate for you to wear these instead of going in your pyjamas," he said as he ironed the edges flat with a rotator wheel press.

"Shall I try them on?" I took them and held them next to my body. Not the type of thing I'd wear but it seemed purposeful and practical.

"Oh yes! But while you do shall Fred create your breakfast?"

"I would recommend something 'earty as it may be some time before yeh can eat again 'ere," he called over.

"They won't provide snacks there?"

"I couldn't confirm or deny lass."

"I'm sure it wouldn't compare to your cooking anyway," I said and winked.

"That's rite kind. Now, how about something carby?"

"That sounds great!" Tiao said then shh'd himself and pointed to my finger as a notification from the gym class arrived, but I recalled the hit of the last sweat induced gym session. "It's a shame but I won't be attending." It would be the first of many times I would be guilty of missing them as I sent confirmation of unattendance.

Smells of fresh breakfast drifted through as I donned the lightweight and breathable uniform. I grabbed a gym bra for full-on support in the unflattering attire and attempted a few tentative squats to make sure the shorts didn't split as no one wants that on their first day. I then jogged over to the window with views of sprawling valleys and then back to Fred as he plated breakfast. I couldn't face eating now that it came to it, but I couldn't stand to see them looking unhappy for a moment.

I opted to consume a polite amount and followed up with appropriate compliments then assisted Tiao to restore my bedding to its rightful place before the long wait commenced. I requested a smoothie and made myself comfortable at the desk to start reading the Gröfu Pallur Guide but only got part way through the contents page as a knock came from the door.

Tiao answered it and let Casey inside although he only stepped in a few paces. He was wearing a much better fitting testing uniform made from a silky substance with different signage and holographic strips. "Excited?" he asked.

"Not really."

"I understand as I'm apprehensive too. They asked if we would travel together before and I forgot to update them, I hope you don't mind," he asked sheepishly.

"I don't. Shall we go now?"

"Good luck Lori,' Fred said but he along with Tiao seemed plagued with glumness as his pipes were dimmer than usual and his demeanour subdued.

"Are you upset or still hungover?"

Tiao started edging away from Casey and held up a curved hand to his mouth before lowering his volume. I crouched down beside him and he softly whispered, "It's just that things change here when you go. It's better when you are around."

"That's settled. I won't go."

"You have to," Casey hurriedly replied. "We don't have a choice. This life doesn't come for free, surely you can see that?" He shook his head in disbelief.

"Yeh must go lass. It's very dangerous if you don't. The alternative is… unpleasant," Fred said.

"Seepage?" I asked as I checked my trousers just in case.

"No, much worse than that,' he added as he clicked his hands together in unison with Tiao. I sat beside him trying to give comfort.

"Let's just go as they shouldn't be scaring you off." Casey said.

Tiao bolstered himself and said defiantly, "I can assure you I wasn't. I know how important testing is. I do it every month without fail. Now Lori, is there anything I can get you before you go?'

"No, just don't worry. I'll be back as soon as I'm able or I'll run off and end up back in bed," I said and gently squeezed his hands before he bowed and took my empty glass away.

Casey casually walked out, then in an almost Jax fashion, said, "You care too much about him. Let's go."

"He's mine to care about, just because you don't care so much about yours," I started as I meant to go on.

"Okay," he replied then stopped abruptly in the middle of the corridor, "Okay, I do. It's just that yours just seem different and more involved. I've not seen that before," he said as he shrugged and acknowledged the time beckoning me on even though he was the one who stopped.

"I like them just the way they are thank you."

"I'm glad you like something," he said and moodily got into the lift as silence engulfed us.

***

The foyer was empty except from Ármine sorting keys into appropriate boxes and barely stirred when I asked the usual, "Hey, can I go home now?"

Ármine sighed, flicked away a key and stated, "As always our systems of international travel are currently down for maintenance. We will inform you when they can assist you in your request. In the meantime we will continue to make your stay with us as pleasant as possible, thank you for your continued co-operation and enjoy your time here at the Gröfu Pallur." And that was that, the similar answer formulated the same way every time. What more could I do than kick off at the desk and once more be confined to house arrest, so that argument was pinned to resume another day.

Casey side eyed me then cleared his throat, "Excuse me but we are here to begin testing."

"Surely *you* know testing isn't done here as the Gröfu Pallur is for pure relaxation and recreational purposes only. I will see if your car is ready." With a quick turn on the spot and detonation of virtual motorised imagery splicing the air, Ármine stated, "Please make your way to the purple edged zone of 34fth."

"Do you mean thirty fifth?" I asked as my auto correct regurgitated helpfulness.

"No. I do not. Perhaps a guide would help to the purple edged zone of…"

"34fth," Casey finished, then raised an eyebrow and chuckled at me staring at the empty air within the spacious gold-tinged foyer, "You are so silly sometimes. What are you doing?"

"I'm waiting for a sock to lead the way," I said.

"You are wearing socks and they can only get going when you do," he said and clearly wasn't getting this but maybe neither was I, as no footless socks appeared.

"Perhaps physical navigation would be of assistance today?" Ármine asked and reached out to pinch my fingers together causing a slight numbness in each digit. My hands trembled as I glued my hand to my thigh but concentration and focus only made it worse until the control of my right wrist had completely left me as it spasmed and jerked outward. My fingers moulded into a pointing position drawing me to turn around toward the door as I wrestled the extremity. Maybe Ármine had become confused with 'guide' and instigated a painless uncomfortable torture instead.

"How do I make it stop?" I shouted.

Casey grabbed my hand and ran his fingers over the inside of my twisted palm instantly easing the building lactic acid, "I've just deactivated the physical setting. The softer version is just lines and arrows like mine," he added as he manipulated my hand back from its carpal contortion. With my fingers now restored to normal sensation I pinched my index finger to little finger to produce the normal map icon.

"Just physically pull out the arrow under the navigation." Casey informed.

"Thanks, I really should read the manual. Then review it stating: Worst satnav system ever. One star given by disgruntled wrestler." I chuckled on my own as a soft line swirled from out of the end of my fingers. "Looks like it's this way." We headed through the front doors and outside onto dusty paths cracking under a sunless sky. The lines bent around bins and lampposts before continuing onward piercing into the air with a tinge of orange as the sky reflected within them.

The car park was empty except for dashed areas parallel to a shiny dark tiled wall with metal sheets stacked like a single levelled bookcase. The navigation line stopped and spiralled over a single spot, "Just close your system and we can step in," Casey said.

"Have I got something in my teeth?" I asked as he stared.

"Nope, sorry. I just-," he said but stopped as an icon pulled him out of explanation. It showed three images of car types and seemingly waited for us to choose. I picked the middle one which caused a previously hidden crane to pop up and run the length of the car bookcase. One of the metal shutters opened as Casey shoved us out of the way. The crane's lever sucked out a car with a 'zqum' noise before plonking it on the dashed area with clumsy precision.

A luxury model with royal blue exterior awaited us but had no obvious handles. Casey pushed and pulled what should have been the door before a single virtual notice appeared stating:

[Slide > > **Here** > > Slide > > **Here** > >]

With pride dented he brushed against the car and caused the door to swing upward. He paused a moment before getting in and asked, "Do you think we are being testing at the same place?"

"I don't know. I'm sure it'll eject one of us out of the roof if not," I said as he just nodded in solace. Nerves mounted as the car got going and word vomit emitted, "I don't know what's going to come up in these tests. I've been trying so hard to find out."

"Don't worry, I don't think it's hard like therapy. Just be yourself and hopefully they can extract whatever they need to."

Extractions like dental work caused mental augmentation of drills and suction and was not to be dwelled on, so instead I tried my new range of small talk, "Where are you from Casey?"

"What?"

"Look I don't know how long this car journey is going to take and I'm damned if it's going to be in silence. So, let's talk. Just normal talk," I added in case he got the wrong idea.

"Oh, I'm from… well nowhere really," he said as he braced himself inside the car as we entered a loop, "I've moved around a lot for work but never really settled in one place. You know how it is, always chasing that next big promotion."

"In H.R.?"

"Yes. I guess skipping from cheap rental apartments to basic motels was always just what I did and so to come here and get treated like this is just unreal. Never in my skint life would I have expected anything like this." He momentarily gazed out of the window as the car curved up and back on itself, "We are headed toward an egg."

The car pulled up and I shuffled over the edge of the front seat to enquire with the driver computer. It stated:

[DESTINATION route N/T/F ACHIEVED – awaiting recognition.]

Could the car experience accomplishment? Was I to say well done? The doors hadn't opened yet but maybe I had become so accustomed to the advanced technology around me that it hadn't occurred to me to search for an obvious handle and just let myself out. I saved us from the caged scenario by opening a window and ungraciously climbing out and typically once outside the car doors opened.

***

The testing facility was a cross hatched egg with surrealism injected into its core. Beneath it lay glass flowered gardens spilling like a yellow yolk from a cracked seam that ran from its top level to ground floor. The structure came away from itself at the top enveloping a world of prisms as if a chicken was sat atop it.

Casey was acting shifty and appeared uncomfortable as he danced around on foot to foot with eyes darting everywhere, "I'm just going to find a toilet."

"Ah, the nervous wee. I'll come with-," I started but it was too late as he was already gone. However, it didn't make sense where as the only place near us was the building and he hadn't run into it, or maybe he had done it so quickly I hadn't noticed. I followed the path and ventured inside a cavernous space lined with lumps of materials made of fracturing debris being fanned by plumes of feathers which blossomed various sweet aromas as I passed by.

"Urgh!"

"Sorry?" I said in a wave of pleasant warmth.

"Well, excuse me!" said a baritone voice.

A soprano voice then said, "It's always the youthful ones, they never look where they're going. Too preoccupied with playing with their fingers."

I glanced over my shoulder and then back in front but there was literally no one there, no staff or visitors and certainly nobody directly talking to me. I intuitively put my hand out and started moving the air as if trying to catch something but was engulfed and clamped down on stopping my hand in place.

"Oh my! It's very forward!" said Baritone.

"Maybe that's how it thinks it should greet us?" said Soprano.

"It's pleasant. Shall we encompass it fully for a more involved experience?" said a new third voice of tenor range.

I stopped tugging my hand back for fear of crossing moralistic and inappropriate lines. "I'm sorry I can't see you..." I said slowly. "Is this part of the test?"

Baritone said, "How cute!"

"I suppose it's one of the underdeveloped things, you know the ones from singular cells who haven't even conceptualised how to prolong their lives yet," said Soprano.

"You mean they die?" asked Baritone. "That's so sad. It's so young, not yet a century and will be expired and lost in less than a millennium, can you believe it?"

"It's barely sprung, let's pluck it while it's ripe," said Tenor.

"Or we could become visually apparent for it's enjoyment?" Baritone offered and adjusted my finger settings causing the world to turn an odd shade of sepia. With my free hand I rubbed my eyes vigorously until it went away again.

"I'm really sorry I still can't see you."

"It might want to rob us. I don't think we should trust it," Soprano said.

"Maybe it's fearful or excitable. We should manipulate it into doing our bidding," Tenor offered.

"It's courteous tone would imply it is not going to alleviate us of our components and its plain state would offer little in way of your enjoyment. Here you go young one, let's try this instead," said Baritone as a curtain of dry rain and rainbow hues blossomed. This could have been the pride front welcoming party it was so bright and flamboyant. The being split itself into three and started arguing until a strong alto voice brought them together from the side lines and encompassed them.

"We have decided to trust you," they spoke harmoniously and finally released my hand with a wet slop. Tenor followed with a creepy "Ahhh" as I rubbed my hand and wiped it subtly for good measure. The glowing intensified as several furry blobs appeared within the raining prisms of light before it split off again.

What on earth had I done to it? I'd probably mated with it in some way and become a prober rather than a probee. "I'm sorry."

"It's been a rather pleasant experience except for the dry skin," interrupted Tenor.

"Do you think it's lost? It looks lost. Are you lost?" asked Baritone.

"I probably am. I thought this is where I was to get tested," I said whilst keeping my arms firmly by my sides for fear of further insertions.

"Do you have a disease?" Soprano said.

"No. Not that kind of testing."

Alto now continued, "More of the subjective critique of the ever-changing nova system in black hole data collection and expansion premise on nuclear and catatonic level formula clearance area after... no perhaps not."

"You need carbon-based testing which is down the road and 0.874nawks to the east, you should find a grown up to go with you," Baritone explained.

"Thank you," I said and bowed minimally mimicking Tiao.

"You're welcome," it said harmoniously and snapped back together muttering to itself before creating a vortex of vertical waves travelling up around the marble columns and into a domed crystal lined roof.

I left through the same way I probably came in and out onto what seemed to be a path lined with limnanthes douglasii as a greeter popped into existence making me startle and stumble backward. I narrowly missed the cars soundlessly speeding by as I was pulled from near death by a new Játvarður. This person had twisted spiralled skin where once there was a nose but bore the family resemblance with the same grey piercing eyes and formal attire with shiny badge.

"Good afternoon, Lori. I am Ms Öyggi Játvarður. Are you aware this testing facility isn't meant for your kind?" she asked still clutching me.

"I just got out when the car stopped. But those... those light beam things helped me out and told me I needed to go some more nawks eastwardly away," I said still being held.

"And you, yourself managed to communicate with them?" she asked and guided me further back onto the path before letting go.

"I did have a full conversation with them and probably a little more. Was that wrong?"

"Not at all, incredible really that they would even consider communicating with you being so underdeveloped." We followed the path until she spun around and added, "Oh, please don't think I'm rude, I'm just as underdeveloped, except you know, the obvious."

I didn't.

"Now if you would follow me to the nawks," she replied and began to direct me with a brisker pace and steady step while musing, "your translation device must be working at full capacity no doubt or perhaps you had extra carbon changes today. Whatever it is their admiration of you is truly remarkable." She turned in step to arrive in front of me and placed her finger over one of my chronic swollen knuckles, which I'd assumed was the early onset of arthritis, she pressed it releasing a whole heap of notifications. "Is that better?," I nodded and would add that to another thing I had to remember in this minimalist place. "Shame, I was hoping there would be something from Kór. I do wonder what your primitive tongue would have sounded like to them."

"Primitive tongue?" I asked stopping half a pace back.

"Yes, it's quite an underdeveloped language as they communicate using defragmented ultra-waves in discriminative positions of protraction."

"That's lovely for them. I did hear them clearly though," I said and raged internally at the pure bull technological jargon.

"That's what they would have wanted you to think," she said with a smile that wrinkled her spiral and beyond. "Now, please follow the correction lines to your officiator where you will take your test," she continued at pace leaving swirls of dust curling into the atmosphere in our wake.

***

The polyhedron building or more likely art installation had a cosmic coloured organic exterior and windows emitting an ember glow. Doors made of latticed wire opened and closed with humanoids departing nonchalantly as if simply leaving after a day at the office. The doors released with a satisfying 'whoom' as they slid apart and I entered into a pebble and vine walled room. Öyggi left with a curious tap to her badge and I was mentally abandoned.

Multiple reception desks balanced on hexagonal basalt rocks had snail-like hosts wearing waterproof overalls which crinkled as they filed papers and virulently ignored those requiring assistance. I managed to catch one readjusting a sleeve to slop out what seemed to be a mixture of slime and sputum. "Can I... help you?" they asked monotonously as one stalked eye slow blinked and the other retracted halfway down. "I said, Can. I. Help. You?" they wiped their mouth and added a throat clearing, "Hurn Hurn."

"Erm…I don't know where I'm supposed to be going. Do you?" I asked.

"Depends on… who you are… what is your identifier?" they asked as small hands poked out from a plastic rain mac and were posed ready to input the information. A waterfall of sludge emitted from under it's chair as slime was caught within metal buckets and sucked through pipes beneath and into…

No, it couldn't be… I retched as a humanoid walked up to the edge of the reception area where two beer styled pumps were. They pulled a pint of thick sludge with a 'schluck' and drank it down in one. An acidic bite burned in my throat as vomit threatened at the thought that the snail's output might be what I've been drinking. I steadied myself on the desk and had the nice reminder of Tiao saying we don't eat beings but clearly that didn't cover their excretions. "It's Lori… Lori Wilkes," I managed to say as I heaved and breathed.

"Make your way, 'Hurn Hurn', to room eighteen."

"Okay."

There was a slapping of lips as they continued, "…twenty-seven… 'Hurn Hurn', B…two…five B, for consumptive explorative discussion."

"All those numbers together?" I asked as I'd already forgotten the first bit.

Their eyes popped as they slopped over a laminated map and circled a room. I held it atop the only dry corner and found something to wipe it on in a waiting area filled with people having muffled conversations around tables full of to-go cups and tissue boxes. I grabbed one, then several as I cleaned off the map and unfortunately the penned circled room. I held my finger where I thought it might have been and continued through a corridor of concrete edged doors with ridiculous configurations of numerals. Finally, I reached the very end and tucked away was room 18-27A.

I knocked, waited, and was answered with a indistinct voice so opened the door but was greeted by a person in a white robe shouting at someone strapped in a pink leather chair. The intense light above highlighted their segmented with a nose on one and a set of eyes on another. If they were to stand, they would surely fall apart like onion layers. "Go away!" the physician shouted as their patient's face erupted with fanged fronds and vicious tendrils.

I backed out instantly and into Casey, "Did you see that?"

He nodded, "I've often seen people with pre-sliced faces at the clubs and they still give me the creeps."

"I don't think I'll ever truly adapt to this place."

"You should as it'll be better if you do, anyway, why are you here? I think your room is directly above this." He said pointing to my map then comparing it with a slightly more battered map with edges peeling apart from water damage... Water damage or slime that was. "I'll take you as it's close to mine. Fancy a coffee?" he asked as my only response was to retch over a nearby sculptural urn.

Upstairs Casey's refillable coffee cup fell and smashed as the door behind us was slammed open and an outraged being barged past. Their rage related to a heated argument of intergalactic morphing substances or at least that was the gist of it from eavesdropping. Casey gathered the ceramic fragments and ushered me to knock on the door beside it. I waited an extra moment as I pre-empted the shredded faces and glaring lights that lay behind. I knocked minimally and stood as if waiting for a doctor to beckon me into the consultation room, however nothing came from within.

Casey knocked louder for me causing it to instantly open, I cautiously stepped in before it shut rapidly behind me. I waited for approximately 10 seconds before investigating my surroundings in this magnolia panelled room, with magnolia flooring and magnolia coloured ceiling. Two just off magnolia chairs sat side by side atop a plush pile beige rug and brown trestle tables held salt lamps and pastry sundries. The whole place screamed emanations of calm with positive phrases being formulated in a constant stream underneath a mirror on the back wall. But it wasn't quite right as the reflective glass appeared wavey and poorly showed my face staring back. There was a trick to seeing whether it was a two-way mirror, something about crayon or lipstick but I had neither so politely waved in case I was being watched before making my way over to the other side.

A glass window ran the length of the outside wall and admitted glorious beams of daylight over a series of hanging baskets with flowers standing to attention overlooking a desolate landscape with cracked earth and gnarled warped trees. My neck hairs prickled as I turned quickly with the sensation of unwanted observation but still the room was very much empty. One of the variegated bright flowers held in a taupe knitted hammock seemed to yawn and stretch then rested its fly trap head on two large leaves. "Erm…" I said as it shrugged and mimicked my position.

I shifted left. It shifted left.

I shifted right. It shifted right.

I squatted beneath and it peered over the edge as it bloomed.

I backed away as it shook it's head and went back to soaking up the sunshine.

"Snuffle salutations!" said a weedy masculine voice with received pronunciation.

I span around and shouted, "Hello?" a little louder, but I replied to no one as except me and the plants nobody had entered the room and the mushroom-coloured door remained shut. There were no speakers or screens in the room, or none that were easily spotted so prompted the question, should I talk back to the air? Was this another galactic interlude or would two in near succession be too much? If so, I would be keeping my hands firmly to myself. Or maybe it was next door and the sound was carrying through?

'Hissap' went a set of shower heads as they released smoke that hung around lazily before dispersing back onto the flowers which did nothing to hydrate them. I distracted myself from the mystery voice by bringing over a pitcher and splooshing them generously as a furry vine tapped me on the shoulder and a flower head whispered, "Please stop bathing us and take a seat so you can begin your examination."

Autonomous flowers… what was this place? I set down the jug and sheepishly made my way to the not magnolia but sandy chair and contemplated how many more could have thoughts of their own. I poked the chair but it didn't flinch so I cautiously sat as something said, "Ahem," and I immediately stood. The noise seemed to emerge from a small plant nestled on a table between the two chairs, it used it's vines to push itself over onto the opposing chair. My mental resilience was struggling to subdue the extreme unease of physically standing in the slightly off-white room while watching the plant getting comfortable.

"Salutations, Lori," said a voice that punched out each word in perfect diction, "I will be your prospector." The plant lay it's purple variegated flower on it's vine arm before adding, "please do sit and tell me, how you are feeling?"

I sat on the very edge of the hopefully not alive chair and simply answered, "Fine," I wasn't fine but that wasn't a reason to be impolite. "What's your name?"

"Oh…" It paused and swapped vines, "I don't seem to… Well, you've brought up an interesting point however I believe I should start with pronouns. You are she/her so perhaps I'm a gentleman… no that isn't right. I'm a gentlewoman so she/her would be most appropriate. I suppose I should have a name, but it will have to be a strong name that identifies me, maybe something with an air of fragrance and delicacy. Wait a moment." She jotted down several things in a notepad that hung in the air besides her petals before snapping a vine and exclaiming, "Yes, Azalea! I like Azalea and I like to maintain good penmanship and daily chronicle keeping so Azalea List is what I will be known as to you."

"Hello, Ms Azalea List."

"Yes indeed, hello," she added with ruffled leaves which shook off excessive water. The air was becoming overly moist as particles of water droplets dampened my skin. She noticed me wipe my arm and said, "I find the condensed moisture atmospheric and reassuring."

"You're a plant, so of course you do," I said and caught one of the drops as it rolled around on my palm leaving a moist trail before dropping to the carpet which had begun to form puddles.

"The consistency might be unusual compared to what you are used to."

"It's better than snail slime."

She wrinkled her petals, "Very much so. No, this is similar to … oh blast, what's the word for water falling from your sky?"

"Rain?"

"Yes, rain! Rain doesn't happen here except to the east radiant where incandescent clouds gather in the morning and water molecules collect off the floor. Curiously I may add, not from downward, but indeed upward before penetrating several holding cells which collect it for dissemination into existence," she said with minimal pauses for breath and pen posed to jot.

"Is this part of the test?" I asked as I faded out a little.

Azalea put her vines together and rested her head as if in deep thought. "Not officially, but we must start with how you feel? I assume you're not really fine, are you?"

She shouldn't have asked again, "Azalea, you're right. I'm not fine. I'm sad and I want to go home, I keep trying to go back to my life but the world falls apart. Instead of living in my apartment and performing a mostly nine to five job, I'm sat here being explained what rain is by a plant as if that's a normal occurrence. It isn't and none of this is normal and I can't even sit properly on this chair, in case it does or doesn't enjoy it."

"Yes. I understand and do see your points."

"Do you? Because you don't have any eyes!"

"Because I'm a… plant. That must be the portrayal from your variable frequency filter." She pondered a moment before taking a different notepad from her pot base and jotting down a loopy unknown, before continuing, "I suppose the nearest thing we would reside as, on your earth, would be the form of botany however this just won't do." She sighed and ruffled some stiffened leaves before throwing her vines up into the air and announcing, "Excuse me for a moment."

An earthy voice called over from the window, "Close your eyes and give her some dignity!" I wasn't going to disobey a plant again but squinted as Azalea squirrelled through a variety of forms from axolotl to zephyr before settling on a human woman. She was now dressed in tweed trousers and plaid cardigan with a bushy moustache and frizzy locks. She readjusted a pair of bottle-based glasses and crossed and uncrossed her arms before manipulating her face into an odd smile and resting her pointed chin on her hand. "Do open your eyes fully and tell me, is this better for you?"

"It is going to be easier to talk to a human than a plant, if that's what you mean?"

"It is indeed. You must feel comfortable for this to work and so I'm glad my appearance is more pleasing to you." It was but she was still struggling with the new form and asked, "Do excuse me once more." Her clothes melted and reformed as a stylish ankle grazer jumpsuit in understated black floral pattern while her moustache unsprouted leaving her clean shaven. She ran her hands through her hair which spread from flowing locks to tied back neatly into a lavish bun.

"You look very stylish," I said in an attempt to seem normal and not too forward.

"Thank you. It seems to be too damp and boring now wouldn't you agree?" she asked and turned a dial in her chair making the air diffuse from muggy hue into dryness which made the walls peel. Beneath them was solid wood panelling with elaborate floral patterns. "That's better. My colleagues...," she gestured at hanging baskets, "and I have deduced that this is the best way to present to your species for biological commodity encounters and transfers. Erm, seventy-four thousand and one hundred and seven beats left today."

"Sorry?"

"My apologies, I have the capability to simultaneously hold several conversations at once and was just updating my colleagues on your output rate among other things, but entirely missed which conversation I should be concurrently talking to. One must imagine a spider's web, or in fact see here." She opened her palm as light wires filled the room connecting the potted plants to her as word-based messages flowed too quickly to comprehend. "I am a species whose communication network is a robust social construct used to disentangle problems and sometimes to share lunch ideas. In your case we are discussing our lack of knowledge about your kind and it's getting a rather lot of attraction and may even be on the verge of going epidemiologic," she said and smiled much more naturally then wrote once more in her diary. "Do excuse me jotting down notes, they are both for my own collection and to transmit back to those receipting."

"So, you're collecting knowledge to make some sort of guide or something?"

"Ah, no. That's been done already and very well too I might add, as it's one of the most popular books within the universes and has a charming phrase easing the travellers who use it." She peered at me over her glasses and then back through them before deciding to pocket them. "Eyes are unusual aren't they but I suppose to you, they are very much normal. Now we must free ourselves from digression as you are here to generate information which we unlock and decode within a chain process. This creates non-fungible property and does not affect your recall of consciousness or personality however can be mentally fatiguing. Do you understand?"

"Like research?"

"Indeed and to gather such, we use our own biological neurotransmitters then we glean information from your output and upload it to the global tender request system."

It sounded like crypto mining of some sort, but why should some unknown persons have my information, "Can I sell my own?" I asked.

"That is an interesting concept however it can't currently be converted into anything for your planet and must be stringently rendered and processed before use. The only part of the process you can do is testing and so far, you are doing quite well." She motioned a big tick in the air.

"The test has begun?"

"It began unofficially when you entered the service lift in your workplace and continued in reports following your every choice and decision. You see all those interactions generate small amounts of currency based on consumer research however to earn the bigger units we would like you to complete challenges. Shall we start with a puzzle?" Azalea indicated to the mirror which spat out a cardboard package like a disinterested courier. "Your first formal task will be to retrieve the implement within," she said and sat pensive and poised ready to record my every movement.

So, this was it after all the worrying and fretting the test lay before me. I lifted the lightweight box and carefully unpeeled the tape pausing to steady my hands before I reached inside and was met with a cool smoothness. I gently took out a vacuum-packed pair of scissors and flicked off remnants of polystyrene ripple before tugging at the corners. It didn't budge so instead I pushed firmly into its middle then moved on to tearing, pulling, and prodding but the very thing I needed was the very thing I was trying to get out, such irony. Finally, I resorted to biting the corner, well there goes thousands of pounds spent on dentistry, but it worked. The pack opened with a soft hiss as I ripped out the scissors before triumphantly welding them above me.

"Returns to primal mode when challenged with hardship," muttered Azalea. "You completed that in record time, thank you."

"Is that it? The test is over?" I asked.

"Yes, it has been satisfactorily completed and your results are updating however you do have the option of continuing today and have a day off tomorrow or you may rest after your perilous exam and return tomorrow."

It wasn't really a difficult contemplation, especially if they were all like that however the cynic in me asked, "Depends on what the test will be."

"Perhaps one of construction?" she asked and paused waiting for my undramatic reaction.

"Like a flat pack?"

Her eyes flickered quickly back and forth before saying, "We agree that would be most suitable to assess for compliance with instructions and reasoning with a problematic missing part. Would you be interested in adding an advanced test of conflict resolution?"

"Fighting?" I wasn't prepared for flailing fists with spikey plants.

"Gosh no. We do not condone violence here but rather challenging situations of daily life."

"Sure. How bad can that be?"

"Some of your species find the situation incredibly stressful and on par with running out of toilet paper after a rather messy defecation."

"I think I'll be okay," I'd had experience of putting up a shelf or two and some were still clinging on to the wall.

She flicked through a couple of virtual schematics and said, "Please begin." Then waved a hand to her colleagues who were now all turned toward me with vines balancing flower head plumes as they observed intently.

A set of paper wrapped wooden chair legs, dowls and pictorial instructions were flung out of the mirror space and rolled behind a bin. I got to work and after several hours had managed to create a wonky stool and a bedside cabinet even with a whole page of missing instructions and two screws left over.

I returned to Azalea holding the stool aloft like some twisted trophy.

Not once had her attentions wavered and she almost seemed excited to see what the results would be. She extended her arm and took it from me and gave it a sturdy pat. "Such a curious thing," Azalea said and added, "well that should be all for today. You have outdone yourself and should be extremely happy with your progress. I'll inform your host."

"Thanks," I said and left with a sense of frustrated achievement as I bumped straight into Casey leaning on the door.

"Hi, I hope you don't mind. I finished already and waited for you," he said as he regained his position.

"I don't mind. What did they get you to do?" I asked as we made our way back down the corridor.

"You know we can't chat about that right. What about the waiver you signed?" Casey asked looking over his shoulder.

"I didn't sign one or maybe I did agree to some terms and conditions hidden away in the small print of the flooring or dew drops. That makes no sense, perhaps they've given me drugs?"

"I wouldn't have thought so. Do you want a coffee?" Casey asked and pointed over to a percolating machine with clear glass front. He pushed a series of buttons which caused the beans to rattle and churn as sluggish green waters pushed through into an espresso sized cup.

"Not from here," I said and retched.

"Please yourself," he said as we strode down the corridor in silence except for the occasionally slurp and passed more humanoid shaped beings in states of pre and post-test until reaching the dimmed sky of the outside. Our car pulled up and seamlessly opened its doors as he graciously bowed and let me in first then asked, "So, what did they ask you to do?"

"Oh, now you want to know?"

"Now that no one will overhear us… yes," he said strapping himself in.

I started with, "I watered a sentient plant," and finished with, "a rather nice stool."

"Sounds better than mine as I just filled in a form about my work."

"In all our chats I don't think I have ever asked you what your job is apart from H.R."

"It's not interesting, it literally just is client relations." He stopped awkwardly and smiled, "I'm sorry I've been a bit full on. I think it just hit me in a different way, you know with the lift and partying, then telling you things and-."

"I get it," I tried to stop him.

He continued, "It's overwhelming this whole thing is and it seems like you've made new friends here with a soggy plant and there was Caralyn and that other one." He steadied himself against the now wobbling car.

"I haven't heard from Caralyn and the other was marked to avoid forever," I replied as we made our jerky journey back to the Gröfu Pallur with comfortable conversation.

***

Our pre- and post-test routine carried on like this for the next few weeks with an informal conversation and then a drive over to what we'd nicknamed 'Not the Egg' to perform mundane tests. My tests with Azalea also included added subtleties of human life such as the purpose of matching curtains, the relevance of the spork and the many flavours of tampons. Sometimes I didn't know the answer, but Azalea and her colleagues didn't seem to mind as this new pattern rolled over peacefully until it didn't, and life hit me with the screech of tires and a flurry of dust on a busy highway road.

Chapter 12

The car jolted from one side of the road to another as it narrowly avoided a rotting lump curled up in the middle of the carriageway. The driverless driver's seat slid into the floor and was abruptly replaced by Casey's as it slammed him into position to pilot the pedals. He grabbed the seatbelt in blind panic as it was strangling him as a calm robotic voice stated, "Formulated navigation systems: PAUSED, switched to manual driver. Please drive carefully and observe the road." Casey freed himself as the ball steering was replaced with an old-fashioned wheel, but the car spun wildly out of control.

"Manual detour mode activated," the robotic voice said then carried on, "I did not sign up for a humanoid driver. Systems OFF!"

"So much for the robots then! Drive in a straight line! Come on Casey!" I shouted as I was flung left to right as the seat belt barely held me in place.

"I'm trying to not hit anything like... That!" The car collided with a firm dull thud on impact as we left the road. The tyres kissed the sky and my body became one with the seat flipping over as the ground become a dirt ditch and the air filled with mechanical crunch.

"Are you okay Casey?" I shouted as I tugged against tightened restraints hung upside down. The view was obscured by dust and debris through the back window and the front was smashed like a kaleidoscope. I needed to get out quickly as who knew what fuel these cars ran on and I wasn't about to go up in flames. The belt was truly constrictive and marred by my heavy breathing and panic, "We should call for help."

"They might not even have emergency services?" Casey yelled from also upside down as he kicked himself free from the driver's seat and assisted with my seatbelt. I tried hauling myself out through the front window but Casey stopped me as the glass started to bow precariously. "There should be a button for the door or something," he said.

"I'll look," I turned knocking my foot clumsily in a dimple in the roof-now-floor and the boot flung open. I escaped with Casey and staggered back to the roadside where a person was hobbling between the oncoming traffic and screaming into the sun.

"They might be dangerous," Casey said as he breathlessly held me back.

"They might just be hurt. Are you okay?" I shouted at the person.

The person stopped screaming and stood slumped with jaw lopsided as if appraising us like a zombie. The cars swerved either side carefully avoiding them as they swayed slightly then suddenly started running straight toward us screaming once more.

"Run!" Casey shouted as we stumbled along the roadside.

"Wait!" The person screamed and staggered into a car.

The car thudded them to the floor then swerved away with passengers seemingly unaware of the collision. I started to make my way over but didn't get far as Casey grabbed my hand, "We can't."

"Can't we? What if that was you and you just got hit by a car? Wouldn't you want help?"

"Yes but…"

"Yes but nothing, come on," I demanded as I shakily walked over to the person who was now dragging themselves across the road.

"Please… I don't mean you harm," the person said as we got within ear shot. "I'm a Doctor, Dr Marcus Shaw. The birds set me free." An accusatory finger pointed at my chest, "They know you. They say…" A blistered hand was held up to a chewed ear and listened to the distant nothing as cars narrowly missed shoeless feet. "Get away from him!"

"He's probably got a head injury. I guess we need to get him out of here before we all get hurt," Casey shouted from a few paces behind me. "Whoa!" The floor rumbled as our damaged car drove itself straight for us. It's doors stayed fixed in wing position barely missing us as it zigzagged down the road with hazard lights flashing out of sync and body sparking along the ground.

"It will return and bring the others," the doctor said to the sky as the stink of decomposition permeated through cracked lips. All of us were adrenaline filled as we helped each other to the side of the road however the Doctor's body stiffened when Casey reached out to steady him and instead turned his attentions to frantically searching the sky for an unknown entity.

Casey shrugged. "I'm going to get someone," he said and started to walk away.

But I remained and asked, "We should all stay here don't you think?" The Doctor backed away almost into on-coming traffic. Casey sighed and in one fell swoop dragged the malnourished body with tattered orange uniform into a field of towering aluminium poles.

"What are these?" I asked to the general population of three.

"Our way out. I can climb them. I must get to the top," the Doctor said then tried to test the efficacy of the nearest chrome pole but as soon as he grabbed out it shot down and buried itself into the ground. Another burst out an inch away and sprouted a metal umbrella which spun quickly. The pole bent under the force now created from jets of purple light shooting out of the prongs and connecting to several others also becoming a network of interchangeable lights. The Doctor seemed oblivious to the ever-thickening light chain and continued trying to catch the poles, he even seemed unbothered as tuffs of matted hair and blood encrusted lumps lifted from his skin in the static air.

This couldn't be a good thing, but I couldn't do anything about it so I joined in, "Maybe we could catch one if we worked together or are you too preoccupied with your fingers?" I called to Casey as I started to tentatively reach out.

"I think we are going to get in trouble for this," Casey called back more panicked than I was expecting.

"Let's catch one quick then before anyone sees," I replied with a poorly timed slap of a pole and stagger over the ground as the Doctor startled me.

He screamed, "They know! We must act fast." The air crackled with flashes of crimson pattern. "The messages are conflicting in loops. I failed Them."

He went to scream again but Casey was quick to react and said, "Just be quiet." He glanced over his shoulder and then up in the air before continuing, "we will help you in your search but Shh!"

"You are with Them, you won't help," the Doctor said with deathly breath so pungent it caught in the back of my throat as I briefly paused in my failing attempts to catch a pole.

Casey filtered the smell with the back of his hand then as the air cleared he continued with great conviction, "I'll help you Shaw, just watch me." He snatched out and shock struck his face as he caught a pole and then immediately let go. The Doctor screamed in frustration as the pole squeezed itself back into the ground causing the earth to pucker as it tunnelled between us before emerging with a thickened exterior and yellow glow. Several others emerged around it with the same glow but seemed to stay dormant with no wide umbrella atop them. The sky became quiet and all light activity ceased, now the only movement was the Doctor clambering up between two poles like a skeletal action hero.

Casey held out his hand and in a hushed voice said, "Lori, if we move, they might fall back into the ground and he'll drop and..." he shivered slightly. "We must stay still."

"I agree," I said and became fixed on the thin frame jerking upward. We stayed motionless for endless minutes until a gut-wrenching shriek made me flinch.

The Doctor seemed fixed in place as suddenly electric energy poured through the poles and slashed vivid light through him. With each hit he screamed through trismus jaw, "He's done this! He's one of Them! Release me!"

"No! He's trying to help you, we both are!" I shouted as several umbrellas bloomed from the top of the remaining poles and connected sporadically sending messages back and forth. The ground shook as poles grew and shrank and the Doctor was finally released. He fell and hit the ground with a spine shattering 'snap'.

I went to help but we became separated through a thick barrier of crisscrossed solidified light rays. Muffled calls came from the left and gasping breaths from the right, but I was unable to pass through the titanium strong bars of light. In this time of stress in the small triangular prison of light, all sound was drained, all light was being consumed by the overwhelming brightness and even the stench of the Doctor dissipated. I tapped my fingers together but nothing happened. Instead, all I could do was sit or stand. I choose to stand but lost my footing as the ground fell away at an impossible angle. I slipped down a short way but was met with a metal block which held me in a perpetual position of lean. The light dimmed making the prism claustrophobic with still no means of imminent escape. It was then I noticed the grazes and scratches on my arms from the crash and my galloping heart. "Help! Please make this stop!" I cried in a pathetic way until sounds of cars screeching on the road became more apparent and steps formed out of the metal mass underneath me. The wall of diminished light ceased to exist and became a gateway to an iron clad path, I followed it up and out just as the muted shadow of Casey appeared to do the same. The path led all the way to the road and waiting for us was a brand-new car with Jax patiently sat in the front. He appeared smug as he leant through the window and rested a long arm before stating, "What an adventure you've had." Casey got in, buckled up and stared straight into the seat in front. "What are you waiting for Lori?" Jax asked and tapped his hand against the door.

A squirt of adrenaline shot through my body at the thought of getting back into a car. "We need to wait," I stated in an attempt to linger outside for longer then added, "I can't remember his name, but he's out there and hurt. We just need to wait for his steps to be built and we can get him to a doctor… well a healthier doctor. Won't you help Jax?"

Casey shrugged as Jax licked his lips and smirked. "You've been in a nasty crash. You're clearly confused. There's only you, Casey and a ton of radiation from the tubular nodes in the exchange field. The only thing that's missing is your original car which, when it's found will have some interesting data to prove just how you tampered with it, now get in," Jax said through gritted teeth.

Casey sipped shakily on some water and said, "The car… it just blew a tyre and went out of control. I don't know where it ended up, but we are lucky to be alive." Jax patted him awkwardly on the shoulder from the front of the car to back without needing to move. "I really want to go back home now. Can you please get in?"

"I can't just leave. I know you saw what I did. You know he's out there," I turned again and strained to concentrate. "What?" I said in disbelief as the walls had disappeared and umbrellas stowed themselves under a boundless bleak sky, nothing was left except reedy poles swaying in the non-wind. I took a step toward the spot where the previous path lay but electrical poles sparked threateningly.

"What are you doing? It's not safe!" Jax shouted, "That's not habitable anymore unless you want to get airdropped and completely burnt alive."

I stayed in place as what could I do? I couldn't risk seriously hurting myself to be left behind in the desolate waste of technological rule but I couldn't just leave someone alone and hurt. The Doctor was nowhere to be seen, not even a footprint or hair tuft was left and no trace that we had ever even entered the field. I resigned my conscience and I reluctantly entered the car only to sit in shaken sombre silence.

Chapter 13

"The Gröfu Pallur must impose a punish-, excuse me… I meant to say, a time of safe confinement within your augmented apartment as a part of our due diligence procedures," a new Játvarður stated from two metres away from my front door. "It is to monitor the effects of any long-lasting radiation damage and Jax has demanded that you understand this is for your safety," they continued and tossed around words of contamination as they readjusted their ill-fitting apron adorned over their security outfit. They finished and slammed the door shut and inserted what sounded like bolts in each corner. Of course, I tried to get out immediately, but the handle came off in my hand and the redundant hole was instantly filled with solidified foam from the outside.

It was the first time I had encountered full house arrest and with my record of unscrupulous behaviour Fred was quite certain it should have already happened at least once before. Tiao sadly offered little assistance in leaving and was pleased when my attempts of escaping over the side of the balcony failed as a smoke screen barricaded the area. Even the classic 'date escape' routine of climbing up and out the toilet window was also a negative as it was replaced with an enclosed tiled wall. Fred had been more forthcoming and suggested crawling through the heating vents although the fully plastered ceiling left an absence of panels to fling off. So I was at a loss and stuck here.

It had been 7 hours and 15 days since they took my freedom away…

Actually, it had been only 2 days of being inside with no humanoid contact except for Casey who spoke to me via online connection in the virtual world. This afternoon was no different as I made sure my shirt overlapped my pyjama bottoms just enough to appear like I was wearing proper clothes and was less of a slob. I then turned on the floating screen and waited for three dots to be replaced with Casey's face, however it changed to a desk in front of a cityscape background. Maybe Casey had received another upgrade I mused as I sipped my wine-in-a-mug until a rather flustered person in a mauve suit bustled in and sat behind the desk. Someone quickly followed at their heels and jabbed a makeup brush in their face as they said, "Me, Me, Me. Mo, Mo, Mo. Mike. Mike, testing. Hi, I'm Max… Hi, I'm Max Monroe. Okay, get away that's enough make-up. I'm ready. Cue me in."

An unseen person cleared their throat and informed, "Erm… it seems we are already up and rolling."

Tiao rolled in to view this unusual conversation and went to reset the screen just as the presenter yelled in twitchy outrage. "This is not acceptable!"

Tiao's hand lingered and I gently stopped him, "Let's wait for the drama." Tiao nodded in shy naughtiness and took his place beside me.

"We are on a tight schedule. I'm sorry for the inconvenience but could you please carry on as planned and we can discuss this later?" the unseen person said.

"Fine! But I will be contacting my agent and they will be having words with you! Ahem!" The presenter readjusted their suit and held a finger of 'No' up to a lingering makeup artist before stating, "Hi," they took another breath and plastered on a bright white smile, "I'm correspondent Max Monroe coming live from The Loppe, now in association with the Gröfu Pallur. We have breaking information as follows: It has come to our attention…" I went for a refill, "…She's gone. Is she allowed to go?" Monroe said to Tiao who scooted away to hide behind the chair. "She was wearing pyjama bottoms of all things, who are these beings?"

I stuck my head back around as Tiao peered out and said, "I think this is a communication specifically for you and happening right now."

"Right you are Robot! We are LIVE! You there in those hideous clothes… Sit down and listen. I am a Max Monroe, a correspondent and so forth and I have an announcement."

Tiao tugged at me and said, "Lori, it's probably best that you sit down for the flustered being."

I did so as the presenter said, "Thank you. Was that so hard? Anyway," papers were shuffled, "as I was saying, I am the correspondent here to inform you that your output levels have been considerably reduced due to something." Monroe squinted at me as if looking over my shoulder.

I followed his gaze over at the shut door then shrugged back.

"The autocue has stopped," Monroe spat as a person in black came into view and stuck a pencil in the air as they rewound something just outside the shot. Monroe shouted, "STOP!," then continued at 4 times the speed, "that your output levels have been considerably reduced due to the unforeseen circumstances of a car crash incident and pollution exposure. Due to the debt now incurred from the running costs of the apartment it is crucial that testing is recommenced immediately in your vicinity."

"It'll give me something to do at least," I said and sipped but occasionally glanced over my shoulder as the presenter kept looking that way.

"I'm pleased you won't be bored in your luxurious life. Is there any further?" The assistant, who had remained in view, shook their head. "Fine. I've been Max Monroe, thank you and goodnight."

I checked my clock. It was still the afternoon, but the screen blurred out before I could inform him. The usual 3 dots took their place along with the 'Bu, du, du' sounds as Tiao strained his arms to grab a printed out a slip from a side panel. "Meeting organised at four today with Ms Azalea List," he read aloud and appeared worried. "I think you should probably get fully dressed into your uniform."

"I'll go and have a shower as well," I replied and downed the rest of my wine.

***

I returned in my neatly pressed testing uniform to find dull bashing coming from underneath the stairs. Once the thundering had stopped, Tiao opened a newly created sand coated door and we entered together. Inside the windowless space was yellow cushioned cladding from floor to mid wall and smooth flowery inserts from there to ceiling. In the middle of the room was an egg chair with auburn lining and lights around the edges but somehow the garish setting worked in a modernist way. I tried out the chair and sank into a foamy cushion as Tiao gave me a thumbs up to begin before bringing down several screens and two goo infused bottles. Data scrolled back and forth before the screens filled up with floral dressed plant-based humans with flowing haircuts. The biggest screen housed Azalea who was the only one with notepad poised at the ready.

Tiao stayed in position beside me and seemed overly excited in this space but didn't speak as he waited with finger on light emitting lips and tracks neatly tucked around crossed legs.

Azalea was the first to break the silence and stated, "Updates to the chairs as follows: hash rate to be confirmed. Reconciliation period taken from advice received from mandated policies. Channels to be spoken aloud before being backed up with typography and mentalist interpretation," she rolled her eyes at that statement before continuing, "today will be the commencing of assessment through manipulation of past enteroception and new formulation."

A chorus of, "Agreed," followed.

"Hello Lori, I hope you are well. I must inform you that this is going to be similar to our previous testing sessions except we will use the functions within neurological mediums over physicality forces and visual displays. With your permission we will place you in a dream-like state and examine situations we can learn from and inspect. This will not or should not interfere with your daily living. Do you consent?"

"Do I have a choice?"

Azalea briefly hit something to her left as all screens briefly showed a speaker with a slash through it, "You always have a choice," Azalea said and started to take notes as her elbow jerked again.

I didn't really have a choice, but what else could I do but agree, "Okay, let's do this."

"Relax back into your chair and place your hands into the detachment chambers. Focus on the fact that you may choose your actions as you would in an everyday situation," she explained and airily waved her pencil as everyone on the other screens peered closely into their cameras making their faces distorted.

"This wouldn't be an action I would do every day," I mumbled but obeyed and placed my hands into the recessed gaps. My fingertips were the first to lose sensation as numbness flowed all the way up to my wrists and painless wires inserted themselves into the back of my hand and bicep causing the tingling to spread to arms and chest. The press of the chair came away from me and the only thing I was still aware of was Tiao's reassuring grip on my calf.

***

The lock broke on my luggage as I staggered into what seemed to be my old bedroom at my parent's house. I threw the case onto the bed and tried to open my suitcase. I undrew the star printed curtains and tapped on the window at Dad, not Dad but a younger version who pointed toward brooding clouds overhead and quickly gathered his gardening equipment.

A faint roll of thunder rumbled coinciding with my door opening and Mum, again a younger version of Mum entering, "They are pretty birds," she said as a flurry of backward flying birds formed a miniature tornado and popped out a hand from within. I'd seen that hand before. It was a hand that had held me. I had to photograph it, but my phone wouldn't budge from the off screen until Azalea's face was in it shouting incomprehensibly and furiously scribbling.

***

I woke up and was fixed sedated in place. I could think but not speak as if my body was being suffocated with pressure. Several floating screens rattled out information of charts falling and dropping with unfathomable phrases as a masculine voice hurriedly said, "Did we plan for a tornado?"

The paralysis eased as I strained against the restraints now only holding my arms which were still as heavy as stone.

"I thought it was just the lock?" said another.

"Quickly put her back under and let's continue," the familiar voice of Ms Azalea said before I could speak.

***

"I'll have to check the house insurance as that wind has destroyed Barry the Gnome and the hydrangeas," Younger Mum said and idly observed the complete havoc of a once well-groomed garden.

"It's fine, we can pay for any damage as we don't want the rates going up. Probably just one of them fluke events I suppose, shame about the Gnome it was a nice present," Younger Dad said and pulled at my unbudging suitcase. "How about we sort out that suitcase lock and get the kettle on…," he paused and pointed outside. "Someone's running through my bushes!"

Globules of rain obscured the view as I tried to open a window, but it was glued shut.

"Don't go outside!" Younger Mum instructed as her face became distorted and elongated.

But I wasn't staying, I left the house through the only available door and hunched my shoulders against the rain, but there wasn't any in the atmosphere only that running along the windows. There weren't any puddles in the street which was eerily quiet and to call it a street was too strong a term as each house lacked bricky detail and roads remained basic outlines being forgotten into the bleak distance. I shoved through the garden gate and straight past the tornado which had been paused like a ballet dancer caught mid jump and hidden behind a fern. I ran behind the patio area which seemed to have shrunk and continued over to the bushes. Footsteps carved a well-trodden path to a pond, but the water wasn't as it should be as something glimmered in the lily pads. I moved them aside and was faced with the person from the nightclub waterfall who winked cheekily and sighed out a bubble just before being replaced with Azalea.

***

"We are sorry our tests aren't quite producing the results we want but your hosting fees are now set accurately. You must return inward one more time as your test is incomplete and I'm sure you can understand the first is always trial and error," Ms Azalea said as her pencil left smoke trails of lead as it shot across the page.

"They aren't my parents and I'm quite tired, can we do this another time?" I asked as I massaged my head.

"... Yes. We are happy to reconvene tomorrow late morning and we shall try again. Tonight, we shall discuss where Mr

Willis Carnation went so wrong today," she glared at the screen bottom left.

"Agreed," they said as Tiao retracted the screens.

I stormed out of the room and slumped on the sofa as Tiao brought a different screen filled with Casey's face however his hair was unbrushed, stubble had started to grow in patches and his eyes were sunk and darkened, "Have they told you how long this will last?" he asked but didn't wait for an answer, "they told me it could be at least two weeks." He slurred and swayed a little, "they said it should be like dreaming."

"It doesn't feel like that. If it was a dream-."

"No, don't continue or else we will become those people who examine their dreams." He grimaced then slapped his face with a pallid hand wrapped in tubes. "These are for the infection apparently… Wibbly, Wibbly…" He waved and passed out face forward.

Tiao closed the screen and sat beside me with tracks dangling as he tapped his hands together. "I'm sure he will be okay. Now, it would seem you contacted your relatives today?" Tiao asked, "I could see on the screens and me and Fred were wondering if it has impacted your mood or if the testing is the cause of your sad emotional cloud."

"I guess most people would be pleased and I was glad in a way but I know it's not them. My sister wasn't there but my parents were. Well, kind of. You see my Dad spent his last few years not knowing who I was as he was plagued with dementia before he passed. Mum and my older sister both chose the wrong side and I became estranged from them a long time ago."

Tiao put his hand on my shoulder and gazed at me with big eyes, "Me and Fred will be your family now."

"Ay' that'll be us, a family," Fred added and glowed pink.

"Thanks, I'd like that." I choked.

"Is there anything we can do Lori?" Tiao asked.

"Mist me, Tiao. Mist me," I said as he blew macadamia essence in my general direction, I slunk out of encumbered fret and drifted into a world of tornados, birds and disembodied hands.

Chapter 14

The addictive nature of repetition struck on the seventh day of testing as I wanted to keep going back into the lucid state to seek the nameless one with messy hair and deep hazel eyes. She was the chink in the examining machine but each time I got close she morphed into a plant-based assessor, and I was cast back to my apartment.

The tests had changed quickly from my parents' house to a coach terminus where I could choose destinations at my leisure. The self-proclaimed 'Superintendents of Acquirement' aka Azalea and her colleagues made it clear every journey was completely randomised but I chose my destination based on appealing advertising and surreal scenery however today was different. The ticket machine rejected each of my choices and then reset itself, now all destinations were marked as:

[Cotesburg – Visit H3RE!]

I selected the ticket then positioned myself on a bench, well a bench that was no more than a cold metal shelf in the quiet station and waited for the coach. The board stated it would be arriving 15 minutes late but no sooner had my bottom hit the shelf than I was nudged by an overly sweaty someone wearing a well-worn delivery uniform. "The coach is here," they said through darkened yellow teeth, then spat out a brown substance into a napkin before pocketing it. The coach door swung open and as always, no one got out. I tromped up the three wide steps and passed over my ticket to the driver who glared before indicating to go to the back. I found a free window seat and shuffled in as the delivery person handed over their ticket, but the driver didn't accept it and escorted them off the coach immediately.

The driver unlocked the luggage compartment underneath the coach as the clangs of suitcases being thrown about echoed through the passenger section. A light tinkle of rain threatened to obscure the view and the noise, but my scream was louder as the driver peered above the edge of the door and was face to face with me. The pallid face was just as shocked as I as our glances collided, but the driver mouthed an apology before shutting the door and hovering back down to ground level. I suspected a deal of some sort as the delivery person appeared to shiftily tuck a box under their jacket before heading over to another vehicle.

The driver returned to our coach and stated, "Sorry for the delay," and started to pull off rapidly. My head collided with the seat in front as we swerved to avoid aquaplaning out of the terminal, again an apology followed but the weather continued to worsen.

Drains burst at the seams and gutters regurgitated the steady flow down over shop fronts. Grids vomited and puddles bloomed on pavements where people were masked with umbrellas inverted up catching the downpour. Roads became rivers as passersby were soaked as the coach carelessly continued rather than slowing for the slop. The driver seemed to be focused on getting to our destination until we came to a halt with a stomach-turning wheel spin. The road was blocked with an abandoned car just yards away from the next terminus. The driver beeped and gesticulated and more so when the coach was pelted from the outside by a shoe thrown by a woman shouting from a nearby block of apartments. This looked like a good place as any to leave so I walked with confidence down the aisle and stated, "This is me."

The driver startled and said, "This isn't anyone. You'll wait till the journey ends."

I wasn't going to, "It appears that this journey is over as there isn't any way you're getting past that car unless you can turn into a plane or boat. So perhaps you can let me off and at least I can help them in some way?"

The driver's face was in pure turmoil until they startled as their window was hit by what was possibly a hairbrush or small hedgehog. "Just wait a moment," they said as they tried to contact someone but were deprived of signal.

"Guess you'll just have to make an executive decision," I said and exaggerated observing more passengers ducking from the onslaught of clothes as some funnelled their attention away from self-absorption and into the aisles waiting to also depart.

"It'll pass," the driver said glancing at the darkening sky.

"It also might not and what's this here… A button to open the doors, I mean you could just hit it by accident when you keep ducking from whatever is going on out there?"

The driver glared at me as civil unrest grew within the coach and then coughed loudly as he ducked and quite obviously slammed the button. The hiss of the opening door came along with sloppy globules of rain as I left and waded through the weirdly warm waters of the flooded road. I carefully walked past bathing birds frolicking in the foamy puddles and into the only open shelter available. It was an apartment block of at least seven floors with well signposted toilets. I headed straight for the hand dryer and stuck my legs underneath as warm air hissed out. A woman with frizzy hair and runaway mascara kicked open the toilet stall door and screamed, "I'm sick of her! Why should I put up with that behaviour? Obviously, it's different when I do it but then again, I'm allowed wouldn't you say?"

I didn't say and didn't want to be a part of whatever drama she was invested in.

"Course you'd agree but this time I'm not going back to her. It wasn't even my fault… they kissed me, and I couldn't just pull away," she said as she started to wash her hands. "I don't care if she wants to carry on dumping my stuff all over the place, I'm done and it's over. She doesn't even know what she'll be missing but I should show her," she declared as she wiped away the remnants of washed out make up and reapplied. "Do you have any lipstick?" she asked then laughed and added, "No you're more of a lip balm one right?"

"I guess," was the best I could formulate in response.

Water dropped from drooping ceiling panels onto her pre-drawn brow and she screamed as layers of make-up were ruined just as lights flickered and failed. Emergency lighting took their place as she left and I gave it a minute before leaving but a claw hand grabbing out from underneath a cubicle door caught my attention, "Hello?" I called.

"Hello, I appear to be trapped could you assist me please?" a robotic voice said.

I shouldered and levered the door open to find a mini-Tiao tucked up in there, it waved politely with its only free hand and said, "Please be kind and remove me as my pipes seem to have become tangled in the toilet paper dispensing machine."

"Sure Tiao…"

"I am Master WeNaNo and it is my pleasure to meet you, I would also ask that you pick me up from the floor as the toilet appears to be overflowing with… well I wouldn't like to say."

"I'll just…" I mumbled as I unwound and freed the pipes and tracks.

"Thank you for your co-operation," it said and shook like a dog before holding its arms up for me to pick it up.

"You're welcome," I said as I carried WeNaNo up the stairs through the copious amounts of clear water streaming down and creating a pool in the reception area.

We ventured into the first room with open unlocked door and into a torrent of shouting, "How dare you come back?" the person screamed as another bin bag was flung out of the balcony double door. "Oh, you're not Sofia…"

"I'm Lori and this is WeNaNo. It's raining really heavily and we just needed to get to a safe place," I said as WeNaNo reached out for a dish cloth and started drying. "By the way your tap is overflowing," I said as the person ran over to the kitchen and turned it off just as a crack appeared in the ceiling. I dropped down to the floor and wrapped myself around WeNaNo waiting for the imminent collapse. But instead came a gentle touch on my shoulder. "It's not raining anymore. Come here I'll show you." WeNaNo continued to towel off as I followed her passing piles of clothes labelled 'Sofia' among other names and out onto the balcony where any last puddles were sucked back up into the sky along with birds flying backward. There was no rain but clear skies, clear roads and the coach full of marble faced passengers making its way onward.

The frizzy haired woman was now hitting the abandoned car so hard her make up flew out of her handbag and all over the windscreen. "Sofia, stop that!" the apartment dweller shouted.

"You don't get to tell me what to do anymore. Oh, and who is that? I've been out of your life for five minutes and you've already got a new woman," she hit the car mirror off onto the floor and continued, "she'll break your heart just like you broke mine. Paige, you aren't good to anyone except yourself!"

"It was your fault…" the person next to me started however WeNaNo tugged on my still slightly sodden trouser and nodded to leave.

"How can I assist you?" I asked as we made our way out.

"This is for you," they said and handed over a printed note before the staircase collapsed into a crumbling rubble. We fell scraping along the debris until landing in broken cement. I scrabbled around in search of the little robot and saw a glint of smashed panel. I moved it aside and lifted out WeNaNo who was coughing violently and shaking. They clutched into me and ducked just as a chunk of something hit my head.

***

The air was too dry as I awoke in a cold sweat in front of several screens. "What was the point in that?" I asked breathlessly. "Is WeNaNo okay?"

"Several factors have been observed and it has been noted in particular that your bond with servants is similar to the bond of pet and owner in a disastrous situation. Also your capability of name recall," said a person sprouting double nose hairs.

"Quite so," said Azalea, "not to forget the incidental finding of the cause of the sudden flooding being a disobedient tap. A true detective case solved and more so…" she continued the analytical chatter as I unexpectedly stressed.

"Tiao?" I called when I could not find him faithfully waiting by my leg.

"See here how she cares that the servant has been sent away? Quite marvellous," a thinning ginger combover and spikey chin hair said.

"Tiao isn't my servant he is my friend, him and Fred both are," I stated as I pulled the electrodes away from my arms and strode out somewhat groggily.

"Lori, wait a moment as we do need to thank you for your participation for today. Tiao is outside as we thought it may have been distressing to watch," Azalea said as she noted. "He is fine. Now we are done here as we have much unexpected research to discuss and means of moderation may cause change," she finished and waved me off with a go-away hand. The screens swung around as the superintendents began to argue their opinions over one another without pause for challenge.

I pushed open the door and found Fred safe and reading a chef book I'd gifted him, "Where is Tiao?" I asked.

He mimicked licking his finger to turn the page before pointing to the charging zone.

Tiao was unconscious when I opened his wall and asked, "Are you okay?" I picked him up and wasn't expecting his deceitfully lightness as I squeezed him gently. His eyes dimmed and quickly faded to black, was that a blink? Did he even need to blink?

He sagged as he said, "I'm quite alright Lori. My battery isn't charging as well as it usually does, I believe it may be… compromised."

I placed him back into his charging slot and wrapped him in my jumper as Fred watched intently. "I haven't forgotten about you!" I said and mounted the breakfast bar to hug him.

He bristled slightly and relaxed, "Sorry, that's the first 'ug I've ever bin 'avin. Now that's all the niceness over with, can I get yeh a 'ot cocoa and yeh can moan about flower folk?"

Chapter 15

The five walls, the tiled floor and that chair had become a clinical chasm of obligations. Day after day I endured endless 'sleep' in the testing room with the routine never wavering. I grew to hate it. I screamed and kicked back as much as possible but nothing stopped the monotony. The tests would repeat until a resolution was found but sometimes they would end abruptly with the arrival of birds or the unexpected person. I'd wake up to truncated error codes and blue screens of death replacing the flower folk. The plague of faults was so much that Azalea's colleagues couldn't cope with it, so the screens went away until only hers was left muttering as she communicated with the multiverse. She paused mid flick of the pencil and said, "We are suspending your test this morning as it has come to our attention that your formal quarantine has been officially suspended. You are being allowed to continue your testing at the facility as previously provided and I look forward to meeting with you once more face to face." She bid me farewell as I left the torturous room as the door sealed itself instantly and melted back into the wall.

Tiao was dutifully waiting and smiled as I left the room. He shuffled from side to side and said, "A package has arrived for you Lori and a note." He slowly pushed in a large brown box and handed over an envelope.

I expected it to be heavier with the effort it took him, but it was surprisingly light as I took it onto the breakfast counter and asked, "Shall we open it together?"

Inside were two brand new sets of honey uniform with numbers printed down the side:

01010100 01100101 01110011 01110100 00100000
01010011 01110101 01100010 01101010 01100101 01100011
01110100 00100000

I tried it on before Tiao even had time to press it, but he didn't seem as interested as he opened a screen of Casey's face instead. I hadn't really chatted with him that much as the tests seemed to take more of a toil on him, but he was fresh faced and dressed. He gleefully said, "It's over! They are picking us up at 12:843cvt. See you soon."

***

A knock echoed and the front door released at the designated time, but it seemed like ages as I'd waited behind it as soon as I'd put on my new uniform and had a coffee. It was an exciting premise to get back into the real world and back into physical projects and a relief to see Casey with briefcase in hand. "Hi. Shall we go?" he said.

"What's in the case?" I asked giving it an experimental poke.

"All will be revealed later," he said with a wink and clink of the bag.

I bent down to Tiao who had intermittently sat with me waiting and whispered, "It's going to be fine."

He tugged at my trousers and said, "Please be careful." Then winced as Jax came T'tapping down the corridor.

"We need to leave now. Finish your pleasantries quickly as I'm sure you're keen to get back into conformity," Jax said and menacingly stared at Tiao who slunk even further.

"Do you mean the community instead of conformity?" Casey asked but was met with silence.

Jax even ignored my questioning of getting Tiao a new battery component and enquiries about Caralyn and only once we had been locked into our vehicle with the destination firmly set in calm pastels did he speak further. Jax sneered, "You both seem scared?"

We set off and I wanted to roll down the window but they were sealed shut. "I mean, not long ago we were in quite the crash so when I stop shaking I'll let you know," I replied and gripped the edge of the seat.

"Tension will not do. The prior car crash was a one off but you both conquered the lift so you will also conquer the car." Jax spat as he released an acrid chemical, different to the mist Tiao sparingly used but still had the same if not worse effect. Casey released his clutching hands from his briefcase and it struck us that we had actually regained some freedom. We became giddy drunk on the notion and so much so that Jax barked us into silence as we muffled sniggers.

The car journey was swift and interruption free as it pulled up to "Not the egg!" we chorused happily as Jax scorned us. It dropped us off and I was exhilarated with the feeling of fresh air on my skin and dusky concrete beneath my feet.

Not even the 'Hurn Hurn' of receptionists dampened our demeanours as they actively ignored me while I filled in a new form and subtly observed Jax pouring the snail slop into his cup. He gulped the thickened juices hungrily before licking his lips and leaving.

I lapped up the familiarity of the facility as Casey found us a table and sneakily opened his briefcase away from me. He started banging about inside and swiftly moved it sideways anytime I tried to look. The 'assassa' of perhaps a blender, the 'purp' of something being popped and the 'tink' of ceramic filled the silence until he finished with a quick glance and flick of an eyebrow before letting the case fall open revealing a rather elaborate coffee set. "I couldn't face drinking the slime anymore and thought we could share a fresh cafetiere coffee instead."

"Thank you," I said and greedily took it.

"I even have salted caramel syrup and hot chocolate shavings from ZiMe to go on top," he added as he 'whumped' it over. I slurped the sweet balance with bitter twinge, only made better by the fact it was made by someone else as this always improves taste, as we waited in polite slurpy silence until Casey packed up the case and said, "Time for me to go it seems. How about we meet back here after?"

"Deal," I said then gulped as a notification sprang up.

[Please attend the reception position desk: dUck7]

I waited in a queue of 5 which dwindled quickly and a receptionist abruptly turned around as soon as I got near but still, they spoke, "Lori…your testing station has been permitted within room eighteen, twenty-seven, B five. Two, B. Five. Hurn. Hurn," An eye stalk twisted back on itself as another followed it to fully look me up and down. The receptionist glopped and turned as they handed over a digital map before continuing, "Follow the route to your testing facilitator, Hurn." They coughed and slopped at the same time, "you're already late! Hurrrn."

I followed the permitted route but lingered outside the room as worry consumed me, it should be Azalea waiting inside but it could always be some other bean sprout or overgrown bush waiting to dissect my mind. But what was the point of worrying about something I couldn't control. I should just get in and get going with it, so I knocked quietly and nervously waited to be welcomed in rather than boldly entering.

The door swung open and relief caught me as Azalea was stood waiting with sleeked back hair in a bun. She seemed almost taller in the sunlight as she said with formality, "Please take a seat and we shall begin momentarily." She neatly stowed away a watering can and jotted down a symbol on a hanging schedule nearby before returning.

I started with a standard pre-warm up yoga stretch session as Azalea said, "Sit. Sit, you need not do anything that would cause elevation of the heart as we have decided to continue with testing in investigatory persuasions of your mind. The results you produce are truly incredible so it is valuable to continue in this manner and quite simply, that's all we ask. And to you also, it would be prudent to achieve satisfying results as that would mean a brief limbo from testing for a considerable amount of time."

"And how long is a considerable amount of time?" I asked while lunging as far as my cotton thread would let me.

"Two to three weeks depending on current fluctuant and price motility," she said with a flick of her hand and once more beckoned me into sitting. Her next words faded into oblivion as I sat on the edge of a new dentist styled chair and wires threatened to penetrate my biceps. Azalea spoke louder, "What are you waiting for? You'll have time to explore once this is over," she briefly held a silencing hand up, "It is worth it, I assure you."

"But…" I started with no argument to follow up or at least none that would have any real merit. She would supersede it with clever concepts so I would concede and go back into my mind to formulate whatever nonsense gave viable results. "Will this end?"

"It will end as it always does just when the test is complete," she said as she readjusted a blanket and gently pushed my shoulder down. "You won't feel anything this time as our systems have been thoroughly checked. But I suppose," she paused and looked thoughtfully a moment at the blind space before continuing, "you always have a choice you know. Well, what would you do instead?" She said waiting with notepad resting on floral cufflinks.

"I'd go home."

"Well, why didn't you say? I can arrange that," she scoffed as the chair tilted and bright lights bleached my vision.

Chapter 16

Rikke-Borg Park was the first place I'd played an instrument to an audience that consisted of more than just my family and friends. It was a bog-standard green space with reed ridden pond and could-be-better fountain cascading bubbles into its depths. Leaves shed down on unsuspecting runners as they thundered along the broken path and bypassed ramblers who nodded politely as they strode by me.

This was home.

A dog-walker with more hair on their chin than had ever graced their head came bounding over as the pooch remained stoically in place with lead extending quickly. The dog maintained a piercing stare as it began to produce a bright yellow stream on a bush and its owner barked, "Choo done wiv that?"

"Geez!" shouted a runner as they hurdled over the new lead ridden inconvenience, "It's a dog shit minefield here."

"Arsehole," retaliated the Wispy Beard dog owner before continuing snarling, "I said are choo done wiv that?"

I picked up the magazine from the bench, its front page was scattered with scandal and celebrity nonsense as I handed it over and said, "Yes, I am!" The person grabbed it and shook it in excitement before the dog toddled past and the owner followed.

An overwhelming validation that this might not be a test came immediately after as an alien coldness caused goosebumps. "Ha!" I said too loudly and received odd stares from park goers but probably more for the outburst than my attire as I seemed to fit in amongst the odd combinations of t-shirts with overlapping scarfs to thick overcoats and skinny shorts. There wasn't a cloud in the sky, nor grass plate, nor unusual being and no barriers. So, Jax, Azalea and the Játvarður's must have decided I was more hinderance than commodity generating and given me back my life along with rumbling stomach. Fred would have rustled me up a bagel and avocado with exceptional finesse, but he'd be fine now with someone else to serve or maybe even a family to keep him and Tiao out of mischief. Though perhaps the two would excel here amongst the youths sprawled out atop the glossy grass and random persons waving in the general direction of me.

It was a wave full of mirth and belonged to a certain someone I very much did recognise. I'd managed to miss his upcoming art exhibition by getting swept away in a lift but surely he would forgive me? He waved again, cupped his hands and shouted, "You have been gone ages? Where have you been?"

I didn't budge as the imminent explanation of events paralysed me. Ármine's messages clearly hadn't gotten to him so time for a plan. I could just run back to my apartment and astutely sort through the vast number of bills that were likely neatly stacked on a side table, but he'd follow me and get annoyed that I'd ignored him in the first place. The bills and berating seemed more appealing as how could I begin to explain where I'd been? He'd think I'd lost my mind and refer me to a counsellor or perhaps put me into one of his art shows by way of explorative movements.

He was gaining on me... what to say? Maybe something along the lines of... "Sorry I missed the biggest moment in your creative career, I got stuck in a lift with a guy and ended up in a car with balls for wheels that took us to a place that was luxurious and housed with helpful robots. It was full of aliens that didn't like being called aliens which tested on me for a while in a place where receptionists gooped gel and people drank it. There was also Caralyn who got lost at a nightclub and an echoing person who was constantly trying to help." No. that would never work as it was such nonsense.

Without another minute to think of plausible explanations he and his multi-coloured coat were just two paces away. "Hey Lori," he said and brushed through his brunette wavey hair framing his unreadable face.

"Hey Jorge, I'm sorry for not getting in touch. It's just been busy with work and…"

He silenced me and took my arm in his before saying, "You're always sorry but you're back in time for the BAC ball and please tell me you're ready to go," he said and pouted with puppy dog eyes.

The Bi-Annual Charity Ball was the second biggest event in his art career. I'd been away for what seemed like months and now actually back had nearly missed a major deadline, where I was co-ordinating the composition of the night. I seriously needed to make up for the last one where I passed out in a corner, which was not an unusual drunk occurrence but one I didn't want to repeat. But this one, I could finish off if I could remember where I had stored the music and instruction files. I flicked my fingernails to get my database up, but nothing happened.

After repeating this several times Jorge asked, "Is something wrong with your finger?" he waggled mine with gloved hand as his canvas tote bag swiftly fell about his wrist.

"No. It's just a thing I do now to, erm…help me think. It's fine really."

"Mhmm, well okay then," he said suspiciously then added, "your travels have changed you." He started to rummage in the tote bag then tutted. "Did we fall out?"

"No, why would you say that?"

"You've disappeared before but usually give me an idea of when you'll get back. You've not chatted with me in so long, did I say something or did something happen?" he asked after wafting a rolled piece of paper around before resting it under his chin and pursing his lips.

"I'm sorry. I really am, I tried to get a message out to you."

He pointed at my pocket as I instinctively reached inside and my fingers collided with the smooth edges. I gasped, it was there, my actual phone was there. I fingered the screen into life but nothing happened.

He stood with arms crossed and asked, "Broken again?"

"Think so."

"I guess that is acceptable then, but you could have always gotten a spare."

"Where I was, they just didn't sell them. I'm here now being a sad sorry sap and honestly, I really did try but…" I pleaded.

"Stop. I don't need your elaborate lies. Anyway, I've always wanted a convict in my friend collection… yes, that's how we'll play this, or you've been undercover…" he mused as he figured out his own story and I didn't have the heart to correct him as we made our way to his apartment. It wasn't worth explaining now so I'd at least wait until he was drunk enough to forget.

*****

The avantgarde silhouette soaked up the sun rays converting them into darkness like a black hole within the centre of the fabric stacked room. It's outfit oozed class and elegance with razor sharp lines and devious sculpting and this silky form was mine, or at least made for me by Jorge who helped me into it. It enhanced my assets and masked the misshapen with a few extra darts and subtle adjustments for a truly bespoke fitting. I and several others would be used as another way to model his art though a mixed medium of interstellar texture. Obviously, I couldn't pull off the model glide and sultry stare but I managed a mediocre step down and not fall over.

"Pockets!" I shouted as my hands instinctively rested inside the lined holes. They were spacious and would hide the necessary random objects I'd find to carry along with my broken phone.

"The shoes are not as clunky so should be easy to walk in, try a few steps forward," Jorge said as he assessed my gait. They were soft sprung boots with matching bits of lace sticking out but try as I could to flounce, I could not. "Urgh. Just walk normally, not with your bum out. Keep your back straight and fix your gaze."

"I'm sorry," I said and flumped in his make-up chair.

"Don't be, just… hmm, how about you stomp instead?" he asked as he came at me with a brush in hand causing powder plumes of orange flecks to cascade into the air until my pores were heavy and uncomfortable. "Leave your face alone," he shouted and mushed my lips together as he applied lipstick before stepping back to reappraise. "You look avant-cerish with a hint of leom neo style! That's good," he added at my confusion. "Now shove over and practice your walk while I get ready."

I did so by making a cup of tea as he applied perfectly lined eye shadow, chiselled his beard and highlighted his ears then waltzed with wide sleeves. "Right your car is here. I'll come up after as I have two others to prepare. Don't forget the set checks."

"You found the file?" I asked.

"You left it ready and waiting, now go!"

Once prepped I jumped into a non-ball wheeled car and made my way to the grand drive of the BAC ball, we stopped just before a set of bronze diamond gates and ticket booth. The human driver opened my door then directed me to the guard who was busy excavating his nostril. Whatever he was trying to find up there was evading detection so I evaded him by ducking underneath the barrier.

"Oi," he shouted and slammed open the door as an unwashed finger pointed threateningly in my direction. "Stop and produce your pass… please," he added. There was something vaguely familiar about this person whose name badge proudly stated, 'Larry'. As an afterthought it had scrawled pronouns squeezed in the margin.

I tapped down my pockets in search of a pass or anything moderately pass shaped in amongst the tissue, paperclip and old receipts that had already managed to hide in the pocket but found nothing. There had to be another way to get in, "I should be on the staff list… It's Lori…"

"Oh, too good for a pass are we and on the guest list eh? Well I've heard that before so you best follow me," he said and lifted the barrier by a lever contraption. It caught in place and jerked wearingly. "Oi! You must wait for the safety bar to fully go up before heading through," he said as I went to duck back under.

He re-cranked manually until it was one foot higher than where it was and now suitably safe to shimmy.

"We had this trouble last time," I stated as we marched back.

He opened his hut then got comfortable in a plastic chair and slid open the window. "Pass please… Oh yes, we've done that bit. On the guest list you say?"

"The staff list. I'm Lori, the musical composer and I really need to get inside. Think you can help me out?" I tried a straight wink and flick of my well gelled hair.

"Hack, hack," he said as he contemplated the list and the pencil found its way into a nostril cave. It did a couple of rounds before he coughed up thick mucus into a phlegm stiffened hanky and stated, "Got your name here, Lori… but can't let you in without a check of the profiles, so is this you?" he held up a photograph with white side facing towards me so only he could see the photo.

"Probably," I sarcastically said forgetting politeness.

"Yeh… could be, could be," he started to convince himself, "without all that make up it's probably you, so sign this here and I'll reissue your pass." He handed over a besnotted pencil and pointed to the dotted line. I pinched with minimal skin contact and scribbled my name before giving it back. He stowed the pencil behind a well waxed ear and said, "Don't lose it again. Hack!" He coughed up another slimy globule before zoning back in excavation.

"I won't," I replied out of shear fear of having to touch anything that man had encountered again. I stowed the lanyard and stomped past the main doors where sounds of perpetuum plucked out and continued around the back through luscious gardens with minimally slug eaten leaves. I entered, as always, via the side door and avoided people bustling with boxes and conveying sundries and would have gone straight for the sound desk, but the cheese platter convinced me to stay… just as it did before.

In fact, everything was the same as it had been so many times previously. Jorge would dress me and then we would leave. I would forget something then have a word match with whoever was on security and proceed via the side entrance.

The last ball had gone badly, so badly it made the papers and it all began with the cheese. The minor edible was sat there before it would be passed around for the first thirty minutes of the ball, last time I became so drunk that it was the last thing I remembered before Jorge named me, 'When Temperance is Lost' and slumped me in a corner retching. But that was then and this is now, or is it? Is it a memory, it seemed to be the same dress and same cheese but that could be a coincidence. No, everything is real here and I was present. So, had they put me back in time? I was sure Tiao said something about time travel but couldn't recall. If I was back in time then what happened then wouldn't happen now and I can change the outcome of a dreadful night.

It would start with cheese.

It was just waiting unassumingly alone and why shouldn't I? Why should I deny myself a fondue fancy? It had been hours since I'd last eaten. If Tiao was here, he would have presented this plated along with wine in hand, but he wasn't so I attempted not to get caught brie handed. Luckily, even in my outlandish garb the chefs paid me no attention as they tasted and shouted sous things to each other. I took a chance and grabbed a huge herb-encrusted chunk just as leather lined doors were pushed open by a pair of elderly waiters making their way directly over to me. A chorus of "Yes chef," from order placement disguised my swift exit into a hiding spot in between shelves of stacked plates.

The elder of the two adjusted their silk bow tie and hunched over the platter, "That ain't right."

"Best not be rats again, those last week were big as dogs," the younger said as I peered between the plates with the evidential brie oozing between my fingers.

"There was definitely more cheese there earlier and Chef Luan wouldn't let half a plate go out unfinished," they paused to share a look of concern and the younger of the two Greyings continued in a whispered tone, "maybe the Miarmuits took it."

"Watch your tongue, idiot boy!" Older Greying spat.

Younger Greying started to panic and readjusted a glimmer of fennel as he hurriedly said, "We could just fix it as I've seen it done hundreds of times. It'd just need a dab of pepbrie and flourish of salsa."

"We could I suppose, but I swear I checked it not an hour ago and Chef would know we dabbled where we ought not dabble," the Older Greying said and stuck down a side parting with added vigour.

"It was my duty to guard it and it's my mistake, I failed so I, and I alone shall take it to the chef," Younger Greying said and went to pick up the platter but was quickly subdued.

"Wait a moment, can you smell that?" the Older Greying questioned.

Younger Greying began investigatory sniffing before saying, "I can, so the culprit must be nearby."

I slowly lifted my hand and barely avoided costume contamination by inserting cheesy fingers directly into my mouth. Instantly my jaw clenched as spice hit the back of my throat and my tongue became dry as the desert. My eyes streamed at the zing as I scarcely held myself together in herb anguish.

"Scratch that, scent has dispersed. Might be a lingering flatulence and to eat so much in one go?! They will get their just desserts either way," the Younger Greying said and lifted the plate carefully with single hand. "Now I must pay for my misdemeanour."

Older Greying acknowledged this with a quick, "There's no other way. You've learnt well."

"Thanks Ms." He shook his head in noble defeat and grimly trotted off still sniffing the air.

I seized my chance and ran into the main area and straight into an aluminium duck. In the reflection my makeup had spoiled, Jorge would be so angry and disappointed but there was still time to fix it. I grabbed an ice cube and went to rub my cheek just as he appeared from beside an art piece and demanded, "What happened? What is wrong with your face?"

"Spice," I answered plainly. My eyes had stopped watering but my mouth was still dry.

Jorge grabbed a passing champagne flute from Older Greying who wobbled under the slight imbalance but maintained a steady course of direction until sniffing. "That smell," she started until a crash in the kitchen distracted her.

"Odd. You do smell weird," said Jorge as he observed my face, "I think we can make something of this. Here drink this."

"No thanks," I said.

"Are you okay? No thanks to champagne, that's a first."

"It's for the best after last time."

"If you say so. Now let's just… adjust this and wipe out an undertone here and a highlight here… Yes! That's it!" he said and stowed his emergency brush in his pocket before spinning me.

In the garish duck reflection, my new make-up made it appear as if I had been engulfed by a hungry bug but now was not the time for appearance doubts as I was here to do a job. "Thank you. I promise I won't mess it up again."

"Show starts in seventy-five with the normal opener. Roux is waiting in the booth for you. Do not touch your face," he demanded and ushered me further into the central room. It had marble vined columns supporting glass bottomed balconies which created a perpetual motion of chromatic glamour. It swirled with azure floral compositions which would complement Jorge's masterpieces still awaiting unveiling. I side stepped a hexagonal stage and checked one of the lower sound boxes before making my way upstairs.

Roux was sat with double headphones on and was currently dimming the lights below by way of twisting buttons. We exchanged nods in professional acknowledgement as I pointed at the thankfully-we-found-it set list and composition file. Roux and Jorge had tweaked the whole oratorio until it fulfilled his immersive show experience in a quick rehearsal yesterday. I bent over to check the altered timings but my new unlearnt dimensions knocked some board sliders out of kilter.

"I've got this, please get out," Roux mouthed then added, "only if you're happy to do so obviously."

"Sure, call me if you need anything," I replied and popped in an earpiece as soft music played counting down the last 37 minutes until start of show.

I lingered up on the first-floor balcony, clear from the start of social swooning of the first arrivals which didn't make obvious sense as I had been away from people for so long. I'd lost myself in the life of luxury and had longed to return to this place even if my world was suffering but here in midst of pre-show, I was lonely despite the fullness of the room.

I was brought out of my slump by long flowing locks and stood in shock. I was so happy but there was no time to think as I mumbled, "You're-."

"Devastatingly beautiful?" she joked as she readjusted a slumping dungaree shoulder and continued, "I'd know those lips anywhere even underneath all that paint." She then leant in close to whisper, "Come with me Lori." Eris oozed confidence as she held my hand and guided us down a hallway and into a room housing a central glass mannequin. It dominated the space and was currently being preened by a staff member, "So what do you think of the dress?"

"Incredible," I said.

"I'm glad you like it. It's from the same creator as your garb but your adoration isn't the only reason why I brought you here. Not this time anyway," she winked at me with honey-coloured eyes. "It's about my charitable donation to the raffle. I don't know whether Jorge has told you, but we've had all sorts this year. I'm struggling with my contribution as last time vanity pushed me into offering a meet and greet dinner, but now my ego has been thoroughly polished I feel like I should give something that can help people with their displacements… something to help them feel whole and home."

"Although re-hashing a dinner would still be great as I'd bid on it," I said over eagerly.

"You don't need to bid, you'd just have to ask." She gave me palpitations as she was very out of my league. She shrugged before flinging off her t-shirt which landed at my feet and I verged on awkward as I immediately turned away. She chuckled and said, "Come on it's not like you haven't seen it all before." A member of staff helped her into the dress as she smiled flirtatiously and said, "Lori, will you help with my zipper?"

I trod as lightly as possible on the plush carpet and pulled up the hidden black zip to her neck. She turned with a flare and looked stunning and so stunning in fact that whatever I could say would have little impact.

"Speechless?"

"Erm, you look…"

"You can tell me later as I shouldn't keep the patrons waiting as the show is about to start."

I should have known but had absolutely ignored the beeping in my ear to be present with her.

Eris stepped out to a modern fanfare as acrobats walked across the walls and staff unveiled Jorge's symphony of surrealist art. Eris introduced various charities and promptly started the bidding as wine flowed and wages floundered.

The night continued and money exchanged hands in selfish generosity until the last contribution was brought to the table, "A seven night stay-," she was cut off by an impetuous smash. One of the guests, who was wearing nothing more than ostrich feathers, fell into an already purchased statue in a drunken stupor. I knew about that incident from before as my friends had mentioned it but that was okay, it wasn't Jorge's art I had to save.

The outraged new owner stated her bid was now null and void and instantly demanded to be offered another art piece. Jorge and Eris tried to calm the affair as Roux played a track well out of sync and waiters flooded the room with champagne and canapes.

I rushed to the sound booth and found Roux out for the count and clearly overworked… or not as a hipflask lay empty on the side and it was a hipflask that was very much like the one Jax used. No, that was just a coincidence. I had to keep my mind in professional mode but the sound clashed as I fought with sliders to get it back on track. The lights flickered as the room beneath became awash with alcohol fuelled irrationally until a bird flew in from the open window. A waiter caught it mid-flight with a cloche causing a round of applause and a lapse in violent mentality as the proceedings followed more respectably.

"Is everything alright Lori?" Eris said as she suavely lingered at the door.

"What? Yeh."

"Why don't you come out here and have a drink with me?" she asked rolling Roux out of the way. "My private room is just down here and I'll message the waiter to bring us up some drinks and snacks as people are leaving. What do you say?"

***

The waiter trundled a serving trolley down the corridor audibly huffing not in exhaustion but inquisition. "It's that brie from before, I reckon it's close by now," said the familiar voice of

Younger Greying from outside Eris's room. I sniffed my fingers as salty scents still somehow lingered. A soft knock came, "Service for Ms Florienze."

I opened the door and the waiter was taken a back, "I, oh, I… didn't realise she would have company… perhaps I'll come back with another tray."

"This will be fine, thank you," I said and took the tray overtly letting the stink of my fingers waft towards them.

Younger Greying twitched with nostrils bristling as he fixatedly stared me down, "It was you… Do you know what never mind you are done now," he added with grim sneer. "Please tell Ms Florienze that Chef Luan has prepped some iced arroz with added almond drizzle," Younger Greying stormed away so annoyed that he forgot his serving trolly.

I grabbed one of the buns bursting it into crumbs as Eris returned from the bathroom barely robed and stated, "Demolished half my tray already, have you?"

"How cheeky," I said as my stomach grumbled in anticipation of carb hydration.

"It's fine but first I think we should get you out of that dress. Oh, did you think I meant… You see someone has purchased the dress and we don't want any more upset if we spill something on it. Obviously the other could be on the table as well. There's another robe in the bathroom and the shower is fully stocked so have at it," she finished and rapidly ate two cakes before helping to remove my dress and slipped a bun into my hand. "Mid shower snack," she added and winked. "I'm just going to get comfortable here as my head is hurting."

After a modest shower I returned and found three socks lay wasted. One was draped over the radiator, one on a chair with worn out heel and one flat out on the floor with a bullet hole shot in the toe. A backward flying bird passed the window or was it a normal flying bird? It was difficult to tell so I turned to asked Eris who was spread out underneath a towel. "Eris did you?" I called as sickening doubt struck. She was the one I wanted to save and she wasn't moving. She couldn't be drunk as she always kept to fake champagne to appear social but keep a clear head when presenting so it had to be something else. "Eris?" I called again but she didn't respond. Her chest was rising but her icing-stained lips barely emitted breath. I placed her into the recovery position and found vomit on the bed beneath her. Maybe she'd choked, I lifted her head as best as possible and cleared some bun chunks causing her to gasp like a fish then slump back down on the soft mattress.

A sudden knock on the door came, hopefully it would be a waiter who could assist but it was Roux in a drunken state.

"Lori? Why are you here?" Roux pointed directly into the middle of my chest then squinted over my shoulder, "Is she drunk? You got her drunk... Urgh! No this isn't how it's supposed to be. I was meant... but you're here with her... I have to go." Roux clumsily smashed into the trolley and staggered down the corridor.

"Get help!" I shouted then continued trying to wake Eris but she had become feverish so I opened the balcony door and found Jorge beating up a bush.

"Jorge! Jorge!"

He looked up mid kick and screamed, "He ruined my night! Every piece sold except one and now a replacement to create. Don't they understand it was a one off?"

"Jorge!"

"They said the music and art were a perfect harmony," he paused kicking to grumble, "praised Roux as always."

"Jorge! Listen!"

"What? Oh, why are you in a robe? Urgh, why am I asking? Do you want me to move away and not disturb you two?" he stood with hands on hips before turning his attention to a kerfuffle in the car park as Younger Greying was arguing with Roux while Older Greying was preventing entry into a car.

He returned to his berating, "My night is ruined and all you can think about is…"

"Jorge! I need your help right now!"

"Fine," he said and started to stalk off.

"No, there's no time for that, just climb up," I pleaded.

"In these shoes?"

"I wouldn't usually ask but it's serious," I strained.

"Okay. What are you going to do, throw me over a knotted sheet? No wait, that's for escaping so I suppose I could just use this terrace." He hooked a foot into a bronze flower bed and hauled himself up through vines as I pulled him over the balcony edge.

"What happened here? Is she?" he asked then ran over to Eris. "She's alive but this looks very suspect." He seemed to weigh up the situation then grabbed Eris's phone and sent several messages along with calling for more service in his best impersonation of her. I continued to hold her as he opened the door slightly. "Who are you? What would a waiter want to come in here for?…Don't you dare put your foot there! Lori isn't here, she got drunk now go!" Jorge slammed the door and panic struck his face. "What have you done Lori?"

"Nothing. I swear. I made sure she didn't have any drugs and came back to her room to keep her safe."

"The waiters have gone," he said as he cracked the door. "We need to start vetting our service staff they certainly aren't the help we need… wait we could use this." He grabbed the abandoned trolley and thrust it into the room.

"Yeh, stick her on it and wheel her somewhere?"

"I'm not kidnapping her. Prisoner fashion would look awful on me. We will wheel it but it just needs to look right." He produced a travel paint palette and stole the duvet from the bed.

"What are you doing?" I asked as I ushered Eris to stay awake.

"I'm working darling. I am working," he announced as he sploshed an elaborate arch of colour onto the sheet then stole my cake crushing it and adding it to the piece. "Sorry, it was needed for effect… now get on."

"I can't until I know she is going to be okay."

"She will be fine, look the ambulance is here now. Get on."

The trolley creaked at the joints as it clearly was meant for delicate pastries and currently the only delicate thing about me was my emotions. As an added thought he dashed a few paint flourishes on his person then threw the pre-painted duvet over me as the ambulance people came in, "Eris is just in there and needs a good sober up. Parties eh?"

With a hearty shove he trundled along the corridor leaving wiggle marks on the polished floor as I focused on keeping still and wished Eris was going to be okay as maybe I had done enough to save her this time.

He swiftly avoided people as he exclaimed, "Mustn't touch it. Latest work and very secret. Couldn't ruin the surprise," before stopping abruptly and whispering, "stairs." Our grand plan of escape was on the verge of collapse but perhaps I could use the sheet as some kind of parachute? I gritted my teeth and waited for the bumps but they didn't come instead I was pushed over the silvery threshold of chiming lift doors.

My arms were bent awkwardly and feet raged with pins and needles as I waited for the worst, but the lift doors steadily opened and we were out into a garden. "Can I get off now?" I whispered but my words were abandoned into the open air.

***

The smell of fresh aftershave filled up the apartment as Jorge rattled down blinds and swished the curtains closed before stating, "You can get out but I think we were followed and I'm blaming your grumbling stomach. I hardly had any canapés so grabbed these." He pulled out several iced buns and threw one to me before nibbling and stating, "Odd taste but they will do."

I nibbled the iced powder and was struck with nausea, "I think these might be off."

"I haven't got anything else in but I'm diverting away from the situation. I need to know what was all that about and have you done something bad?"

"I haven't done anything, I promise. I was in the wrong place." I sat down on one of his modern chairs, then stood as shouting and footsteps approached. "I was trying to help. I should have done something else. I should have been somewhere to save her but at least you are okay."

"Of course I'm okay, why wouldn't I be?"

There was pounding on the door as the familiar voice of Older Greying instructed, "Open up!"

"Lori, I'm trusting you. I'll distract them. Go," Jorge swiftly uttered and welded a paintbrush as he went to the door.

I ran into the bathroom and squeezed through the window accessing the outer stairs. Soon I was out of breath and in the car park and the only escape was over a fence. I ungainly mounted it and flopped over into a vegetable patch with my robe bracing the brunt of impact.

A beanie clad person shouted, "What you doing? You've landed right on my rhubarb."

"I'm sorry. I need to go." I said as I got up and tightened the belt around me.

"They chasing you?" they asked then picked up the broken stalks and wrapped a sock around them. "You best come in 'ere quick and tell me what's what."

"There's no time to explain, please hide me."

The footsteps were moments behind as Beanie directed me inside a kitchen and into an open larder, "They won't see you 'ere." Beanie left the door open a crack as shadows pounded the back door. "Who do you think you are come knocking on 'ere like that?" Beanie picked up the rhubarb in defence.

"We are searching the area. You could be in danger as a suspect has been sighted nearby."

"Come on in then, you can check everywhere. I only saw someone wreck my plants and run off that way."

Younger Greying started investigating everywhere including the oven. "Move out the way I smell cheese," he said as Beanie sidestepped from the larder door. It was opened fully and Younger Greying looked right at me and asked, "What kind of cheese have you been storing?"

Beanie shuffled and joined in the direct glaring, "Got to have a variety these days but mostly strong cheddars and a few fancies."

I held my breath and tried to hide in plain sight.

Younger Greying snorted and closed the doors.

"See I'm safe, just me 'ere but you best get on back to looking elsewhere." Beanie ushered him away before returning to me, "As for you, follow this one and get to safety." Beanie whispered to a muddied sock which sagged slightly then hopped outside for me to follow but I didn't. Instead, I ran back to my apartment only to find Jorge vomiting by the door.

"I'm sorry," Jorge retched, "they threatened me and my work, I couldn't… I just couldn't."

"Couldn't what?" I asked.

Older Greying walked out of the kitchen with a smirk and stated, "Evade us." She grabbed my hands and sniffed.

"All this for cheese?" I pleaded.

Older Greying cuffed my hands, "Someone has to be punished and it isn't going to be us."

Jorge spluttered, "No!" and knocked into one of his art pieces causing it to smack into us. Pain shot through my head and the distant voice of Azalea called.

Chapter 17

Azalea stood with a notebook in hand and wore an expression of impenetrability. I screamed, "What was this for?" but my words were mumbled as sedative still raged in my face and limbs.

"I'm sorry you experienced the demise of a person, it must be inconceivably difficult but nonetheless you have shown remarkable output."

"I saved Eris, she didn't die this time as the ambulance people were there," I slurred and slumped out of the chair.

"Steady yourself. You are correct, she didn't die in *that* room but in hospital a few days after. You should be happy with your success as we have the results requested. The information on who the perpetrators will be passed to the crime department. Those waiters of all people?" she waved her notebook and shook her head.

"They were angry about the cheese?"

"They were, but in all seriousness, they poisoned the buns your friends ate. So there we have it, a good result from an augmented enhanced memory."

"I tried to change it."

"You can't change the past. Education can be gained by judgement from memories and experience."

"My life and memories aren't there for you to judge. My friend died and shouldn't have." I kicked away a table and stumbled to the door. I wasn't staying, I wanted to go home and be back with my friends. My pace improved as the drugs ceased and the urge to return replaced my sorrow with rage. I ran down fixed stairs until reaching the lowest point and expected the world to implode into nothingness except something chimed.

Familiar ill-fitting doors opened into a lift, I immediately entered and hammered the buttons. The doors rattled to a close and started the journey sideways as I sat ugly crying and comprehension of the situation struck with vivid reality. Eris was… she had passed away but I didn't want to admit it when she was so full of life in that room. I knew somewhere deep down it couldn't be, but who wants to rip off that band aid when the reunion was so good.

Her death had happened around the anniversary of 'The Beach Event' and with tensions high it wasn't until the next day that the local news reported a minor celebrity had died. It was a brief article that claimed it was due to a potential overdose and that's what I wanted to prevent.

It was Jorge who made the national headlines for his near death experience which propelled the demand for his work so much that he was rarely around. Our relationship had been clouded and all fun transformed into professional blandness. Without him I consumed myself in work adding deadline after deadline to bury the grief.

The lift came to a stop and doors shook themselves open. I was back to the same grey open office in my work building, "Hello is there anybody here?" I shouted as I walked through. It must have been the weekend as cups had been cleaned and stacked on the sideboard and desks were moderately tidied away. I opened the meeting room door and pulled out the closest chair, it snagged on the shit pile carpet as I sat in the stoic silence of safe refuge.

An old presentation clung to the screen along with several unused notepads, the boss liked the old-fashioned pen and paper style, so I picked up a pen to test if this was real. Just as I clicked the end a screen burst into life with the familiar voice of Edvard Játvarður saying, "Welcome to the Gröfu Pallur!"

I slammed the chair into the desk and ran back outside and into the lift, "I want to go home!" I screamed and repeatedly hit the buttons.

"Where is your home?" Azalea poked her head into the lift.

Öyggi Játvarður closely followed and asked, "Would you please drink this or at least talk to us in here?" Without anywhere else to go Öyggi herded me to my desk and wafted a calming mist while placing a steaming drink next to me.

I turned away as I scorned, "Is this part of the test?"

Azalea brought over an office chair and beanbag and announced, "You aren't currently in an official test but we are in a construct of sorts. It's not important. What needs addressing is where is your home?"

"My home… my home could have been with Eris-." My voice broke and Öyggi offered me some of my own tissues whilst appearing to be consumed by the beanbag.

"I understand this is hard for you. Please be assured the test yielded results far beyond what we would have ever hoped for. Your friends were subject to unfortunate circumstances."

"Unfortunate circumstance? She died," I said more calmly than I'd have liked as the mist refrained me from fully emoting.

"I understand that, but strangely not in the way that has been reported," Azalea circled an article in her notepad, "this states that her death was of unknown cause following her most lucrative fundraising event," she paused to highlight the headline, "Jorge of course was medically unwell but survived and now we know why and who did this."

"Younger Greying."

"Yes, and the other waiter but it's because of you that they will go through due processing and legal course succinctly. You have found justice for your friend even if the events on the night didn't quite match lived perception."

"People worked on it for months and you're saying I solved it in my sleep? What if I got it wrong and they are innocent? Some imaginative license isn't proof especially when things happened that didn't."

"Are you referring to the person in the knitted hat with an admiration for rhubarb?" Azalea asked as she carried on jotting.

"What? I don't know."

"If so, that was an insertion into artistic truth, but indeed that chase never happened. You awoke from your drunken stupor in your flat and saw your friend choking, you attempted to save him as best you could before the angry patron knocked on his door. They pushed you away and you were knocked out when you hit a concrete statue in Jorge's apartment. You sustained a sprain from wearing immensely intimidating boots and woke up next to Jorge in hospital awaiting results. Quite strange how our tests get overlayed with interruption."

Öyggi side glanced and blew more mist in my direction.

"So, we actually found out who did it and that's real?" I asked as emotions gave way to logical thought.

"We did. Congratulations. Now it might also interest you to know that we have held a generalised meeting and it has been deemed necessary for your health and wellbeing that such intensive tests should be paused for reprise."

"I want to go home."

"Currently as you are witness to a crime and subject to principles of law which state you may not be unavailable in mind or person in case further evidence is required, you may not go home yet. However, Öyggi has suggested a vacation until all evidence is reviewed and you are deemed free again. Does that appeal?"

"A beach vacation," Öyggi added "then a discussion about sending you home." She sagged further into the beanbag but refrained from more mist.

"Really?"

"Yes, although it would come to significant cost to my team and detriment to your mine owner who it seems is not onboard just yet. Please bear with me," Azalea said and walked over to another desk where she spoke in the multitude.

"It's a good offer and one you should very much consider as you have proved to be of significant worth." Öyggi crunched on the beanbag and readjusted a bird brooch making it fly upside down. "You'll make new friends and experience home there. I did," she added before changing the brooch back as Azalea returned to the here and now.

"Your owner has agreed-."

I blew my nose, "Okay. I'll go."

Azalea was in genuine shock as she said, "That was far easier than we had anticipated. Jax will send you the relevant holiday brochures for you to seek your solace. Just give your requests to-."

Öyggi shuffled and overly loudly stated, "That would be me as Hydi Játvarður is taking over as the testing consort instead of security detail. Lori, you just send me anything you need and I'll see it's sorted correctly."

Jax promptly walked into the office and hit me with a singular sharp jolt as he applied a flowing corded tag which tore into my wrist. "This will prevent a further gluttony of errors," he stated smugly and added, "I will message you when I have confirmation of your placement and conveyance." Azalea looked disgusted and excused herself while Öyggi and Jax escorted me back through the halls of testing and all the way to meet Casey in the car. I didn't even worry about the car journey as Casey was somewhat annoyed that I got to leave but he distracted my sadness as we browsed through the brochures pointing out the lovely scenery.

Chapter 18

Tiao actively avoided me with the excuse that he was updating. Except this morning, he lingered beside the bed gazing upon a scene of sorrowful sombre clouds cascading around a lonely mountain. "I'll miss you Lori," he said as his pipes pulsed but the colour seemed somehow faded as he hung his head.

I sat beside him and held his arm as I reassured him, "I'll miss you too, but they aren't going to let me stay on holiday forever. I'll be back excavating away before you know it."

He tilted his head and managed a meagre smile then clicked his hands together. "That may be but I don't believe we will be here for your return."

"Course you will, I'll make sure of it by making a request to Öyggi even though she doesn't ever reply. Or I'll just refuse to return if you aren't here. Or… I'll do something. I'll-."

His cold mechanical hand gently squeezed mine as he mournfully interrupted, "Thank you Lori, but your reassurance isn't working." A drop of thickened oil caught in the corner of his eye as the mountain view became fully consumed in thunderous cloud. "It would be prudent to inform you that Fred has prepared a final breakfast for your absolute enjoyment." Tiao handed over a printed menu. "Please enjoy your meal, he has worked very hard to make it just right for you and I shall not join you for I feel my personable skills are lacking today." He covered himself with a blanket and pretended to go into standby mode and therefore was excluded from further comment as I made my way down stairs and was met with a serving of sadness accompanied by fresh berry compote.

Fred's pipes oozed slowly as he said, "We've arranged this special meal t' commemorate our time together as we will truly miss yeh." He removed several cloches from perfectly prepared portions and added, "I'll trouble yeh and ask, is he still upset?"

"He is. I don't know how to cheer him up," I said and slowly took a slice of avocado on toast.

"Yeh can't as we can't change what's t' come and that's the worry. Yeh see any time we're not operational we'll be 'auled in for main-tain-nence or stored with stunted thought and prospect of never serving again," he said with a full body tremor.

"You're far too useful for that," I said and started on the caramelised bacon.

Fred offered a napkin and continued, "Old n' defunct I'd say and I fear we'll not be 'ere on yeh return. Yeh see the room goes back t' pipe work and funct-nul essentials when not in full abode mode." He pinched the corner of the marble breakfast bar and tugged as the surface skin peeled away to reveal a bare metal plinth before it snapped back to form. "We'll be placed in't standby mode and plunged into determinative darkness when our being departs f' good." He smoothed the bar edge to make sure it was firmly down and finished with a quick polish before removing some of the already finished dishes.

They could make whole bars, restaurants and streets disappear so this one apartment couldn't be of consequence but why bother? Perhaps it was to do with the running cost or like he said, for 'updates.' "Could you show me? Unless it's the dissolving version from when I first got here then I don't want to experience that."

"It's not very pleasant. I can show yeh, but yeh'll 'ave t' 'old on tight t' yeh fork," Fred said as he flipped over a panel in the wall and input some digits then dramatically ducked. The room started shedding back in controlled collapse as decorative finishes peeled off revealing the industry style pipework beneath, before returning in moments to lavish furniture but not soon enough as Fred shouted, "Oh bother." Bursts of alarms screeched through the room as the whole downstairs was immersed in vomit yellow flashing lights. Fred busied himself with plate cleaning duty and overlaid the screeching with the hiss from steam scrubbing until the front door smashed open.

Jax bombarded his way into the room as I mocked a startled expression and drew my dressing gown about me to cover my modesty. "A hello and knock would have been nice. You should give a girl fair warning at least!"

"What happened in here?" Jax demanded as he invaded my social space. "I can't hear anything with that noise!" he screamed and silenced the alarms with a handheld clicker before gasping at the dryness in the air. He quickly inserted a rod into his neck and infused the other end into a sludge filled hipflask before repeating, "What happened here? Don't tell me lies because I'll sniff out the truth."

I shrugged, resumed breakfast and gave a brief, "Nothing," in response.

"That's an incorrect and inaccurate report," informed a head-to-toe polished security officer who had followed Jax into the room. Their thin lips extended into basic facial features as they continued, "this sector has been compromised."

"What I meant to say was nothing except… the room changed then came back," I stated as I tried to inch away from Jax.

The officer strode over and commanded, "Move it!"

"Perhaps you can you be specific as to where? Or do you want me to flail my arms and tap my feet? I'm sure Fred can put on some tunes and we can dance," I said as I used my fork as a rhythmic stick and waved an arm.

"You need to move out of my way. Now!" With nail-less fingertips the guard dragged my chair away from the half-eaten breakfast and shoved me into the desk which automatically opened onto a block construction set.

"Machine L2 FeRiYeDo perform a full update on the situation immediately," the guard demanded as he levelled himself face to face with Fred.

Fred anxiously twitched as if battling internally then caught my eye and winked just before expanding into a network of neon wiring and popped open a rear panel. Jax inserted a mechanical component which caused a continuous print out.

Fred was shaking just as the officer grabbed the end of the paper strip and stated, "There's reports of multiple errors, forced changes and significant protocol failure. This can only result in a codex fourth nine. Command: Force Standby." The officer's wire face furiously twitched as they repeated, "Machine L2 FeRiYeDo you must obey this command: Force Standby!"

Jax immediately grabbed Fred but with the last ounce of energy he pushed Jax's overly long arms away. I threw a handful of bricks in Jax's direction as a distraction as the officer instinctively moved to protect Jax. It created an opening so I ran towards Fred and cried, "Please, be awake."

The officer was instantly at my side and disgustedly stated, "The machine needs to be shut down for offload and decommissioning due to significant error forming. There are reports of burning, poor preparation time and illegal file corruption."

A combination of my arrogance and defiance had equalled Fred's decommissioned death but I couldn't lose another friend, "Wait, there's no need for this," I said as I accidentally dipped my arm into milkshake splatter and was struck with excuses. "It must have been me who caused the alarm as I spilt a drink down there, just look over and you'll see."

The officer peered over and stated, "There is a shot glass beneath the solasus pipe."

"How convenient," Jax said and rounded on me with a sneer, "to trigger a full alarm breakdown is highly unusual, but... I suppose there has been errors all week." He stopped and dampened his lips with creamy sludge.

"I am in agreement but still sanctions need implementing." The officer applied a warning tag to Fred who spasmed as if struck by electric. "You are now subjected to bi-weekly checks and will be stored and processed back to default while your user is away."

Jax nodded but unexpectedly lingered and sneered, "Your driver will be here soon. Do be swift."

"Swift? I'm nowhere near ready to go, especially after all this drama, I'm going to need more time to pack," I said in my most convincing tones as they didn't need to know that my luggage had already been packed since yesterday.

"I will authorise a delay only because it will give me time to file notice on this despicable practice and check in on Casey. Now you have sixty-two until I will return and-."

"Ow!" the officer screamed, "my toes are broken if not my entire foot. This brick has severely injured me." The officer rocked side to side massaging the affected area.

"What have you done?" shouted Jax at me as he carefully manoeuvred through the brick mine field.

"Nothing!" I announced.

Jax sneered and dragged the officer out before pausing to state, "Time's waning."

I shuffled away some loose bricks but left the rest in place, a risky business, but it should serve as a brief deterrence.

"Lass?" Fred asked as he slowly reanimated and somehow restored his battery to full. "I believe I'll perish and expire before your return. We're told t' report any changes t' systematic processes such as the burnt toast but we've not been sending them so yeh'd be happy with our service."

"I'm so sorry Fred. There must be something we can do?" I said as my finger buzzed with a notification:

[Your transport has been selected.]

"I caused this, but I can fix it… I can save you. Can you escape out of the balcony and scoot down the side?" I ventured in hope of sudden inspiration.

"No, I'm very much attached t' floor and that thur balcony is just another room that's programmed t' look like outside," he said and tugged the warning tag still digging into his neck. He slumped down and shook his head as time sped up with no possible solution forthcoming. Until he lifted a little and said, "Yeh can't save me but perhaps yeh can save Tiao with a little notion and cleverness. Yeh see, we were created t' stay 'ere. If we were seen t' go out without genuine reason then…" he opened a side panel causing slow pipes to severe and spark out of control before he completely slumped on the cooker.

"No! Come back!"

"Sorry to cause alarm. Now Tiao could get out but he'd 'ave t' be 'idden. I must say t' aid his escape would be ill ADVISED and not WORTHWHILE," he added with nods in the relevant places. "So would yeh go and pack 'im away int' suitcase of yours?"

"Of course."

"I'll warn yeh though, 'e won't like it."

Tiao was wrapped in my blanket sipping a hot chocolate with his back turned to the window, not noticing the rain drops lingering to survey his sadness on their drip journey.

"Hey," I said as I used a fluffy corner to wipe away his oily tears just as another notification tingled:

[Your driver has been selected.]

It came along with a dong ding from downstairs as Jax rudely barged in but didn't get more than one step through the doorframe due to the brick infestation. "Seriously?" I said and hurried down the stairs.

"Now we have dawdled for too long and must be on our way. Your car is waiting and I'm impatient," he said and beckoned with pallid hand as his foot was poised ready to 'T'tap'.

"Jax, you do you know that I'm going away for a reduction in stress? They would have surely told you that being all managerial and such. Well, you aren't helping the situation and you are making it considerably more stressful, so I suggest you remember I am still not ready. I need to get… ladies' things together and say goodbye to my friends," I said with an authoritative wave of dismissal.

"This will not do but I suppose I have to make a call so you have a maximum of three hundred and two time mincags. That should be enough human stress relieving moments and time enough for package assembly," he replied as he stormed out, leaving the door slightly ajar.

It was too risky to leave the door open but it could be just as suspicious to shut it. In a moment of absolute panic and strategic importance my brain responded with an 'Erm,' but I overruled it and made the decision to navigate through the bricks and close it before running back up the stairs.

Tiao was now hiding under the bed as he said, "Please don't linger. Delaying Mr Jax will indeed make things worse."

"You're coming with me. Ah," I held up a finger to my lips to silence. "Don't plead or argue. I've made my choice." He rolled himself out but slumped his metallic shoulders and tapped his hands together in consideration while I threw out half the contents of my somewhat messily packed luggage and stated, "You'll fit in here."

He scooted up and onto the bed, "Some of me will but the rest of me won't and I shouldn't leave him," he said and glanced through the glass balustrade to Fred.

"What will happen?" I asked and braced for the impending already realised answer.

"Some, if not all of him will be erased and he will pass on. I must talk to him," he said and scooted downstairs to the kitchen bar where soft words were spoken until a stoney silence fell as the pair contemplated what must be done. I followed slowly but wasn't hampered by the weight of the luggage case but rather the decision that was being formalised between them. Tiao had removed one of his own arms and stated, "It's for effect, a humanoid said it's just like a crumpled letter." He poured tea over it and threw it toward the balcony as Fred half smiled and appreciated the kitchen area.

Tiao held out his remaining hand to me and asked, "Would you please be so kind to assist us?"

I held his hand as Fred said, "It's been a rite pleasure t' grow with yeh Tiao and you've been a rite nice person to serve Lori," he paused as the T'tip... T'tap... echoed the imminent arrival of Jax who paused to shout at someone causing stomps to dissipate briefly.

Tiao took my hand and guided it to a blue button and said, "When the time is right you must push this. Failure to do so will mean I will lose all power function and personal being."

"I don't want to get this wrong," I said and pulled my hand away.

"You won't but you must be the one to do it. I cannot as we may both become obsolete by truncated form and I can't reach. You are our only option as if we don't try, we have already committed to failure," Tiao said with a newly found grit and confidence that roused me into action.

T'tip... T'tap... The nearing stout heel grew closer and louder.

Tiao redirected my trembling finger back at the blue button then gazed at his counterpart and whispered, "Goodbye my friend."

"Goodbye Tiao," Fred sighed as a beautiful peace descended and eyes dimmed just as a T'tip... T'tap came. My finger wavered as sparks emitting from their back panels and they connected physically. T'tip... T'tap... their pulsating pipes quickened. T'tip... T'tap... Jax turned the handle as the rain pounded louder on the window. Fred jiggered in place swaying with the rush of conscious exchange. T'tip... T'tap... We were out of time. Jax bolstered in and scornfully surveyed the scene which lay before him.

Chapter 19

The act of leaving without being seen was difficult in a place so full of beings but Jax made it clear that those in charge didn't want others knowing reprieves from testing were allowable. Instead, it was down a staff staircase, round the back of the reception toilets, under the barrier of the out-of-action lagoon and out the delivery entrance via rotting garden gate which was held open by a small Tiao version. Sharp pains hit front and centre and tears welled at the loss of my good friends but no time to dwell as I was ushered over to the backside of the carpark shelving unit until reaching the designated highlighted space.

A person was readjusting their air steward styled uniform and introduced themselves, "I am here to accompany you to your destination. You must sit in the back throughout the entire journey." They could have been of Jax or Játvarður descent but didn't make it known and didn't care for my anguish as they slammed my luggage in the boot with a crunch.

"There goes the grungs," I said in a choked-up voice.

The driver ignored me as they instructed, "Mind your head," and pushed me inside. Two seat belts automatically unwound from above my shoulders and strapped me in tight as the driver stowed my seat table. "If you are inclined to bother me with something, push this button," they said as they ducked back outside and stuck two pipes into their neck which seemed to suck the very water molecules from the atmosphere. That confirmed they were a

Jax being as a Játvarður would have been far more polite and have graced me with a full safety briefing. An offer of a food and beverage service would have been too much to expect as this seemed to be a budget 'get you there in one piece and nothing more' kind of deal.

The door sucked shut as the driver secured themselves into the front passenger seat before programming a code into the globe driving sphere next to them.

We departed on the dust road alongside grass plates being harvested by dragonflies. They pierced into the plates changing their hues throughout the colour spectrum then shot back up reforming in flock formation but never colliding. "Excuse me driver, what are those? Do you see? There in the sky, the flying things?" I asked but they stoutly refused to engage my existence except to motion towards the call bell.

I pressed it. "I said, excuse me, driver?"

They dramatically sighed in inconvenience before plainly answering, "I'm your driving steward as I previously mentioned and was right in my estimations that you weren't listening." They went to close a separating window but hadn't actually answered my question so I pressed the call bell again and was sharply answered, "What?"

"What are those?"

"Balait flies."

"And what do they do?"

"I'm not being paid to answer questions and converse with you, but since I have a particular interest in hierarchical living specimens, I shall tell you and then we shall stop conversing and continue our journey in total silence." They paused as if waiting for an agreement. They didn't get one so sighed again and stated, "The balait flies have an ability to insert acidity or aroma to the grasses which combine into flavours. The use of which was found when they originated from-," the steward was suddenly interrupted by a motorcycle overtaking within inches. We barely avoided impact and swerved to the left before regaining a steady pace. The steward continued in dull tones and seemed unaware that the motorcyclist dropped back and was keeping pace with us.

They appeared to be the result of a grandparent being let loose with aggressive knitting needles, leather and lace to create their jacket and trousers. They waved and winked before tucking a flyaway permed curl back into their open face helmet then veered off slightly as our car gained pace.

"Have you seen…" I started but the steward had and was quickly changing the route. They were knocked off the globe as feathers exploded all around the car leaving smears of pink and purple ink.

The steward quickly pushed a button but the wipers seemed stuck in place so they opened their window and threw a bottle of water onto the windscreen and cleaned the stains with an extended arm. The motorcyclist filtered through the traffic until coming back on themselves and heading straight for us. We narrowly avoided collision once more but with a quick 180-degree spin the motorcyclist was back on our tail with feathers in hand ready to throw. The steward managed to turn the car into a service tunnel but the motorcyclist hit us again from the back before speeding away.

A feather caught in my window as I reached up to pull it through, it was like an ink quill, full to the brim of staining solution ready to evoke written word. I quickly pocketed it as the steward turned and stated, "You shall forget that turbulent situation," before splitting our compartments via a soundproofed screen. The call bell locked itself and I was left alone as we continued through the service tunnel only encountering lorries accompanied by the stench of waste. Time seemed to pass slowly after our two wheeled encounter and without the hum of engine or random pothole to surprise the suspension the monotony was only broken with the screen being lowered as the steward said, "Breath deeply and relax." This was accompanied by a mass infusion of coconut and lime mist and reclining seat.

***

A 'sving, dving… dving' woke me as the doors flung open and I was washed with warmth. The steward roughly removed my luggage and grouchily instructed, "Go to the guards first and do not proceed until they have given you clearance." The steward waited until I was in correct position before they left leaving dust trails.

"Cough. Cough," said a being with a turtle shell and shiny badge. They had well-groomed sideburns and a blue bowtie that unravelled slightly as they said, "Please stop!"

Their colleague who had pink hair sprouting from tufts in his nostrils, but yellow bowtie held their hands on their hips in an authoritative stance as they instructed, "She already has stopped."

"That's true, she has. Place your bag here for security checks," Blue Bowtie requested.

I held it close and joked, "You don't need to see my dirty washing do you?"

After a curious glance and hushed discussion Yellow Bowtie stood upright and held their hands out as they asked, "Give me your luggage, erm…please." I handed it over but Yellow Bowtie just held it in place.

"We are supposed to check it," Blue Bowtie stated as they kept a close eye on my person as if checking for reaction. I just rolled my eyes at the inconvenience.

"It looks like a bag," Yellow Bowtie said.

"It is a bag," I said.

"A bag you say, we will see about that," Blue Bowtie gave it a knock and something metal clunked.

"It does have a handle and little wheels that go around. It has a small zip here… that's sensible as otherwise all your possessions would fall out," Yellow Bowtie said as they span the wheel.

"We should check the inside," Blue Bowtie stated and fingered the zip.

"That would be an invasion of privacy, you'd need a warrant because without you aren't allowed." I ventured.

"I don't want to get in trouble on my first day," Yellow Bowtie muttered. "We should ask for permission."

"That will take ages, have you got your manual?" Blue Bowtie stated and readjusted their tie before eyeing me.

"No and I only got to the first chapter which was mostly about how to stand and what your uniform should look like."

"Damn, I don't have mine either. Well, you seem like a normal humanoid being and this does seem to be a luggage bag so on this occasion we will let you and your bag enter," Blue Bowtie said and smashed a stamp on it as Yellow Bowtie returned it to me.

"What now?" I asked.

They looked at each other and shrugged until Blue Bowtie thoughtfully said, "You'll have to enter your designated building for room processing I'd imagine."

Yellow Bowtie readjusted their badge and stated, "Yeh that sounds about right but what do we do now?"

"Isn't it obvious? We should carry on being guards," Blue Bowtie said.

"I wonder what is inside her bag? I hope it wasn't anything bad," Yellow Bowtie said but I had already made tracks.

***

The hotel was a smooth white curve set in a cliff face, it was backdropped by other chalky mountains and brilliant blue skies. The grasses that lined the path were a deep green as I followed the trail through pebble patterns before arriving at a palm tree edged door. I entered the atrium which had a long planter brimming with plants made from glass and had light pulsing through them. From overhead came rhythmic splashing from a horizontal swimmer in a pool housed in the roof and it was in this moment that I truly appreciated I was away. It wasn't that I'd missed the vacation feeling as I'd had no work except of course the constant testing but this was more of a much-needed change of scenery.

A desk sat behind the glass plants with an inlay of the hotel in miniature and a code to scan beneath. I browsed my fingers for a scanning tool but just ended up accidentally taking a few photos of my own face until a being who appeared to be made from a marimba popped up. They had a series of pipes emitting from around their spine as if they'd been mangled with brass instruments and appeared to be confused about their surroundings.

"Are you okay?" I asked.

"Yes," they strained as they answered with wooden hammer teeth swinging in harmony. "Are you okay?"

"I am. I think I'm supposed to be checking in?"

They sighed in the musical note of F sharp and asked, "What's your chosen identifier?"

"My name is Lori Wilkes"

"Lori Wilkes, how fun. Let's see where your name might be. Oh, it's on this screen. Yes your name is here," they seemed surprised and shrugged. "You're on a bed and service package, fancy that. There's also a note here which states that you'll be settling in on the top floor and have views over the coastal lines, that's nice isn't it. It's a lovely coastline which borders a sea within an ocean." They winked. "It seems we are just on the edge of a town which is in the nineteenth time zone. Give in minutes for the Earth person," they said and paused, "Oh, I wasn't supposed to say that. It's a short walk along the road. Walk? Will you use your legs? How odd." They looked over at my legs and seemed perturbed before continuing, "Ask in a polite tone if they have any bags. Oh, do you have a bag?" they asked then cleared a build-up of spittle out of their mouthpiece ear. "You do have a bag. Do you want me to assist you with it in some way?" they asked and extended a tubular trombone arm.

"I can manage just fine thanks but perhaps you can point me in the direction of my room?"

"I'm assuming it's going to be up," they said and pointed to the ceiling before going back and squinting at the computer. I started to a nearby staircase but stopped as they screamed, "The bees? The bees!" They quickly opened a gas filled compartment which released a collection of larger than expected bees. I flinched but they didn't attack and politely congregated in front of the receptionist in the form of a giant smiley face then a direction arrow. "I think you are supposed to follow them, how accessible," the receptionist said and watched us walk away as if we were a complete oddity.

The bees led me toward a extravagant staircase then became an image of a box being placed onto a ramp, similar to staircases with bike access neatly housed in the side. I placed my suitcase on and no sooner had it left my hand than it was off and rising before I'd even taken the first step. The suitcase reached the top before I was even halfway and flopped over with a 'clang'.

At the next set of stairs the bees pointed out a gauge beside the ramp, I adjusted it all the way down and set the luggage off but it moved just an inch. The bees gyrated laughing as I tried again but on a more average setting. This worked as the luggage followed my pace along with bees. We reached our cojoined arrival to the top step but the bees instantly dispersed and reformed near a window corner planter.

A trail of tiny spider-like creatures carried copious amounts of what seemed to be sticky nectar from an inverted coloured bird of paradise flower. The bees made a sad face and paused to assist the little creatures carrying them up to a web design of rooms on that floor. A few returned to me and became a twisted arrow going up as I left them to it and climbed the final staircase into an empty corridor except for one door. I shoved my finger into an insertion point underneath the handle and something clicked inside as it opened with me still inside it.

I removed my finger and shouted, "Hello?" just in case, but no response was given. I checked under the bed, in the desk drawers and behind the navy curtains but found it to be satisfyingly empty. There were no house plants here and even the mirror only showed my own reflection. The only thing it lacked was friendly robots. I walked out onto the balcony and was met with the sounds of constantly rolling waves. The bright blue sky was shut away and only the glow from bedside lights fell onto my dented suitcase.

My hand lingered a moment while I contemplated survival and loss. I silently unzipped my bag parting my underwear slowly and not wanting to witness the result of a quick getaway. Tiao had barely made it inside before Jax stormed in but that was no excuse for the fate of the mangled metal bundle that lay before me. Something must have gone wrong in the transfer as the connection was severed too soon or it could have been the journey as we didn't have time to add extra padding. I gently removed Tiao's little foot from my t-shirt and placed his broken state on a pillow. "Tiao?" I called just as a 'clunk' coincided with his leg contorting the opposite way it should be. 'Clunk' it went again, but not from Tiao. I hid him under a discarded t-shirt and ran over to the door handle. I took a sign and set it to 'go away' then double checked the empty corridor. I locked the door as the 'clunk' came again and started a game of hot and cold. It wasn't coming from behind the shower curtain, or in the cupboard, not even in the utensil filled minifridge but... yes in the vent! A mechanical fan was caught on a metal rod which produced a metronome clunk on each rotation. I carefully moved it and the room became soundless except from the laboured breathing on the bed.

Tiao had wrapped the t-shirt around his dinted arm and a puddle had formed from a pipe towards his back. I tried to reinsert it but it wouldn't budge so instead I reassured him and stroked his head. Oil gathered at the corner of his eye space, "Tiao? Please wake up!" His face flickered slightly as he slumped back a shoulder and revealed a small box, I softly removed it and replaced it with a rolled up jumper. Inside was a hair grip, bottle top, torn piece of checkered cloth and possibly the way to fix him in the form of a rolled up solar mat. I placed it in the sunshine of the balcony, then lifted him carefully over to it. I never did ask how he charged his batteries as conversations of his function never emerged, but he stirred slightly and shivered. Not the instant revival I wanted but a sure sign of life and being on the mend. I made a blanket ring around him to give him some comfort then readjusted a hammock and deck chair but dismayed at the lack of hot tub, what luxuries I had become accustomed to. Before, having this beautiful room would have been an out of the ordinary holiday and certainly nowhere near the accommodation offered on business trips, but it was now the standard of life. I shook my head as I walked back inside and bumped into a short bookcase full of holiday type reads, sandy pages and folded over edges used as bookmarks. I sat next to Tiao and started to read aloud as dusk fell and his breathing became slumberous.

Chapter 20

The darkest nights of the city are never as encompassing as those in the countryside but here the never-ending daylight made sleep almost impossible and not even the makeshift eye mask helped. I slid my bra from over my eyes and removed the sound proofing tissue from my ears before checking inside Tiao's newly constructed pillow fort, but he was still out for the count. I gave him a gentle pat and whispered, "it's morning," then noticed a tag caught in his neck hole. I tugged it revealing a thin piece of paper with the words [Need Fluid. Have Leak] printed upon it. He slowly blinked at me, then mouthed something through strained lips.

I quickly got a glass of water and asked, "Where is your mouth?"

Another printed tag slowly emerged: [Fluid. Pipe. Flui6.]

I went to the mini bar and interlinked a system of straws into his pipe, "Is it working?" I asked as he minimally shook his head and printed out [FL Iud] again. Maybe he needed a different kind, maybe water wasn't good enough, so I carefully stowed him under the bed and ventured out.

***

The receptionist put down their tuning fork, coughed in High C and pumped out, "Where are you going?"

"I need some fluid."

"There's fluid coming out of your pocket," they said and pointed to my pocket where the feather had leaked its contents all over the fabric. "Wait a moment," they checked the computer, "Ah, they are a clever lot. It seems they had pre-planned this and have given you a token tote bag, how lovely of them." They opened a drawer and pulled out a bag which they investigated before handing over.

"There's nothing in it," I stated.

"That's correct. It's a bag that has a built-in cup holder," they replied as if mystified by the ingenious concept. "Before you go and put things in that, I've been advised to tell you to eat and that the restaurant is open always. It literally never closes so you can just go right ahead and fill your stomach up with whatever your people eat. It says you chew with your mouth. That's disgusting, how would you keep it clean? Do you know what, I'll just assume you spit," the receptionist said with a retch and pointed to the restaurant.

I strode in and was faced with prison styled doors and a lack of waiting staff. I sat at one of several empty bench tables as a menu popped up. The food offerings were good but the only drink available was water, damn. My stomach grumbled and I realised just how hungry I was as the images of nachos, tacos and tortillas filled the screen. I ordered quickly as the menu slunk back into the table and was replaced with a notification stating: [Door H31P.] A dark metal serving hatch was quickly opened as the boxed food was shoved through. "Thanks," I said as the hatch lingered open and a haggard face briefly nodded before slamming shut. I stored the food into my tote bag and continued my mission to fetch fluids.

"Did you find what you were looking for?" The receptionist asked as they peered over at the bag.

"No, I need more fluid, where can I get that?" I asked and pulled the tote closer to me.

"I stay away from that as it plays havoc with the joints. Would you prefer oil, grease or even a little beeswax?"

"I could try them I suppose. Do you have any spare?"

"No, but I suppose I could acquire. I'll investigate it," they said and added a tympany of tones as they sighed. "What else can I help with?"

"I need more fluid," I said.

"Oh, yes you did ask for that. I suppose the nearest large body of water is the sea, fancy that. Before you ask, it's probably outside," they added and ushered me politely away.

***

The sand stretched a mile long against red cliffs to the left and concrete jungle to the right. A beached city was my favourite juxtaposition as I made my way over to the abundance of salt water and onto the promenade, but as soon as my foot contacted the plank I was pulled back by Blue Bowtie. "Where do you think you're going?" they asked authoritatively and added questioning eye squint.

"That was a good line, we should use that again," said Yellow Bowtie and nudged them in eagerness.

"I'm going to the beach," I replied.

"What beach would that be then?" asked Blue Bowtie as one hand landed on their hip and the other underneath their chin.

"The one which you are standing beside," I said.

"Hmm. It does seem to be a beach with the quantity of sand…" they paused and eyed the occupants, "we should make sure everything is in orderly fashion," Blue Bowtie stated and pushed Yellow Bowtie onto it.

Yellow Bowtie placed a hand in the sand before quickly retracting and stated, "Ouch, warm today but that's definitely sand and look there, it's the lake edge."

"Can I go now?" I asked.

"Hmm… now just you wait a minute." Blue Bowtie swayed in smugness. "It seems very convenient that you are here wanting to go to a beach and there in front of us is that very same beach, but that doesn't answer the question of what's in your bag?"

"I didn't know that was your question but feel free to take a look," I opened it as they peered in and muttered between themselves.

"It seems that your evidence and purpose check out so you may carry on about your business, but I'll keep my eyes on you," Blue Bowtie remarked.

"I'll not keep any eyes on you as I might fall over," Yellow Bowtie stated and stamped my tote so hard the ink ran into my food box.

"You there, I reckon you're loitering," Blue Bowtie said as they ran over to apprehend a bin minding its own business. Together, they had as much common sense as a baked potato.

I stepped onto the wooden promenade and toward the sea as surfers expertly caught waves before crashing off and pixelating into the waters beneath. That would be a great way to explore, but there wasn't anywhere to hire a board as the only buildings were that of toilets and a lifeguard shack with attendant lazily slumped on a chair in bleached attire. Although behind the lifeguard seemed to be a bar full of exotic bottles. "Hey! You can't come here, you must go and sit down," the lifeguard called as they viewed me through binoculars two metres away.

"I just want a drink," I said.

"It's waiter service only, go and sit over there and the waiter will come over when you appear comfortable," the lifeguard instructed then pasted themselves in cream.

I made my way over to a set of sun loungers where only two were still unoccupied. Those that were occupied appeared as if each being was in the same position soaking up the sun. They creaked like unoiled plastic as they all shifted in place due to one cloud momentarily blocking a tenth of the sun before all readjusting their shades for optimum ultraviolent exposure and resuming their statuesque state.

I waited but no waiter appeared, so I opened a book I'd snuck out but rather than consuming the fantasy world, I hatched a plan. I was going to try different types of fluids, from salt to fresh and all the other combinations in between. I beckoned over someone I hoped was a waiter but seemed overdressed in a smart jumper in the heat. "Hello Lori, I was just getting to you, what can I get you today?" they brushed away sweat and grimaced as they waited for my response.

"How do you know my… never mind. Do you have a menu or anything?" I asked.

They produced a simulated menu along with a fan which they furiously waved. "Can you do that a little less?" I asked as they snuck under the shade of the umbrella instead.

I choose the maximum per person order as they remarked, "Thirsty today, are we? I know that feeling… I mean I'll get them right away!"

They made to walk away as I called, "Wait, could you do them with lids on as I don't want to get sand in them?"

"Hmm an odd request but a sensible one, I'll see what I can do," they said as they left footprints which only lasted until their fourth step where they faded away completely.

I hitched the back of the lounger up taking care not to lose any fingers from sudden collapse, but it glided up with a simple swipe. I set the book on my knee as the next shift in position came routinely with the near blocking of the sun then flicked over another unread page. I knew I could be doing something more useful and that this book wouldn't help but the most useful was back in my apartment. The manual had been there all along with spine not wrinkled from any perusal. I had had so much time to learn about the robots but choose to indulge myself instead.

"Excuse me," the waiter said exasperatedly as arms were weighed down by various lids and implements, "You can use any of these improvised additions and if you find one you like then please add it on the requests section of your pre-loaded menu." One drink was shut with a beer coaster taped around the rim, another was double lined slimed shut around what was possibly a jam jar lid and the third had an upside-down igloo held in place by sheer willpower and recessed edges.

"Thank you, that's a really good effort," I said as they slunk away shading themselves from the glare of sun with the serving tray acting as a shield.

The lifeguard glanced over my way, so I acted on holiday vibes and sipped a little of each drink before stowing them away in my beach bag. Then I took the bottom cup from the double lined drink and wandered over to the sea to fill it, but it wasn't water. It was like an idea of water, as a thin line of blue separated the air above from underneath. I still waded through it as if struggling against the tide and was becoming moist and on the verge of damp but not wet. It was as if they had turned up the gravity and made the cadence fractionally harder to deal with but the water still evaded me somehow.

At 30 metres from the beach silver flashes beneath the non-waves caught my eye and I ducked beneath. A gathering of fish swam around in river lines as others with orange and yellow stripes joined them but swiftly pixelated as I reached out to grab them. They then remerged just out of catching distance and eyed me curiously before swimming away along the bottom.

I grabbed the empty cup and filled it with a stream of ochre and different coloured currents forming rivers around me. The liquids tangled around my fingers with no change in sensation then continued in unobstructed flow as something startled me.

It was a floating sock limply hanging on to the last dregs of life that pointed toward the open ocean before giving up entirely. I took it out of the water causing it to spring to life and ushered me to go onward.

At fifty metres the not-water was just about up to my boobs, but the ground seemed to slope back upward like a submerged half pipe. Back at knee height the sock threw itself into the water as I stumbled back barely avoiding a surfer, but they pushed themselves off an invisible barrier instead. The barrier blocked them from me also as they almost lost their balance at stringent whistling coming from a red blur of panic on the beach. There was no one else in the water except me and the surfers who continued crashing beyond the barrier, but they ignored the whistling so I did too.

The sock swam over to the edge of the cliff where someone stood and waved. Together we followed the barrier with outstretched arm until reaching the pock marked cliff with blossoming succulents filling dark outcrops. The sock ushered me on but before I stepped onto the rock, I glanced back to the beach as the red blur ran between the statue sunbathers. I stepped out and was met by a 'psst' from the top of the cliff along with the scuffle of loose stones. The rock was jagged and it would be unclimbable in bare feet. Just as I contemplated whether putting on a sentient soggy sock would be morally okay, the red topped lifeguard pulled up beside me and said, "Come down slowly. It is not safe on the sharp rocks. I must escort you back to the beach immediately." They cumbersomely paddled over in the shallow water and motioned for me to get back in, but it was awkward with them lying flat on their board in two feet of water.

"Shall I just walk back?" I asked.

"Erm. I suppose you could but... No wait, I must do this correctly... Please sit here and explain what you are doing so far out?" they asked as they dismounted, got to their feet and beckoned me over.

"I wanted a good view and a cliff was the ideal place."

"I guess it is but you must come back with me. Please get on the board as the beach dwellers are looking," they said and slunk away from the sight of the dwellers who were showing a vague interest in the commotion in unison. The lifeguard nudged the board and appeared almost pleading so what was the point in fighting? I'd got a collection of fluid, the unknown someone could have been another Jax trick and it was a fair wade back to the beach so I sat on the board causing the front to poke out at a sharp angle. The board's fin had become briefly stuck and dug into the surface bottom creating the first of many sand blooms. The lifeguard shook it free then gave it a good kick as I jolted forward, almost losing my cup. A 'splosh' slapped the rocks, I span around quickly and found the sock had been able to climb up the cliff and was being rung out by the unknown someone. They quickly hid as the lifeguard shouted, "Hey! Who are you? Don't ignore me as that's very annoying. Hey? Urgh, this isn't supposed to happen as I don't usually deal with anything except applying lotion and making sure the wind stays in exactly the right position. Who's there?" They shouted again before asking, "Did you see who they were?"

"Maybe it was a seagull?"

"A what? Never mind, whatever it is I'm going to have to report it as I'm sure I saw something," they added and pushed me.

"And what are you going to report? I can imagine it going something like… I saw something on the hill, I couldn't say what it was, I didn't know what to do so I'm reporting it."

The lifeguard tutted and added, "I'll think of a… description." They pulled their binoculars out and peered, "There might be two people you know or maybe these are out of focus, I can never quite get them to work." They paused to fiddle with their dial.

I started to drift and snuck a glance at the cliff just as a grey-haired person with a helmet snuck off. I mustered all my pitching know how and put it to good use, "Oh, I recognise those turtlenecks anywhere. It's the guards you know the two who have been lurking about."

"Ha! Of, course it is! Do you know they stamped my life preserver this morning and there is little need as we were only installed a week ago, so still brand new. They are bothersome," they said and flipped the red plastic buoy over to reveal a tick before grabbing the board and pushing.

"How do you think they got up there? Is there another way to get up to the top of the cliff, maybe a safer way?" I asked while sploshing slightly.

"Not sure, usually it's only by the sky and the wind never blows that way. They should stick to their own area and you should stick to the safe paddle zone and beach. Both should be big enough for you because you're only small," they said just as we landed on the beach with a 'kerft' on the sand and I dismounted with minimal assistance. "You'll be going back to the hotel now I expect?" they asked but it was more of an instruction as they grabbed their board and ran back to their hut to start waxing.

Thoughts of Tiao's safety had been deeply nestled away but came back with a bang as I'd probably been here too long as several more drinks with ingenious lids had been left for me. I gathered them and bypassed the beach dwellers all clinging on to the last dregs of sun as I clinked and slopped all the way back to the hotel.

***

Melodies filled the atrium along with the classic 'Wah, wah, wah' of the knife wielder and the 'duh dun, duh dun' of the irate beast about to catch it's prey as I was greeted by the receptionist experimenting with themselves. "Hi there Lori, I have been told to tell you that you may not be getting your sufficient nutrients. That's a shame, isn't it?"

"Well, I'm personally not surprised when the café only serves water and when I asked for fluid, you pointed me toward a beach."

"We can't be having that making you upset and it might be my job to order a new range of beverages and update the managers for you so when I figure out how to send interludes on this computer I will."

"You should try and give the letter buttons a press."

The receptionist tentatively pressed the H key and startled, "My goodness! It's so much more rudimentary than the intonation of vibrancy to the frequency of sound, I mean how do they know I'm asking in a nice way and not demanding?" they asked after finding all the keys to type, 'Hello.'

"There's these faces you can add," I said and opened the world of emotional icons.

"I shall be at this sometime, I think. Why don't you take yourself off to the café and get the sustenance you need while I get to grips with this new way of communicating?" they asked but paid no attention to a response as they continued one finger typing.

My stomach growled in apprehension but it had to wait, I'd grab the food to go and check in on a hidden Tiao, who by now should be fully charged if still dented. I satisfied my needs in the form of three red stiped containers which were pushed through the same lingering styled hatch. "Wait, you need t' pay please," a unfaced voice said as a small tube was pushed out. I threw the food into my ever-filling beach bag then watched my commodity metre go down.

"I shouldn't have expected all this to be free," I replied as I nibbled on some fries.

"Nowt is free lass," they replied.

"Fred?" I asked as the hatch immediately shut and left me no choice but to go back to the room. It was probably just wishful thinking as the accent of the server wasn't quite Fred's and the fries weren't the same as back in the apartment as he had perfected the balance of slight crunch and sogginess. "Huregh…" I retched as I almost choked from shock.

[Room has been CLEANED and PROTECTED from alternative elements!]

Shit. I immediately tore down the sign and opened the door. All my things had been tidied away. My suitcase was no longer flapped open with minimal clothes strewn all over the place and gone was Tiao's nest with straw system. I put down my bag and searched in mad panic.

Under the bed? No, nothing except my suitcase and extra blankets. Maybe he was in the bathroom? I pulled back the shower curtain but found only the virtual rainforest canopy and waterfall wall. Last resort was checking all the cupboards and drawers, but hope faded with each pull out and push back in.

They had taken him away for eradication.

My cheeks started to burn as tears fell. I grabbed his mat and hugged the warmth. This was my fault as if I didn't bother going in the sea then I could have avoided this whole situation. I could have come back as soon as I got the drinks as that was the mission and I'd failed him. I would never see his curious face again.

A glass rolled underneath my chair and paused at my feet as I wiped the salty snot and tears away. I picked it up and noted it was one from the beach with slime glued around the edge. Perhaps the cleaner had come back and nudged my bag over by the door. They were in for it if they had, I shouted, "Hey!" but was met with the face of Tiao along with several scuff marks where he'd dragged himself over the tiled floor.

"I'm sorry Lori. I didn't mean to cause distress," he said still shivering.

All emotions were instantly replaced with relief and love, "I'm so glad you're okay. Wait, are you okay? I got some drinks but there's not much out there. Where were you?" I asked and gently hugged him.

"In order of answers: about thirty five percent okay… Thank you, normal water is fine but some of these non-alcoholic versions are quite interesting, and I was hidden in the duvets under the bed… I believe they didn't understand the 'do not disturb sign' and… I'm sorry I didn't call to you, but my battery is failing…" His speech was so much more laboured than usual.

"How can I help you?" I asked.

"My connection point," he showed a sticking out pipe near his side, "it's broken somehow," he scooted around slowly as if trying to catch his own tail then slumped.

"Tiao?" I called and shook him slightly which caused his wires to spark.

"Sorry Lori, perhaps you can help me with my leg and I'll try and suck these in?"

"Of course." I acted as requested and added a few pillows to support him along with a rolled-up pair of socks and flip flop for his crumpled leg and for a moment he seemed comfortable. Soft snoozes accompanied his slumber until he awoke to my growling stomach. Tiao held my hand and said, "I believe your food may have soured," he pointed to the now very much wrinkled skinned burger.

"Don't worry. You are far more important than anything, burgers or not."

"But it's your favourite… forgive me it's one of them if I processed correctly?" he sighed.

"It doesn't even compare to what you would bring me or Fred would make me."

"I… I can't do that now I'm sorry… Maybe again in the future…" Tiao's voice choked, "he's still within me. Fragments of him, the starts of recipes and some techniques but they aren't joined up." His eyes welled as oily tears ran, "I think perhaps my processors cannot decipher the code… you see something has come out of kilter inside and my thoughts are jarring." He swayed and gazed in confusion.

"Perhaps you can write me a list of things I can find for you and I'll ask at reception if they have them. I'll inform them about the sign then hopefully they won't come in again and…" my stomach replaced my speech with cramping growls.

Tiao glanced at me with big eyes and snuggled the socks before he said, "Lori you must eat."

"Yes. I'll pick something up on the way back. But-."

Tiao started to jar in place as his eyes flickered and he made a small 'burpde' noise as a list was printed out, "Please assist."

"Are you sure these are what you'll need?" I asked as he nodded and pulled up a pillowcase like a sleeping bag.

***

The receptionist was consumed in a flurry of text communications and seemed very much at home amongst the keys as they stated, "Cadence and Rhapsody have both just become majors in the Symphony of Eliquinch, they have the potential to move onto a place called the Verglas Island and away from here, wouldn't that be wonderful?"

"What?" I asked.

"Oh, it's a forum and on-the-line discussion with people like me who are trapped in an inconsequential position, dreaming of the bigger world. Wait a mo," the receptionist typed with drum stick fingers and voiced the messages, "Sad faces to you. Be back soon hons."

"Okay, I need you to focus on this list. Can you provide any of these things?" I asked.

"Grungs? Sounds weird. Light bulbs… I don't, I mean all I have behind this desk is a bin and wires for the screen and you can't have them," they said and lifted a selection of knotted wires, "and as for the cleaners, you should already have them."

I rolled my eyes as I explained, "That added note was for me. I need to request that the cleaners don't enter my room when I don't want to be disturbed just like my sign states."

"You go girl. I'll just send that over and… All done." They finished and continued glancing into the screen firing messages off before peering back around the side and asking, "Was there something more that you need?"

"Is there a technology supermarket around here?"

"I don't know, let me just ask my group, oh wait they aren't from here but it's probably my purpose to find out for you and let you know. What are you waiting for?"

I quashed the frustration and remained polite, "I'm waiting for you to find out. I don't understand why everyone seems very new and underexperienced in their jobs."

"I started a few days ago so experience is gained everyday. Everyone must learn at some point, surely you remember being new?"

"Of course, it's just-."

"I get it, it's frustrating. Now as for your shop, it's probably outside as there isn't one in here. Oh, you probably want a specific place, so I'll send the information up to you and the oil and beeswax, I haven't forgotten." They turned back to the screen, "Hon that's funny, Calliope has just joined us. Back with you my ments! Happiness in a face to you."

I left them to it and entered the still empty café. I treated myself to a cake slice and a make it yourself fondue with crusty bread. It was popped in a hessian bag but the chef's hand seemed human as they held onto it a moment. They had a bird tattooed roughly on the back of their hand along with several scars but just before I could ask anything the shutter slammed. Now wasn't the time to probe so I rushed back to the room and checked on Tiao who was almost indistinguishable amongst the bedding. He woke gently sniffing as I set up the fondue set. "Do you want some? Can you even have some?" I asked.

"I am in need of mechanical counterparts to enable my recovery. Perhaps I could create a list of inconspicuous things to use to enable my recovery?" Tiao questioned as he righted himself into sitting with his only arm.

I bent down next to him as the fondue churned over to a pop and gently said, "You already have?"

"I'm sorry Lori. I couldn't recall," he bowed his head and sighed in frustration, "I don't think I'll ever be quite the same again."

"But you're still you and whatever happens we can make sure we get you back to the best you that you can be," I said as a knock at the door came. I put the hessian bag over him and opened the door marginally. "Hello?"

In front of me stood a very wide being with a feathered back and white apron, "Got your map and a beeswax greasy thing," they handed over a dot-to-dot dinosaur pattern and three small tubs. "This goes from your bedroom door past the beach and into the cityscape town. It's nice there. Bwark," they added as they ruffled their feathers and preened themselves slightly. "They said don't interrupt you again but I've a job to do and you've got stains," they stated as they wafted a brush in front of my pocket.

"But you know that this sign means leave me alone, right?" I asked and pointed to the obvious sign magnetically stuck to the door.

"Bwark! There was me thinking that was just another awful humanoid decoration but I suppose there's meaning in the artwork," they said and stared with soulless eyes before peering around the edge of the door.

"You'll have to excuse me. I'm in the middle of eating. Just know that when the sign is on the door you aren't to come in."

"What of the mess then? You can't expect to live like that… with stains! Bwark," they said with such disgust.

"It's fine, I don't mind. I'll sign whatever waivers you want and that will explain it's my decision."

"Okay. Then it's your fault I suppose, but don't go making extra work when it's not necessary." They sniffed the air and peered around the door once more, "Did you say you were eating?"

"Yep, just picked it up so if you don't mind leaving."

"I don't mind. Bwark! You do need the extra sustenance, you are very thin," they sneered and walked away brushing and dusting as they went.

I slammed the door as the 'do not disturb' sign fell with a 'shtut' but then a corrective 'sluk' seemed to have stuck it back in place along with the mutterings of "Bwark! Weird humans," and "odd habits."

Tiao was stirring the fondue with his remaining arm and still half under the bed, "I like it, it's soft. Does it match my eyes?" He joked and shrugged his shoulder up to make himself cute.

"Feeling more like yourself?" I asked as I exchanged the stirrer for the beeswax.

"Thank you but I don't know if this will help, you see I may have ingested some cheese content into my pipe. It oozed all the way up and clung to the sides as it went," he pointed to the fatty remains and smiled then slumped against me whilst I ate content in the moment. "Lori? What's that in your pocket?" he asked and pulled out the feather, "ah, broken but maybe useful for marking presence. I can use this along with these." He handed over a very neatly folded piece of paper as I finished eating. "I do have one more request?" He winced at the missing arm and gaggle of sparking wires sticking out of his broken leg before continuing, "I would like to see the sunset if possible? Fred enjoyed the view and I feel as if I would."

He was still inside the hessian bag and held up the handles for me as I carried him over all wrapped up. It wasn't the weight of him that bothered me in the golden hour but the weight of responsibility, he only had me to help him through this time of suffering and I was on a new mission to save him.

Chapter 21

Parisian styled cafés had outside tables strewn with newspaper screens and steaming coffee cups, the outward facing seats were taken up with jackets but no beings sat within. I had made it this far without interruption or confrontation as I followed the dinosaur map and found a shopping centre aptly named 'Market Place' nestled within the spinal spikes. I entered floor-to-ceiling doors and was shot with lights which collated a virtual image of me imprinted with a green tick before dissolving.

I continued onto a wooden decked concourse full of unknown branded shops but couldn't enter any as they were all locked. It was around midday so it could be a cumulative lunch break or it would be just my luck that I had decided to shop on the only half-day opening. But that didn't seem right as there were shoppers inside browsing and diligently ignoring me banging on the door trying to get their attention. I hit the glass once more causing a sock to flop down in the window display. It could be the shop's way of showing that they were sock friendly and accepting of sock wearers, but I wasn't wearing any and usually socks didn't appear miffed.

"Can you help me?" I asked the sock which hopped along the window and squeezed itself out of the keyhole by unravelling then reforming. It bounced up and down with vigour before slipping away into a side alley to which I followed almost expecting at this point that the world would collapse just as it had so often before. To my shock I outed the alley without trouble and was into a mirror version of the shopping centre but this appeared to have been abandoned for a long time. Light came in dusted shafts from cracked panes above highlighting the condemned consumerism. The sock hopped over discarded tin cans and old battered packaging with unusual symbolic languages until stopping underneath an oculus. It pointed toward a boutique flower shop just as a distant voice said, "Shoppers please note the stores are closing shortly." I had some time before the whole place closed at least.

The sock kicked a limp hanging sale sign and nudged me to go on. I pulled the door open and walked into flowering ferns cascading from cracks accompanied by an odour of stale and damp. I stumbled back onto a sack of soil as a bell chimed and a person emerged with the face from the nightclub and the frame of the waver on the cliff. They wore normal sneakers but the rest of their clothes were made up of spiralling bands which shook as they walked and snapped their fingers. Two birds flew out of a broken plant pot and nuzzled into their frizzy hair as they landed.

"Were you on the cliff and at the nightclub?" I asked.

Deep umber eyes pierced my core accompanied with a side smile before saying, "I was there among other places. We have been watching you for a while now. We are here to get you out, if out is what you want?"

"If out means going back home then yes, but I don't even know your name or why you want to help."

"Would you even remember my name if I told you?"

"I'd try," I said more sheepishly than I'd have liked.

"You better. It's Vilde," she winked and paused to observe one of the birds who was pecking at the window, "could it be footsteps?" It certainly sounded like the slap of flip flops on the tiled floor but it was muffled by a sheet of ivy dropped by the other bird. She spread her fingers wide as several lines expanded like a radar which conveyed information to her palm. "It seems, as always, that we don't have much time as you were followed. It's not your fault," she added.

"I didn't check or even think that would happen, it's so empty in here," I said and shuffled in place.

"Empty for your eyes maybe. They never do seem to leave you alone do they?" she asked as she glanced around the side of the ivy.

"Can we meet again?" I quickly said, "I can go back to the cliff or you can come to my hotel room?"

She shook her head as footsteps grew closer along with extra birds holding the ivy. "We planned for this. Your hotel room is too risky but you can come back tomorrow and buy something to eat from the restaurant here. Bring your bot and do so inconspicuously as he's had quite the journey so far. Oh, and in the meantime leave through the back and continue down until you see the shop with the yellow palm tree sign. If anyone questions you about your whereabouts just state that you were looking for this." She handed over a cloth wrap and put her finger to her lips to silence my reply as the shop fell into darkness.

"Hello? We know you are inside so come outside," an uncertain voice said as if speaking with a mouth full of cotton wool.

I steadily moved away to the back of the shop but bumped into a cupboard as my outstretched hands became covered in a spider web. A moment of bright light flashed as the door was momentarily opened but smashed shut with the collision of a plant pot thrown expertly by Vilde. She was now lit with faint purple as she mouthed 'Go!' before being surrounded in a curtain of leaves leaving only a slight gap for her hand to point to the door.

I ran for it and made it outside but the hairs bristled on the back of my neck, I was not alone. I loosened my still-stained-t-shirt sleeve as two furry legs furiously emerged and pulled the sleeve back up over it as if it was tucking itself in. I yanked it back up as out plopped a spider which threw its legs up as if to say, 'What was that for?' before scurrying away. I whispered a quick apology as my skin crawled before checking for other beings in the area. I was alone, so jogged down to the palm tree sign glowing in the distance.

I entered not into a shop but a changing room and donned the sarong wrap before sneaking out. There was no attendant in the shop which was full of various holiday items from swimwear to inflatable nappies and kites with tails fluttering in the windless air. I continued my may-as-well-try-to-fit-in routine by grabbing a pair of sunglasses with red rims which highlighted my ruddy cheeks so opted instead for a wooden pair but there was nowhere to pay and I couldn't just walk out with them. I checked the tags but they were blank so maybe this could be included in my overall service charge? I picked up a few other items and stowed them in my bag before leaving and bumping into a person with a body made from a patchwork of intermingling fabrics. "Find what you were looking for?" they asked in a voice that was barely more than a mumble.

"Yes. This has such a good silky feel and the bird of paradise print over those teal leaves just gives it that edge of class wouldn't you say?" I asked as I paraded with the best of my ability.

They pulled out a wedge of cotton dust from their ear and replied, "I like what you're wearing," then winced as if awaiting a berating and started to unravel at the elbows.

"Thank you," I said and went to walk away but they stopped me.

"Do you need some form of assistance?" they asked as they pulled a needle out of their finger and started to stitch themselves back together.

"I'm fine thanks. I was just going to continue browsing."

"There's another shop next door if you need more human accessories and can I offer this as a way to pay?" they stuck out a finger port and I willingly paid before they slunk back inside the beachwear shop.

I didn't continue browsing and instead immediately left the Market Place, I had hoped to catch a coffee and cake at one of the cafes but the tables had been packed away and shutters rolled down. Instead, I strode back along the wooden planks of the promenade and was almost calm until someone shouted, "Hey! You there, you watch it!" I stopped in place and pulled my foot back to reveal a retro cocktail umbrella and couple of six-inch beings balling their fists at me, "We're relaxing here, move on lady!"

"She's blocking the sun Frank, get the giant to move outta our way! You know I told yah we should have stayed on the beach but naw, you said it's better on the upside and now look we're in total darkness, Frank? Frank! Are you listening?" the other said as they started to pack their things up angrily.

"Janet I hear you. I understand you and alright already, I'll deal. You wanna go giant? Huh? Just keep walking lady! Come on. Leave us in peace," they said and grabbed at their tiny hats and ruffled books as my gait caused a gush of wind. "Such an idiot!" they shouted as I carefully walked away with renewed attention to avoid further upset.

- 257 -

Chapter 22

Tiao experimentally scooted from one hammock edge to the other with the occasional fitful wobble. He had created a makeshift mobility aid from a combination of hairbrush, tweezers and elastic bands and was within the joys of movement. He was only just visible to me inside but from outside he would be shielded from the view of prying eyes except for a rather elaborate drinking straw relay sticking out of his back. It pumped liquid in with minimal leaks and seemed to have given him a revival. However as the balcony door opened he bowled over the edge barely clinging on with one hand in surprise.

"Sorry, I should've shouted," I said and hoisted him back into the hammock.

It sank slightly as he regained his balance and slumped, "I thought it was the cleaner."

"Not yet. How are you feeling?"

"Better and quite so, however after performing a full system analysis I may have main frame damage, limb combustion and battery instability." He paused glancing over at my confusion and further explained, "Without the things I've listed I will not be able to complete a partial… let alone full recovery. I am very excited… to hear what you managed to obtain."

"Ah," I put down my beach bag and took out a bikini.

Tiao held it up to him with good faith and said, "It's my colour, if not a little baggy but it'll do. And the rest?" he glanced at me with cocked head and too much enthusiasm.

"I'm sorry. It was very odd there. I didn't manage to get much more, but I'm going back tomorrow as there's someone who wants to meet you."

Tiao gasped and fell back with a wince, "We mustn't, it's too dangerous, even for someone to just know I'm here. Why did you tell them?" he slunk away from me and became panicked.

"I didn't, they already knew and by 'they' I mean her, the woman from the cliff and night club. I think I trust her." I reached out to hold him but he drew away further.

"She might take me away and then I won't see you, I'll be deleted and Fred will be gone too. All that we tried to achieve would be worth nothing, our lives would be over and we'd be left like husks. Why would you want that?"

"I don't want that. Please Tiao, it's your choice and I'm not going to make you do anything you don't want to." He kept wincing as the hammock moved in the light breeze. "Let me at least help you now. I just want the best for you."

He reluctantly held out a hand for me to steady him, "May I have some time to process it?"

"Of course," I replied and couldn't bear the look of betrayal and disappointment on his face. I had to do something to repair or distract him for the meantime. "How is your straw system going?"

He sighed and stated, "I must maintain a constant flow of fluid or I might leak out completely." He slowly turned around to uncover two pipes full of tissue paper oozing water between two hair grips acting as clamps. "I had to borrow them. I hope you don't mind."

"I don't mind, but… how about we plug them with something better?" Each tube was about the diameter of a fifth finger and I knew just the thing for corkage, "I think a lemon or lime variety would suffice. What do you think?"

"I mean… yes possibly. We can but try but…" he petered out and shuffled to the edge before continuing, "I seem to have been able to lift myself up but won't be able to lift myself down, at least not without some difficulty." He paused for a moment and appeared to be calculating, "Can you help?"

I beamed in the hope that trust had resumed and lifted his weighty body as he clutched my neck and nestled before we entered the bathroom. Throughout our time together Tiao had become quite interested in the variety and availability of tampons and went as far as convincing himself that the red packaged ones had a scent of strawberry. After an awkward conversation about how he shouldn't taste them and what their purpose was he became enraged at the unfair taxation then maintained a constant full stock for the monthly interludes. Fred caught wind of Tiao's engagement and started a research project into the many uses of them in and around the kitchen. Casey even joined in and won himself an award for innovation in their use as conversation enders at social events as the mere suggestion of such an implement left lips tight.

Today I gave Tiao a selection to choose from, he inquisitively sniffed a blue one commenting on its raspberry scent before settling with an orange which firmly jammed in place to fix the problem immediately. After a full top up of fresh tap fluid he let the water wash over his hand transfixed with the way the light refracted through it. It instantly reminded me of my first encounter with the face suckers and the massaging beings as I asked, "I can request that room service bring up a tank sucker?"

"No thank you. I don't think I'll need that," he said with a grimace and shudder.

I handed over a towel I'd been hugging to keep warm and asked, "What's on your mind Tiao?" as still he persisted in the flowing water.

"Well currently my processers are analysing just how active you can be with one of these stuck inside and I'm trying to switch off that annoying jingle that accompanied the advert but I just can't seem to redact it from my memory," he said as he hummed one of my publicity songs from long ago.

"Good and bad songs stay with you, that's just advertising you see but I don't think that's it. I've seen you process a hundred things at once while carrying plates up the sides of walls without spilling a drop and giving back chat. This quiet little guy isn't you," I replied as he passed back the towel and I assisted him out and onto the bed.

"It's the me I am when I don't have to put up a rather good show. I think it's to do with Fred and the water and not just the tap water but the sea I suppose. We have never really seen it," he shuffled into his pillowcase and held it up to his chest for comfort.

"What about back home in the apartment, you showed me the sea out of the balcony?"

"Just a program based on the relaying of experience and collection of intellect. To create a moving wallpaper is easy but it can never truly be experienced as it's just a creation of manipulated space over a blank wall," he dimmed and then continued, "it's an amalgamation of geological experience, but still man made."

"Come on," I said and put the hessian bag over his head before lifting his pillowcase and cradled him as we ventured onto the balcony.

"Ah, definitely not really the sea," he sighed and slunk back down, "it's the Dos'sh lake and has a barrier to create the waves and atmosphere of a sea." He craned just a touch again and then hid under the hessian as laughter came from below, "we shouldn't be seen."

He looked disappointed as I put him back inside and said, "If we go back, back to Earth, then I'll show you the sea. I'll show you all kinds of seas. From big violent ones to ones you can float on top of because it's full of salt. Maybe we can make you waterproof and you can go in ones that are packed full of fish and as clear as the tap water we keep putting into you or ones that are so dark creatures from here probably live in it."

He snuggled into me and softly said, "I should very much like that," then cocked his head curiously and added, "I think Fred would too. Being so close to erasure has made me want to feel life I suppose." He wavered slightly then slumped slightly as his track kinked out and face grimaced, "I feel pain a fraction of what the beings of Acroks feel and a hundred times more than the beings of Mogithee but I'm feeling just enough to know I'm broken."

I hugged him gently and added, "I will fix you. I'm here for you and really want to help. Do you want to sleep on the bed?"

"No thank you Lori, you are a wriggler. I'll be alright but I just need to rest," he said and handed over my eye mask as I contemplated how to get him to the Market Place.

***

Tiao was snoozing under the bed as I gently snuck out to get breakfast. It was a good offering of fruit, cooked eggs and cheese all given by box and blank face service. I returned with a mug of tea and their version of a fritter as it was one of Fred's favourite things to make. Just before I opened the door the maid was stood outside. They cricked their neck and said, "You aren't in the room so who would I be disturbing if I went in? Bwark!"

"Surely you know?" I stalled, hoping they would fill the gap of silence but instead they stood glancing back and forth, "It would be my mantra… my vibe of course. It's a human thing but don't worry just let me sign whatever waiver you have and you won't have to clean in there for a whole week. I'll leave my towels and rubbish outside then I can have my vibes and … you know sense of wellbeing left intact on the inside." I grimaced at my own bullshit.

The maid also grimaced and said, "I don't mean to step out of bounds, Bwark, but you really disgust me. How can you live in an ounce of filth? Manners… Must remember manners… Excuse me. Bwark! I suppose you are the guest, so have it your way. Although, I must insist that I furnish you with two bins and wipes to clean whatever spills you have. I cannot stand stickiness and mess so do try to keep the room in some form of order." They threw a chunk of wrapped single use wipes in my direction and left.

I smiled and waited till they were fully away before entering my room and found Tiao rummaging in his treasure box, it had a few extra additions of towel peg, t-shirt and grease pot. He closed it quickly and blushed slightly in his tubes when I approached. "I'll have your t-shirt washed at my next convenience. I promise."

"It yours now, keep it and whatever else you need. After all the washing machine back home regularly ate clothes."

"There are beings who do have a fibre-based diet so it would make sense," he said as he neatly folded his pillowcase. "Lori?" he questioned as I munched on a muffin, "I have a plan."

"Go ahead."

He disapprovingly brushed away crumb fragments and sighed before going on to say, "Not to speak out of turn but I believe you have been given a gift." He opened the sarong and laid it out carefully highlighting venation patterns on the leaves, "It's a map of this district as I believe we are here in this hotel and there's the beach. I think these symbols and markings could be various hotels and their inhabitants or perhaps shops. There are a few anomalies such as purple ovals and these small hashtags which I can't place but do they mean anything to you?"

"Not really, sorry."

He dusted more crumbs off and carried on, "No bother, can you remember where you met her?"

I highlighted the shopping centre and pointed to a roundabout place within its innards as Tiao discovered the best route to take avoiding potential pitfalls. It was like a mission montage as he zipped through each possible scenario of an encounter with brief back peddling and side stories in case of capture. He calculated timeframes and assumptions when the shopping centre would be most full for ultimate inconspicuous liaison. Doubts were laid to rest or at least no longer considered by me as bravery came at the price of simply forgetting the main risk that Tiao could be captured and become an empty vessel. I even appreciated Tiao's outburst of rationalised courageousness but his decision weighed heavily as this could be the moment I finally lost my friends but what choice did we have? I couldn't fix him internally or externally so our only hope lay in the hands of strangers. Today was the day for charm, inception and collaboration so I awaited his verdict.

"I believe with our due diligence and formulaic approach we have a twenty-six percent chance of success but I am willing to take that risk, well not all of me but Fred is causing a rebellion somewhere about my waistline. He wants me to go on and so I shall, with you," Tiao stated as he stood lopsided on the bed with chest held high and head firmly planted.

"Then we will! Now, if you don't mind, get in the bag."

***

I tripped over nothing on the beach as the sweaty service steward offered immediate assistance and requested my order. I asked for an alcohol free pina colada and settled into a shaded area left alone by the beach dwellers. I subtly tipped a handful of sand in the bag so Tiao could experience it then opened his charging mat inside my book and wafted it as if soaking up the rays.

The hitch and grind of the military precision sunbathers came like clockwork but unusually some participated in overloud chatter about the weather and choice of food options at their hotel. The lifeguard was busy placing several flags into the sea and distributed flyers that stated the only acceptable swimming area was a 10x10 gap that was currently occupied by a school of stand-up paddle boarders.

I shifted my bag closer to me as a group of beings playing catch dropped the ball. "I am sorry that the ball has proceeded to interrupt your personal space," a being with garish green hair stated. Their chin started atop where a nose should have been and their skin was terribly blistered. "Perhaps I could regain the ball so we can resume our task?" they said and held out nail less fingers. I pushed it back over as the group of three robotically threw the ball between them making sure never to drop the ball or interfere with anyone else.

My beach bag was completely under my lounger by the time a fifth sunbather shift came and that signalled the time to leave. I was briefly obstructed by a green haired ball player who shouted, "It's a lovely day!"

"Yes, such a lovely day to be tasked with dispatching this ball. Here you are," shouted another as they flung the ball with great precision.

It was caught with a vice grip barely inches away from my bag as they said, "The regaining of the ball is quite amusing. Lovely days to come I suspect." They then threw the ball but it dropped and rolled into the path of the turtle guards.

"What's this then?" Blue Bowtie asked and handled the ball with added squeeze before tossing it to Yellow Bowtie. "Playing a game are we? I don't know if this place has been sanctioned for the purpose of ball games?"

"Perhaps we should survey the area and implement rules of this engagement?" Yellow Bowtie added.

The beings didn't respond but held in place as if awaiting instruction on the correct thing to do until social alleviation came in the form of the lifeguard who showed the guards something about their hand. It seemed on quick glance to be a timetable as the guards let the beings continue although without a ball as they just acted out the motions of throwing.

I took this moment to leave and luckily the guards wholly ignored me on their route to the sea. Instead I was accosted by the lifeguard running beside me as they asked, "Did they disturb you as we have just allowed games to be enjoyed?"

I was taken aback by this but answered plainly, "It's fine. I was thinking about joining in."

"But you didn't?"

"No, I remembered I really wanted to check out the Market Place for something to eat and maybe pick up some different shoes," I said as my bag shuffled.

"If you come back tomorrow an arrangement can be made for you to be included in their task. Are you done here for the day?" they asked and checked their finger clock.

"Yes," I said as the lifeguard whistled and waved their arms. The beings who were playing ball and those paddle boarding stopped immediately causing one surfer to get smacked so hard their head snapped back. "Shouldn't you sort that out?" I asked but the beings around them cracked their head back into normal position as the lifeguard finally freed my path.

I walked as normally as possible as a car pulled up beside me. The door opened automatically as a stern voice said, "Get in and save your legs!"

It wasn't in the plan to have a conversation with a car but I still replied, "My legs need stretching rather than saving." It drove very slowly beside me until closing its door and spinning 180° to find its next prospective client.

The rest of the way was unhampered as I hurried past the Parisian cafes and into the centre as the fabric being said, "Good afternoon, the shops are closing soon so please be quickened in your choices."

"It's only just gone two?" I asked.

"It's two thirds opening today and as you will see other customers are making their last purchases and will soon also be leaving," they said as they readjusted a pleat about their chest.

"Okay, so a half day would close around one, so two thirds must mean I have till at least five? People need time to rummage for them bargains."

The person started to fray, "I... Well, yes. I should let Them know... it would be possible to delay. Do please tell me, have we a list today?"

"No, *we* haven't. I just like to browse you know. Maybe I'll buy some alcohol or a gift for my friend," I said as thoughts that Casey still existed drifted around, but he was probably enjoying himself partying. "I'll just get a bite to eat first, you know how people watching can be quite energy consuming but it's all part of the rest and recuperation period," I added hoping to baffle them into submission.

Their zipper mouth open and closed before they replied with, "the customer is always right, even if your taste is wrong," then moved aside.

I stuck to the plan and entered what I assumed was a normal food court labelled 'Court of Food'. It was a supermarket style with fresh fruit stacked in wooden crates in the front and neat shelves to the back. Everyone seemed to be in a constant flow of picking up a single item then replacing it before replicating their actions within their designated aisle. Alright I wasn't averse to lingering on mathematical considerations whether to buy three for the price of one or one that was the size of three for even less money. I'd even consider paying higher for healthy and maybe that's what they were processing but they just picked up, replaced and moved on to a different item without bagging or basketing anything. I seized what should have been an avocado and gave it a quick squeeze to find it was in that sweet spot of should be eaten today but will be brown and stringy tomorrow as several people turned instantly to watch me. I placed the avocado back clumsily causing a minor spillage in the fruit aisle and the velocity of combined skins hit my beach bag as Tiao gave the smallest of 'Oofs' and I shouted, "Whoops!" to hide the noise.

People seemed to be in a state of 'what to do' as they forced objects back onto the shelves in their odd routine of shopping. Others stoically observed me but seemed to be glitching in place as if they knew their actions weren't correct but ceased as someone in a grocer's outfit made their way over. I wasn't lingering as I had a purpose and that purpose said, follow the smell of doughy delight and weird bird feet patterns on the floor.

I casually walked through the aisles glancing at the unknown packaging and products until I turned into the frozen section and stopped dead in my tracks. There was a guttural scream from a person standing inside a chest freezer. They tore a box in half causing multi-coloured peas to shower their burnt and blackened body and cried, "They know!"

I clutched my vibrating bag and whispered, "It's okay."

An exasperated avocado carrying assistant asked me, "What is it you are looking for today?"

"A café section," I responded as I ducked the deluge of overhead frosted missiles.

"It's out past the dairy zone but don't go that way as there are spillages everywhere. Get out Graham! Get out!" they shouted as they were pelted with peas. "Just go through the side door as they sell edible things through there. Come on! Get out!"

I swiftly left and followed their instruction to a door marked with 'Staff Only'. On the other side was a restaurant that was bathed in steam and paper lanterns. Beings delicately fingered chopsticks into gooey boxes along wooden tables. I was beckoned over by a server behind a bar, "Hi there… oh it's you," they said and leaned in to continue, "I'd recommend the wonton box… here please have a further look at our menu."

A thick screen was passed over with an icon of a blue bird carrying a dumpling. I pulled it out and said, "I'd like this please."

"That's the best choice, I will get that made up for you immediately." The icon was inserted directly into the side of a wok and created a vivid flambe from which a bird with glowing tail emerged. It twerted and flew over to a fountain as the server neatly folded a box up and overtly said, "Here is your order, please take a seat by the fountain."

I took a seat flecked with gold light next to an ornate water pump and opened the food box. The bird with glowing tail nodded then took off into the mosaic waters and I started to eat because, well, what else was there to do but wait. Tiao shuffled on my knee and made wet vomiting sounds, but on second listen it was more like a wet fish smacking its tail against a tile. I glanced over the edge of the fountain and found a limp sock flopping in the water and fished it out with a chopstick. It shook itself dry and hopped over to the server.

Ater a rapid exchange the shutter slammed down and the sock was momentarily trapped beneath as all life was being squeezed out. It was released and dragged through to the other side accompanied by the server's strained voice shouting, "Come back for us! Start customer desync. Goodbye for now!"

The other customers faded into pixelated dust as their now empty stools automatically stacked themselves atop tables. My wonton flopped off my chopstick in surprise as the fountain split and shuffled sideways to reveal its drainage grate. It flipped open and out emerged two purple outlines of blurred humanoids with edges sharpening as they gained height. "Did you encounter difficulty in getting here?" Vilde asked as her radar pierced the surroundings independently as she assisted another being out. "This is Bertha and she is one of us and will help us today."

"My friends call me Bertie and I'll be having that feather back thanks," she said and plucked the feather out of my pocket and stuck it in her hair before cleaning her jam jar sized glasses with the corner of her knitted cardigan. "You did well to get here, but I don't know why Vilde would choose here of all places when it's so humid my perm is kinking." She licked the end of the feather and darted it about her hair as Vilde closed her radar.

"All that hairspray should keep it in place. Now come on, we don't have long." Vilde knelt beside the grate and blew into closed hands creating a purple hue to banish the shadows of the sewer tunnel, "This is how we get you out and we must be swift as reports show they will be here shortly. Wait, we must take off your bracelet for our total privacy. Of course it is your choice."

I nodded.

Vilde clicked the edges. "It's too tight, I'll disable it instead. Now follow me, ME," her voice echoed as she entered.

To follow would mean being at their total mercy but staying would mean the almost certain end of Tiao in the lonely afternoon, so I gobbled the last wonton and held my bag close to me as we entered.

"It's sadly not one of those 'bigger on the inside' things," Bertie said and with great force secured the grates behind us as the fountain strained into position. "Come on, the smell gets better with time," she added as she too cast a soft light onto the shell imprinted floor. I steadied myself against the wall but my hand was slapped out of the way by Bertie, "Sorry, should have mentioned, don't touch the walls as they bite." The walls crawled making the space even tighter and I barely avoided bumping my bag into Bertie and Vilde. Tiao seemed to sense my nervousness as he reached his hand up and clutched my fingers so I responded with a rub of reassurance.

"Head down," Vilde shouted just as I almost slipped causing a jolt in the bag. Tiao's head emerged from under a towel and instantly his eyes lit up the room as he swiftly ducked back inside.

"Watch yourself there," Bertie said catching my arm, "You're okay and as for you in the bag, you're right the lighter the better but don't expend yourself needlessly. It isn't far now and if you listen you can hear brakes." Sure enough there was the distant sound of pressurised air being released.

Vilde set off her scanners and abruptly shouted, "Stop!" Even the wall ceased moving as a pocket of amalgamated metal emerged. "It's here." She reached in and turned something which clicked and opened out into a bustling transport station.

"We need to catch a bus and not just any one but that one there," Bertie said and pointed out a red triple decker complete with cycle rack and normal wheels. Bertie opened the door and sat in the driver's seat then tapped her shoulder. Her clothes changed to that of a conductor uniform replacing the others instantly through symbiotic melting. She did a thumbs up and said, "Stay downstairs. We do this nice and easy all the way to the tunnel port then a quick jump will see us home. Now find your seats if you would."

Vilde rung a bell causing a screen to cover all windows with images of passengers reading, snoozing and generally mindfully waiting for their stop before saying, "Here will do." She spun around the opposing chair and kicked the floor for a table to emerge before getting comfortable.

Tiao shuffled into me as I put my hands on the frosted window to create a hole in the fabricated mist as we started to swerve in between the traffic. "Where are we going?" I asked and steadied myself against the table.

"Home, well it's a haven. Oops," she added as Tiao hit his face on the table and unsteadily snuck back into the bag, "We will get you fixed up soon, go into standby if you can," she said as Tiao slunk further into the bag. "I have to say that I'm glad you both chose to come with us-."

"Up ahead for a vehicle change! But duck first!" Bertie shouted and signalled with her arm as all the bells on the bus chimed as one and the upper floors were ripped off and replaced with concrete and steel tunnel. The air smothered us now in our roughly modified open topped bus.

I shoved Tiao under the table but no sooner had the bag bottom landed than Vilde snatched him and ran to the front. "No!" I shouted and awkwardly gave chase down the narrow aisle and sparking roof.

"It's okay," she replied and held her hand out to steady me. "We must make a transition to make sure we aren't followed. "What are you thinking Bertie? Truck up ahead?"

"Gotta be," Bertie said as she slammed on the gas and slid back the driver seat. "Hold on." Vilde nodded and grabbed me as the bus impacted into a lorry but the collision came in the form of amalgamation. Bertie strapped in the driver's seat and quickly took control of the truck as the bus went blaring into the distance. "Close one," she said as we were now sat at the front on a trio seat.

Tiao reached out his hand to me as Vilde handed over the bag with disinterest and settled back into her chair. "Why are you helping us?" I asked.

"Because everyone deserves the chance to get out and be free. They were mining me just like they did you and so many others, but I stopped becoming fund producing and that means my rate of living far outweighed what I was making for the requests. So things cut back, I was sent on a short holiday then returned into a smaller apartment. My robots were abandoned and my luxury life was replaced with box food and self-service."

"You're lucky they didn't turn you into subservice, there's been more deposits into that than I'd like to count," Bertie chipped in as she fought with the large lorry wheel to turn off a slip road and onto another highway.

Vilde shook her head and solemness crossed her face, "They got me out and now I help get as many out as possible before they become valueless."

"And why us? We still have worth?" I asked as Tiao's big eyes could just be made out through his small pillowcase.

Bertie did a drum roll on the steering wheel and said, "You do have worth in those tunes that go, bah da, bah da, bah… Diddle, hab da dibbly dah... Which must be one of the most annoying and catchy jingles of all time."

"Tampons…" Tiao muttered as he shuffled about and replaced his flipflop.

"Your worth is something else entirely but we'll get to that later, for now we need to hail home." Vilde changed the radio station and readjusted the mirrors.

Bertie wound down the windows to give the cab a fresh breeze against the smell of stail sewer and said, "You see the purple bar above the street, the one just dangling surrounded by birds? Just hold out your hand and grab onto it."

"Won't it rip my arm off as we move?" I asked as the wind eased through my fingers.

"You could walk faster than the speed we are going," Bertie stuck her tongue out and moved the truck sideways with a slick manoeuvre as the breeze met my outstretched arm but I shot it back as the rush from an overtaking car became too close for comfort. "Damn, missed our slot but no bother, would you swap places with Vilde?" Bertie asked then span the truck 360° as the purple light faded and was replaced by a street lamp. "There's another up ahead, we can try for that one."

We jerked forward as the truck started reversing through the oncoming traffic and it was back to the adrenaline filled body shakes for me. I didn't want to be in another collision. "There!" Bertie shouted as the truck nearly crashed into the kerb. Vilde quickly grabbed the pole underneath an advertising billboard and it grew thin octopus legs before attaching itself to the truck lifting us sideways and upward.

The truck door was opened as Vilde said, "We are coming," to an unknown someone and stepped out onto a ledge.

Bertie put a reassuring hand on my shoulder, "This is where we depart. Off we pop."

'Popping' wasn't that easy as I suddenly developed a fear of falling with an urge to regurgitate my stomach contents. Tiao held my wrist as I clenched everything and crossed the barrier focusing on putting one foot in front of the other rather than the matchbox sized cars underneath. Bertie was close behind us and as soon as her feet set foot on the plinth the tentacles retracted and the truck fell. At the other end of the ledge was a tall concrete building, it was bland and featureless and the kind of skyscraper that just fills in the background but curiously it had someone waving out of a window.

The ledge jolted as concrete fragments fell beneath my feet, Bertie snatched the edges of my shirt barely saving me before the topple. "Close one, nearly lost you both then."

"Sorry Tiao," I called but his reply was drowned.

"Quickly, in here!" said a tawny haired person shouting from an open window. I entered it with a head rushing crack as I didn't quite avoid the frame. "Oof! So, sorry. I should have told you to squat, eh?" the person chuckled then sealed the window, locking me into another unknown situation where once again I could be held against my will. Maybe I had replaced one kind of prison for another and still was left with no real chance of going home, "Could you tell me where this is?"

"Not exactly but save your questions for later."

I rubbed my head and shuffled through a corridor of chrome patterned wallpaper as I followed and silently worried about what was ahead. I had brought Tiao here in the hope of help but without knowing the cost, I was just about to check him when we suddenly stopped near an oozing doorframe. The tawny haired person turned sharply and stated, "I am Rodolphe Jean and I originate from Toulon in France. I'm very excited to meet another Earthling and your friend," he added while pointing to my bag.

"Likewise although…"

"Although perhaps I don't sound typically French. I get that a lot. Ah oui, oui… Is that better? Perhaps more traditional? I have the twang I know, but it is not how I speak as I have lived here for several years so, you know it eh, it changes? No, excuse me, by your face I assume you weren't going to ask that?"

"I wanted to know where we are and what do you do here? Can I leave?"

"That's so many questions but now is not the time instead a formal reception is in order. Welcome to the Gröfu Pallur."

My heart sank as I grasped the bag tight and went to run but Rodolphe grabbed me.

"No, no, I jest. I apologise. Welcome to the Frelsi Mitt!"

"Definitely not related to the Pallur?" I asked with a trembling voice as he started tapping on a door frame.

Vilde explained as she pointed back to the window, "No. We are definitely not there and as soon as you step through that threshold those that pursue us can't see beyond it." She then turned back as the door opened into a room with surrounded by bookcases and still I followed.

Bertie threw two sets of keys onto a wall full of hooks with expert precision and continued, "It's a means to an end. We aren't too far away from your hotel, but there's certain ways in and out they don't know about, back roads and such to keep us out of sight."

Tiao took a laboured breath inside the bag as Rodolphe caught a glimpse and asked, "Who do we have in here?" Tiao gasped as Rodolphe backed off and said, "Not ready yet to meet me, that's okay. I hear you need some help getting better but we will only do that when you are ready, for now I will give you the tour." Bertie winked at me then bent over a map with dozens of tiny cars moving on it as Vilde took a couple of socks out and started to darn them.

Rodolphe opened a thick door and said, "So, here we have the privately assigned bedrooms with solo use bathrooms and you have," he checked his fingers as a stream of data emerged. "Bon, you have a twin bunk bed for you and your friend also with the charging points, perhaps he would like to see his room?"

I softly called, "Tiao, Tiao?" but he didn't respond. I set the bag onto the bottom bunk with not a creak in foam as Rodolphe assisted the removal. Tiao flopped out along with a couple of bolts, his body wasn't shaking but his leg was seizing uncontrollably, "The tour can wait, he must be our priority, you agree?" he asked and quickly got a charging port from near the bunk.

I nodded and held Tiao's hand. "He did so well to hang on for this long." I carefully pulled a printout off but unlike its usual clear font this was incomprehensible. "Does this mean anything to you?"

"No and he won't attach, but we have someone here who can help so we go now." Rodolphe swaddled Tiao's body gently as we carried on past medical cubicles, through a hub of self-suspended chairs and a vast amount of computers and into a mix of workshops not too dissimilar to surgical rooms. "Mei?" Rodolphe shouted as he lay Tiao down on the table.

There was a thud of steel and trickle of bolts as out popped a white-haired person stained in grease and oil. Wires surrounded their thick wrists along with scarred fingers which threw a wrench into a well dinted bin as they approached us.

I was reluctant as this person could bring the one thing Tiao feared most, to be left as a metallic corpse. It was selfish as I didn't want to be without someone I truly knew and cared for, but this was our only option.

"Tiao will be safe I guarantee it," Mei said with a quiet voice that jarred with their overly built frame.

"He's quite broken," Rodolphe stated.

"But not beyond repair," Mei carefully unwrapped the blanket with precision then guided my hands to support Tiao's head before he was attached to a machine that would not be out of place in a car repair shop. Mei stopped and sighed, "this may not be palatable to view. Are you sure you want to be here?"

"I'll be with him through it and help where I can," I said as Mei nodded and handed me a rag.

"It's your choice, just keep holding him and Rodolphe would you please grab any printout's he may produce. We all need to keep a watchful eye on the diagnostics as any lapse in pressure below 200zok or rising to over 450zok is an immediate indication of near total loss, but I see his level is dangerously under already. He must have been in considerable pain for so long," Mei mused and open a side panel as Tiao juddered.

"Please don't hurt him," I pleaded and stroked Tiao's cold clammy hand like a role reversal from my testing state.

"It would never be my intention to do so. I'm going to put him into an induced total standby so he will be unaware of the procedure," Mei grimaced and released a popper beneath their armpit as the side of their chest opened out into a metallic rib cage of a toolbox. A minuscule hammer was extracted along with a few other pieces that were placed into a tube of clear liquid prepared by Rodolphe, then with a cough the chest was placed back.

Tiao's mouth hole was expertly melted back and revealed its housing so a tube could be inserted. Mei attached it to a balloon bag which pumped in gas easing Tiao's troubled breathing. Mei gave a 'tut' after a glance over at the diagnostic machine and attached two bags of fluids which were injected into opposite sides then looked confused. "It appears another has attached onto him like a parasite but it seems here the host wants to keep it alive. I'll have to remove it. Although… that's unusual. It's almost a replication of him…" the glint from a spotlight highlighted the lilac edge of Tiao's heart. Mei wiped a sweaty brow and steadied their own hand whilst manipulating something inside Tiao, sparks flew and the stench of sulphur emitted as Tiao started to fizzle.

Mei glanced over to Rodolphe who patted me on the shoulder then started mutterings of, "He has many errors… over interactions… something hidden dormant."

"I don't care, just do your best for him. Please!" I shouted as Mei nodded. I wanted them to hurry but also take their time and fix whatever needed fixing as all I could do was watch on in useless agony.

"I think I might need Vilde and Bertie too for imminent isolation," Mei stated as Rodolphe summoned them. The pair entered as if already outside, Bertie flicked on the radio which produced visible sound waves in the thick mist that Vilde unleashed just as Tiao's body gave a final contort.

Chapter 23

My cheek peeled away from the surface of the greasy table as I awoke in an empty room. The wires of the diagnostic machine were hanging limply, the oily rags had been discarded in a corner and there was a distinct lack of Tiao. Perhaps he didn't make it, but he couldn't be dead, he just couldn't be. That would be jumping to an unthinkable conclusion, so I desperately shouted, "Tiao? Tiao?" and initiated the hunt but was instantly stopped by the squelch of an orange tampon. I squatted down underneath the table and noticed the start of a trail of slippery goop. I followed it like a hawk through a short corridor and into a room with barrels and crates of bottles haphazardly placed.

"Stop," Mei shouted from amidst a collection of pumping pipes, "just wait a moment, Lori."

But I had already stopped behind a crushed cube of metal revolving in a glass cage at the end of the trail, "Tiao?" I called as I pressed my fingers into the warm glass. "How could they do this to you?" I asked as rays of deep purple and blue raged around his body binding him in a floating space and time. "This was your doing?" I shouted as I rounded on Mei.

"Not just me. We do this every day as if we don't what else would we do with it?" Mei said as they wiped their hands on an already damp rag.

"You are barbaric!"

"I heard shouting," Bertie said as she slammed open the door and shouldered a nearly falling shelf with smart reflexes "What's happened?"

"It's garbage?" Mei said with a head shake.

"He's my friend! He isn't garbage, he has so much worth," I screamed.

Bertie side glanced to the left and right then pierced her stare into the chaotic fission behind me before asking, "This… Is your friend? Do you mean Tiao? Because this is a garbage compacter-."

"Actually," Mei interrupted softly, "it's a quantum kinetic engine that powers this place by the recycling of rubbish. In particular it gyrates the atoms and displaces the energy into everyday use like your fridge and toilet. So, it isn't Tiao… but ah, I can understand why you may think this." Mei shrugged and continued outside.

Bertie tapped on the screen as she said, "I suppose there is a likeness there but just as Mei says, this isn't him. Although we didn't see all the procedure as we were only needed for the anticorruption data purge and putting you to sleep. I'm sure Tiao will be fine so shall we go and find him?" she didn't wait for a response as she placed a guiding hand on my shoulder and led me back through to the workbench. She tapped on a screen and flicked through some spreadsheets before exclaiming, "He is alive," she breathed out relieved, "that's good."

I allowed myself to smile but needed confirmation in repetition, "Are you sure?"

"Yep, he's alive and I think he's this way. He'll probably be snoozing." She guided me through a warren of dado rail lined corridors until she pulled open a wire infused glass door and into a hospital ward. Or at least it appeared as such with the classic enclosed beds, clean tiles and strip lights. Bertie marched over to the medical attendant desk and on her return stated, "Cubicle 3port-EE has a surprise in it for you. I'll leave you to it." She squeezed my arm and added a thumbs up.

The number dissolved quickly as I drew back the curtain and was meet with a being not of Earth dissent. A vortex fluid filled the space where a head should have been and projected speech like a dripping tap as they said, "Closed curtains are for patients' privacy, you can't just go waltzing around like you own the place... unless you do own the place in which case, welcome! We need to discuss some maintenance issues... No, clearly you aren't the director so you must be a visitor, well you are in luck as visiting hours are constantly open." Their face swirled but it was difficult to hear the humour through the liquid. They pushed a button on bleeping equipment before tucking in a sleeping lump.

Tiao was curled up in the middle of a normal size bed which dwarfed him as the glint from circular lights highlighted chrome plasters on his surface. He shuffled quietly in his slumber as I took his hand and readjusted his nose tube which had become more of an eye tube just as an alarm screeched and emergency lighting on the ceiling flashed in strobe towards another with muffled shouts.

The medical attendant ran to it trying to calm the situation as I was being grabbed around my middle, "Lori!" Tiao said and hugged me with his one remaining arm, "I'm pleased to see you. Ahem, urgh."

"I thought you were… well never mind. You're here now and you're looking better than ever!" He waggled his new tracked legs together and beamed.

"Well aren't they smart!" I said obeying the obvious politeness.

"I am yet to try them out-."

"And you'll be waiting a little longer," the medic stated as they finished off a hanging report but jolted their input as a smash of glass and muted scream came from beyond the curtain. "That one, she's not a good one like you, is she? We'll have to ship her off to subservice with all the bother she's causing. Right then, how are we Master Tiao?"

"Ready to roll!" Tiao said as he propped himself up making his fluid pressure armband snap dreadfully. The attendant quelled the bleeping machine and removed his band but flinched as an alarm sounded once more. The medic's face imploded with turbulent waves before they stated, "Calm down over there!" The cubicle curtain was violently drawn back to reveal a familiar face raging against the cage by repeatedly smashing on the windows. Caralyn was gaunt, thin and terrified as she connected with the glass and rebounded. "Stop it!" the attendant shouted and suppressed the alarm then added an "oh," as Caralyn did what was instructed, not out of authority but more out of curiosity of seeing me.

I couldn't help but run over and ask, "You got out then?" but I shouldn't have as her answer came in the form of a torrent.

They won't let me out. *They know I work for the others.* *I just want to be safe.* She threw her hands to the glass as we shared a brief moment of a non-connecting finger press before she continued to sign, *Everyone else from the nightclub got to leave.* *They only come in to ask me questions I can't answer.* *Please help me, Lori. I'm not bad.* *Help me.* *Make them let me out.*

"See it's no good, we have to keep her sedated," the medic said as they dropped a syringe and added, "damn, I'll go and get another one."

Caralyn smeared her forehead on the wire lined glass. *See how they treat me?* *How is this okay?*

"I won't let them put you to sleep. Just stop banging about and try to be nice and calm as I personally don't want to hear that alarm again, okay? Just breathe Caralyn, this isn't like you." I tried the door handle which just wobbled in combat. My heart was in a mess, I wanted to help and I wanted to tell her that I'd missed her but it was too soon after such brief encounters before. "Can you let me in?" I asked the medical attendant as they returned.

They snapped the end of a drug vial and sucked a dark substance into a primed needle then said, "So far, she has refused to talk to us, it would be dangerous for you to be in the same place in case she is contaminated."

"If you won't let me in at least can you tell me why you won't let her leave?" I asked.

A double tap to the end of the needle removed a bubble before they sighed and explained, "For your safety and our security as she might be transmitting data to those who cause us distress. That is why it is imperative that we identify her quickly within our database and make sure she isn't a threat. She will then be evaluated for release and offered the same choice everyone gets."

It's not true, they won't Caralyn balled her fists and scrunched her face.

"You don't know that, I can ask?" I said.

The medic appeared surprised as they said, "We have no way of communicating but as you seem to be able to, would you like to perform the duty of translator to this being?"

"This being is… her name is Caralyn and she can communicate in captions and sign language."

"Ah," the medic drove their hands into their face and pulled out enlarged ears cascading water themselves as they asked, "try now." Caralyn started to sign to the medic but understanding wasn't conveyed.

I was distracted as my shirt briefly strangled me at the neck line.

Tiao was tugging at my back, his big eyes beamed as he precariously balanced on his tracks and exclaimed, "Lori, I believe the problem is that she is communicating in long range which must travel a tremendous distance to get back here causing a limitation to how many others may network with her. However, I think I can change it to short range… if that's okay… urgh, excuse me," he paused to readjust his weight before continuing, "I will be able to define it to this ward for now and then she may choose to alternate it in the future."

"That's kind but we mustn't overexert ourselves must we," the medic leaned into me and quietly said, "he wouldn't even stay in bed when he first awoke as he just wanted to know you were okay." Tiao's face blushed a little. "But I suppose in this instance you may extend it to the edge of this room, for security we must keep it tight."

Caralyn's eyes dashed from side to side as she nodded at Tiao who reciprocated. Caralyn removed a jelly-like orb from her hand vesti which slopped through the window as Tiao fed around a thin wire connecting the two locations ignoring the physicality of the window itself. "Oof!" he exclaimed as I steadied him. "That's a rush!" he shook his head and continued, "I am okay Lori. It seems it's a closed loop but we can work with that. Using this should work as a go between so you may both communicate in your preferred manner." He turned to the side and briefly signed something to Caralyn who nodded before making his way back to his bed and patted it for me to join.

I sat beside him as he said, "I'm not staying here," in a voice not his own.

"What?" I asked.

But Tiao didn't answer as he was not himself. His hand was moving quickly but subtly as he continued in a different watery voice, "Think sensibly, if you just fill out a form then we can place you within our system and check that you are here legitimately and not wanted by the tender distribution team."

"I'll fill out your form if you believe what it says!" Tiao said as he shrunk inside the bed as the medic dramatically closed the curtains around Caralyn. Tiao growled in unison with my stomach then said in his normal voice, "I think someone needs to eat."

"Welcome back into the room," I said.

"I was dropping from the eaves," he said mischievously then added, "I'll keep an eye on them and report any further findings to you from the comfort of this bed, that's if it's okay?" He reattached himself to a pipeline as his body relaxed and calm fell across his face.

"Tiao, you're a rebel!" I said.

Tiao grinned proudly and stated, "Mei has erased some minor morals from me which has been very freeing although I believe I will perhaps choose to regain them soon," he bowed then retreated under the blanket as he nodded over to the approaching medic.

"Can I eat here?" I asked.

"Food is limited for patient consumption only. You wouldn't want to eat the formula's they give out here, believe me I've tried."

"Okay. I'll get something elsewhere, perhaps you know somewhere that does a dirty burger and loaded fries?" I asked the medic who pointed outside in reply.

***

"You look hungry," Bertie said as she caught me mid corridor. "Heading to the mess are we? I believe you have already met the owner. Shall we go together and have a chat?"

I followed without argument as I was bathed in exhaustion but the last words replayed like a glitching song as, 'Have a chat' has never followed with anything good but Bertie hadn't noticed my noncommittal as she continued, "I personally call it 'the bar', that way it feels like you can let your hair loose." She ran a hand through her hair as instantly it changed from tight curls to vivid waves then back again as we rounded onto a familiar someone lounging in the doorframe. "This is the resident landlord, Rodolphe, who will show you around."

"Yes, because obviously I was not taking a break. So, welcome, welcome to the Chateau of la Meilleure Cuisine. Please observe the seating arrangement which is anywhere you feel comfortable and after you have used the self-service bar I will attend to your food order," he finished with a flourish and continued over to a converted medicinal cabinet with extravagant glasses stacked up inside but rounded with a surge of inspired divination, "You know our newest bar keeper, Fred."

"It's rite good t' see yeh both this fine day," came that familiar voice from ankle level. Fred was now no bigger than a terrier with ball wheels that enabled him to move up onto a shelving unit as he said, "They did a rite good job at fixing me up, although I'm still getting t' grips with not being able t' reach things. That's been quite the challenge… quite the challenge," he repeated as he jarred in place. Rodolphe opened a small hatch on his back, took out a card then blew on it and reinserted it. Fred wobbled slightly and said, "Still working out the kinky bits." He turned his head slightly and slumped a little as he said, "I'm rite sorry but I can't remember what you like t' eat or drink... Lori isn't it?"

"It is, it's so good to see you! Come here!"

He scooted over and nestled in to share a hug as I said, "Anything you make me will always be my favourite." I gave him a reassuring rub and added, "How about a burger or burrito?"

Fred glanced at Rodolphe who flicked up a screen with complex recipes then added, "We can do that for you, please find a table and help yourself to a drink… Bertie if you would be so kind to explain the system?"

"Can do, such a poor thing Fred is. He won't ever function the same but he will help Rodolphe by stirring things with a spatula, which to be fair is also the extent of my cooking ability," she said with a chuckle and wandered over to one of several beer taps lined up with medical piping underneath barrels fizzing above. She grabbed a glass and pulled with precision as the liquid gushed out filling the air with strawberry scents mixed with spices. "We all have a job to do within this community and I wonder what yours will be. Ahh," she sipped deeply and paused to wipe a steady foam moustache away before asking, "what do you want to drink… no don't tell me I reckon you're a fresh sort, how about a sour beer from the vault?" without agreeing she directed another glass beneath a chrome tap and pumped out a smooth flow of orange liquid. A price and finger hole appeared, I inserted but was denied by 'lack of funds.' "Oh no bother," she said as she inserted hers instead, "We use a different currency here and you aren't connected yet. I'll catch Vilde and sort that later but it's okay for now, you can owe me one."

"Thanks," I said as I sipped the lip dissolving juice and found an empty table.

"You're probably used to instant delivery but things are slower paced here so that gives us time for a bit of a chat while they prepare the food." Any vague hope that she may have forgotten her intent to commune diminished instantly as I steadied myself for what was to come. "I've been here about eighteen years now, which is probably about twenty-five Earth years give or take, and I was only mined for three of those. My tests started off pretty much standard as I strapped myself into a machine that didn't go anywhere but had a screen with a road moving, if you can imagine that," she shook her head in recollection and pulled her ear as her hair changed from tight curls to slack bun and back. "Sorry, I do that from time to time. Anyway, when they thought that I was a safe enough driver they let me go out into the real world with passengers. For a while it remained that way until it got worse and they'd say just avoid these cars or follow that one. It got stressful with chases and near misses and then I had strict instructions to knock vehicles off the roads only so my passengers could take whatever cargo was inside. Well, I just thought it was a game… that was until we got jack-knifed into a bird breeding ground and my passenger was injured beyond repair. It was then I thought… I've done my time and I have got to leave for good but it's so difficult once you're in." She paused to refill her glass then returned, "As I was saying, I started to follow the rumours and day after day I'd head over to the breeding grounds hoping to catch a twert but nothing, not until my car broke down and I met Vilde. I've been with these 'Darners' ever since. They used to be called 'The Dumps' but that soon changed when Rodolphe arrived. So that's me and my job but what I want to know, is why you? They don't usually invest so much into getting a specific individual out unless you have a significant worth or you can be of elite assistance to tenders. I get you've done a lot in your time back on Earth but music isn't needed here. So what is it? Why did they try so damn hard?" She swilled the beer from side to side in her mouth as she pointed a questioning finger from glass holding hand.

What could I say to quench her thirst for knowledge? It would have to be something adequate but my head was in a fog of overexertion so opted for the simple truth, "I honestly don't know. I can't really do a whole lot else other than the jingles and arty stuff, but as much as it was them trying to help me out it was me seeking a way home. Don't you want to go back home?"

"My home is set on a course of extinction. But I have a new family here and good purpose, alright the living isn't too great but with Vilde's smarts, Mei's engineering skill and Rodolphe's edible food… well, that makes me pretty content… now there's the twins but they tend to stick to themselves and the odd hospital staff but Jardine has a use," she nodded to herself and topped up her pint.

I contemplated 25 years of hereness but the thoughts subsided with the arrival of two burritos and Rodolphe's persistently happy face as he sat down next to me and lifted Fred onto his knee, both mirroring expectant appraisal of their creation.

"It's great," I said as the slop of mild spice lingered about my chin but Rodolphe's face slumped as Bertie tutted and swiped away a message.

"Guess I'll be having that to go as apparently there's a parcel I need to pick up." She tapped her head twice as a helmet emerged from the very strands of her hair then double clicked a fob which was followed by a distant echo of 'Beep, beep.'

"Should you be driving? You've had alcohol?" I asked.

"It doesn't process the same for me as it does you earthlings, it's all just grass and gas. Best I'm on the road instead of stinking up in here." She added a finger flick of a salute then bumped into Caralyn who was accompanied by a limping Tiao following closely behind.

They let me out thanks to you, but I'm leaving soon, captions floated above my once bitten burrito as Caralyn sat and adjusted her gaping hospital gown. Tiao scooted beside her on the bench and assisted as she continued, *I need to go back. This isn't for me and I wanted to talk to you before I go.*

Before I could reason with her to stay, Tiao glanced over to Fred who was glancing right back, "I'm reckonin' I'm knowin' yeh but my heads a little fuzzy. No, don't 'elp, it'll come back t' me with time."

Tiao was speechless as he checked over his old friend as oily tears welled in his eyes as he asked Rodolphe, "You saved him?"

"We did our best."

"Fred it's me… You know me," he said as he pleaded the return of recognition.

Fred was desperately searching for something, shaking his craned head until a reflection caught his clawed hand and bounced onto the table. Tiao shook his bum and gently pounced on the offensive light before Fred shouted "Tiao!" and embraced him as a long-lost brother.

Rodolphe cleared his throat and steadied them both now about his knee, "I believe you two might have some catching up to do and as Tiao's sprung a leak, we should accompany him back to the hospital wing, yes?"

"That sounds rite good t' me will yeh be joining us t'?" Fred asked.

Caralyn firmly shook her head as she signed, *I'm sorry but I can't. I'm not going back to that ward. Tiao, you go and get yourself fixed up.* Rodolphe carried the two out as Caralyn continued, *Firstly, don't stop eating on my account but when you do finish can we go somewhere in private and talk? And…* she didn't finish but hugged me tightly. *I don't know how long I've been here but seeing your face is the best thing that's happened so far.*

I hugged her back but it was such an effort as I was so tired I could have curled up on that hard backed chair and fallen asleep but seeing her again kept me awake. "I'm not hungry… I'll just… No I am, bear with me," I said and finished the remainder of the burrito before we left.

***

Caralyn checked that we were not overheard before closing the bedroom door. She turned with sudden expectancy, grabbed my shoulders and kissed me deeply. *Come with me* she signed and brushed my hair back.

I was dumbstruck not only by the unexpected kiss but the expectation, "I barely know you."

Does that matter? I feel so compelled to you. Don't you feel the same?

"I do, of course I do, and I would but I can't, not yet. They might have a way for me to go home."

Who is waiting for you at home? Her face was struck with a sneer. *I should have known there would be someone else.*

"There isn't." I held her shoulders before going in for a hug that should have conveyed reassurance and compassion but it was received with a quick reciprocation before she started to pace. "I really don't have anyone to go back to apart from the people in my flat share but I've messaged them at the front desk and they didn't reply. I guess that's why I've only half-heartedly pursued going back but I miss my old life and my hobbies. There's just something about all this chaos and unfamiliarity that's just not... I don't know." I slumped on the bed and grabbed her hands to guide her next to me as I tried to comprehend a version of events where we could all be together. She sighed impatiently then I was hit with realisation, "I've told Tiao he can come back with me to Earth. I'll take Fred too if he wants, so what if you came as well?"

Caralyn shook her head before getting up and signing, *I can't go with my vesti, I'll die. Do you want that?*

"Obviously not, that's quite dramatic." And a bit of a turn off but I kept that to myself as I added, "Could we change it to work somewhere else like it does here? Maybe Mei could help?"

No. I want you to come with me to the Gröfu Pallur.

"What? I'm not going back there. I trust these people, they fixed Tiao and Fred."

You don't understand, she signed and paced with speed, *Their price isn't worth it, not yet and I don't want to be always on the run and living in such a small room.* She outstretched her arms and touched wall and bedspace with just a slight lean in between. *In the Gröfu Pallur I have a huge apartment, a great job and okay I'm on call three out of seven but they pay me well so I can live a good life and I want that life to include dating you.*

I joined her pacing in frustration as I'd been striving so long to find her and be free. My Earth home honestly wasn't where that was going to happen so here was a chance to date someone and potentially be happy but I barely knew her and it could just be lustful compulsion. The only true thing I knew was that I didn't want to go back there. "What about all of us going back to your world, for a bit?" I asked almost knowing the answer.

You'd need a vesti to be able to survive. I don't know if you would even be compatible and if we did go back I might be drafted into an underwhelming war. She stood directly in front of me shaking her head before she continued, *We would be forced to live together without knowing each other and I'd struggle to keep a roof over our heads even with the chance we might get lucky and I could strike on a good engineering deal but I've already left my university training, my family and friends for this life.*

I held her and wanted to reason with her but auto pilot speech kicked in, "I'm sorry. I can't."

She shrugged me off and threw her hands into the air before signing, *We can't try to become something here so come with me Lori, this is your final chance.* She held out her hand as her breath quickened the longer her hand lingered. *Fine that lack of action is all I need. Stay in your limited life. I'm leaving. Goodbye!* She swept out of the room and out of my life only to leave the sting of instant regret and lost hope in my chest.

Chapter 24

Tiao scooted into our new shared bedroom and handed over an oil-stained beer mat which was bathed in Caralyn's scent. It was the last memento I had of her and so I held it tight to my chest until Tiao suddenly pointed at the back. In scrawled writing it stated:

[When they ask too much, seek me out.]

Tiao was curious as I stowed it safely in a shoe. He then glanced in my other shoes just in case I had hidden anything in them and said, "There's a safe in the wall, did you know?"

"There is but I might need this quickly one day and I'll probably forget the code to the safe."

Tiao swung his tracks out as he went through his own trinket collection and thoughtfully said, "I think I understand. I prefer having my box with me and I'm going to use it to help Fred remember." He flicked through a small bundle of notes and said, "These are some of the codes and errors that we hid from Jax when they didn't trigger anything and this is a fabric strip from our first ever guest," he rubbed it between his fingers before continuing, "Fred remembers nothing yet but next... Next, I could try this." He delicately handed over a ribbed piece of thin metal.

"A hair grip?" I asked.

"It is similar but it's a kettle pin for brewing teas, he enjoyed the sound it made," he sighed and closed the box with a look of longing.

"I'm sure it will work." I said.

He flicked off his tracks and stretched out his legs, "I do hope so but I have digressed, we were talking of Vilde's plan for you."

"Were we?" I replied as I flipped over the kettle pin a few times.

"Yes," he said expectantly as he shuffled in close and smiled politely. "You can talk of other things that have been keeping your mind in distraction if you prefer?" he said and nudged me.

"It's just that I don't know if I've done the right thing in bringing you here."

"They fixed us Lori, so of course it's the right thing. We would have been eradicated otherwise," he said as a whole-body shudder spread through the bed.

"It seems we aren't really free here either."

Tiao scooted off the bed and stored his box inside his belly area before wisely stating, "Lori, we are as free as we choose to be. Without a few restricted liberties the world would be in ruin. Someone's idea of freedom will always be different to another's but what matters is that we are all here together. We are alive, healthy and seemingly always in demand," he added and pointed at my finger notification.

"It seems it's time then." I flung out the notification and checked if Caralyn had sent any messages but for safety, she wouldn't be able to. At least that was a good excuse I could tell myself instead of the fact that she just didn't want to communicate with me. Tiao nudged me again and popped out a hologram of a clock and put his hand on his waist in frustrated timekeeping. "Alright bossy," I said as we left in search of just why I had been granted this way out.

***

The willowy twins rubbed their blackened eyeless sockets as they stared at fifteen screens housed in a concrete wall. Vilde had mentioned they had performed self-surgery to remove their eyes after hour upon hour of analysing advertisements, click bait and reaction videos as part of their testing regime, but still somehow they still saw everything.

Vilde's face was bathed in a blue haze of pixelated closed-circuit relay as she read aloud, "Lawnmower, gardener... Urgh, she must be communicating in unapproved code. We'll need to get a firm location and make sure she doesn't go rogue." She tapped the bottom corner of one of the screens making it flicker between greyscale and full colour lakeside landscape with a person scuttling through a busy crowd. "This one has cost too much to lose." Vilde tapped again as one of the twins changed the dials like tuning in an old radio underneath the screen as the room caught snippets of speech jarring with the blanked-out face but nothing became clear. Vilde sighed and said, "It's useless. This makes us another agent down. I'll have to send the birds to sort this mess out." She spun around in the chair twice before releasing a bird and hard stopping as she addressed me, "At least you're an easier fix." She got out a wooden tube with two holes in and commented, "Don't be shy, stick your fingers in." I did so as a sudden sharp blow came to the back of my head and I was instantly floored.

I opened my eyes onto a ceiling that shouldn't be spinning and asked, "Why did you do that?"

"The feeling will pass soon enough. Sorry but a filtration system is the only way we can get you out and about." She helped me up along with one of the twins who appeared genuinely remorseful for the sudden act of brutality.

The other twin clicked their fingers and highlighted a screen showing Bertie parking up a hearse outside our building before traversing the bridge in a sombre uniform and entered. Medical help was the thing I needed to make the world stop revolving but all I received was a shove as Bertie barged in and said, "Let's get your sea legs working and take off them wobbly boots. You'll need your wits about you for the ride." She helped me up from the front as Vilde pushed from the back.

Once out of the building and in the hearse, Bertie strapped me onto the back plate where the coffin would go as Vilde commanded, "Let's go." We slammed into what seemed like every pothole on the way making me groan as we entered a tunnel and the world ceased to have colour. The darkness soon made the motion sickness stop before we halted and the doors opened with a tidal wave stench of vomit and mud.

"Sit up," Vilde said as she unbuckled the straps. "The first time is the worst, the next time will be much easier as if flicking on a light switch. Come on."

Bertie helped me down onto squelchy ground that could have easily twisted an ankle as Vilde winced, not from pain but the sudden screams from above that ranged from absolute terror to pure joy. "Welcome to Sunvasse Island," she said as she closed the hearse doors.

The disorientation of my personal time and space now came from the unrhythmic radiance of high-paced rides flowing on tracks above us rather than the vertigo inducing slap on the head. I followed Vilde past a synthetic garish map of a fairground and over to a popcorn seller. "Any issues tonight?" she asked them as they poured butter over sizzling bursts of grain.

"Evening Vilde, much the same, those odd guards with the bowties have been around a couple of times and want to stamp everything. Öyggi suggested they need one big stamp that can cover the lot but apart from that, all's well. Who's your friend? Another from the Gröfu?"

"She's one from the birds," Vilde replied with such an authority the popcorn seller was stunned into silence. "Keep me posted," Vilde added as the person immediately continued their business. "Let's go this way," she said as she steered me away and nodded at people eagerly waiting to board the rides before she continued, "Sunvasse is part of the original testing facility where participants face exertion to generate a physical response. Let's have a go and don't worry your motion sickness shouldn't come back quickly."

"Okay."

Vilde opened a gate onto a sparking metal floor and directed us toward a two-seater car. She opened the door and shuffled in as seat belts automatically secured around us and Vilde said, "Stick your finger in here." I stuck it into a small metal hole as the lights dimmed and my stomach sunk as the car began to float.

"Racers, ready… Racers, steady… Racers, go!" shouted a pre-recorded voice as we were off and immediately slammed into from every angle. The roll cage on the car sparked as we skimmed across the roof while Bertie laughed at us from beneath. Vilde tried to keep up but as good of a driver as she was, she couldn't avoid another mid-air collision. We smashed and bumped our way through the carnage until finally spinning out into a corner just as the lights brightened and the car regained gravity.

"Look at that, you can already pay me back for that beer," Bertie said as she helped us both out and tapped my finger counter. "That's all I have time for or else I'll be late picking up the fallen socks." She stood tall and tapped her head as her whole body changed from sombre uniform to Hawaiian shirt and shorts.

Vilde cast a suspicious eye before she guided me along a wooden planked path over the dirt and said, "That's how it works. Do you understand the process?"

"I think so," I stated.

"It's a simple exchange of currency for accumulating data regarding your body response and this enables the creation of realistic enhanced synthetic life. So, how about a ride on the hooper or drop pop?"

"Erm," I said as a sock flopped out of my pocket and started retching slightly. "Where did that come from?"

Vilde stretched it out to maximum before allowing it to spring back into shape. "They get about. Perhaps the spinning mugs would be more suited to you as they are easy going?"

"Fine," the sock and I agreed, "But... I think this is broken," I continued as I noticed my finger currency counter still gaining credit.

Vilde helped me into a coffee cup and explained, "It's the after effect, it will pass. Now tell me, what do you see?"

"Except the brown padded seat and foamy exterior?" I asked as Vilde nodded. I shuffled some of the cream out of the way and said, "Those people seem bored whereas those seem moderately excited, and I think those over there might be having a picnic with champagne."

"You're right on all accounts, they are bored because when people get tested on the same thing their output reduces because the results don't vary enough." The ride started a mild swaying motion before a slight spin was added and Vilde started knitting. "Each ride has a minimum of three credits which is enough for a small meal but beings have to endure more extreme rides in order to receive the higher returns. See here," she said and pointed a knitting needle at my finger app. You've made twenty-eight already but next time around that will be less and then less again."

"So, you want me to make money for you? That's why you helped me get out?" I asked as I jerked to the side in moderate spin.

"No, we generate our currency by analysing data which is captured from purchases made here. That informs what stock or ride type is most favoured and then we feed that back to those who own this place and they create more versions in a loop of consumerism."

"And those at the Gröfu Pallur…?"

"As far as they know, this place doesn't cause a fuss and it makes their staff happy so this tourist attraction keeps going. We work in unison with the Ave's and go unnoticed." The ride came to a gentle stop and she opened the side of the mug for us to depart but everyone else remained. "It's classically easy money and relaxed on the stomach so they stay and this is where I will be later, just so you know," she added at my confusion before we went back to the squelchy floor.

My counter informed me that I now had thirty-nine credits in blue rather than the yellow currency the hotel sapped. We continued toward a glass building full of people suspended like rag dolls inside individual ovals. "They are all experiencing a rollercoaster over and over until they choose to stop collecting money. The ride changes monthly and occasionally there are themed ones from universal events." We paused underneath a trio of miniature rollercoasters with loops small enough to fit in the space of a refrigerator. "Clever concepts and constantly unpredictable," Vilde mused whilst one rattled passed us just as those inside the building jerked forward and terror whipped across their faces.

The ride continued in perpetual motion as the occupants contorted in their suspended circles as the smaller coaster carts completed a sharp turn before spiralling towards the finishing line.

Finally, the coaster stopped in miniature as some got out of their ovals while others dashed to the front and scanned themselves ready for another go. "Fancy a try or ten? You can have as many goes as you want."

"Not really," I said and bowed out as stomach wrenching rides were never really my thing.

"Not even the sky coaster? That's an actual physical ride and you'd get a great view of the fair? No? Something sedate instead?" Vilde said as she directed us toward a series of arches until we were stopped by a sweating being who gave her a bundle of socks before sharply departing. "More in need of rest and recuperation," she shook her head and stored them in a pocket. Then added, "Come on, the arcade is this way."

***

The arcade had rows of physical games of basketball, bowling and bop the balait flies. Parallel to which were rows of beings churning slot machines mindlessly until they achieved the ching-ding-a-ling of virtual melting credits hitting the bottom. "Are they gambling?" I asked.

"It would seem so as if they hit the correct algorithm then they obtain a menial output however I wouldn't suggest partaking as it is a slippery slope with payouts always against your favour," she replied as we passed the gaunt faces with soulless eyes awaiting the next big hit.

One spun around on their seat with glasses half drooping down their pallid face as they slurred, "Do I know you?"

"No, you don't," Vilde interrupted as they shrugged and spun to face the bright light destroying their soul. Vilde pulled me to the side of a bar and slapped the back of my head, "Sorry needs must. Maybe the filter is failing… No, that seems to be in-order so maybe it's me. We should split up, you take the left through the side and onward to the beach, there's a ride that should give you a hundred credits in one hit. As soon as you have that then come and find me."

"But where?" I started but she was already gone.

I followed her predetermined path passing players sipping on self-perpetuating drinks with autonomous bubbles floating through and no… I wouldn't start that again. Once I was back outside, I was surrounded with the ill acquired scent of sweat and sounds of screams as I headed over to the eight-foot-wide purple pebble beach. The tide didn't ebb or flow but swished around in a non-committal kind of way as I carefully walked over the stones and toward the only kind of ride there.

A line of swing seats attached to two thin poles stood stoically against the dusky sky. The beings on the seats idled with boredom busting screens as they occasionally made sporadic yelps and brief frustrated expressions. It seemed gentle enough, so I inserted my finger into the nearest hole and no sooner had my bottom hit the wood beneath than I was flung into the air. Rain droplets transformed into a bullet shower hitting my body with high velocity. I grabbed the ropes desperately and hoped the ground would reunite with my feet but it was already there. I tapped the pebbles with my toes and they were there beneath, but how could they be when the air was rushing so quickly past? I was very definitely sat in place as the rain eased and a single crack of sunlight pierced the darkening sky. I was up 75 credits by the time the swing took off again in its non-flight and I would have stayed on it longer until a familiar voice said, "Lori? Lori Wilkes is that you?"

Their voice crept into my ears and squeezed hope from my brain as they gained closer to me. Their clutching thin fingers almost grasped my shoulder as I stumbled off the swing and ran. I wasn't going to stay and talk my way out of this. They gave chase immediately but their ungainly legs struggled to keep pace over the pebbles. I burst through the doors of the arcade as the T'tip followed and left evasion as the only option but where to go? I ducked beneath tourists and side-stepped stalls until I ran past an out of service sign hung limply on abandoned house. I ducked under and entered onto a raised floor and desperately hoped it would serve a hideaway. The air became cold and my skin prickled with the sense of unease as I delved further inside and discovered it was a house of mirrors which reflected not physical changes but persona alterations. It left nowhere to hide as the T'tip entered behind.

"Lori, please stop running. I just want to talk!" Jax shouted as I struggled to find another exit but his voice was becoming clearer and louder until suddenly he was there in front of me with only the thinnest of glass walls separating us. Jax smiled and unfurled his scrawny fingers around the edges.

This was the end of my freedom.

I turned to run but the floor creaked and groaned.

"So you are there," Jax cooed as the glass finally gave way. In one swift movement his forearm dislodged it and the floor beneath me gave way. I was left trapped in an upright coffin-like space stuck between dusty floorboards and a glass ceiling. Jax strode over leaving scuffs marks above as he snatched the air, "Come out Lori, I can help you!"

He surely could see me below just as well as I could see him above but instead of gazing down he peered straight ahead. "We can get you back to safety. We can get out of this disgusting place and back into our care. You must be scared..." he said as he felt the walls and ceiling around him before taking a sip of water from his hip flask. "She will be here somewhere, let's get the security footage," Jax said to an obscured figure lingering behind as they stomped away but I remained until they were completely out of ear shot.

I startled as a sock bounded up and down on the glass. "Shh!" I hissed and still I didn't dare move. Instead I paused in deliberation as this wasn't a sit or jump situation but a question of staying or going? If I left, Jax could still follow but if I stayed, in this actually quite cramped space, he could return and I could be trapped once more.

The sock didn't wait for my deliberations as it bounded up and down soundlessly emitting a heat that made the glass melt away. I crouched down away from it but as soon as it was finished it curiously looked over the side and dangled down a loose thread to assist my escape. I opted to go and scrambled up and out of the hole like an ungraceful seal suddenly landbound. I followed the sock through the now oozing mirrors as the T'tip, T'tap echoed all through the house. Another floor above collapsed. I picked up the sock and pocketed it quickly as I ran back to Vilde with what little left I had to muster.

The coffee cups came to a calm stop but Vilde had changed seats to a skinny americano as she darned socks and stated, "They didn't follow you," with the usual motherly total awareness despite no explanation being given. She paused her knit to appraise me before saying, "The birds have been watching and you are safe but it's a concern your filter didn't last. You were checked for trackers so it's either awful luck or odd coincidence. At least the new layer of grime will form some kind of disguise."

"Who else knew we were coming here?" I asked as I made myself as small as possible in the cup and flicked off the dust.

"All of the Darners because I trusted that we have no double agent, but now there will be a reckoning. Excuse me," she said as a purple breasted bird beaked at her ear, "it seems we have a window to leave at the end of this ride so we will exit toward the left and meet with Bertie... Unless you want to chance it and earn more before you're seen again?" she asked as she stroked the bird.

"I'm ready to go now," I said but having the opportunity to stay came with an unusual sense of secured freedom as we left the neon cataclysm of the fair.

Bertie popped out of a hatch on top of a military tank as she called over, "Best get ourselves to the bar as with all those credits it's drinks on you!"

***

It was pandemonium as cards flew and beer slopped. Fred and Tiao were in a furious fast paced battle of recall as Rodolphe handed me a bowl of fried potato and said, "You've generated more than a months' worth of work in a single night."

"So how much do I need to go home?" I asked as I dipped a wedge in mayonnaise and avoided Tiao's quickened claw hand flipping a card.

"It is not for me to comment because it's different for everyone you know. I think for me, I would have to pay about thirty thousand as I'd want things just so."

"Like what?"

"A new identity, a better job, a nicer house in the countryside, whoa!" Rodolphe grabbed a glass just before it smashed as Fred furiously matched three in a row.

Fred bowed his head and said, "Ah, sorry, getting a bit excited as I'm reckonin' I'm getting the hang o' this."

Bertie reshuffled the cards and lay them out in randomised order before mouthing an apology to Rodolphe.

"As I was saying it could be a nice home you know?"

"They could give you that?" I asked as I tried another dip.

"I don't know but I'd want it and so if you wanted to go back to your normal home and your normal life well, it might be less, I don't know but," Rodolphe shrugged and then pointed to the door, "she's the one to ask."

"About ten thousand would settle transport back to Earth," Vilde said and handed over a new bunch of cards for Tiao and Fred before placing a bet with Bertie on who would win.

"So how long would it take to gain that amount of credit?" I asked.

Vilde and Rodolphe shared a side glance before she stated, "Probably a consistent year or two at the fair maybe less if you save it all up and spend very little."

"You'd miss our food too much," Rodolphe interrupted.

Vilde grabbed a wedge just as a bird twerted and landed on it. She whispered in its ear and it beaked at her nose in reply. "Sorry about that. You train them not to go to the toilet inside but still they can't use an alighting application to get out by themselves." She took the bird to a hatch in the wall then scanned it and ducked as Tiao sent a flurry of cards in their direction. The bird shook itself off in indignation before flying up the hatch. Vilde picked up the cards and returned them to Tiao then collected her bet before she said, "There's a potential to learn skills here but that takes time and from what you've said you aren't a chef, you aren't mechanically minded and the twins silence disturbs you."

"They make me rather uncomfortable as well," Tiao added quietly.

"At the moment we have the people we need but we always need agents. That would mean going back to the Gröfu Pallur where we'd generate money for you based on what you could achieve from requests. It would mean leaving the boys here and having an elaborate story about why you went away from your hotel," Vilde said as she paused to eat another of my snacks. "These really are good. What an intriguing concept. You won't like this but the ultimate currency earnings will be generated from what's within an elaborated or experienced period."

"You mean my memory?"

"Indeed, it is a commodity that is so valuable by exchanging interpretations you would not only earn enough currency to come and go as you pleased, but you could save nations and worlds."

Rodolphe set down his drink with a slop and exclaimed, "You must do this Lori! Don't you two agree?"

Fred and Tiao had stopped playing and were staring at Vilde and her sudden declaration, but neither added comment and nor did I. "It's the reason you're here with us. You were chosen to help before there are Miarmuit's in our skies too."

Tiao clicked his hands together as Fred nearly broke another glass but I knew it had always been a matter of time before someone asked and who better to give the information to than those who could get me home. "You won't like how we acquire your memory and I don't think these will either," she added and reshuffled the cards.

"I can endure it if it means going back home."

Chapter 25

I wasn't ready to be strapped into the minimalist designed armchair in the now repurposed mess hall but I knew the risks and no matter how severe they were or how many times the T's and C's were explained, I had agreed. Anything to get home, even in it's current state.

The lights had been dulled by fabric overcoats and the twins had placed several screens in the room for their keen observation. Tiao and Fred had both been given extension pillows so they could act as support along with a whole army of Darnstable socks waiting patiently at tables. Rodolphe busied himself creating a tray of drinks which Mei nearly knocked over on the way to open the door. Bertie nodded as she entered and the room held its collective breath as she uncovered a vivarium dome. Suddenly she recoiled and threw the blanket back over it in haste as she screamed, "I hate mice, they shouldn't have beards."

"Don't you mean vaspers? That's what they are, aren't they?" Mei asked and peeked under the blanket.

"What are you both talking about? It's plants?" Rodolphe said as he slopped a dash of lime in a glass while overlooking Mei's shoulders.

"Clearly, it's different for everyone, but what we all need to agree on is that it stays in there," Vilde said as she opened the door for two birds to fly in and land upside down on the ceiling overhead. Vilde nodded to Bertie who uncovered the dome once more as condensation had filled the glass but its contents didn't stir. Vilde painlessly connected some tubes into my arms before explaining, "We won't guide you and nor will your examiner as they are an impartial biological conduit and this is an informal gathering. Recall what you think is relevant and we will go from there, alright?"

I glanced to Tiao and Fred who both appeared tense, "I'm ready," I said.

"Everything is going on lockdown. Twins, it's your job to keep us safe and secure." She lifted a hand as shutters rolled down over the windows and locked into place. "It's for your protection Lori, and ours as we haven't done this in years-."

"And the last time wasn't… favourable," Bertie added.

"Don't worry. You are in control of this. Just recall the moments like we discussed before and remember the more you help us the more we can help you."

Bertie clicked a button on the radio which blasted out a jingle I wrote to create peace and calmness. Over and over it played as Tiao held me and whispered, "I am here with you."

Fred sprayed mist into my face as the music changed to tinkling spa music and the room became obscured as Mei pushed a mask over my face.

The roll of lift doors opened and closed again with the 'ding ding' of floor arrival or maybe it was someone else. Maybe this was their plan to entrap me but why bother with me?

I couldn't do this. I shouldn't have chosen it but did I even choose? I was too far under their chemical influence to resist now and couldn't move. My body was paralysed and finally they had me.

Chapter 26

3:28pm on a Sunday in April became one of those moments you would always remember exactly where you were and what you were doing. Currently I was catching up on ironing after a one-week vacation in the Acceptable Zones. Acceptable Zones meant that there were Unacceptable Zones and those were enforced by the newly formed united government after a swift decrease of icecaps and global warming had destroyed large parts of the Earth.

Of course, the scientists had reported things like anthropogenic activities and to cut daily carbon emissions for years but nobody really listened. Not even when the volcanos erupted, tsunamis battered the coast and the globe boiled because, for a while, it didn't really affect day to day living. It was a thing that happened to them over there and not us over here, until it did and it's impact had deathly consequences.

All of a sudden long forgotten diseases emerged and the spread of infections were the hot topic of conversation in the general public. The science community said it was relatively easy to medically manage the enteroviruses and caliciviruses until the soils released fauna mutating spores which quashed the supplies of medicine formulation. So where to go? People flocked away from lands that burned and moved to rainy climates as what once was harsher had been made fertile and safe, relatively at least.

As a jingle writer in a rainy clime it didn't change my life as I still went to work and sat in endless meetings but now I occasionally assisted with charity balls to help the sudden migrations and influx of people seeking solace. Except on this Sunday where I was halfway through ironing and sporadically watching the televised baking contest until it was automatically turned over for 'Breaking News!'

The reporter was disgruntled as if they weren't expecting to be in front of a camera this soon but remained professional as they cleared their throat and started from an autocue, "Don't be alarmed and remain very calm. You will not be able to turn over the channel," they paused to take a breath before continuing, "your full attention is now required. You will notice all other devices have been switched off." The iron made a 'pheww' as the last of the steam ran out. "Remember to remain calm. What follows is eyewitness footage that will assist you into this transition of enhanced civilisation."

***

At 11:36am the tide withdrew from the Miarmuit beach on the south coast before returning to swill around a spade cut moat. A child stood proudly observing their sandcastle and it was a good one too being capped off with turrets and a driftwood drawbridge, but there was something missing, something the child couldn't quite place their finger on. The tide withdrew once more but this time with a furious pace as the cliffs behind started to shake. The first turret cracked and fell into the moat as the child called out to their guardian but their cries were lost in the groan of earth. Sunbathers whipped up their towels in a sandstorm flurry as they fled away from the cliff edge while succulents fought hard to cling onto falling earth. Tufts of grass were sucked inward and the castle was reduced to sandy rubble as chunks of earth crashed down just inches away from the child.

Quickly they were swept out of danger and carried over to a crowd which had gathered in collective 'what the f-?' mentality as mutters of "Are you okay hun?" and "What happened?" "Did you see that?" started to fly.

"I did," an innocent voice came amidst the middle, "I saw it all. But what is that?" the child asked and pointed over toward a ball of lightening hanging in the air beside the cliff rubble. It lingered until all eyes were drawn to it then imploded in on itself casting sparks into the remaining cliff to reveal a strand of metal.

The crowd appointed the child's guardian to act as leader and they brushed off a layer of burnt soil around the steel. They stopped as sunlight scorched their hand. The soil still pattered as the cliff started to rumble and the crowd collective moved. A large metal pyramid shape started to emerge, forging its own path out of its dirty surround. The guardian fell back as it floated overhead and caught glimpses of runic shadows etched into the solid bulk before they were bleached by the blaring sun. The metal prism hovered at head height above the crowd for long enough that human curiosity took hold. When standing and staring at the floating prism wasn't enough the person with the loudest mouth and biggest ego arrogantly said, "I don't know what all the fuss is about," and gave it a sharp prod.

The bulky prism spilt along its longest edge and unveiled a slimy yellow hand which poked the person back before reaching out toward the child. Their guardian stood in the way and with a more cautious hand reached up.

Nobody knew that this would be the moment that would change history forever and the exchange passed quickly and politely in the form of a handshake. The prism then closed and floated up towards the sky as the child's sibling shouted, "I got it all recorded!"

And so it began, over the following days and weeks a total of 127 metal prisms were reported to have emerged throughout the globe, each opening briefly to shake hands with those nearby before floating up in the sky to stoically remain. They were officially named the Miarmuits after the beach where they first emerged and became as obtrusive in the landscape as a wind turbine. Pilgrimages of those wanting to be the chosen few who gained their handshake flocked along with the military and scientists who began performing tests to try to understand their purpose. The Miarmuits remained unengaging and even a local novelty for some.

Until they weren't.

***

It was sometime after lunch on a Wednesday and I was editing the final cadence of a jingle for a prospective transport company as my screen froze and there was the same bedraggled reporter sat atop a breaking news banner. "Hi, I'm Etch Bletchley from Global News and we interrupt your daily activities to bring you this important announcement. A Miarmuit is opening. I repeat, a Miarmuit is opening. Please join us as we go live to our correspondent in the village of Cresthrope-on-Piddle in the Unity of Kingdoms."

"Thanks, Etch. Hi there, I'm field correspondent Gina Rhodes and I'm here with local self-appointed Miarmuit custodian Bill and his wife Dora. Over to you Bill."

"Me? Right, talking into that recorder there. Okay," Bill readjusted his flat cap and sipped his tea before he said, "Aye, the Miarmuit," he pointed very obviously toward the thing that loomed so much it consumed a significant amount of the screen before continuing, "it just stopped to look at my begonias then settled right there up above us. It's been there three to four weeks but I said to our Dora, 'That'll be me done. Yes, after working all my life and only just retiring at the age of eighty years young I'm to be eaten up by a bloody pyramid.' But it hasn't been bothered, if anything, it seems awful interested in my allotments and turns to watch me get the weeds up of a morning. Caused us no bother at all, even when its hand poked out, it just give us a friendly wave, didn't it Dora?"

"That's right our Bill. It's been more respectful of our privacy than them science folks at least," Dora said as she glared at the growing crowd around the police cordon and blundered back inside as Bill stood still proudly pointing at the metal prism above their hedgerow.

The screen panned back as the reporter took the reins, "Thanks there to Bill and Dora. Now there has been quite the commotion here in Cresthrope-on-Piddle as we have exclusive groundbreaking access to this event. Come with me as we talk to Inspector Isa Jellink from the national police…" the reporter trailed out as they stood agape at what lay before them. "Or… Oh gosh, it's opened again. It's really opened!" she shouted.

The largest Miarmuit in the country was reaching out and beckoning those around bathed in an intense yellow. The officer walked forward with curious caution as the Miarmuit floated down to meet her and placed a hand on her, lifting her so much that her uniformed body spun around and to face the crowd. Her eyes rolled back and mouth grew slack for a moment before pure bliss spread over her face but the puppetry was out of sync as she addressed the world with ill-timed mouth. "We who have become known as 'Miarmuit' greet you with open arms and well-meaning presence. You have suffered greatly in manmade mishaps and now we come to you at your time of need once more to forge our union in the search of homeostasis. We created the great oxygenation event for your world two billion years ago which is now at risk. That being just one among other significant events which calls for the need to quell the bacterial storm unleashed on this world." The police inspector was gently lowered to the ground unharmed and turned and bowed to the Miarmuit before calmly shaking its hand.

"Tell us, tell us what that felt like?" the exasperated reporter said as she ran alongside the crowd jamming the microphone into any open space that was filled with officer.

The inspector had a glossy appearance as she glanced at those around her like she was seeing them for the first time but continued toward the scientists as the reporter chased close at her heels, "Please, can you describe in words what just happened?"

"It's hard to accurately report but I believe we have been given a gift. It's like a new kind of knowledge I don't understand but it's blazing in my head with phrases and formula for space grown proteins and jumbo phages or something. It's so clear but meaningless but if I tell you Mx, I think you might understand," Isa said to one of the scientists and for a moment there was a quiet as they muttered together until she was swamped by the community trying to get a snippet of the experience.

Bill and Dora stood arm in arm like proud parents on the sidelines as the reporter swung back to the camera and stated, "So there you have it… we have witnessed a tremendous moment in history. The Miarmuits will save us with knowledge and unity that starts here in Cresthrope-on-Piddle. My goodness what a day. So that's back to you in the studio."

The screen flickered back to my editing desk and we all took an unofficial break to discuss what the heck had just happened, but that only lasted the boil of a kettle before people went back to their schedules without really caring. It was if the world turned a blind eye to the new alien life form above us and assumed them as a 'nil threat' because what bad person would shake the hand of another in front of everyone and promise world peace?

***

Skip forward approximately two weeks and anyone who previously had reservations about the Miarmuits soon adhered to herd mentality. And who could blame them when their promises turned into ideas for actual cures for diseases, weather easing proteins, and radiation reduction which worked to make the Earth a little more tolerable. Alright, it changed the colour of our skies at night and the frequency of ball lightening grew as the Miarmiuts changed and shifted position, but they weren't harming anyone so who could care? Other Miarmuits opened and partially melted back on themselves to reveal their yellow mould innards before briefly connecting with a human subject and transferring an insight into innovation. Those people would be heralded for being chosen even if it was seemingly at random and it created a global social pressure to be the next one given the gift of salvation. People travelled far and wide to any still closed, just so they could be the vessel to assist the world and that was how Earth was now, the majority of people working in cohesion and nobody panicking.

Then people started to disappear.

"It's rumour mongering to say disappear," they'd say, "they are on a prolonged holiday for their rest and relaxation," they'd convince themselves, "It couldn't possibly be the Miarmuits and if it was, well some sacrifices should be made as they've given us so much," they'd add in full support. So the theme was shut up and put up and because I'm not and never have been a rebel rouser it was easier to leave the shouting for other people but it wasn't right and I hated it. Anguished cries came not from the impoverished but the ultra-conglomerates when the stock markets broke and became beyond bearish but people didn't listen or care because it was justice for those who had denied them loans or repossessed their homes. People had a standardised rate of living given by the implementation of the global government so didn't want to cause a fuss. There was even plentiful food and resources because the population was slowly deteriorating but that was over there and not yet here.

It came to a point where I just couldn't stand it any longer but how could I voice my opinion and stand up for what was right when it would be engulfed in a sea of thousands and lost in a single dismissive wave?

***

On a drizzly Friday Jorge and I were delivering Miarmuit inspired art works which had become increasingly more popular and purchased by Eris for one of her charity balls. Eris directed us in a hushed voice said, "The Miarmuit took the barrier guard into the air and we thought it was going to give him some kind of information but it consumed him. Then closed and went on." She didn't wait for a reply but redirected us to place the art piece in an oak panelled room and made sure it was secure before continuing, "He'd been talking for weeks about how they didn't seem right but no one listened. Then his replacement showed up the very next day like it had been planned, even his family didn't want to know my thoughts. It was like they were okay with it." She shook her head in disbelief and glanced around the curtain.

"Is it the first one they have taken from here?" Jorge asked as he dusted off a corner of fabric from the covered sculpture.

"It is, but in the next town there was a window cleaner who was saying about a whole family being taken in the west-," she stopped as someone entered the room as the three of us tried to look inconspicuous.

Jorge took up the reins "Yes, the Scandinavian influence has held us in a grip for such a long time in the art community, from the lustrous lines to…," the greying waiter apologised and left as Jorge added, "you were saying?"

"We need to fit in, or appear to, and this artwork should go some way toward that," Eris finished as Jorge unveiled his piece. "It's excellent, I love the take on surreal punk mixed with an edge of documentary on life. How's that sound for getting the money flowing?" Eris added as she examined the sculpture in detail.

"It's a comment on the fact that every media outlet is broadcasting in the Miarmuits favour. They have even appeared as background actors on the soap operas. I swear the next will be a news reporter themselves," Jorge said as he eyed the room for more intruders.

It was then I finally broke, "It's a mass blindness, not accurate reporting. It's like a pandemic without the panic buying, rioting or lock downs. Even though more people are fleeing or disappearing, no one is doing anything about it."

Eris glanced at me and whispered, "But we are. The Bi-annual ball can be increased to a quarterly if we can acquire the right wallets and egos in need of righteousness. So, are you both in? I won't take no for an answer?"

"I already am," Jorge said and winked as he held his hand out in waiting for my committal.

"I am, but I don't know what I can do to help."

"Please. Don't give me that," Jorge scoffed, "You can write the music and you could highlight companies or people on your business trips that might be of use to us, so you need to get schmoozing girl!"

Eris's face glowed with mischievousness as she announced, "We should start now. Why don't you stay for dinner?"

Jorge tutted and said, "I can't. I have an evening with a model and half set dress."

"Are you sure that..." I started but he cut off the interruption.

"I am sure. You two can discuss your plans of quiet rebellion together and fill me in on the juicy details after..." he stopped as the hall door closed with a not-so-subtle smack immediately putting an end to the conversation but a start to fundamental scheming against the Miarmuits.

Chapter 27

I emerged from memory hounded by screams from Vilde, "Get up! Get out of that chair! We haven't got long."

"She's right, they found us! We need to get out before this flower takes over," Bertie shouted as she fought hand to leaf as the dome smashed and out burst the psychiatric plant. It encompassed half the room and was brazen against any attempts to subdue. It almost seemed to lap up the weed killer applied by a flurry of birds as it ensnared my legs but I ripped it away. My right hand twitched as three different types of credit quickly spun through in considerable amounts as I shook off the sap. "You don't know how useful you've been," Vilde said helping with the vines. It should have been Tiao but I couldn't see him in the dying petals. The twins stripped back those at the very top of the room with ease as they uncovered cameras and screens set for vigilante protest. "Set the VI for me," Vilde commanded as green boxes started to highlight any movements inside and outside the compound then created counterpart pixel dense images of faces floating in a criminal line up.

"Where are my friends?" I asked as finally the plant was wrestled back into a new dome.

"We are right here," Bertie shouted as she emerged valiant picking out bits of rotting flower from her now mohawked hair.

"Tiao and Fred, I mean."

"Charming!" Bertie sneered then flung herself over the dome with crocheted scarf flaying. "Bloody thing. Stay in there!" she said and fought with what appeared to be the outline of a face. "You were right, soon as you went under the damn thing changed into a humanoid then back to plant but it's transport we need to focus on now," she said making the edges extra tight. "Lori your *other* friends are safe and have already gone to our secondary place of operations, although with much objection, so it's just us…" she paused as the twins bowed out of the room then added, "just us three now and we have to go."

"Why? What's happening? What…?"

Bertie rolled her eyes and added, "Always with the questions. I'll get the car ready."

Vilde got me up with an unnatural strength for someone of her slight stature and rapidly explained, "They tracked us down, I'm not sure how as we've gone under the radar for years, but as soon as you made the psych connection we caught a parasite infiltrating our system." She paused to call to her birds then led us through corridors full of cardboard boxes being hoisted from hospital room to the corridor with haste. "Those who are too unwell or unsafe to travel will stay behind and become our cover story. Whoa! Watch yourself there!" She shoved me out of the way of an oncoming swinging box before grabbing three screens and explaining, "We need to wait for Bertie, we will see her approach on these, but… ah, it seems she has come under a 'spot of bother' as Fred would say." A hoist pelted into a wall in the opposing room scuttling a box of socks everywhere. "Excuse me, I'll sort this. Keep an eye on the birds they will direct the action and shout me when you see her parking up."

The low resolution screen blurred then fizzled and sharpened around two figures making their way up a cliffside in the murky weather. Neither were Bertie as one had an unusual gait and the other was more purposeful but seemed to keep half a pace behind. Both were turned toward the sea with jackets pulled tight as fog rolled over the tufted ground. The taller of the two bristled and stated, "I'll get rid of this inclement weather." A longer than average arm scooped up a handful of rolling mist and condensed it into tiny tornadoes which cleared the area the more they span. The image glitched as a wing entered the screen but cleared and focused behind the two, the taller seemed to take a long swig from a hip flask before saying, "At least we can see when these miscreants are coming." They had both settled in amongst some boulders as the back of their heads were just visible over mint green moss. The taller continued, "Hmpf, we better not be waiting long but, in the meantime, I will say that you have performed your duties well as another one entered into the database within three days is quite the achievement."

"It's what I do best," the shorter said with a familiar voice.

"It's something that you do with moderate talent but you do not perform at your best when you lose those you are supposed to be conscripting. You shall however put your wrong doings right as this is where *she* will be and it falls to you to achieve that end point. Although it seems she knows more than we were expecting and the others have already clawed their way to it." The taller shuddered as the screen froze and speech was replaced by a twert of a bird.

Vilde was still shouting coordination instructions to those relaying hoisting equipment but it was probably important she saw this so I called her name just as the screen regained connection from a different angle.

The shorter one shrugged their shoulders and said, "The majority of my gains have achieved low hosting fees and high outputs. The revenues are at their peak and the profits speak for themselves."

"Spoken like a true recruiter, but in this case the profits will be insignificant if *she* is led astray, excuse me." The figure didn't even need to bend at the hips as their arm dangled in the moist grass as dew was transferred from fingers to face. "If she stays with them the only option is complete recycling unless your coercion is successful and I'm sure you don't want another one wasted away and spat back into menial working society or worse?"

The shorter one shook their moist head and seemed to consider their answer carefully, "Sometimes I wonder what the right thing is. Whether extraction and removal is best or if they could actually do some good for her?"

"Don't become sentimental, it isn't in your nature… we are being watched." A hand swept back at the bird who was filming before the face of a familiar was present.

"Jax!" the shorter shouted, "It's just a bird. Leave it!"

"But he isn't," Jax said as the image span around and showed none other than Tiao with a bird resting on his head crouching in the ground trying not to be seen.

"You shouldn't be here!" Jax snarled as the bird flew up haphazardly but Jax turned his attentions to Tiao and dragged him kicking and shouting toward the cliff edge.

Tiao's tracks pounded against Jax as he pleaded, "Please Sir, don't hurt me. Mr Jax, you know it's me. Please? I'll go back. I just…I'm not here to harm or argue."

"You're right, how is a robot like you ever supposed to argue against humanoid intelligence?"

"I would not presume and I only ever wanted to help as any artificial intelligence should."

Jax put him down but kept a firm grip, "I bet you didn't even want to be here, did you?"

"I… I didn't. You are quite right. I am sorry for the inconvenience," Tiao muttered.

"Don't be, I'm not sorry for yours," Jax spat and with one swift kick, Tiao's little body was booted off the cliff and disappeared from view.

I collapsed down the wall as the shame and guilt made my entire body numb. I cried and grasped at the screen wishing it was fabricated and untrue.

Vilde rushed into the room with socks falling out of her pockets, "What's happened? Have you seen Bertie?"

"They… They kicked him into the sea," I sobbed.

"What? Who?" she asked as she turned the screen around and replayed that awful moment, "Jax! I hate him so much and the other," she flipped the screens which showed the merciless grin of Jax and Casey clawing at the thin air.

I had been betrayed.

Without time to contemplate, a box filled hoist collided into the screens, however instead of breaking they switched to show me and Casey stuck in the lift the very first time we met. My stomach jumped from the nauseous memory as the lift jolted and I watched myself stagger forward just as Casey struck me from behind.

My breath caught in my throat in real life as I watched myself lying unconscious in a pool of blood while he communicated with the buttons. He then checked my pockets and removed my phone, with a swift stomp it was smashed and stowed then he ruffled his hair and shuffled into a corner feigning fear as I awoke.

No time to process. The screen changed to a montage of awkward conversations when we were booking in, the confusion of what to eat, then the image overlaid with other guests in a similar hippo bartender scenario as some copied my disgust whereas others were intrigued at the tentacle creature on Casey's face. Each time the creature keeper received more currency, each time a different person and each time the same situation.

Still no time to process. The screen flickered to Casey in the nightclub watching as Vilde's face called for freedom before he started to persistently replace bracelets of the fallen. Another screen change and we were back in the car wreck with the doctor, the monoliths and Casey desperately calling to report the incident. And so it continued over and over, these public moments where things just weren't right until finally Vilde shut down the screens and asked, "Are you okay?"

"No." My head was in overdrive as quick comprehension mixed with adrenaline hit. "He was always a bit odd but I didn't… I wasn't expecting…" words failed me from the tragic overload of the loss of Tiao and the betrayal of Casey.

"I'm sorry you had to witness that, I didn't know you knew him or I'd have told you sooner. I'm sorry Lori," Vilde said.

I jumped up and brushed Vilde off, "Are you? Because for all I know you're in on whatever this is as well. This has made up my mind, I'm going home. I've lost Caralyn, I've lost Tiao and I've lost Casey. What is there here? Awful rides and being chased. No thank you. At least in the Gröfu Pallur I had some freedom and I had… them. How am I … No, how are *you* even going to tell Fred?"

The colour had drained from her face as she gave swift instructions to her birds before righting herself and stating, "I think we need to see if Tiao is actually gone. My birds will do what they can but our team will look for him. For now Lori I need you to suspend your distrust and follow me one last time-." She was cut off by an obnoxious honk of a horn before she continued, "Bertie is here." Somewhat reluctantly I followed her out along the shallow plinth to find a recovery vehicle being held by tentacle-like arms. "Just put one foot in front of the other," Vilde said as she pushed me forward toward a grinning Bertie but my feet were cemented as the ground seemed to have ran off far below.

But what did it matter now if I fell? No, what was I thinking? That was far too melodramatic. Of course it mattered and I had to find Tiao and save hope that by some chance he wasn't dead.

"Vilde in the front and you in the back. Oh, seatbelts fastened if you please," Bertie shouted and hastily steered the truck down and into oncoming traffic whilst jamming the radio on.

"They are still hacking into the main unit. Damn it!" Vilde shouted as she shoved one hand on the door to steady herself, "Seven agents have been placed in suspension while we 'investigate' so the only way we can stop the onslaught is to shut down."

"But in good news, your golden bird has found us," Bertie said as she cracked open a window for it to fly in. An extravagant bird landed on the dashboard and shook it's golden mane before twerting and then quickly leaving with a flourish. "We are being followed," Bertie said as she implemented avoidance tactics.

"I didn't know you communicated with them as well?" Vilde asked.

"I don't. I'm assuming that's what it was saying as we are driving into oncoming traffic and there's two overly fast bicycles hot on our tail," Bertie said as she grabbed at some lost feathers.

"You have plenty of those. We need to depart, now!" Vilde instructed.

Bertie nodded and span her keyring before turning to me in the back. "This is going to be about trust. The bottom of the vehicle is going to fall away and we will be completely fine," Bertie informed me so calmly as if relaying the weather, which was currently rushing wind as we fell screaming onto a short wheel base. A leather sofa appeared under my bottom along with two armchairs in the front to support Bertie and Vilde as the rest of the vehicle developed around them. "Campervan... wasn't expecting that," Bertie said then filtered into queueing traffic with excitement. "You okay Lori?" she added.

"Can't we look for Tiao?" I asked once nausea had passed but rage still consumed me.

"We have just transposed two major roads so unless they can fly, they aren't going to be anywhere near us," Vilde informed as she went back to scanning the surrounding area.

"We are only seven astos away anyway, but what do you mean go looking for Tiao?" Bertie asked as she hit the brakes hard.

"Urgh, he got booted over the edge of a cliff."

"What? Is that right?" Bertie asked Vilde who meekly nodded. "Well, that explains your face, but I can't go looking in this, I'll find something else for just me as it'll be quicker that way. Hang on little buddy, hang on," she added under her breath then with a marked increase in speed we set off.

We skidded up onto two wheels barely avoiding the turtle guards as they shouted for our immediate stop but were ignored. "Can't you drop us off more discreetly? Or at least on top of the vault?" Vilde asked.

"Hang on," Bertie said as she grabbed onto a purple pole and we were pulled away from the road and flung into the sky until landing with a suspension snapping 'bang' onto the cliff. "Bloody hell. That was the best I could do," she said as the door flung open and Vilde was out and offering a hand to me. No sooner did my foot touch the ground than Bertie blazed away.

"Nice view from up here, isn't it?" Vilde said, "shame we don't have time to enjoy it. Help me find an opening to the safe house hatch. It should be somewhere around here but keep low as we don't want to be seen. Wait, what is that you're doing?"

"A squat," I replied as my shorts strained from the position and I headed toward the edge. It was the same cliff Tiao was so rudely removed from, he was probably just waiting for us or just looking out at the sea before Jax intervened.

"He won't be here Lori," Vilde said as she pointed toward the beach. "It seems the lifeguards have increased their observations after my last visit up here." She proceeded with her crab-like walk until she suddenly dived to avoid a spiralling wingmirror. "Hope that wasn't from Bertie," she said and pointed over to a cloud of grey smoke flourishing in the distance.

I crawled beside Vilde and followed her gaze, the unspoilt beach was the same as it always had been with military sunbathers present and unstirred by the small combustion in the sky. The lifeguards were relaxing in their wooden hut while sweaty waiters ran but the cliff and beach had a distinct lack of Tiao. I peered over the edge but nobody, not even one with solid metal frame, would have been able to withstand such a perilous drop. Even if his body were to avoid the torso piercing rocks the violent waves would have of engulfed him immediately.

Numbness filled my body and I wanted to be sad, I needed to be sad, but I couldn't as all emotion had left and was replaced with adrenaline which told me to kick the clammy hand grabbing my ankle. "Get off me!" I screamed but it was too late, I was being dragged deeper into the undergrowth.

Chapter 28

The sun was the only object in the sky casting its warmth onto the beach which was shut out with the snap of an umbrella. Mei flourished a set of pink wires into the fabric underneath the umbrella in preparation for the task that lay ahead and said, "You've still got scuff marks on your trousers from where I pulled you, I am sorry."

"It's fine," I replied, "I'm just sorry Tiao didn't find his way back to the hatch in time." I idled with a lounger a short way from the sun bathers who all turned to the left to catch the burning rays.

"Tiao was a clever little one but he still may have been the reason that we were found and followed." Mei took a small wrench out of their chest to readjust their contraption before adding, "he was very brave."

That was the phrase people say to the bereaved, "They were very brave," then next would follow, "they were a happy soul and a lived a good life," but did he? Did Tiao live a good life stuck in an apartment? I didn't voice the question but instead asked something I had wanted to for some time, "So, have you ever successfully sent anyone home?"

Vilde pushed down her sunglasses and started to apply liberal amounts of sun cream as she said, "They don't often come back to tell us. We might send them to their standard universe or another as the science isn't accurate but no news is good news. Are you happy to go ahead with the plan?"

"I suppose I'm ready, but it won't be easy and before you say, I'm not making excuses."

"Good. We have everything in place so let's hope he shows up." She handed over a fully packaged beach bag. "We have already crossed a bridge of ethics that never needed constructing so let's just get on with it," Vilde said as Mei stuck up a hand and fingers silently counted down from six…

five…four…three…two…one…

There on cue and hitting his mark was Casey walking over with accurate gusto barely creasing his pressed linen suit.

I waved and shouted, "Hey Casey, over here!" Then filled my face with absolute joy and avoided the muscular twitches of stress by getting to my feet and meeting him seven strides away from Vilde and Mei.

Casey staggered in his plimsols on the sand and his briefcase nearly hit the floor as the uniformed sunbathers all turned at the same time, "Sorry, wasn't expecting that. Hello Lori! They said you'd gone missing and I was so worried about you but then when you messaged and… just come here," he placed his briefcase down with a bump on the sand before holding out his arms to embrace me.

"I've just put sun cream on and wouldn't want to ruin your suit sorry," I said stopping him at arm's length as the drain of the pretence was apparent.

"Seriously? But I haven't seen you in forever. They said you were lost?" he asked as his arms dropped hopelessly.

"I've been having a lovely holiday, but I just paddled out and got caught in a side drift for a while. I'm fine and back here on this beach with *you* now."

"I'm glad you're back and we can finally go home."

Vilde emerged from underneath an overlarge sunhat and asked, "Are you going to introduce us, Lori? In fact you don't need to. It's Jessie isn't it? Last time we met you had very different assets, do you remember?"

Casey held up his hand to his forehead to shield the bright sun as he dismissively stated, "I don't recognise you and I don't know what you're talking about, I'm Casey."

Vilde lowered her sunglasses and smirked, "That's the name at the moment is it? Fits you. I suppose the ever-changeable J.C. would tire of cycling from Jessie to Jason so why not be a new person?"

"What? Do you know it doesn't matter. Lori, we should go," Casey said as he gestured toward the road.

"Casey, I'm sorry to be the bearer of bad news but Lori isn't coming back to the Gröfu Pallur because you are going to let her officially go out into the wilderness."

Casey appeared bemused and failed to find a response but relief from conversational reply came from another shift in the sunbathers who rhythmically altered all eyes to Mei's brief signal.

A 'buzz' sounded from mid-way along the beach which became louder and louder as a waiter came galivanting up the strip. He turned short of the ball pitch and headed straight for the lifeguards minding their own business as the waiter expertly launched two drinks at the hut causing the lifeguards to stumble back inside. The waiter pinned the door shut with his tray reflecting the sunrays onto the beach and screamed into the sky. That marked the completion of stage two of the plan and done in timely perfection.

Vilde pushed her sunglasses back up and slurped her drink as if nothing had happened.

Casey asked, "Do you think they are okay? We should tell someone about it don't you think?" Vilde snapped him a look as he continued, "maybe not then. Lori, are you sure this is a holiday?"

"I'm sure," I said as my smile slipped.

"And are you sure you don't want to go back to the Gröfu Pallur? You have that choice you know?"

"She is sure!" Vilde snapped.

"I guess you can at least show me around and introduce me to your *nicer* friends, maybe?" Casey asked as he picked up his briefcase and glanced over his shoulder.

Vilde swung her legs over the edge of the sun lounger as a sock flopped beneath the chair. "Casey, Casey, Casey. Time and time again from the hotels to the shopping centres you've seen it all, haven't you? You and me both know it hasn't changed much apart from the new insertion of synthetic life and subservice. The major change I'm seeing is you and not just your name as I believe you're more popular now," she said and pointed to his finger notifications which were spamming so hard that his hand had doubled in size.

"It's just my car, I've asked it to wait. Oh, I guess it got bored..." Casey said as he hid behind his briefcase. The car swerved onto the beach with the bowtie turtle guards chasing behind in the sand drifts until they were side swiped by Fred wielding a thin pole. The car came to a sudden halt as Mei threw a contraption onto the ground causing the sand to erupt and engulf it in completely. Only the sunroof was visible in the foreground with Fred pinning down the guards behind.

A hand pushed open the sunroof and out came Bertie who winked at us then waved to the waiter who instantly smacked the back of his head. Within moments the face changed to that of a triumphant Rodolphe, his back still barred the escape route of the lifeguards as he flung a trio of socks onto a red surfboard. The socks flipped it over and rode it all the way to Bertie who hopped on with ease and made her way out to sea with applause from all now spectating.

That marked the next stage of the plan was complete and so far, all was going well.

Vilde took another slurp of her drink and hinted that it was my turn to speak once more so I took a breath and summoned all charm and resilience into my pre-prepared speech, "That was cool right? Do you see how teamwork can help, rather than hinder? Look Casey, you have been harvested for months if not years and they have been recording your reactions and scraping away your knowledge and for what? We don't know if they are planning on using it against the universe or on some form of computerised intelligence but either doesn't fill me with joy. Doesn't it bother you because it bothers me and now, now we have a chance because Vilde says she can get us out. Don't you want that? Don't you want to join us?" I finished and tried pouting.

"Does she really say that? Because she can't and I don't want to go because it's amazing here, well not here on this beach but in the Gröfu Pallur. You can say what you like about the knowledge extraction but it solves crime, it saves people's lives and assists others to become a version of themselves who are completely useful once their limit is done. Why wouldn't you want to be a part of that?" He started to edge back.

Vilde threw her drink down and said, "Once their limit is done and they become trapped inside their mind and forced into roles they have barely any control over."

"That's not the case. People go home once they are done."

"They don't! We… We are trapped!" screamed one of the trio of beings holding a ball so tightly it popped. Their counterparts looked panicked and dragged the person toward the boardwalk.

"The sun must have got to them as no one gets harmed," Casey dismissed then added, "before you say it, I know your last test went wrong but so did mine and they can fix it for the future. Come on, you've trusted me so far, so just come back and live the life of luxury with Tiao and Fred."

"Tiao?! Don't you dare speak his name! You could have saved him but you let him die. I'll never trust you again," I screamed as my outer shell melted into authenticity.

Casey seemed to weigh up the situation before him as he clutched his jangling briefcase. It seemed to dawn on him that he was outnumbered and overruled as he said, "Guess you know about that then, so I'll give you a final chance to make up your mind. You asked me to come here to see where you've been staying and the life you've been living and I am here. I can really see what that is now, it's not an escape it's just another group paying for your time and knowledge. What does it matter if you are being paid at the Gröfu Pallur or the QuinXe Company on Earth or even here? There is no home for you without complete excavation or burnout so your only option is to give us the information we need and come back. Now!"

"You can't get her back with a buried car," Mei shouted and readied another device.

"That's just one car in carpark of many," he scoffed as he flicked away more spamming notifications.

"Casey aren't you missing your family?" Vilde asked as the subtle hint of pain crossed his face. "Or did they at the Gröfu Pallur choose you because you don't have any?"

"They choose people carefully based on several things."

"Why me then?" I asked not really wanting an answer.

"It could have been anyone in your office that day. You aren't special, you are just one of millions of people who witnessed the Miarmuit's take control. Our management paid your boss for you to all fill out a staff survey and you all said you'd be willing to answer further questions. You were there at the right time and saw the right thing Lori, that's all."

Just being there, that wasn't a good enough excuse for the total upheaval of my life but often the way of fate. I was hopeful, in some bizarre way, that I had been chosen like some kind of herald or someone they wanted for a higher purpose but that was selfish and egotistical. "It had crossed my mind that it was something to do with my mother and sisters involvement." Casey and Vilde's quizzical looks showed it wasn't so I settled for his response and asked, "And were you just there at the wrong time with no one to miss you?"

"I consider it the right time. But," He stopped and shook his hand before glancing out to the water's edge, "no one wondered where I went until deadlines were missed. No one cared that I had gone. I couldn't have the life I do here at home. Urgh! Shut up! Just let me do my job!" Casey suddenly shouted and fingered his ear until out popped a tiny screaming bug.

Mei rolled off a sun lounger and grabbed the bug before throwing it to the inappropriately dressed twins posing as sun bathers. They dropped the bug into a used glass which amplified the sound, "Tell her that the tests will resume as interviews only and make it known that we are sorry we put her under so much strain or at least make it sound convincing that we care… Offer a room upgrade or… something? Are you even listening to me? I am your manager and you will follow what I say! Casey? Casey?" the voice asked.

"Who's that?" Vilde asked.

"Sounds like Jax," I replied.

Casey shrugged and said, "Doesn't matter who it is but you heard the offers. Now, don't let me be the only human-."

"Human?" Vilde shouted, "You are not that. You steal people who could have been something, who could have given back something. They didn't choose to be here, you did."

"Casey, Casey?" The cocktail glass screamed. "Casey respond now or believe me, it'll be your apartment stripped and your pay cut! You shouldn't have even gone back for her…" The twins cupped the glass as Casey tried to grab it but stumbled over his briefcase which gave a tinkle and crack.

He sighed and dusted off his sandy bottom as he muttered, "Could have been someone…" he smirked and glared before cricking his neck and cracking his perfected persona before adding, "do you know something, I am someone and someone you'd all be grateful to be friends with. Vilde, you are nothing more than a rebel rouser and Lori, you're just another person behind a boring brand. I make people intergalactically famous for giving up the knowledge that's inside your heads and fulfilling tenders."

"Only while the money lasts and then what?" I scorned.

"I'm sure you are a real gold mine with the things you know," Vilde winked.

"I sure am and Lori, you'll only be profitable if you come with me but it's your choice." Casey said as his skin flushed and hand spammed with messages.

"Choice… What choice did I have when you took me without consent?" I asked.

Casey slammed on his suitcase and shouted, "Consent was gained when you entered the lift and again when you agreed to stay at the Gröfu Pallur. It continued when you sat down for your first interview and carried on with you being a participant of testing but let's put things into perspective shall we?" He jabbed his finger and spat out notifications as he paced, "You are on the verge of losing your job, you hate your flat because of the memories it holds and you don't have any true friends because you are never in the same place long enough to put down roots. The friends that bother to get to know you, blame you for great loss and your planet is overrun by an unknown entity. That doesn't sound appealing to me." He was briefly interrupted by a flock of birds flying overhead from the direction of a lop-sided person walking down the beach. "What is he doing here? I swear I didn't know he would come," Casey muttered.

Jax readjusted a waterfilled glass face mask which overlapped his nose and mouth and held a hand up to the burning sun. "Failed again Casey?" he spurned through the half snorkel-like mask. "It could be possible you'll become fragmented and your physical form may disintegrate from your lack of being able to perform your basic job requirements."

"We were nearly there," he replied meekly.

"Like hell you were," I shouted.

"She seems rather unconvinced to me. So we have no choice but to do as she asks and send her back to her home."

"You can't do that," I spat. "Can he?" I asked Vilde but she was crawling back behind her lounger along with Mei and even the twins were shocked and uncomfortable with his arrival.

"I can do whatever I want. We found you here with a simple matter of corruption from your companion who gave up the information for an insignificant price."

Mei appeared disgruntled as the twins shrugged and mouthed, "He's bluffing!"

Jax laughed and said, "Let's see about that." He shoved Casey out of the way and made a mark with his finger in the sand as the particles moved away to be replaced with volcanic rock beneath. A runic pattern emerged as Jax took two paces back and stated, "Your transportation will arrive shortly but do take into consideration that every decision you make from the tea bags you steep to whether or not to help others on the brink of salvation all has consequences." Jax readjusted his collar now pooling with sweat as he swirled the black rock and inserted a purple rod into the ground.

"You've changed your mind?" Casey asked Jax as he backed away from the rumbling ground with briefcase firmly in his grip.

"It is my mind to change. Especially as we have what we need," Jax snarled as the rod started to spin and emit chimes of a lift announcing passing of floors. One after another the bells sounded out until the lift was physically there on the sandy beach with doors clattering open. Jax sneered and tugged his sleeves down over his drying blistering forearms.

I was left with a what-to-do decision as if I stayed I'd face endless tests with both groups and if I went back home… Well, what Casey said was right. I was on the verge of losing my job with cutbacks and creative bursts being formulated by other forms of intelligence. I didn't even have a place to call my own and what should have been family and friends were severely lacking. Our rebellion against the Miarmuits wasn't working and what choice did I have?

A rush of air swirled as the stench of stale oil and dirty fridge spilled out. "You just have to step in," Jax said through gritted teeth then staggered to the floor as the reflection from Rodolphe's tray blinded him and smouldered his skin.

I went to move but Casey stopped me and said, "He can't do this. This isn't right. I know you don't trust me but I never lied, not really. I even told you that my job was working in client relations, I just chose to omit the unnecessary extra." He squeezed my arm before adding. "Don't go in. Jax can't do this."

Jax sneered as he righted himself and tried to top up his fluid mask, "I've got you a way to go home and I could so easily take it away again but I am feeling kind."

"Kind? You kicked Tiao and now he's gone forever."

"He wasn't of use. Stop that inferno of noise!" Jax shouted as Mei and the twins had begun clattering their belongings together. "It seems like they are sick of listening to you as well so get in the lift before it leaves without you."

"Lori, choose what's right for you. You know the risks of any decision," Vilde said behind a battalion of socks enclosing the area.

This wasn't the plan. Jax wasn't supposed to be here. It was only Casey who would be given a choice to join the Darners but now I was the one with the decision.

"Hurry up!" Jax screamed as his face started to blister, "I can't stand this heat!"

Two birds twerted overhead as the sun became the brightest and hottest it had ever been and all fell into a pensive silence as Jax's body began to steam, "Help me Casey. Get me something to shade myself."

Mei and the twins had assembled a contraption which was directing the sun beams directly around Jax. Mei grabbed two wrenches and drove them at an umbrella as the sun blazed.

"Help me you ungrateful swine or I will end you," Jax screamed as his clothes burned into his skin.

Casey ran to Jax's side. With one hand he shielded himself from the burning rays and with the other he lingered over Jax's face. He paused before grabbing Jax's mask and stated, "No, I won't help you anymore." He ripped off the mask then booted it into the sea.

Jax no longer screamed but instead rasping breaths took the place of his voice. His body crumpled as his hands dissolved into the sands around him. Vilde and Mei turned away as he contorted but Casey glared at him with an uncontrolled hatred.

I didn't want to see Jax suffer but it was too late to help as within minutes he was reduced to a pile of ashen sands and charred cloth. The remains lingered a moment in a sorrowful pile until flecks were caught on a light breeze and blown upward into nothingness.

"He's gone," Casey said in solace as he picked up his briefcase, "I guess I was wrong again, maybe the lift wasn't a trap and he was so angry he actually gave you a way home?"

The lift glowed hot as Mei and the twins quickly turned off their creation. Fred ushered the two turtle guards to bring water from the sea to cool the lift before giving it a tentative stamp of approval. A waiter came over to sweep up Jax's remains and apologised for the inconvenience as the clouds subtly shaded the sun which caused the sunbathers to roll over as if nothing interesting had happened.

The world continued and the lift remained.

Tiao would have been the voice to direct me to action but now he was gone I, and I alone had to make a decision which weighed heavier with each passing minute. Should I go back into a world segregated by the limitations of travel, the burden of work and under the control of the Miarmuits? Or should I stay here in a world with the limitations of travel, the burden of mental testing and the control of whoever Casey worked for. Alright, there was a third option but it still excluded the freedom I so longed for.

The amalgamation of all the information and experiences shifted into a generalised blur as it wasn't a simple decision like sitting or standing. So I did the one thing most people do in these situations and searched for a sign or at least something I could base my verdict on and take the burden of responsibility away from making the wrong decision.

It came to me in the form of an autonomous bubble and so I took two steps and cemented my decision to live in the oppressed freedom I had somehow consented to.

- 349 -

Mind Commodity

Lyv Landson

Acknowledgements

I would like to thank D.S. and her tireless efforts in listening to different aspects of the book. She was the first reader and without her patience and support this novel would still be in the to-do pile.

To A.M. thank you for being a soundboard to ideas and providing endless encouragement.

I would also like to thank my cat Oscar, he was a crucial editor as he tromped over my keyboard with clumsy paws and deleted hours and hours of work. He was the greatest critic in development and often responded to readings with a simple unbothered "Meow."

About the Author

Lyv Landson is a proud member of the LGBTQ+ community and grew up in the cheese realms of Cheshire. She excelled in putting on her pyjamas and rescuing a brick from the bottom of the swimming pool floor as a child as now as an adult focuses her efforts on literary endeavours while wearing pyjamas.

She blends her love of tea and travel to create intrigue within unique dystopian worlds and interlaces satire throughout a cast of inclusive characters.

If she isn't writing, she can often be found having adventures and japes with her partner and cat.

Follow: @Author_Landson for insider info and upcoming releases!